VAUGHN L. TREUDE
FIDELIO'S AUTOMATA

DEDICATION

For my son, Lowell Rand Treude, whose kindness, intelligence and sincerity have always made me proud.

Fidelio's Automata

An Adventure in Alternate History

Vaughn L. Treude

Nakota Publishing © MMXV

Fidelio's Automata

ISBN: 978-0-9882442-6-9 (paper edition)
978-0-9882442-5-2 (e-book)

Published by Nakota Publishing
http://nakotapublishing.com

ACKNOWLEDGMENTS

I would like to thank the following people:

My parents, for giving me the freedom to explore my surroundings.

Frank Lewis, my eighth grade history teacher, who instilled in me a life-long love of the subject.

My friends and fellow writers of Nexus, for their critiques, feedback and motivation

Kyle Dunbar, for the awesome cover art.

Margaret Grady, for her painstaking editing.

Melissa Choyce for her unique "Time to Get a Watch" font which I've used for scene dividers.

Kovid Goyal, creator of Calibre, the free program that I used to convert this work to e-book format.

The developers of Scribus, the open-source desktop publishing application (version 1.4.5) which enabled me to create this paper edition on Ubuntu 14.04.

And my very best friend Arlys-Allegra Holloway, for feedback, suggestions, love, and support.

"Without friends no one would choose to live, though he had all other goods."
~ Aristotle, *Nichomachean Ethics*

Chapter 1 – A New Land

Fidelio Espinoza emerged from the gondola into blinding sunshine and a stiff gust of icy wind. His hand flew to his head, just in time to save his prized bowler hat from flying into the void. As he entered the causeway, into the shadow of the great airship *Suwannee Maiden*, he shivered. Just two days before he had sat in the garden of his father's estate, enjoying the rich Cuban soil beneath his bare feet.

Despite the biting cold, Fidelio stopped in his tracks. The vista below made him gasp. Here lay the metropolitan heart of America, that haven of science and progress. To the west he could see the tree-lined streets of Lakehurst, New Jersey. Eastward lay the sparkling Atlantic and the bustling Brooklyn harbor. In Manhattan, to the north-east, modern buildings soared fourteen, fifteen, even twenty stories high. These were the fruits of man's progress, so tall they had earned the name "skyscrapers."

The wind gusted once more, and the airship groaned against her tethering cables, causing the suspended passageway to sway from side to side. Fidelio dropped his bags by his feet, clutched the safety railing, and removed his hat, as the wind threatened to take it once again.

"Espinoza," called a voice from behind him, half-shouting to be heard over the wind. "Enjoying the view?"

Fidelio turned to face his fellow passenger. "Indeed. It is spectacular."

The man gave a hearty laugh as he approached. He had spoken to Fidelio in the airship's lounge, detailing at length the accomplishments of his young sons, whom he was accompanying back to college after the Christmas holiday. "Take care," he warned. "The winds up here are strong, and it would be a long fall to the ground."

"Do not worry," Fidelio said with a smile. "Though I apologize for blocking your way." He stepped back and pressed himself against the railing. "Please, proceed."

"Thank you, sir. Welcome to America, and best of luck on your endeavor." The three men sidled past him and continued down the causeway.

"Thank you, and farewell." Fidelio realized he had dawdled long enough. He donned his hat, picked up his satchel and overnight case, and followed the men down the walk toward the tower elevator. The sons, he recalled, were amateur pugilists.

Unlike their robust physiques, Fidelio's slender frame was unimpressive. In reality, he was in top physical condition from sports such as fencing. Still, he envied the young men's well-defined musculature.

Compared to most Cubans, Fidelio was fortunate. The son of a Havana aristocrat, he had never wanted for anything, except the mother who had died bringing him into the world. Now in his late twenties, he was still new to many experiences. As a boy he had often sat in the stands under the tropical sun, as the horses thundered past in the steeplechase. He had imagined himself sailing over the hedges astride one of those magnificent animals, but such dangerous pastimes were forbidden to him. Only by attending a University abroad had he escaped his father's suffocating restrictions. There, in the mother country of Spain, he met Rodrigo, the man who had changed his life.

The memories brought such a flood of emotion that in his distracted state, Fidelio almost collided with the three men before him as they approached of the end of the walkway. Here, adjacent to the docking tower, was the elevator that would carry them to the surface. "Going down!" came a shout from within.

"Hold the door, please!" The eldest of the three men held up a hand and quickened his place.

"Sorry, sir, the maximum is four passengers." The operator pushed the elevator open, revealing three people already on board: a tall colored man, his wife, and a small boy.

"My sons and I have urgent business in the city," the tweed-suited man declared, casting a stern eye toward the tall man within.

The colored man cast his eyes down. "I guess we're in no hurry, so go on ahead." He and his wife and child stepped out through the elevator door onto the platform, as the three white men shouldered their way in.

"How about you, sir?" The operator, a gangly red-haired boy, poked his head out the door and looked at Fidelio. "There's room for one more."

Fidelio shook his head. He preferred not to benefit from such a crass act of injustice.

The elevator doors closed and the four of them remained on the platform. Here they were in the sunshine, but the air was still frigid enough that their breath was visible. The dark-skinned man regarded Fidelio as if he'd just grown a second head.

"Good day, sir," Fidelio said, "Ma'am." He tipped his black bowler, revealing his dark, curly close-cropped hair. "That was courteous of you to let those three men proceed, but quite unnecessary. During our journey, I conversed with them in the forward cabin. They had no urgent business; their journey was strictly a pleasure tour."

"Ain't no big problem," the dark-skinned man grinned. "Me and my family are just glad we had enough saved for the tickets, and that they had a place for us. You see, my poor momma recently took ill, and a train ride from Florida would have taken way too long."

"I am sorry to hear about your mother, and I wish her a speedy recovery," Fidelio said. "Still, I am appalled by that man's boorishness. He seemed agreeable enough when I spoke with him earlier."

"You're not from this country, are you?" the wife remarked. "Best get used to the way things are done here. White folks always get to go first."

Fidelio shook his head. "I am sympathetic to the plight of all the downtrodden, but this concerns me in particular, as I am of one-quarter African ancestry myself."

The black man let out a whistle. "You don't look it, if you don't mind me saying. My wife and I were discussing that very thing. She said to me, 'That man's passing,' and I said, 'No, woman, the man's Italian, or maybe a Jew.' I bet her a chicken dinner against a new cotton blouse. She sure enough beat me this time." He studied Fidelio for a moment. "Unless maybe you got some Italian mixed in."

"No, I am Cuban," Fidelio said. "Of predominately Spanish ancestry."

"Then that's what you'd best tell folks," the man continued. "In this country, a drop of Negro blood's enough to put you in the back car of the train."

"Daddy said your clothes were way too fancy for a colored," the boy said. The child wore a thin jacket; he wrapped his arms around himself and shivered as he spoke.

"That's absurd!" Noticing the child's alarmed expression, Fidelio added, "I did not mean to criticize your father's words, just the fundamental unfairness of the system."

Actually, the notion that his clothing was *fancy* was rather comical. Fidelio's attire that day was strictly casual; his tall, slender frame was covered with a long gray flannel coat and a matching waistcoat and trousers. His clothing was 'fancy' only in comparison to the colored man's worn dungarees and his wife's simple gingham dress.

Before they could resume the conversation, the elevator door opened again. The four of them entered and rode down in silence. Fidelio took careful note of the unusual sensation of falling. It was the second time he'd ridden in one of these amazing moving closets, the first time being at the start of his journey. He marveled to think there were people in New York City who rode them every day.

As Fidelio emerged from the elevator, the sights and sounds of the Chester A. Arthur Airfield assaulted his senses. He wrinkled his nose at the odor of diesel from the fuel wagons and the smoke of a dozen tobacco pipes and cigars. Thankfully it was a crisp winter day in Lakehurst, New Jersey. If this were Havana, those smells combined with the perspiration of the assembled passengers and crew would have been overpowering. Here the unpleasant aromas were mitigated by a cool breeze from the harbor.

About a dozen people waited in line for Customs inspection. As Fidelio understood it, the United States government derived a majority of its revenue from duties on imports. Hence the passengers from foreign ports of origin were required to shuffle along for upwards of an hour as government functionaries repeated the same perfunctory questions.

"Please state your name and country of origin." The Customs official was a short, stocky man with a thick Germanic accent.

"Fidelio Ludovico Espinoza Cruz. I am a citizen of Cuba."

"The purpose of your visit?"

"Business."

"Do you have any taxable goods to declare?"

"No, sir, I do not." Fidelio was not an acquisitive man; he did not travel with jewels or other finery. He did not smoke and he very rarely imbibed alcoholic beverages, which eliminated two more items the United States saw fit to tax. As for the Spanish gold coins in the purse in his vest pocket – well, those funds were his own business.

The inspector stared for a moment at Fidelio, then at the steamer trunk which he'd brought with him from Havana. "Please unlock your trunk for inspection."

"Is the use of the word 'please' an implication that I may decline?"

"I'm sorry, sir, you may not. We'll try to be brief. Mister O'Malley over on the right will assist you. Next, please?"

Reluctantly Fidelio inserted the key and opened the lid. A second man appeared, presumably O'Malley. He wore the same Customs service uniform plus white cotton gloves. He briefly examined Fidelio's clothing and toiletries, and checked his collection of technical books, which were mostly written in Spanish.

The inspector paused when he noticed the insect-like device which had been wrapped carefully in a woolen scarf. "May I see that?" Without waiting for Fidelio's answer, he picked it up gingerly, and then flicked a switch on its underside. When the creature's legs began to move, he dropped it in alarm. As it hit the ground the automaton performed its self-protective function, and shut itself off.

The customs agent's face broadened in a smile, and he laughed out loud. "I apologize, sir, I didn't realize it was a toy. How clever! Where did you purchase it? My grandchildren would love one of these."

"Thank you," Fidelio sniffed. "This 'toy,' as you call it, is not yet available for sale, but I expect that someday it will." Quickly Fidelio re-wrapped the device and closed and locked his trunk. The inspection had confirmed what he had already told the Customs agents; there was nothing taxable in his luggage.

Now that this indignity was finished, Fidelio stopped at the side of the road and retrieved a hand mirror to check his appearance. With a tiny comb, he redid the curls at the end of his waxed moustache and reshaped the point of his neatly trimmed goatee.

His next move was to hail a taxi to his destination. It would be a twenty-yard trek down the boardwalk to the street. It was a good thing he had devised a set of wheels for his steamer trunk. The four rubberized disks were mounted on pivots which allowed them to be folded up for the voyage. He now swiveled them down, attached the leather harness to the handle on one end, and headed down the walk.

When he reached the street, he was overwhelmed by the number of vehicles, horses, and pedestrians. As he stood by the curb, a haggard-looking man pulled up in a horse-drawn wagon. "Do you need a lift, sir? Just twenty-five cents."

Fidelio looked up at the man. "First I must ask you a question. Are you a member of the teamsters' union? I do not wish to contribute to the exploitation of workers."

"I'm my own boss," the man explained. "So for me it ain't necessary. But if I was workin' for somebody else I sure would be."

"Hmm..." Fidelio pondered a moment. The driver's coat was tattered, and there were smudges of dirt or grease on his face. Surely it was no crime to be poor, and if that were the case, he was the kind of person Fidelio wished to help out. On the other hand, the man's lack of attention to hygiene could be an indication of bad character.

"Well?" said the driver. "Sorry, sir, but I don't have all day."

Fidelio shrugged. What could it hurt? It would not be a long ride to East Orange; surely he could tolerate the man's smell for that brief period. "Very well," he said finally. "But take care with my trunk; some of its contents are fragile."

"Certainly, sir." The driver got out of the wagon and lifted it with an ease that belied his wiry frame. He closed the back gate and scrambled back into his seat. As Fidelio put his foot on the step to the wagon's passenger seat, the pale man extended his palm. "Sorry, you got to pay before boarding. I been cheated out of my fare one too many times."

"That is reasonable, I guess. But I do not have any silver coinage in my purse; I need to retrieve a quarter-dollar from my trunk."

"No problem. Just walk around and reach over the rear gate."

As Fidelio did so, the driver snapped the reins and the horse sprang into motion. "Wait, man! I have not retrieved my money. I am not aboard."

Without another word, the pale man drove the horse even faster down the cobbled street and disappeared into the traffic.

"That man is a thief!" Fidelio shouted to the surrounding crowd. "He has absconded with my luggage! Someone stop him!"

All around him, people stopped to stare, but said nothing. A well-dressed lady hid her face behind her parasol and hurried off. Two young ruffians chuckled in delight at his misfortune. One of them called out, "Serves you right, dandy boy!"

"What is wrong with you people?" he shouted. "Can't any of you be troubled to apprehend a detestable rogue amongst you?"

"Tell it to the cops," said a portly olive-skinned fellow.

Fidelio let forth a few choice Spanish curses, then stopped himself. *I will receive no cooperation by acting like a lunatic.* He kicked a few cobblestones for good measure and considered his options.

"What a fool I have been," he muttered. The driver had not been an honest working man; he had been part of the same predatory element which a capitalist society such as this one invariably fostered. It was the main reason he'd hesitated to come to this country, but at the time he'd calculated the opportunity to outweigh the risks.

He sighed. Would it be productive to report this crime to the police? In the absence of a more expeditious way to achieve justice, probably not. Yet if there was even a slight chance to recover his belongings, he would do it. He saw an elderly man passing by in the other direction. Fidelio approached him and asked, "Could you direct me to the nearest police station? I have been the victim of theft."

"You're not from around here, are you, sonny?"

"No, I only just arrived in this country."

"You don't say? Other than the accent, your English is pretty good. Okay, then; you should go that way," the man pointed, opposite the direction he had been going, "down this street and turn right on Cherry Avenue. In two or three blocks, you'll come to a station on the left side of the street."

"Thank you, my good man." The station was a bit further than the stranger's directions had implied. As Fidelio walked he was overwhelmed by thoughts of loneliness. For the millionth time he mourned the loss of his beautiful Rodrigo. Had his lover not met his tragic, untimely end, Fidelio would likely have stayed in Spain permanently.

After Rodrigo's death, Fidelio had vowed to avoid emotional entanglements, and to be as independent as possible. Yet even the strongest person required assistance at times. For this very reason, his philosophy advocated the solidarity of the working classes. So he would seek help from the police, even though he expected them to be as corrupt in America as they were as in Spain and Cuba.

When Fidelio entered the door of the precinct station, he approached the front desk. "I would like to report a robbery."

The man at the desk regarded him suspiciously. "Fill out this form," he said in a thick brogue, "and we'll be getting right back to ya."

Fidelio took a seat in the station waiting room. He set down his satchel and opened his copy of yesterday's *Times*, which he had not had the opportunity to read. There was a long article about England's new king, after the passing of Queen Victoria, a short item about the Vanderbilt wedding, and another about the founding of a league for 'baseball' players.

He saw nothing whatsoever about the Philippine conflict. It was a topic of great concern for Fidelio. Having 'liberated' the islands from the Spanish Empire, the United States nonetheless denied the inhabitants the independence they desired. Would they also do this to his own country? Or would American troops depart Cuba soon, as President McKinley had promised?

Frustrated, he paged through the periodical until he found a most noteworthy story:

"Nighthawks" Win Bloodless Victory in Muscogee

An entire Army platoon under the command of Col. Thomas Chivington were taken captive Thursday in Indian Territory, as they attempted to arrest members of

Vaughn L. Treude

the Cherokee, Choctaw, and Creek tribes who refused to comply with relocation orders under the Dawes Act. The captors identified themselves as the Keetowah Secret Society, popularly known as "Nighthawks." Sources said the soldiers were amazed to have their weapons wrested remotely from their hands by an "invisible force." This is believed to have been accomplished by the use of magnetic ship grapples, which are manufactured at the Wehali Industries factory in the village of Muscogee. Vice President-Elect Theodore Roosevelt, who is personally traveling by rail to negotiate terms of the soldiers' release, stated his intention to "perform a thorough review of effects of the Dawes Act on the Indian Community."

The story cheered Fidelio greatly. One of his misgivings about coming to the United States had been the many injustices in its society, not just to colored people, but to its native peoples as well. Perhaps the powerless and exploited would finally get their due.

By the time they finally called his name, an hour had passed and he had read almost the entire paper. The detective apologized for his long wait and patiently listened to his story, nodding every now and then.

"We'll keep an eye out for your belongings," the policeman said. "If we come across any property matching this description we'll send you a letter. May I please have a mailing address?"

"I do not have a residence as of yet, but I can give you the address of my employer." Fidelio pulled a business card from the breast pocket of his jacket and read the inscription aloud: "Thomas Alva Edison – Inventor, Llewellyn Park, East Orange, New Jersey."

"Thomas Edison, the inventor? By George, you must one smart fellow to work for the Wizard of Menlo Park. Anyway, we have your information so you may be on your way. I wish you the best of luck, sir."

Fidelio trudged sadly down the street. His visit to the police had been a waste of time. Worse, darkness had fallen and he was stranded in a part of town that was bereft of street lights. The heavy traffic from earlier in the day had now dissipated. After he had walked for quite some time, a coach drove by with the word 'TAXI' inscribed on the side. Fidelio jumped off the curve and waved his hands, but the

14

driver did not slow down.

The best thing now, he decided, would be to find the nearest hotel. Hopefully it would have a dining room so he could get a hot meal. It distressed him greatly that he had missed his late afternoon appointment with Edison. From all he had heard, the man was a stickler for punctuality. He cursed himself for not attempting to find a telephone. Edison's laboratory would certainly be equipped with the newest technology.

Still, his excuse was legitimate, and considering that he had been recommended by his father's friend the mayor of Havana, he expected that Edison would let this matter slip. Fidelio counted himself lucky to have this opportunity. To work for such a brilliant innovator and businessman would give him an education that no institute of higher learning could equal.

Fidelio felt horribly discouraged. He wondered if his decision to come to this country had been a mistake. Yet he was loathe to turn back now, thus admitting his father had been right. He stopped and gazed into the starry sky. The points of light reminded him of the hundreds of candles that the townsfolk of Almadén, Spain had lit in the church for their lost husbands, brothers, sons, and fathers.

In his mind's eye he saw the rows of the miners' coffins, all closed. All the bodies had been recovered, but all were too mangled and disfigured for their loved ones to see. To Fidelio, it made no difference; he did not even know which held Rodrigo's remains. He wanted to remember his lover as a living, vital man. It was then that, as he sat in the far back of the church, weeping quietly, he had made a solemn promise that he would do his best to see that this tragedy did not repeat itself, that men would no longer die in their quest for the treasures of the earth.

Though perhaps he had been fooling himself. He was just one man, a man foolish enough to have lost his prized invention to a rogue in a foreign land.

Then he remembered what his father had told him shortly before he'd boarded the dirigible for New Jersey. They'd argued late into the night. His father saw himself as Spanish and could not countenance his son going to the land which had made war on his homeland. In the end, though, he reluctantly gave his blessing. "Fidelio, you and I may not always see things eye to eye, but you are my son, and I love you and believe in you. Never, ever abandon your dreams."

Chapter 2 – Reprieve from the Reaper

"Doctor?" As Hank MacMillan knocked on the door of his physician's office, his heart hammered in his chest. He imagined this was how a convicted killer felt as he went before the judge. Would the Fates have mercy and spare his life? Or would he face the gallows, figuratively speaking?

"The door is not locked," said a voice from the other side. "Come in, my good man." Hank turned the knob and entered cautiously, as if expecting an ambush. "Right on time, Mr. MacMillan. I was just looking through your records."

Doctor Stieglitz sat on a stool facing a roll-top desk in the corner of his cramped office. He was a short, bald-headed Austrian with a thick German accent. The doctor peered at some dark photographs through some complicated spectacles with multiple lenses and a tiny incandescent bulb on top. The latter was powered by cable to a battery that rested on the table.

The doctor unhooked the battery and flipped the lenses upward, revealing the deep wrinkles around his eyes. "So, Henry, how are we feeling today?"

"Well, Doc," he answered, "I feel a darn sight better than last year, and I'm grateful for that. But please, call me Hank. The only folks who called me Henry were my Ma and Pa, and sadly they're long gone."

The doctor nodded and smiled. "Of course. Hank it shall be. Please, sit down." He motioned to the examination table in the center of the room.

Hank sat on the edge of the table. "I hope you didn't have me sit 'cause you aim to deliver bad news."

The doctor shook his head. "Not at all." He held up a small sheaf of dark images. "Do you remember the fluoroscope photographs we made of your gastric system?"

"How could I forget?" Hank laughed mirthlessly. "The stuff you made me drink tasted like the backside of a billy goat."

The doctor's haggard face broke out in a smile. "You have a quaint way of expressing yourself. In any case, I want you to remember my warning that the fluoroscope is a new discovery, so you must take these findings with a grain of salt, so to speak."

"I hear you, Doc. You don't need to sugarcoat it. How much time have I got left?"

"If you take care of yourself, eat a better diet and stay away from the liquor and cigarettes, you may just have another thirty or forty years or so."

"Well, I did give up smokes like you suggested, much as I miss 'em. And I haven't had a drink in... Wait, did I hear you correct? Did you say thirty or forty *years*?"

The doctor smiled again. "To be frank, I am surprised also. It is quite common when removing a tumor that we miss some portion and the cancer metastasizes, that is, it spreads to other parts of the body. So far we see absolutely no sign of that."

Hank stood up and put a hand on the doctor's arm. "You're not pulling my leg?"

"Pulling the legs of my patients would be rather in poor taste wouldn't it?" Stieglitz chuckled at his own joke. "But I reiterate; this diagnosis is not 100 percent certain. The cancer could reoccur at any time. For the moment, though, you are a very lucky man."

Hank sank back into his chair. It seemed like the room was swimming before him. "I can't believe my ears, Doc. You said my chances were one in ten to live past the end of the year."

"Perhaps it was the new magnetic therapy," Stieglitz said. "Since it is an untried technology, I did not want to offer false hope. Or perhaps it's simply that you are the one in ten."

"Well, glory Hallelujah!" Hank sprang up from his seat and put his arms around the doctor, who patted him on the back and moved back as far as the limited space would allow. "I've been praying to hear this news." Tears of joy streamed down Hank's face.

"So, young man," Stieglitz said as he gently freed himself from Hank's impromptu embrace. "For the time being, you have a reprieve. What is next in store for Henry MacMillan?"

Hank smiled at being called 'young,' having seen more than forty summers. "I'll be danged, but I ain't hardly considered it." He sniffled as he wiped off the tears on his sleeve, causing the doctor to offer him a paper tissue. He blew his nose loudly, and then composed himself. "First thing, I guess, is head back to Arizona. My Uncle Malcolm, the man who raised me, is getting on in years, and I'd like to spend some time with him, God willing."

Doctor Stieglitz nodded. "Of everything in life, family is by far the most important. A brush with death has a way of clarifying one's priorities."

"By the by, Doc, what do I owe you today?"

"I expect to receive payment soon from the Veterans Department, so as you Americans put it, we are square." He smiled broadly and clapped Hank on the shoulder. "I'd love to converse some more but I have another patient arriving soon. So then," Stieglitz extended his hand, "I wish you a pleasant journey back home, and continued good health."

Hank shook the doctor's hand and thanked him once more, then left the office.

What now? He had no plans beyond heading home to Arizona, and he would have done that regardless of the diagnosis. Hank thought back to how he'd been wracked with pain, just a few months prior, nauseated by the doctor's potions and enduring hours on the table under that confounded electromagnet. Before that time, he hadn't been much of a Christian. So he had promised the good Lord that if He saw fit to spare him, he would change his rambling ways, find himself a wife and start a family. Luckily, though, he hadn't thought to set a deadline on his promise to the Almighty. As far as Hank was concerned, there was no hurry.

His first thought was to head to the nearest saloon for a stiff drink, maybe several. He'd avoided hard liquor these last few months, partly on the doctor's suggestion, and also to make up with the Lord for all the sinning he'd done in the past. On second thought, it was best to keep it that way. The Demon Rum only led to trysts with the kind of wild women he'd sworn to avoid. So he headed off down the street in search of a good meal.

After hoofing it for some time, he came to an Italian restaurant called Mamma Peroni's. This was another thing he'd never seen in Arizona – an eating place where they had all their meals on a list, and you could pick anything you wanted at any time they were open. It happened to be about mid-day, so the establishment was quite busy, filled up with workers from nearby offices. "My apologies," the hostess said. "We cannot give you a table before one o' clock."

Hank consulted his pocket watch. The wait would be over thirty minutes, but what of it? He had nowhere else to go. "That'll be just dandy, ma'am." As the woman returned to her duties, he glanced at her departing derrière. He'd always taken a fancy to the dark-eyed, buxom beauties of Mexican extraction, and Italian ladies tended to be built similarly. His mind wandered to thoughts of how she'd look undressed. *No*, he told himself. *Lead me not into temptation.* Then again, if he was looking for a wife, he had to start somewhere.

With nothing better to do, he sat down on a bench the proprietors had kindly placed in front by the entry. As Hank waited watched the throngs of people pass by, he reminisced about his life – his home in Arizona, the women he'd known there, and the War.

In more ways than one, Hank felt reborn. These last few months, he'd finally made peace with his impending mortality. More than once he'd pondered the irony of his fate – to evade the bullets of the Spaniards' guns, only to be kicked in the belly by the hoof of an Army mule. That in itself was trouble enough; it cost him two weeks' recuperation in a field hospital.

Months later, though, the pain came back, and got a lot worse, leading to the dreadful diagnosis of cancer. So the former cowboy ended up traveling to New York City. The Army surgeons, who were no experts in that deadly disease, sent him up there to the Cornell Medical College, where he'd lost a piece of his liver to the surgeon's knife.

Finally the lady returned and beckoned him to enter and take a seat. Hank was pleased that the woman who arrived to take his order looked like a younger version of the hostess. He was glad he'd shaved today, and had gotten a haircut earlier in the week. "I'll have the twelve ounce New York Strip with a dish of spaghetti on the side."

The waitress smiled, showing white teeth between red lips. "With that cut we recommend a red wine."

Hank paused for a moment, trying to remember exactly what his promise to God had been. Then he recalled how the Savior Himself had turned water into wine for the wedding feast at Cana. "All right, you talked me into it. And how about you, honey, could I talk you into sharing a glass with me after you get off work?"

"Sir, I have a husband," she replied with ice in her voice.

"My apologies," Hank said with a smile. "Let just say that he's one lucky fellow to have a pretty thing like you for a wife."

The compliment seemed to appease her a bit, though she was noticeably less friendly when she returned with his food. *If she wasn't wearing a ring, how was I supposed to know?* The dinner was tasty and satisfying. Just to show her there were no hard feelings, Hank tipped her a silver quarter.

Now what? He was free for the rest of the day. His boss at the machine shop had given him the entire day off, probably figuring the doctor's news would be bad. Not wanting to return to his tiny room in Mrs. Miller's boarding house, he resumed his trek through the streets of Manhattan.

When Hank had first arrived in New York, he hated it, with all the crowds and traffic and folks who wouldn't return a friendly greeting when he passed them on the street. Today he saw another side. There was a sense of purpose and industry as people went about their tasks. He admired the newfangled motorcars, their drivers equipped with goggles to guard against smoke and dust. There were also horse-drawn carriages of every description, as well as young men and even women riding tall velocipedes.

As Hank trudged on, he marveled at the march of progress. In these neighborhoods near the University, gas-powered street lights gave way to electric. Everywhere there were telegraph poles, some with extra lines for the new voice telephones. It would no doubt be some time before these advancements made their way to the Southwest. He began to wonder if he could be content with the slow pace of life back in the Territory.

At that moment Hank happened upon the church of St. Thomas. This majestic structure would be a fine place to kneel and thank the Lord properly. Prayer had been a big part of Hank's life in recent months, and he'd attended numerous Sunday meetings, but had yet to find a place where he felt at home. *Did I really mean to change my ways?* Hank asked himself. *Or was it just that I thought I was dying?*

As Hank approached the big wooden doors of the church, he heard a female voice speaking out with great urgency. Turning toward the sound, he noticed a commotion in that direction, so he headed over to investigate.

On the street corner stood three people: two women and one man, attired in plain gray dresses and suits. These were not the form-fitting dresses of current fashion, but the simpler, shapeless dresses like those that proper ladies wore back when Hank was young. One of those gray-clad women stood on an apple crate, a brass speaking-trumpet pressed to her lips. It was tough to make out her words, because the device distorted her voice, but she seemed to be saying something about the Philippine Islands.

A small group of spectators had gathered. Hank joined them, curious about the speaker's motivation. The situation made his stomach churn with fear. Ever since the War, he hated being in crowds, or anyplace noisy. Doctor Stieglitz, who had studied psychology for a time with the famous Sigmund Freud, had offered Hank this advice, "Focus your attention on something other than whatever is causing your anxiety."

So Hank listened intently to the lady who was speaking. She was not comely, being on the near side of elderly, but she stood tall and straight, and her voice rang out with conviction. "President McKinley claims to care for the well-being of the Philippine people. If that be true, why does he send soldiers to destroy their homes, terrorize their women and murder their sons?" Her words struck Hank like a punch in the gut. Was that what it was, when he and the Roughriders had fought their way up Kettle Hill? When he'd shot that Spanish boy between the eyes, was that murder? How about the Moorish looking fellow he'd stabbed with the bayonet?

"The Sixth Commandment says, 'Thou shalt not kill.' So why do we send our brothers and sons to foreign lands to defile the Holy Law?"

That remark brought a hiss from the crowd and a chorus of boos. "Traitor!" a man shouted. "Defending our country is not a sin!"

"Un-American!" cried another. The woman ignored the cat-calls and continued speaking.

Who was this woman, Hank wondered, who had the guts to face these people? Stuck in the ground behind and on either side of her were two wooden poles, holding a cloth banner which read, 'New York Society of Friends.' It was mighty peculiar. The woman's speech, brave as it was, wasn't exactly winning her any friends.

Hank turned to a man standing behind him, attired in a dark blue suit and top hat. "Who are these 'Friend' people?" he asked.

"Confounded Quakers," the man said, shaking his head. "Bunch of crazy radicals."

"Quakers, huh? I didn't know those folks were still around." Hank remembered reading about William Penn in his *McGuffey Reader*. He recalled that Quakers had gotten themselves booted from England for their strong Christian beliefs. Yet the preacher back in his home town of Prescott had been all in favor of the war. It was one of the reasons Hank had joined the Army, figuring to make up for all the sinning he'd done in his life. According to this lady, though, he'd only gotten himself deeper in hot water with the Almighty.

"Who here believes in the Golden Rule?" the lady proclaimed. A hand or two went up in the audience. "What does it say about our treatment of the people of the Philippines? Our leaders said we were fighting to free them, yet we put them back in chains."

"Liar!" screamed a woman in the crowd. "You say my son died for nothing!"

Did he? Hank wondered. *Or did he die because the Spanish War was Satan's handiwork?* Maybe that was the real reason Hank had come down with cancer of the liver. At the time he'd suspected it was divine punishment for drinking whiskey and consorting with wild women. What if it was the killing that God was most riled up about? After all, Jesus did say, 'Blessed are the peacemakers,' and 'Turn the other cheek.' As he thought once again of the men he'd killed and the friends he'd lost, Hank's eyes welled up with tears.

Hank pushed his way through the small crowd up to the table. The other Quaker woman stood to the speakers' left, and was passing out handbills. She was considerably younger. The hair that showed below her scarf was a golden shade of blonde. "I just wanted to testify," Hank said, quietly so as not to interrupt the other lady's speech. "That what the sister is saying has touched my heart."

"Dost thou mean about the Philippine insurrection and the suffering of those poor people?" the young lady whispered. "Here, take a leaflet which explains the horrible atrocities done in the name of America."

"Thank you." He accepted the leaflet from her. "But not that exactly. I'm a sinner who broke the Lord's Commandments in the Spanish War. I'm ready to pray for forgiveness and accept Jesus into my heart. He *will* forgive me, won't he?"

The woman's face broke out in a broad smile. "Of course! As the Bible says, 'He that believeth in me and is baptized shall be saved.' Hast thou been baptized?"

"Yes ma'am, when I turned thirteen and they took me down to the river. But I can't rightly say that it took. If I could, I'd like to tell the folks about my time in Cuba."

"Thou wast in Cuba?" said the Quaker man beside her. "I have recently returned from Havana. I have seen the injured in the hospitals and the graves of the fallen."

"Sorry to say, I was not there on a mission," Hank said. "I was a corporal in the Army. Though I volunteered and went to kill folks I didn't even know, I now regret what I done."

"Surely the Holy Spirit has touched thy heart," said the young woman. "We would be delighted for thee to testify when Sister Agnes has finished speaking."

"This is an outrage!" bellowed a man's voice from behind Hank. "You people dare quote scripture in the service of iniquity. You deny the sacrifices of your forefathers and the virtue of service to God and Country."

Hank turned to face the speaker, a red-faced man in a black parson's outfit complete with broad-brimmed black hat and wild gray locks. The folks behind him seemed to be of like mind, all angry and muttering.

Hank's heart beat faster. He felt like he was back on San Juan Hill, with men shouting and bullets whizzing over his head. In his mind's eye he saw himself frozen in his tracks, a perfect target for the Spaniard's guns, when friend Willie whacked him in the back with the butt of his rifle. "Move your ass, you dad-blasted fool!"

At last the gray-haired Quaker woman took notice of her critic. "I hear you, sir, and I respectfully disagree. Nowhere in the scriptures does the Lord condone that His children kill other human beings."

"You are wrong, impudent woman! When the Lord led the Israelites to the land of Canaan, they encountered its wicked inhabitants. First Samuel chapter 15, verses two and three: 'Thus saith the Lord of hosts, I remember that which Amalek did to Israel...'"

As Hank looked back and forth between the antagonists, the panic grew within him. *There's going to be a battle; all Hades will break loose.* He felt a hand on his arm. "Good sir, art thou ill?" the young Quaker woman asked him. "All color has left thy face. Please come and sit down."

Hank felt like a complete fool. This dainty Quaker lady was fearless when he, a former cow-puncher and war veteran, was fixing to faint dead away like some delicate lady. "Thank you kindly, young Missy, but I've got to go."

He whirled around in a panic, and ran directly into a burly policeman. Hank was well muscled from years of physical labor, but this fellow, being just as fit and well over six feet tall, made him feel like a midget.

"Now, where are you going in such a hurry?" said the cop in a gruff voice. "Settle down or I'll have to run you in." He tapped his hand on his nightstick. "As for you folks," he addressed the Quakers, "City ordinance prohibits congregating in such a way as to cause a breach of the peace, and also to block egress through a public right of way. All of you are ordered to disperse."

"But sir," said the Quaker woman, "we were merely preaching the word of the Lord."

The red-faced parson turned to the policeman. "Officer, these so-called *Christians*," he said, the tone of his voice matching the sneer on his face, "have been advocating sedition of the worst kind."

"That's of no concern to us," said a second lawman, who had just appeared behind the first. "Everybody's got to move along, including you. There's a wagon on the way, and we'll arrest anyone who disobeys a lawful order."

"I'm not the one you should be harassing!" The preacher pointed at the Quakers. "These treasonous blasphemers are the cause of this commotion. I insist you arrest them at once."

Behind him, others joined in. "Arrest them! Down with the traitors!"

Now Hank felt a full panic. *Run!* his inner voice told him. Again he was in Cuba, facing up Kettle Hill. By sheer dumb luck, his terror had sent him charging into the battle rather than away, or he'd have been disgraced as a coward and a deserter. Right now, though, there was no clear way to escape. He was hemmed in by people and had nowhere to run.

"Very well, we shall disperse," the blonde woman said. She placed a hand on Hank's arm. "Brother, wouldst thou come with us? Our meeting house is nearby."

"I – I'd like that," Hank stammered, and turned to follow her.

As the Quaker man and woman were taking down the 'Society of Friends' banner, the red-faced parson rushed in to confront her. "The nerve of you people, slandering our soldiers as murderers! I demand you apologize to the veterans in this crowd."

The gray-haired woman picked up her crate and looked the man directly in the eyes.

"And the King shall answer and say unto them, 'Verily I say unto you, 'Inasmuch as ye have done it unto one of the least of these my brethren, ye have done it unto me.'"

"Be still, harlot!" yelled the red-faced parson. "I won't have you perverting the Gospel! And *you*," he turned to face Hank. "I heard what you said about the war. How dare you insult the memory of your comrades in arms!"

Hank's eyes went wide. Slowly he began to back away, but his path was blocked by people standing behind him. "Take it easy, friend. We're all God's children, aren't we?"

"You, sir, are a yellow-bellied coward." The preacher advanced menacingly.

As he'd done in a dozen tavern brawls, Hank instinctively raised his hands and balled them into fists. Then a revelation hit him like a shaft of light from the heavens. It was as if St. Paul was standing there beside him saying, "Bless them which persecute you." Hank smiled, unclenched his fists and extended a hand in friendship, only to be punched in the stomach by the angry preacher. He fell to his knees on the sidewalk, clutching his stomach.

"Curse you, traitor!" the parson yelled. Several men from the crowd, as big and tough as dockworkers, rushed forward and jumped on Hank. The policemen blew their whistles frantically as the assailants pummeled him in the face and back.

"Stop! You're all under arrest!" yelled the first policeman. The attack ceased as two cops pulled the assailants off of Hank. He felt himself being helped up by rough hands, which then pulled his arms behind his back and fastened cold metal cuffs around his wrists.

"Officer, must thou arrest this man?" said the elderly Quaker woman. "He never struck anyone. That other man attacked him without provocation."

"Sorry, lady, this cowboy is going to the Precinct with the rest of this riff raff."

"I thought you Quakers didn't approve of fighting," said another policemen. "So run along, or you'll be sharing a cell with these hooligans."

As they led Hank away with the others, he looked back at the Quakers. The blonde angel knelt on the sidewalk, collecting a mess of spilled handbills. At that moment she looked up and met his gaze, as if to say, *be strong.*

"I'm sorry, miss!" he shouted at her. "I didn't mean to start nothing!"

"You did nothing wrong." She stood up and once again confronted the police. "Officers, where are you taking him?"

Hank didn't hear their answer, because two cops shoved him into the big horse-drawn wagon with the others. Now he was certain this woman was an angel, even if she didn't have wings, sent by the Lord to help him through this difficulty in his life. If only he hadn't lost his wits and gotten himself arrested. Would he ever see her again?

The officer pushed two more men into the wagon and locked the door. One of the horses nickered and the wagon lurched down the street. "Hey, there's that coward who wouldn't fight back!" someone shouted from the front of the wagon. Hopefully whoever it was wouldn't be able to reach him back here.

Hank ignored the taunt, shut his eyes and prayed to God for guidance. He was headed for the hoosegow. If they kept him longer than overnight, he'd miss work, and Old Man Skolnick would fire him for sure. Without a job, how would he afford a train ticket back to Arizona?

Then he realized that all was not lost. The blonde Quaker lady had said they had a meeting house. Maybe he would go to the Astor library and see if they had a directory of houses of worship. He'd been to that amazing house of books several times while convalescing; it was a quiet place where he could collect his thoughts and catch up on some of the book learning he'd missed as a boy.

Others might hate the Quakers, but Hank found them inspiring. He admired the way they stood with their convictions against the anger of the crowd. They reminded him of the early Christians in the Bible, who kept their faith even when the Romans threw them to the lions.

In any case, Hank vowed that he would look up these Quakers, and learn more about their brand of Christianity. Maybe he could even find himself a wife.

Chapter 3 – Encounter with Genius

"Mr. Espinoza! How is your work progressing?"

Fidelio looked up at his employer. "Very well, thank you. I believe that this new compound will be far more reactive with the Roentgen radiation."

Thomas Alva Edison nodded. "I'm glad to hear that. So why have you not yet tested it?"

"With all due respect, sir, I am concerned about the safety of the fluoroscope, after what happened to poor Clarence." Seeing Edison cast down his eyes at the name of his gravely ill assistant, Fidelio added, "Not that the tragedy could have been foreseen. Still, I'm inclined to take further precautions before testing."

"What kind of precautions?" Edison snapped. "I'm not asking you to volunteer as an experimental subject. Clarence did that of his own accord."

"I understand. But I fear the Roentgen emissions may radiate in a broader pattern than we anticipated. I recommend we emplace some form of shielding, preferably lead foil, on the walls of the room containing the device. We could then wire a remote switch and buzzer so the device could be operated from outside of the room."

"Hmm..." Edison stared at Fidelio for several seconds. It seemed the man was pondering whether to respond with anger or praise, but then his mouth formed a smile. "Then that is what we shall do. Let us begin with the remote actuator. That will give us some distance from the source. The lead may take some time to procure." Edison laughed and clapped Fidelio on the shoulder. "Some people might doubt that a man of your youth could show such talent for the sciences, but the moment we met, I believed in you. Perhaps it's the Spanish in your blood. I find your people an adventurous and enterprising breed."

"Thank you, sir. I appreciate your faith in me." Though Edison's remarks sometimes seemed patronizing, Fidelio knew that his praise was sincere.

"I'm not a man who believes in re-inventing the proverbial wheel," Edison said, taking a seat beside his assistant. "So I hope you've been keeping abreast of the literature. Have you read Herr Roentgen's notes?"

Fidelio nodded. "Recently I read a monograph on the dangers of X-rays by a man named Nikola Tesla. Are you familiar with him? He seems to be working in areas of research similar to your own."

Edison's smile disappeared. "Yes, I know that man." Without another word, he rose from his chair and left the room.

His employer's unexpected reaction aroused Fidelio's curiosity. He resolved to make some inquiries around the lab. If this Tesla was some sort of rival to the great Edison, Fidelio wanted to learn more about him.

On the following day, Fidelio was sitting by the wall, using a screwdriver to fasten a round ceramic switch to the plasterboard, when Edison appeared behind him.

"Fidelio," he boomed, "I have a new assignment for you."

"Yes, sir." The Cuban stood up and used a handkerchief to wipe his hands. "I was just finishing up. I must say that I really appreciate this incandescent lighting. It makes it much easier to work after sunset. Would you care to see a brief demonstration of the fluoroscope's new controls?"

Edison waved his hand. "That won't be necessary; I have nothing but complete trust in your work. This new assignment is urgent, and you being one of my brightest assistants, I thought you'd be perfect for the job."

Fidelio smiled. "Thank you, Mr. Edison. I will do my best to justify your faith in my abilities."

"Of course you will." Edison put a hand on the young man's shoulder and gestured down the hallway. "Follow me; I'll explain as we walk."

Edison was an impatient man with a quick stride, but with his long legs, Fidelio had no problem keeping up with him. "Back in '85 I made a proposal to the US government to develop a mechanical tabulator for the Census. I lost the bid to my old rival, Hermann Hollerith. The sly dog went to work for the Census Bureau, and as such he had an inside track."

"Yes, I'm aware of his work." Fidelio had investigated Hollerith's Tabulating Machine Company as a prospect for employment here in the United States, but had decided that Edison's wide range of interests would provide greater opportunity for experimentation.

"Losing that bid stuck in my craw. Then I thought, if there is opportunity for such a device in government, how much more so in private enterprise? Anything that Hollerith's machine could do, mine would do better. Thus I created the new discipline of magnetonomics."

"Yes, I read about that in the Rutgers College bulletin. Your patent combines celluloid film with magnetic dots arranged in patterns similar to those used by

Braille's reading system for the blind."

"Indeed. I'm gratified to have such a well-informed young man as an employee." He chuckled, "If only my Madeleine were a bit older I should have to introduce you."

Fidelio's response was a bemused smile. He certainly could not tell his employer that he had no interest in the opposite sex. Though Edison was relatively enlightened on issues of race and class, Fidelio doubted the inventor would be as tolerant of a so-called 'sexual deviant.'

He followed Edison to a room that had until recently contained a chemical laboratory. The wooden benches bore the stains of numerous spills. A young red-haired man in a white lab coat was sweeping the floor. "Thank you, Hopkins," Edison said, "you may attend to your duties in the Fluoroscopy Lab."

"Yes, sir." The man nodded and hurried along, casting a cold glance at Fidelio.

It was curious. He had attempted on several occasions to initiate conversation with Lloyd Hopkins, yet the other man seemed to view him with disdain. Fidelio resolved to make another attempt to win the man's trust. He had yet to make any close friends in this country.

On a table in the center of the room lay a pile of the circular metal reels used for Edison's famed 'moving pictures.' One of the reels had been partially unraveled. A length of film passed into a rectangular metal box.

The inventor held up one end of the film and explained, "This is a copy of the census data for Trenton, New Jersey, transformed into the Edison magnetic data recording system. This medium has several advantages over the Hollerith punched-card system, including reduced size and greater ease of duplication. Another advantage is that the dots are visible, thus making the text readable by any sighted person familiar with the Braille system." He inserted the film into a slot in the box, feeding it out the other side and onto an uptake spool.

Edison then engaged a switch, and a row of clear glass tubes mounted next to the box glowed to life. "Are you familiar with Geissler tubing?"

"Of course," Fidelio replied. "The tubing in each cylinder is divided into segments. When subjected to an electrical potential, the rarefied gases within a segment will glow. Illuminating some segments and leaving others dark allow the tubes to display readable letters."

"Correct. Now observe." Edison turned a crank, drawing the film through the box. The cylinders formed letters, spelling 'ADLER ISAAC 59.' "The names are arranged alphabetically, and each person's age is appended afterward." He turned the crank further, and the name changed: 'ANDERSON ARTHUR 33.'

"What an amazing innovation! So what will my assignment be?"

Edison flicked the switch off and the tubes went dark. "You will create a method by which the tapes may be rapidly searched for a specific name, age, street address, or whatever information its operator may desire. It will be challenging, but I believe you are up to the task."

"That will require replacement of the manual drive with a Faraday motor, am I correct?"

"Very insightful. Here, let me open this up and show you the device's internal wiring."

They spent the next two hours reviewing the details of the project. Fidelio was quite enthused. This technology would have applications far beyond the processing of statistical data.

Late on Tuesday of the following week, he and Hopkins were leaving work at the same time. His coworker was mounting his velocipede, one of the newer practical versions with equally sized wheels. "Mr. Hopkins," Fidelio said, "I have a brief question. Do you know anything about a man named Nikola Tesla?"

Hopkins smiled. "No need for the 'mister,' Espinoza, we're pretty informal here. Sure, I know Tesla. He used to work here, until he and the boss had a falling out over a matter of payment. Brilliant fellow; a bit crazy as well. Was always going on about magnetic resonance and such nonsense."

"Well, they do call this the Age of Magnetism," Fidelio responded. "I should have realized he and Edison were acquainted. As for Tesla's ideas, I must say that we shouldn't be too quick to judge. Often the most revolutionary work seems fantastical at the time it is proposed."

Hopkins snorted. "I wouldn't go on about Tesla if I was you. Mr. Edison may be a genius, but he can sure hold a grudge."

After that brief exchange, Hopkins became friendlier. Fidelio was glad; with the amount of work Edison had assigned him, he did not have time for any rivalries. The magnetodatascope took most of his attention. He often found himself staying two or three hours past the time when most of the lab's personnel, save Edison himself, had returned to their homes.

Nevertheless, Fidelio endeavored to spend at least two hours per day on his own project. He had secured lodgings in the workshop behind the home of an elderly couple, the O'Reillys. Mr. O'Reilly was no longer interested in tinkering, so the shop had been idle for several years. In the corner they set up a cot and a chest of drawers, on which Fidelio kept a few amenities such as a mirror, water pitcher, and washbasin.

It was an ideal place to work on his invention. Though his father in Cuba had sent him a copy of the plans he'd archived at their home, Fidelio had made numerous changes since then. The drawings he had been heavily annotated in Spanish and Latin. Hopefully, the cretin who had taken them was too dim to understand their significance.

Over the ensuing weeks, Fidelio recreated his earlier changes to the document, and built a replacement for the lost prototype. He christened it Tarantela, as it resembled an over-sized spider. This new version was better than the first. It now walked with a fairly natural gait. In addition, it had movable arms with pincers that could grasp objects.

After his day's work at Edison's laboratory, Fidelio would eat a quick meal and go right to work on his project. He did not mention Tarantela to his employer. Edison was extremely possessive of his ideas, and the work of those in his employ. Though Fidelio had initially planned to demonstrate the device for Edison and thus document it as his own invention, the robbery had prevented that, so he labored on his brainchild in secret.

Many nights Fidelio worked well past midnight, returning to work after four or five hours of sleep. He wished he could subsist on 'cat naps' like Edison. Unfortunately he found himself quite drowsy the following morning, even after downing several cups of strong tea.

"Long night?" Edison said when he entered the optics lab to see him yawning broadly.

"Do not worry sir; my work is moving ahead on schedule."

Edison smiled. "As long you continue to do so, I'll have no cause for complaint."

Fidelio was pleased that Edison had assigned him to such a fascinating project, even though this area of technology was unrelated to his own invention. Yet his subconscious mind found a connection.

One night as Fidelio labored over Tarantela's schematics, he leaned back in his chair and closed his eyes, and was soon asleep. Usually his dreams were like snippets from his everyday life, but this one was quite strange. In the middle of the shop there appeared a giant celluloid film covered with metallic dots arranged in rectangular blocks. Tarantela crawled across the film in a strange dance, skittering from one block to another, sometimes turning around, at other times snapping its claws. Fidelio realized that the dot patterns determined the creature's action.

"That's it!" Fidelio sat bolt upright in his chair. The kerosene lamp was still burning, and the clock said it was well past midnight. He grabbed a notebook and began writing. "Dots on film need not be data. Designate some patterns as commands. Operator might select a pattern to start an operation such as search."

Though the concept was elegant in its simplicity, it would require considerable effort to implement. The next morning at work, Fidelio began sketching out the new wiring. The motor controls would need to be completely redone. He decided to construct an entirely new circuit, so it could be easily substituted for the existing one.

Early that afternoon, Edison appeared at Fidelio's work table. He watched with rapt interest as Fidelio tightened connections in the new circuit.

"Why have you redesigned my control system?" Edison asked. "You were merely to test and refine the existing one."

"Just a moment, sir," Fidelio said, "and I will show you."

Edison cleared his throat. "Damn it man, face me when you talk. You know I can't hear well." Fidelio turned, intending to apologize, but Edison continued. "If you are having problems with the controller, you must tell me. We cannot afford to be late on this project."

"I beg your pardon, sir. I am working on an idea that came to me in a dream last night. Observe." Fidelio switched on the power, then cranked it manually to the entry labeled 'Adams, Albert.' He pushed the 'start' button and the motor ran forward until 'Baker, Mary,' upon which it changed direction.

"The motor is reversing itself? What is the purpose of this modification?"

"Last night I realized that entries on the tape could be used not simply as data, but also as instructions. In this prototype we arbitrarily select particular names for this purpose, but in a real system, we would encode such instructions as 'begin search' or 'finish.'"

Edison nodded. "Young man, I applaud your ingenuity, and normally I would encourage such experimentation, but for this project, it is not a priority. I cannot afford to pay you to fritter away your days on theoretical research. Let your professor friends at Rutgers do that."

"I apologize, sir. I will make up the time this weekend."

"See that you do. And Espinoza," Edison's faced darkened. "Are you working on other inventive pursuits and not informing me? That would be a violation of your contract."

"No, sir." Though Fidelio hated prevarication, sometimes the situation required it.

"I do not mean to be harsh," Edison said. "I sincerely appreciate your talents. However, if you cannot abide my simple instructions you will need to find employment elsewhere."

"Yes, sir."

After Edison left, Fidelio stared at the film with teeth clenched, breathing deeply.

"Don't take it personal." Hopkins' voice startled him out of his angry musings. "Sorry, I couldn't help overhearing. I think your idea is brilliant. But Edison is a stubborn man. If you question his decisions, he will have you digging ditches like he did to Tesla."

"I appreciate the warning, but you need not worry about me. I have no desire to argue with our employer." As Hopkins walked away Fidelio realized that this scheme would work for controlling Tarantela itself. *If Edison does not see the value in this idea, I shall use it myself.*

Fidelio went right to work. He disassembled the new circuit and re-connected the previous one. Thereafter he redoubled his efforts, often skipping his noon meal to work on the magnetodatascope. He installed a new motor, and made other improvements. Soon it was twice as fast as Hollerith's paper tape reader.

Finding time to work on Tarantela after his long days at Edison's lab was a challenge. It did not help that the walk from home to work and back took 30 minutes in each direction. If only he could have brought his horse from Cuba, the journey would take a fraction of that time. In any case, he had nowhere to stable the creature.

He considered buying a bicycle like Hopkins, but that conveyance would not do for hauling equipment. Since he frequently went to Newark on his days off to acquire components for Tarantela, he found himself spending a considerable sum on taxicab fare. The answer, Fidelio realized, was to purchase an automobile.

After a bit of research, Fidelio decided upon the Stanley Steamer. It had a fine reputation for safety and durability. Since arriving in this country, Fidelio had managed to save a thousand dollars, but for the Steamer he would need a thousand more. One could practically buy a *house* for that amount of money.

His schedule, demanding as it was, could ill afford to wait. There was only one option. Fidelio sat down with pen and paper, his stomach tightening as he touched pen to paper. "Dearest Papa," he wrote. "My sincerest apologies for not writing you last week. My work here is progressing, but it is hampered by a lack of personal transportation. I have diligently saved my money, and I have half of the purchase price of a motorcar. If you could please loan me one thousand American dollars, I shall reimburse you as soon as possible. Love, your son Fidelio."

Due to the urgency of his request, Fidelio sent the letter via 'airship mail.' He received the response in less than a week. "I will lend you the money," his father replied, "if you will promise to be mindful of the dangers of the motorcar. Just last month four souls perished as two of those contraptions collided in downtown Havana. In addition, there will be no further loans until you have repaid this one. I do not wish to foster in you a sense of continued dependency."

Fidelio threw the letter down in disgust. "Does he think I am still a child?" The anger quickly gave way to remorse. Fernando Espinoza had endured the heartbreak of his wife's death in childbirth and raised his son alone. Though the old man had been strict at times, he always made sure Fidelio had the best, from toys and books to education.

He immediately sent his father a letter expressing his heartfelt thanks, and promising to be cautious. The funds arrived at the Newark Western Union office a few days later. From there, Fidelio went immediately to the nearest seller of motorcars.

The Steamer was everything Fidelio had expected and more. Its design was both efficient and elegant. Its curving aerodynamic body was superior to the boxy shape of its competitors. Better still, Stanley had redesigned the boiler to eliminate that bane of steam automobiles, the long warm-up time. The new Steamer could reach operating temperature in under three minutes.

Early that following Monday morning, Fidelio encountered Edison as he arrived at the laboratory in his electrically-powered Phaeton. "Mr. Espinoza, is that your automobile?"

"Yes, sir, I have just acquired it."

"Then congratulations! You have joined the modern world. Is it steam powered?"

"Indeed. I am already quite fond of it."

"It will be a great convenience," Edison said as the two of them entered the front door. "Even considering the warm-up time, which electrical vehicles do not have. By the way, there will be an important lecture next week at Rutgers College on the comparative advantages of different calculating engines. Though I am fascinated with that technology, I am far too busy to go. If you wish to attend, and agree to inform me of what you learn, I will grant you the day off."

"I would be delighted. As I told you earlier, I have been corresponding with some of the professors in the mathematics department, and I would welcome the opportunity to converse with them in person."

"Since your vehicle has room for two, perhaps you could take Hopkins along with you."

Hopkins, who was at a nearby work bench winding a transformer, looked up from his work. "A lecture? What's the topic?"

"It's something you should both find useful in your work: a comparison of the Babbage Mathematical Engine versus the Hollerith Data Entry System."

Hopkins nodded. "That does sound interesting, but New Brunswick is nearly 30 miles from here. Are we to take the train?"

"If you wish. However, your colleague Mr. Espinoza has just purchased a new horseless carriage. I'm certain he'd allow you to ride along."

"Really?" Hopkins looked intently at Fidelio, as if to say, *how can he afford one of those?* Instead he said, "I would appreciate that. What day next week will it be held?"

"Friday. Considering the distance, and the fact that those professors can be quite long-winded, the two of you may as well make a day of it. I must remind you not to discuss any details of your work with outsiders. If asked, simply say we are working with electrical devices and making steady progress."

⚙ ᚠᚦ ⚙

On the day of the lecture, Fidelio arrived at the East Orange laboratories as the sun was rising. His coworker arrived on his cycle a moment later. "This will be a new experience for me," Hopkins said as he climbed in to the passenger seat. "I've never ridden in a motorcar before."

"It's fitting, then that your first ride is in the best." Fidelio depressed the throttle and headed southward on the town's main street.

"I'm sure that Edison would beg to differ," Hopkins said, "since he holds the patent on the country's best-selling vehicle charging station."

"That is true, but a steam-powered car has a much greater operational range."

35

Fidelio had not realized how noisy automobile travel could be, especially when one went from the paved streets of the city to gravel-surfaced country roads. The two men attempted to converse despite the difficulty.

Lloyd Hopkins had an attractive young fiancée named Elise, and the couple was currently busy planning their upcoming wedding. "I hope you will able to attend."

"I would be honored," Fidelio said, half shouting to make himself heard.

"How about you? Is there anyone special waiting for you back in Cuba?"

"Sadly, no," Fidelio responded. "At present I am too busy for such matters."

"As was Tesla," Lloyd said. "I don't envy the solitary life."

Fidelio nodded, thinking sadly of his dear lost Rodrigo. Few heterosexuals understood "the love that dare not speak its name," as Oscar Wilde had called it. Sadly, the world would likely stay that way for the foreseeable future.

Soon they arrived at the venerable institution of Rutgers. Fidelio was gratified to see that his Stanley Steamer attracted stares from students and faculty alike.

The lecture itself was a dull affair. The speaker, Doctor Edmund Brown, was the author of several interesting articles scholarly articles on mathematical engines. Fidelio marveled how the man's monotonous voice could make such a fascinating topic seem boring. It amused Fidelio to see Hokpins' eyes close, his head droop, and then jerk awake.

Afterward they headed to the podium to speak with the professor, who was currently conversing with two other well-dressed, gray haired gentlemen. Fidelio introduced himself and Hopkins. "It was a fascinating lecture, Professor."

"Thank you. It is my belief that this technology will transform the world." Brown pulled a pipe from his jacket pocket and filled the bowl with tobacco. "I am heading back to my office, if you gentleman would like to accompany me."

"If it would be no trouble," Fidelio said. He and Hopkins followed along as Brown and his colleagues exited the building.

"Espinoza, I apologize that I did not remember you at first," said one of the other fellows. "You're the Cuban gentleman with whom I've been corresponding."

"The same," Fidelio said. "Then you are George Rogers?"

"Yes, and this is William Laplace, who was written you was well. It's so good to finally meet you in the flesh."

"We've been quite curious, because we hadn't heard from you in a while," Laplace said. "How goes your, ahem, special project?"

"Unfortunately I have had very little free time," he answered, glancing nervously at Hopkins, who gave him a quizzical look.

"Yes, of course, your duties for Mr. Edison." Laplace drew closer as they walked. "Are you free to speak of this matter?"

"I am sorry; it is not a good time for discussion."

"We fully understand the need for confidentiality," Rogers cut in. "If you require any help with the patent application, I have considerable experience in that area."

"No, I have set that project aside for the time being," Fidelio said. "Anyway, my primary motivation is not monetary gain."

"That, my idealistic young fellow, is beside the point. You need to establish your claim to what's yours before some else discovers it independently. In addition, there is the issue of your stolen prototype. What if that ends up in the possession of someone who understands its value? Some stranger could lay claim to your work."

To his credit, Hopkins kept his questions to himself until they had gotten into Fidelio's automobile. As they departed the campus, it seemed like he was about to burst from curiosity.

"I hate to snoop in your affairs, Fidelio, but I can't help being concerned. What was stolen? The boss is really strict about locking everything up. How could it have gotten by him?"

"The incident they described happened before I came to work for Mr. Edison."

Hopkins sat for a while, obviously mulling over the implications of this new information. "So you've been engaging in independent research? Edison would not be happy to hear that."

"I am aware of the intellectual property clause, but this falls outside the agreement. It was something I created when I lived in Havana. I brought an early prototype with me to America. Unfortunately, my trunk was stolen shortly after I arrived in this country. Not just that, but the plans as well. Luckily, my father in Cuba was able to send copies of the earlier schematics."

"Still, you should have informed Mr. Edison. You could easily be using information you got from working in his laboratory. That wouldn't be proper."

Fidelio exhaled in disgust. "I assure you that it is based on work I performed before being employed by Mr. Edison. The plans were signed, witnessed and dated."

"Very well, then," Hopkins said. "I will take your word for it."

It was not until they stopped at a café for supper that Hopkins broached the topic again.

"Fidelio, I've been thinking. If your device is as valuable an innovation as the doctor believes, I would like to be in on it. My Elise has her heart set on this charming little bungalow downtown, but on my salary I could never afford it. If you were to take me on as a partner, I will ensure that Mr. Edison never finds out about your project."

Fidelio put down his fork and stared at Hopkins. "Lloyd, if I did not know you better, I would conclude that you were blackmailing me."

"What?" Hopkins opened his mouth in surprise, his face pale cheeks reddened. "Fidelio, you misunderstand. This is no threat. I simply believe that, as your friend, I might be given the opportunity to participate in your project."

"Friend?" Fidelio laughed mirthlessly. "Friends do not speak to each other in such a fashion. I am beginning to question my judgment in considering you as such."

"That goes both ways. Friends don't keep secrets from each other, and you never told me about your side project."

"That is very presumptuous of you. If you do not respect my privacy, our friendship is over."

"Suit yourself. I'm not the one who was breaking the rules."

Fidelio lowered his voice and leaned in toward Hopkins. "I warn you – if you disclose my private business to Mr. Edison, there will be serious consequences."

For the remainder of the journey, the two men shared a hostile silence. Fidelio was tempted to order Hopkins out of his car and let him walk home, but his upbringing forbade such a discourteous act. The sun was setting as they arrived at the laboratory once again. Fidelio had barely rolled to a stop when Hopkins flung open the door, jumped out of the car and cycled away without a word.

Chapter 4 – Crisis in Buffalo

Hank stood outside the Temple of Music with a small group of Friends. They watched silently as the visitors to the Pan-American Exhibition poured into the ornate structure. He and his companions had expected the autumn weather in Buffalo to be cool and dressed accordingly. Though the morning had been pleasant, in the afternoon they encountered an unexpected Indian summer. There was no relief from the merciless sun. Under his dark clothing, Hank felt the sweat rolling down his back.

Robert Barton finally spoke up. "Brothers and sisters, I suggest we end this vigil and return home. No one is paying us any attention."

Hank exhaled in frustration. Robert was a sincere Christian, but having been raised in the Quaker faith, he didn't have the enthusiasm of a recent convert like himself. "Please, let's stay a little while longer. The President is speaking now. A whole mess of people are in there listening. They'll be pouring out in a few minutes."

"I agree," Nola Parker said. "If this journey was for naught, what do a few more minutes matter?"

Even after several months in the church, Hank still felt like an outsider, and he was grateful for any kind of acknowledgment. "Thank you, kindly Sister Nola. Sorry, I meant *thee*." The Quaker 'plain speech,' as they called it, took some getting used to.

Robert had been right, though. Most folks barely gave them a sideways glance. Of the few who actually noticed the protesters, the majority seemed downright hostile. That didn't bother Hank; he believed if people would just speak their minds, the truth would win in the end.

As for the Quaker philosophy, Hank had occasional doubts. The Friends were brave and true disciples of Christ. They were among the first to take a stand against slavery. But sometimes their way seemed too passive. Hank wanted to grab people by the collar and shake some sense into them. Just because he'd taken a vow of non-violence didn't mean he had to stand around like a wooden Indian.

Considering all the injustice in the world, even a silent protest was better than none. Hank was particularly proud of his sign, though his arms ached from holding it up. It was a simple placard attached to a thin piece of lumber, the type carried by the New York City dockworkers when they went on strike the previous summer. Its inscription, in broad brush strokes of black paint, was the sentence, "I have seen the horrors of war."

In addition to Hank's message, the ladies of the group wore broad sashes bearing legends such as 'Christ Opposes War' and 'Love Thy Neighbor.' Hank's favorite was the one that said, in the words of Jesus himself, 'Blessed be the Peacemakers.' That was because Nola wore it. The sweet, chaste angel had inhabited his dreams ever since he'd met her.

"I applaud thy faith, Brother Hank," Robert said. "But what shall we do? We don't wish to chant slogans like a gang of laborers."

Hank turned to face the group. He cleared his throat. "We could sing a hymn."

"Brother Hank, this was to be a dignified, silent protest," Robert sniffed.

The man's dour personality took some getting used to. Folks said he'd been morose since the passing of his wife, so Hank tried to be sympathetic. Though sometimes, he felt like he was being ridden like a ten-dollar mule.

"That's true," Hank replied. "But standing here hushed up isn't helping our cause any. Given the thousands who've traveled from far and wide to hear the President speak, we have a unique opportunity. And uh…" he stammered for a moment, "Christ tells us to help those who're suffering, as the poor Indianos of the Philippine Islands surely are."

"What would thou have us sing?" Damiana asked. She was Robert's sister, a matronly woman married to an older gentleman whose infirmities had prevented him from attending today's vigil. Her warm personality helped counter-balance her brother's doctrinal strictness.

As everyone looked at Hank, his mind went empty. Silently he prayed for help, and a thought sprang into his mind. "How about 'How Can I Keep From Singing?'"

"I concur, Brother Hank," Nola said. "Because that hymn is most appropriate. Yet others among us wish to remain silent. Can we reach a consensus?"

That was just like the Quakers, to take a vote on everything. Though some could be bossy at times, Nola always made sure every member felt included. If only he didn't feel so tongue-tied every time he was around her.

A loud voice startled Hank out of his reverie. He found himself face to face with a burly, round-faced man with a dark bushy beard.

The stranger's face was flushed with emotion. "What's this traitorous bullshit

I hear? Have you actually served this country, or are you one of the ungrateful slackers who didn't?"

"Please, sir, mind your language, there's ladies present. And yes, I did serve in the Spanish war, but I have seen the light."

"So you would disgrace the memory of your comrades who fell in battle? And the sailors who died on the Maine due to Spanish treachery?"

"Gosh, mister, if I hadn't served you'd say I didn't know squat about war, but since I have, you accuse me of disloyalty." Hank felt self-conscious for lapsing into his Western lingo, but he felt foolish using the Quaker speech with outsiders. "Either way, I don't get to speak my mind."

The stranger stepped closer and began rolling up his sleeves. "Speak your mind, *sir*, but don't dishonor my country, especially when the President's here."

Hank looked at his companions, desperate for some to help him carry the argument. All were silent. He turned back to the furious onlooker, now flanked by two muscular fellows who looked just as belligerent. In his younger days, Hank would have called that even odds, but he'd sworn to follow the Savior's command to harm no man, even these no-account ruffians. He swallowed hard. "Please don't take offense, sir, but... do you remember in the Gospel, the part where Christ talked about turning the other cheek?"

"Ah, now I get it, you're a yellow-bellied coward!" With that, the bearded man slammed his massive fist into Hank's unprotected face.

In his past life out West, Hank had traded punches with many a cowpoke in dozens of tawdry saloons. In the Army, he'd been in numerous scuffles while on liberty in the island's cantinas. Certainly he'd lost his share, but he'd made sure his antagonist came away with at least a sore jaw or black eye. This time, he had no chance to block the attack. The man's fist hit Hank's chin so hard, he thought he heard a gunshot, and then he fell to the ground and blacked out.

When Hank awoke, he opened his eyes and saw a canvas ceiling glowing golden. *Must be around sunset.* For a moment he thought he was back in Cuba, in the field hospital after he got kicked by that blasted mule. But the pain was in his head, not his stomach, and he remembered what had happened. How long had he been out?

Hank propped himself up on his elbows and looked around. A few feet away stood a young man in uniform. On his hip was a holster containing a revolver. He stood next to a white sheet or curtain that hung from the roof of the tent. From the shadows moving about on the sheet and the sound of hushed voices, there appeared to be quite a few people in there. Hank meant to ask the man where this place was, and who or what he was guarding, when someone arrived at the door of the tent.

"We have the fluoroscope," said a voice from outside.

"All right, come in," said the guard.

As the guard opened the tent flap to let them in, Hank realized that there were a lot of people outside as well, talking loudly, maybe arguing, Was he still at the Fair? There was the sound of squeaky wheels as two workmen in dungarees entered the tent with a cart laden with a massive electrical device. The metal, glass and wood monstrosity looked just like the machine they had used to photograph Hank's insides at Columbia Medical Center.

Someone pulled back the curtain and allowed them to proceed. Hank craned his neck but couldn't see anything. After they passed through, the guard turned and looked Hank in the eye.

"I see you're awake," he said.

"Yep," said Hank. People spoke in hushed, anxious voices. "Can you tell me what's going on in there?"

The man regarded Hank suspiciously. "I'm sorry. My duty is to provide security for the individual behind the curtain. I'm not permitted to say more than that."

"Can you at least tell me where I am?"

"Certainly. This is the medical tent at the Exposition."

"That figures," said Hank as set sat upright on the cot. "The fellow out there knocked me cold. Did they arrest him? Or am I the one in hot water?"

The young man shrugged. "Sorry, sir, I know nothing of your situation, or why you're here. Is there a reason you would expect to be in trouble?"

"Not at all. Like I was telling you, I was in a bit of a tussle, but I didn't lay a hand on the man who slugged me."

"Then you should have nothing to worry about."

"You're military police, aren't you? Did you serve in the war?"

"No. sir. Though I was sent to Cuba to keep order after the armistice."

"Ah, you were in Cuba? Me too, with Roosevelt's Roughriders." Usually that statement got an awe-struck response, but the guard made no comment, so Hank continued. "Couldn't I just have a quick peek behind that curtain? This business has got me mighty interested."

"No, sir. You'll have to read the story in the papers tomorrow, I'm afraid."

"Never mind then. Am I free to go?"

"I've been instructed to hold you here for possible questioning. Please relax, sir, I'm sure your wait won't be inordinately long."

That might be so, Hank reflected, but when a man had nothing to occupy his mind, without a hint of how long he'd be waiting, even a short spell could seem long indeed.

Eventually two Erie County sheriff's deputies arrived. "Henry MacMillan?"

"Right here! Have you fellows come for my statement? Never mind that; I got no plans to press charges. I'm sure the fellow honestly believed in what he was saying, and I can't fault a man for sticking up for his beliefs – even if he did get a bit carried away."

The men gave him a blank look. "That would be up to you," one of them said. "Our orders are to transport you to the sheriff's office."

"But– I was here with a group, can't I get a message to them? That's the Quakers who were here on vigil. They might be real worried!" As he said it, Hank realized how ridiculous the request was. How would these men know where to find them?

"Just come with us, sir."

"All right, officers." Hank stood up. For a moment he felt dizzy, and staggered a bit.

The other deputy took Hank's arm to steady him. "Easy, take it easy. The medic says you've had a wee concussion."

"Sir, I notice a bit of the Old Country in the way you talk. Tell me, do your people hail from anywhere near County Donegal?"

The man shook his head. "I'm an American, Mr. MacMillan." Then he smiled slightly. "Though my mom and pop were indeed from the Emerald Isle."

As they exited the tent, Hank was astonished to see that the medical tent was surrounded by a throng of onlookers, packed ten to twenty deep. The front rank was dominated by a line of men in fancy suits, carrying notepads. Standing front and center was a man with an enormous camera resting on a tripod. Every reporter was trying to speak at once.

"Officers! Officers!"

"John Van Dyke, *New York Times*..."

"Can you say anything about the President's condition?"

"No comment, gentlemen."

As soon as they got past the bulk of the crowd, Hank turned to his escorts. "What's this about the President? Did something happen to him?"

"Sorry, Mr. MacMillan, we'd best not say," said the deputy with the Irish accent.

They came to a small black carriage with the word 'POLICE' painted on the side. The Irish deputy opened the side door and bade him enter, then got in behind him, while the other man got in front to drive.

"I'm relieved, Officer, to see I'm not going in the paddy wagon this time." That remark earned him a glare from the deputy. "I didn't mean no insult to the Irish; it's a figure of speech, right? With a name like MacMillan, you know I've got Celtic blood myself."

As they rode in silence, Hank said a silent prayer of thanks that the trouble had passed. Though his head still pained him a bit, that would go away in time. Likely he wouldn't spend any time in the hoosegow, either, though he was mystified about what they wanted. Most likely ask him about what happened to McKinley. Too bad he wouldn't be able to help them.

Finally they stopped in front of a red brick courthouse. The two officers flanked him as they walked up the steps to the door. They passed the reception desk and climbed a flight of stairs to a small room where two other men were waiting. One was bald-headed and stocky; the other was rail-thin with a shock of flaxen hair. Both wore dark slacks held up with suspenders, white long-sleeved shirts, and long neckties. The stocky man nodded and the deputies departed.

Hank looked from one to the other. The room was hot and stuffy, and they did not look happy to be there. "Gentlemen, if I may ask, I'm puzzled about the reason for this interview."

"We'll ask the questions, sir," the portly man snapped. "I'm David Hancock of the Secret Service; this," he gestured at the blond man, "is my colleague William Wright." Hancock cleared his throat and looked Hank in the eye. "What is your opinion of President McKinley?"

"I never did meet the man, and I don't follow politics, but I've got no beef with him except the war in the Philippines. Those folks have a right to be free, just like us."

"And would you say he should be made to pay for what he's done?"

"That's not for me to decide, but he will have to answer to his Creator someday."

"What do you know about anarchism?" Wright cut in.

"What, you mean the lack of government?" Hank shook his head. "I reckon if

44

men were angels that'd be the way to go. Otherwise we need a bit of law and order, even if we don't always approve of the folks in charge." He gave his questioners a puzzled look. "Why do you ask?"

"Just answer the questions, please." Hancock pushed a sheet of paper across the desk. It bore a pencil sketch of a face, dark-eyed and scowling. "Do you know this man?"

Hank stared at the face. Something in the eyes, in the tightly drawn mouth, told him, *this is a man who thinks life gave him a raw deal.* "Sorry, I never laid eyes on him." He pondered a while longer. "No, I take that back. I can't say for sure if it's him, but there was this tall hombre I saw who came in all by himself. I remember 'cause he was looking around all nervous like."

"So he was definitely alone?"

"Yep. He looked real miserable, but we all were, from the hot weather and all. He was wearing a heavy jacket, which seemed a mite strange, but then my party and me were gussied up for the occasion, too. Now it all makes sense."

"Why? Was he doing anything else unusual? Carrying something perhaps?"

"Not that I could see, but he had one hand in his jacket pocket. There was plenty room for a gun in there, if that's what you're suggesting."

Wright, who had been mostly taking notes, looked up from his pad and asked, "What were you doing at the Exhibition? You didn't come to see the President?"

Hank shook his head. "Nope. I was on a vigil for peace, with my fellow Friends. Society of Friends, that is. Most folks call us Quakers."

"Quakers?" The chubby man interjected. "The cowards who refuse to serve their country?"

Hank sighed. The Apostle Paul talked about suffering for one's faith, and of course in Bible times they had it a lot worse. "Sir, I did serve, in the recent campaign in Cuba. I was with Colonel Roosevelt's Rough Riders. That was before I joined the Friends."

"I understand," said the fair-headed man. "My mother's family hails from Philadelphia. I don't agree with your interpretation of Scripture, but I respect your beliefs."

"What I'd like to know is," Hank said, "what happened to Mister McKinley? I can't abide what he's done abroad in the name of my country, but I don't wish the man any harm."

"The President has been shot," Hancock said. "He is currently in grave condition."

"Really? And was that the scoundrel who did it?" He pointed to the sketch.

"Indeed," answered the stocky agent. "Though he may not survive either. The crowd attacked him after the shooting and gave him a savage beating. I can't say I blame them."

"The President had no guards to protect him?"

"He refused our protection. Actually, we had several agents discreetly on scene, but they were not close enough to prevent the tragedy."

The interrogation went on for a while longer. The two men asked Hank many more questions, some of which were differently-worded repetitions of earlier ones. Probably they hoped to trip him up or make some connection between him and the shooter. They never did ask Hank about the man who had punched him in the jaw.

In the end they thanked him for his time and sent him on his way. Just outside the courthouse, two familiar faces awaited him.

Nola left Robert's side and hurried up the steps to meet him. "Brother Hank, we are so relieved to see thee. Did the authorities treat thee harshly?"

"Nope, they treated me fairly enough," Hank responded, looking at them both in turn. "They were mighty upset about what happened to McKinley. I reckon they were just trying to find out whatever they could."

Robert nodded. "We thank the Lord thou art safe and not under arrest. Our kind has been wrongly accused before." He glanced quickly at Nola, who smiled but said nothing.

Hank realized with a shock that grouchy old Robert was sweet on Nola. Did she feel that way in return? *Please Lord,* he prayed, *let it be the brotherly kind of love.*

Robert hailed a horse-drawn taxi, which took them back to their hotel. They sat together in an awkward silence. Hank gazed out the window, trying to summon his courage.

By the time they reached the hotel, Hank had made up his mind. "Sister Nola," he said as they exited the carriage, "I would have a word with thee, in private." He looked briefly at Robert, who nodded calmly. Did that mean the two of them weren't sweethearts after all?

Robert waited by the doorway as Hank walked with Nola along the sidewalk bordering the hotel. "Sister Nola, I've never been good with fancy words. Thou probably already know that I'm sweet on thee. I may not be the best catch in the river, but I'm a hard worker and the woman I marry, I'll treat her like a princess. In other words, what I'm trying to say is, I love thee, Nola. Would thou do me the honor of being my wife?"

Nola's pretty mouth was twisted with distress. "I do not mean to hurt thee, but I am promised to another." She smiled uneasily. "Henry MacMillan, thou art a good, kind, and honest man. If Providence had intended differently we might have ended up together."

Hank hung his head. He hated to appear weak, but he knew if he looked at her, the tears would come. Nola put her hand tentatively on his arm. "I am certain that a handsome, devout man such as thee cannot help but find love."

"I understand." Hank said, setting his mouth in a smile. "I apologize if I upset thee." Of course Robert was her beau; he'd been a fool not to notice. He prayed to the Lord to give him the strength not to hate the man. After all, who could blame him? If the shoe were on the other foot, he wouldn't want Robert to hold a grudge, either.

The next day, Hank bought a copy of the *New York Times* at the train station. It told how a foreign-born 'anarchist' named Leon Czolgosz had shot the President. They had rushed McKinley to the Exhibition's medical tent and used the Roentgen machine that had been on display nearby to locate the bullets lodged within McKinley's body. The President was expected to make a full recovery. Hank said a quick prayer for the man's health, which he figured was his Christian duty, even if the man had been responsible for some terribly sinful things overseas.

On the following Sunday, at the close of the weekly prayer meeting, Robert and Nola informed the fellowship of their intent to marry. Hank shook Robert's hand and congratulated them both, though the joy of the occasion was lost on him. Although he intended to continue serving Christ in any way he could, New York was not the place for him to do it. It was time for this old cowpoke to go home.

The very next day, Hank packed his things and settled up his rent with Mrs. Miller. He also wrote a letter to Mr. Skolnick at the machine shop expressing his regrets, but he had to leave town. The Old Man, as everyone called him, was a crusty old fellow who had his favorites, and since he'd gone Quaker, Hank was no longer one of them.

It was only a few blocks to the railway station, so Hank didn't bother calling a cab. As he walked along, carrying his heavy bags, he gazed wistfully at a graceful Zeppelin departing the Buffalo Airfield. He had always wanted to take a ride in the sky and see God's creation from the air. In his daydreams he had planned to take

Nola on such a ride for their honeymoon. He had enough in his pocket for an air ticket to Chicago, but the thought of going alone tore at his heart. Besides, the cost of the ticket would leave him precious little to spare for living expenses when he arrived back home in Arizona.

He cast his eyes down and kept walking. When he reached the local rail station, he bought a ticket for a westbound passenger train on the Buffalo, Rochester and Pittsburgh Railway. Thirty minutes later, he was on his way out of the Empire State.

Chapter 5 – A New Direction

Fidelio had never been one to waste his time and energy in worry. Yet he found Hopkins' threats unsettling. Certainly he did not want to lose his job at Edison Laboratories, but being accused of impropriety upset him far worse.

Since Fidelio had not been fired immediately at the start of the week, he concluded that Hopkins had decided not to inform their employer. Yet Edison surprised him by calling him into his office late the next Friday afternoon. Never before had this request turned Fidelio's stomach in knots.

"Get the door, please," Edison said. It was an ominous sign. His office was small and cluttered with precious little air circulation. He did not close his door without a good reason.

"Fidelio," the older man began, "You have been an exemplary worker, but recently I have heard some very disturbing accusations. I have been led to understand that you have been spending your spare time working on an unauthorized project – a project that quite likely uses ideas you have come across in my employ."

Fidelio forced himself to wait a moment before responding; any outburst would likely appear as an indication of guilt. "Sir, with all due respect, the allegation is preposterous. From whom did you hear this?"

Edison held up a hand. "Easy, son, I didn't necessarily say I believed it. However, I take this issue quite seriously in light of the contract we both signed when you came to work for me. Such a violation would normally be grounds for your immediate dismissal. However, I value your services. If you were to hand over the project you've been working on, including all the plans and blueprints, I will not press charges."

Damn that Hopkins! Fidelio would not allow the scoundrel's scheme to be successful. "Anything I may have worked on was my own concept from long before we were associated, and was outside the range of the activities of Edison Laboratories. The agreement was quite specific in that regard."

"Then it should be a simple matter to show me proof of this fact, such as notarized drawings which predate our association. If you are an inventor, you must be aware of the importance of such documentation, since, according to the US Patent Office, the initial discoverer is awarded the rights."

Fidelio exhaled. "You have my word as a gentleman, but regretfully, I cannot provide proof. My trunk was stolen when I arrived in this country early this year. I filed a report on the incident with the Newark police."

Edison stared at him for a moment, and then burst out laughing. "Young man, I have heard some cockamamie stories in my life, but I'm sorry, I'm not falling for this one. I've given you a choice. Will you hand over the device, or shall I be forced to notify the authorities?"

"No." Fidelio stood up, fists clenched, face flushed with rage. "I will not give up my invention, nor will I have my reputation sullied. My father has copies of the original plans in Cuba. I will request he send these here by airship mail. You may then inspect the device and verify that it is derived from the original plans."

"If that is indeed the case, I shall pursue no legal action. However, I feel that you have violated the spirit if not the letter of our agreement, and as such our business relationship must come to an end."

"I agree. Had you not terminated my employment, I would have tendered my resignation. Good day, sir." Fidelio grabbed his satchel and stormed out of Edison's office. Before he left the laboratory, however, there was one more issue to resolve.

Lloyd Hopkins sat on a stool in the magnetonomics lab, peering into a microscope. "You Judas! You betrayed my confidence!"

"I beg your pardon?" There was a smirk on Hopkins' freckled face. "I don't know what you're talking about." He returned his gaze to the microscope, reaching across the table for another sample. "Unless 'Judas' is some kind of traditional Cuban greeting."

"Look me in the eye and say that!" Fidelio grabbed him by the wrist.

"Unhand me, you thug! You had best leave, or the management will call the police!"

"Then I will be brief. You befriended me, then betrayed my trust. I refused your blackmail so you told Edison a tapestry of lies and half-truths."

"I swear it was not me who informed him of your extracurricular activities. You know that Edison corresponds with the science faculty at Rutgers. Have you asked them?"

"I discussed the matter only with Laplace and Rogers, and both of them swore on their honor to keep my confidence." Fidelio glared at Hopkins, wishing that the 'evil eye' he'd heard about as a child was not a fairy tale. "You are a liar, and a poor one at that. In my country, such slander would be grounds for me to challenge you to a duel."

"Now you have offended my honor as a gentleman by *your* slander. Dueling is illegal in New Jersey, but we can still settle this matter like civilized men. Did your fancy university teach you to fight, or will you slap me with a glove like some kind of fop?"

"Ha! Your jest is every bit as insulting as your libelous accusations. I accept your challenge, at any time and place you wish to name!"

"Then make it tomorrow evening, at 7 o'clock sharp, Tenth Street Gymnasium. Do you know where that is?"

"On Tenth Street, I presume. I shall see you there."

With all the worries of the previous week, Fidelio had been plagued with stomach trouble as well as difficulty sleeping. Now, surprisingly, it seemed as if a crushing weight had been lifted from his soul. That night, he slept soundly. Early that next morning, he sent a telegram to his father, requesting the notarized documents. He spent the rest of the day working on Tarantela.

Fidelio was so occupied with his creation that he almost forgot his appointment with Hopkins. He drove the Steamer to Tenth Street, easily finding the gymnasium. As he entered the facility, was surprised at how many men were here, most of them young, hale and well-muscled. If Hopkins were not a member, this would be an excellent place to frequent.

On the far side of the room, he spied the familiar shock of red hair. Thankfully there was no sign of the wild blond curls of Hopkins' fiancée, who usually accompanied her man like a rosy-cheeked Siamese twin. He approached his nemesis. "I have had no opportunity to purchase boxing gloves."

"Mister Salerno will lend a pair to you." Hopkins nodded toward a paunchy bald man with a huge handlebar mustache, apparently the gym's owner or manager. "You will need them, because this gym observes Marquess of Queensberry rules. Are you familiar with them? Or do Cubans fight no-holds-barred, like the savages they are?"

"I am well acquainted with the rules," Fidelio sniffed. Seeing that Hopkins was already bare-chested, he removed his shirt. His fencing breeches and boots would suffice for boxing regalia. He procured the gloves from the owner and quickly laced them up.

As he climbed into the ring, Fidelio realized that Hopkins was more muscular than he'd realized. The man's quiet demeanor had misled him, which was unusual, given that he was well-accustomed to appraising other men's physiques.

Salerno paused to strike a match and light a huge cigar, then rang the bell.

The two men leapt into motion. Hopkins threw one punch after another, but Fidelio dodged and kept up his guard. At the University they had criticized his fencing technique as too defensive; here that strategy was to his advantage. Still, Fidelio quickly lost his initial overconfidence, because by the end of the first round he was panting heavily. Having avoided physical labor over the past months, his fitness had suffered.

"Round Two!"

Fidelio raised his gloves, but was momentarily distracted by a handsome young trainer at ringside. His focus was restored when Hopkins landed a ferocious blow to his chest.

Fidelio ignored the pain and put up his gloves, guarding himself more carefully now, but still he did not strike.

Hopkins punched again, grazing Fidelio's ear. The breeze of its passing was almost as disconcerting as if the blow had connected. That moment of disorientation cost him, as Hopkins punched again, this time connecting to Fidelio's stomach. Thankfully, the second round was over.

Think! As one of the trainers furnished him with a much-needed drink of water, Fidelio admonished himself. *You are far cleverer than this red-haired baboon.* That mental picture reminded him of a difficult opponent he'd faced in a tournament during his sophomore year, and the gambit he had used to defeat him.

"Round Three!"

Now! Fidelio charged forward, swinging wildly. Surprised, Hopkins stepped back. Then Fidelio fell back, holding his gloves up by his face, deliberately opening his midsection to attack.

Hopkins took the bait. He lunged forward and swung a mighty blow, which Fidelio dodged by a quick jump to the left. When the punch did not connect, Hopkins continued his trajectory, stumbling and almost losing his footing.

Just as quickly, Fidelio whirled and jabbed at his opponent's new location. There was a sickening crunch as Fidelio's fist connected with Hopkins' nose. The red-headed man's eyes went wide. Two scarlet rivulets appeared below his nostrils. He wobbled for a moment, then collapsed to the floor of the ring.

Fidelio stared at his vanquished opponent and caught his breath as the mustached man counted to ten.

"The winner!" Salerno proclaimed in a rumbling voice. He approached Fidelio as he exited the ring. "Young man, your technique is unconventional but effective. It so happens that I'm setting up a league. You'd be perfect for our light-weight class."

"Thank you, but no." Fighting the urge to vomit, Fidelio removed the gloves and donned his shirt. As he glanced over his shoulder, he saw two men lifting the unconscious, bloody-faced Hopkins from the ring floor. He was in no mood to check into the extent of Hopkins' injury. He left the gym, disgusted that he'd agreed to this barbaric contest.

As he walked, he sensed a presence behind him and turned quickly, expecting an ambush.

"Oh! Excuse me to startle you! Where did you learn fight that way?" The man behind him was tall and wiry; his broken English had a strong Slavic accent. Though his features were harsh, there was a certain stark beauty in his blue eyes and high cheekbones.

"I am from Cuba," Fidelio began cautiously. "But I attended university in Spain, where I was on the fencing team."

"Ah, fencing. I did not have opportunity in my country, but would like to learn now that I am in America."

"Indeed. It is a fine sport, though I am hardly qualified to teach it. Are you by chance Russian?"

He shook his head. "My home country is part of Russian Empire, but I am Ukrainian. My name is Ivan." He extended a beefy hand.

Fidelio shook the Ukrainian's hand and eyed him suspiciously, recalling the incident with the thieving driver upon his arrival in Brooklyn. Yet something about the fellow's mannerisms – the way his eyes held his gaze, how he stood just a bit too close – told Fidelio that Ivan shared his own predilections and appetites. "Pleased to meet you, Ivan. I would like to talk with you further, but I know how vile my appearance must be, not to mention my hygiene. Do you know Elena's Teahouse? We could meet there tomorrow at midday. By the way, my name is Fidelio."

"I know, they announced when you won. This is fortunate meeting. I share house with brothers two blocks away. You can wash up there, then we talk further."

Fidelio nodded. "I would greatly appreciate that."

Luckily, Fidelio was in the habit of taking an early morning constitutional, so Mr. O'Reilly was not overly surprised when he encountered his tenant at their gate, heading for his quarters behind the house.

"Fidelio!" O'Reilly waved as he walked up to greet him. "Were you out `enjoying this fine beautiful morning?"

"Indeed," Fidelio said. Although he had bathed at Ivan's, his clothing reeked of sweat, and he hoped his landlord would not notice. "Is Mrs. O'Reilly feeling better today?"

"Much better, thank you. She must have eaten a bit of undercooked pork roast." He reached in his vest pocket and consulted his watch. "My stars, you'd best hurry, or ye'll be late for work!"

"I am currently on hiatus from Mr. Edison's laboratory." Seeing O'Reilly's look of surprise, he added, "Do not be concerned, I will not be late with my rent."

As Fidelio opened the door to his modest quarters, he sighed and sprawled out on his tiny bed. He did not, however, have time to rest.

It was high time he considered his options. Though his employment with Edison could not be salvaged, he had gained invaluable experience there. Indeed, the relationship had served its purpose, and allowed him to earn some money as well. There had to be other opportunities for employment in this huge country.

Several possibilities came immediately to mind. The first was Nikola Tesla, whom he had written a few weeks prior. Tesla had apparently assumed the letter was a request for a job, rather than a scientific inquiry. In his response, he had thanked Fidelio for his interest, but "We have no openings at present." Perhaps that had changed; every few weeks Fidelio would see something in the scientific journals about one of Tesla's unique and ground-breaking ventures. He resolved to write another letter soon.

Another name that came to mind was Henry Ford, the noted automotive innovator. His Detroit Automobile Company had just barely survived the last business downturn, so he could certainly use some young talent to help turn things around. However, Fidelio remembered that Ford was a good friend of Edison's, so it was not worth trying. Tragically, a personal reference which would have been a valuable asset was now a liability.

Then there was the inventor of the telephone, Alexander Graham Bell. He divided his time between Canada and the Washington, DC, area. Unfortunately, Bell and Edison were also acquainted, though more as rivals than allies. Yet it would be a simple for Edison to contact Bell about him; he had little doubt that Hopkins would encourage him to do so. For a moment, he felt a sense of despair. Would he be forced to return to Cuba, his dreams defeated?

No, an Espinoza would ever give up so easily. According to his father, the name derived from the Latin meaning 'thorny brush,' and the members of their family had appropriately been known for their stubborn, 'prickly' character. Even if Fidelio never again found employment with any notable inventor, he could take a more mundane job until 'Tarantela' was ready to be unveiled to the world. He wracked his brains; wasn't there some other possibility?

There was one more fellow, a visionary of sorts whom Fidelio had read about in the *New York Times*. Antoine De Vallambrosa, or as he was better known, the Marquis De Mores, lived in a desolate region of North Dakota known as the Badlands. He was a French aristocrat who bought property in this cattle raising area in hopes of becoming a meat-packing tycoon. After declaring bankruptcy and working for the French government in French Indochina, he returned to the town he had founded with the idea of shipping the choicest cuts of meat to the cities by dirigible.

The article had so intrigued Fidelio that he'd written the man a letter. An innovator such as the Marquis was a potential investor in his automaton project. As of yet he had received no reply. Most likely this was not for any personal reason; a rich man like Vallambrosa would certainly receive a great deal of mail regarding business opportunities. If he did not receive a response within the week, Fidelio decided, he would send the Marquis a telegram.

Fidelio checked his pocket watch. Yes, Elena's Teahouse would be open. He changed clothes, then went to the O'Reillys' pump for some water to splash off his face. When he returned he would be in a better frame of mind for planning his next move.

While Fidelio was out, he stopped at the mercantile to buy some new shirts, since he would soon be looking for work. On his return, he opened the gate to the O'Reillys' yard and, as was his habit, he pulled the Steamer under the shelter of the extended roof line behind his residence. As he disembarked from the car, Fidelio heard a strange noise. Was Mrs. O'Reilly nosing around again? He'd politely requested that she wait until he was home before seeking out that misplaced set of knitting needles, or whatever she thought might be back there.

Might it be an intruder? Annoyance turned to fear as Fidelio unlocked the car's glove box and withdrew a wide-barreled pistol.

He crept to the front of the workshop, taking care to duck down as he passed the side window. The front door was closed, but there were unmistakable scratches on the wooden door frame next to the knob. Fidelio braced himself for a confrontation.

He flung open the door, gripped his weapon in both hands and cried, "I have a gun!"

"Don't shoot!"

"You!" Though the intruder's identity was initially a shock, it made sense. Who else would have a grudge against him?

Hopkins stood, pale-faced and shaking, with both hands pointing at the ceiling. "I'm unarmed," he said.

"Do not worry; this weapon fires only a burst of lead shot; a discharge would not be lethal at this range – *probably*. Nevertheless, do not try to escape!" He paused. "Did Edison incite you to this? This is an outrage; I'll sue the man for all he's worth!"

"No, I swear that Edison had nothing to do with this."

"Move away from the wall," Fidelio ordered. "You cost me my job. Now do you wish to rob me as well?" He started for a moment at his former friend. "You look frightful."

"That's your doing. Since you disfigured me with that cowardly blow to my nose, my Elise no longer loves me."

Fidelio ignored the accusation; it was just like Hopkins to cast blame on someone else. Still, there was no denying the man's nose was now enlarged and crooked. "If your looks were all she valued, that was a good thing."

"Not so! She hated boxing. I had promised her I would give it up. We had one hell of a donnybrook after I came home from the hospital." His eyes shone with hatred. "You goaded me into it, you son of a bitch."

"You insult the mother of a man who points a gun at you?" Fidelio laughed. "You are a bigger fool than I imagined. If you are not here to steal, why do you invade my home?"

"I was looking for evidence. I cannot believe that Edison is giving you the chance to cover up your deception. I'm not so trusting. I want to put you behind bars where you belong."

"I see. Since, I am not a trusting man, either, you can tell your story to the police."

Hopkins smiled, which, given the man's circumstances, was frightening. "I wouldn't do that if I were you." He gestured with his chin at Fidelio's bed, where one of his dresser drawers had been dumped. "I found some very interesting photographs. Funny, I didn't see what was right in front of my face. I should have known you were a homosexual."

"How dare you invade my privacy!" Fidelio didn't ask what the 'evidence' was, because he recognized it from across the room: several nude photographs of Rodrigo. "You are an uneducated bigot. Those pictures of the nude human form are art, not erotica."

"Then why are there no pictures of naked *women* as well?"

"My personal life is none of your concern." Fidelio's finger caressed the trigger. "I am tempted to shoot you and place this weapon in your dead hands for the police to find. Leave now, before I change my mind. If I ever see you again, I will not be responsible for my actions."

Fidelio stepped aside and pushed open the door. Hopkins edged toward it, slowly at first. Once he'd cleared the threshold he broke into a run, leaping over the O'Reillys' fence as he fled.

"*Ese puto!* I should have killed him!" Fidelio muttered as he put the photos back in the strong box he kept under the bed. This time, he remembered to lock it.

He had to get out of this place before his head burst. *Post office;* he thought, *I have not checked my box today.* Fidelio locked the door behind him and jiggled the knob – not broken, so Hopkins must have picked it. He would speak to the O'Reillys about getting a better lock.

The post office was only a few blocks away, so Fidelio went there on foot. He entered the combination on his locked box, expecting it to be empty as usual. Instead, there were two letters inside. He opened the first and glanced at it on the walk home. It was a note from Doctor Laplace. He had enclosed a pencil drawing from a Sears Catalog labeled 'Toy Spider.' It was nothing like Tarantela, that much was obvious, though Fidelio appreciated the professor's concern. He promised himself to check these sources in the future. The second was even more of a surprise. The return address was inscribed, 'A. De Vallambrosa, Medora, N. Dak.' He opened it and read it as he stood on the street corner, oblivious to the stares of passers-by.

"Dear Mr. Espinoza," the letter began. "Your letter was most intriguing. As I have been seeking suitable investments, I would be interested in learning more about your invention. Per your request, I would be happy to sign an agreement of non-disclosure. I am willing to pursue initial negotiations through the mail, but it would be most helpful if you were to bring your plans and prototypes and meet with me at my company headquarters in the town of Medora."

Fidelio grinned. This was the first good news he had received in some time. He would send a reply immediately. The documents would likely arrive soon, and once he had settled his dispute with Edison, he would be on his way. In the meantime, he would pack his belongings and get the Steamer ready for cross-country travel. This unfortunate incident had been the catalyst for a new adventure.

Chapter 6 – Painful Recollections

Hank's first choice for his journey westward would have been the celebrated *Great Lakes Zeppelin*. How glorious it would be to gaze down on God's creation like a soaring eagle. Sadly, the purchase of a passage on an airship was financially beyond Hank's reach. Instead, he bought a ticket to Chicago on the *Lake Shore Limited*. Once in the Windy City, he planned to catch the Santa Fe back to his old home in the Arizona Territory.

After arriving at the Buffalo station and delivering his steamer trunk to the courteous young Negro porter, Hank boarded a Pullman car near the front of the train. To his dismay, it was fully occupied. There were well-dressed businessmen, soldiers in uniform, laborers, couples on holiday and families with children. Since the war, he crowds of people made him feel really hemmed in, and his run-in with the law in New York City had only made the problem worse. He continued on to the next car in search of a seat.

As he walked down the aisle, Hank felt like he was slogging through quicksand. In his last few months with the Quakers, he'd had some happy times, and had begun to almost feel like he belonged. Now with the passing of his dreams, the entire world looked bleak. He tried to cheer himself with Scripture: "Ask the Lord and He will provide." If Nola would not be his bride, he'd find some other lady just as sweet – though at present, he didn't feel too confident.

Toward the end of the train, Hank finally found a car with some open space. He selected a forward-facing seat in a group of four which was occupied only by a burly man whose face was buried in the *Buffalo News*. The fellow wore dungarees and a long-sleeved dark colored shirt, probably a common laborer like himself, but at least he had some schooling. He noticed a golden ring on the man's finger. Probably he had a wife and family waiting at home. It made Hank feel very lonely.

Hank fell into his seat and exhaled deeply. This was, he told himself, the beginning of a new chapter in his life. What would he do when he got back to Arizona? Hopefully his old boss Oscar Tillman would need an extra hand on his ranch. If not, Hank would look for work with one of Tillman's neighbors. He would also join a church – there were several in Prescott – and later on, he could recruit some folks for a prayer group in the Quaker tradition.

As Hank sat and pondered his next move, the conductor appeared. He was a big, bald-headed man with a handlebar mustache, who looked more like a prize-fighter than a ticket-taker. The man checked Hank's ticket, then turned to his neighbor. The laborer proffered the slip of paper for inspection without even poking his head out from behind his periodical. Minutes later, the train pulled out of the station with a shuddering groan.

Those thoughts of churches and prayer groups reminded Hank that it had been several days since he had witnessed his faith to anyone. Evangelizing did not come naturally to him. Just thinking about it gave him a knot in the stomach. He'd need to develop a more social outlook, if he wanted to spread the Gospel in the Arizona Territory.

Hank sat with his hands folded in his lap, staring out the window as he pondered on what he should say. It was only when they had cleared the Buffalo rail yard, and the clack of the wheels on the rails had steadied his nerves a bit, that he steeled himself to speak.

Hank cleared his throat. In a rather loud voice he leaned forward toward his neighbor and said, "Um, sir, have you heard the word of the Lord?"

His neighbor lowered his newspaper, revealing a ruddy face, a bushy mustache, and a fearsome scowl. "Do you take me for a simpleton? You religious zealots view us working people as if we were raised in some foreign land that has never seen the Bible. I'll have you know that I was raised in the Catholic Church, and took my first communion at the age of seven."

Hank's face flushed red. "My apologies, I didn't aim to cause offense."

The man exhaled, and laid the paper on his lap. "I'm certain you had only my best interests at heart. So let's get it over with. Tell me how the Church of Rome is really the Whore of Babylon."

"Heaven forbid! Whatever kind of Christian church a person chooses to attend, I'm all for it! As our Lord says, 'He that believeth in me and is baptized shall be saved.'"

The man continued to glare at him, so Hank felt obliged to explain. "I lived a sinful life, even though I grew up knowing about the Bible and such. I mean, who doesn't hear the Christmas story as a child? But it never truly stuck in my heart, 'til last year, when I got really ill. That was when I prayed to the Lord for deliverance. When I regained my health, I realized the power of the Lord and committed my life fully to Him."

Feeling uneasy in the face of the man's continued silence, Hank continued. "So anyhow, I hope you'll pardon my interruption. My church is the Society of Friends, and everyone is welcome there, no matter what creed you call your own."

"Quakers!" the man snorted. "Blasted pacifists! No thank you, sir, I'll pass." He stood up, grabbed his bag from the rack above the seats, and stomped away, claiming a seat at the furthest end of the car.

Hank leaned forward with his head in his hands, trying to console himself. Here was a man who claimed to follow the Son of God, but clearly did not understand His message. Hank felt like a failure. At least, since the Lord was all-seeing, He knew Hank had tried.

For a while he sat back and breathed deeply. His doctor had recommended it as a counter to his recurring attacks of shell shock. Yet that did nothing to chase away the lonesome sickness in his heart. Hank sighed. Through his bunched fingers, he saw the abandoned periodical on the empty seat. The paper would be a welcome distraction. If the man returned for his copy of the *News*, he would cheerfully return it.

He unfolded the paper and frowned. The headline was not encouraging: "PRESIDENT DEMANDS SURRENDER OF PHILIPPINE REBELS." Below this lurid banner was a sketch of William McKinley, who had recently been released from the hospital. The President's near assassination, and his subsequent battle with the resulting infection, had not softened his un-Christian disregard for the people of that nation.

Hank was familiar with this story through the Friends, who opposed all war as part of their philosophy. Despite the capture of their leader Emilio Aguinaldo earlier in the year, the Philippine rebels continued their fight against American rule. How two-faced of Americans, to celebrate their independence on the Fourth of July, and then deny it to somebody else. Worse yet, the Army was using torture like the 'water cure' in their interrogations.

It was not the only article about the war. At the top of page two the heading read, "Vice President to Oversee Campaign against Tagalog Bandits." Hank remembered Theodore Roosevelt vividly from his time in the "Rough Riders." He hadn't been surprised to see that Roosevelt had risen to such a high station. The man was a natural born leader, and it didn't hurt to come from a rich family. After Vice President Hobart's death in 1899, McKinley needed a new running mate, and the 'war hero' Roosevelt stepped in. When that maniac shot the President in Buffalo, Roosevelt came within a heartbeat of the highest office in the land.

Hank put the paper down and raised a hand to rub his aching forehead. The awful memories of war were still fresh in his mind; he'd relived them in dreams almost every night. Even now he could hear the boom of the Spanish guns as they rained death from the sky. He heard the whistle of the shell and felt the blast that knocked him off his feet. The explosion sent his buddy Will tumbling down the slope and into a stream. A red cloud leaked into the water.

As the others scrambled for cover, Hank clambered down the slope. Will might be alive, and he'd drown unless someone pulled him out of the water. Another whooshing sound caused Hank to hit the dirt. When he looked up, there was a muddy crater where his friend had been.

"Attention, men!" Lieutenant Colonel Roosevelt's profile was outlined in fire by the tropical sun. "This position is not safe. I will not have my comrades slaughtered while waiting to act." He drew his saber and held it aloft. "Onward, to the Spanish fortifications!" He sheathed the weapon and headed his horse up the slope.

Hank fell in with the others, anxious to leave the place of Will's demise. The tropical heat was stifling as they marched up Kettle Hill. There was a twisty feeling in Hank's gut. Would he be the next to meet his Maker? Though he had never been much of a praying man, he silently mouthed the words of the Lord's Prayer: "Our Father, who art in Heaven, hallowed be Thy Name..."

There was another crash, this time much closer. It was so real that Hank jumped from his seat and dashed down the aisle. He had to get out of this place. In the back of his mind, he knew it would be crazy to jump from a moving train, but it didn't stop his panicked flight. He slammed into an elderly woman, knocking her to the left into some man's lap. "Beg pardon, ma'am!"

Suddenly, Hank saw in his path a rumbling metal monstrosity, much like a small version of Spain's dreaded *carro de combate*. He was running too fast to stop himself; he stumbled and slammed into it head-first. As he tumbled over the machine, there were shouts and shrieks all around him.

"Damn it, man! What the devil is wrong with you?" Two rough hands grabbed Hank by the collar and pulled him off the floor.

"What's the commotion?" a man shouted from behind them. "Any altercation is grounds for ejection from the train."

"It was not my doing," said the angry passenger. "This lunatic came running down the aisle and overturned the drink cart. My wife and I were both doused with scalding coffee." He pushed Hank away. "Please get this maniac out of my sight."

Still dizzy from the blow to his head, Hank stumbled into the well-muscled conductor. Even in his saloon-brawling past, Hank would have steered well clear of this fellow.

"I'm so sorry!" Hank pleaded. "I... There was a noise, and..." He saw the culprit, a shattered glass platter at the far end of the aisle, "And I done lost my head for a minute."

"I'll say you did. You must come with me." He grabbed Hank's sleeve. "We do not allow drunkards or dope-fiends on this railroad."

"I ain't never done dope in my life! I didn't mean to go crazy; the noise set me off. I've been that way since the war." He looked around for sympathy, but the passengers all glared at him. "I'll pay for whatever I wrecked."

The conductor was unmoved. "Come along quietly now. I do not wish to resort to violence." He grabbed Hank by the collar and physically lifted him off the floor.

As the man dragged him toward the rear of the train, the passengers broke into applause. "Good riddance, you ruffian!" came a woman's voice.

One man sprang up from his seat. "Wait!"

The conductor stopped in his tracks, loosening his hold on Hank's collar. "Sir, I will be with you momentarily, after I handle this trouble-maker."

"Didn't you hear the man?" The speaker was a stocky olive-skinned fellow with a thick gray beard and a distinct Spanish accent. "He's a war veteran. He risked his life for all our sakes. Can't you see he's suffering from shell shock?"

"My good man," growled the conductor, "Do not trouble yourself. The situation is under control. Whether or not this man is a veteran is of no concern to a foreigner."

The bearded man straightened up in indignation. "I am no foreigner. I am Lieutenant Colonel Miguel Rivera, retired. I served in the Civil War in the New Mexico Volunteer Infantry."

The conductor raised his eyebrows and frowned. "Beg your pardon, sir; I had no idea. Very well, if you insist on helping this fellow, you may accompany us to my office."

Rivera followed Hank and the conductor to the back of the train. At the front of the caboose was a tiny office with a desk and two chairs. The conductor motioned for Hank to sit.

Hank did so, and looked up at the conductor. "What happens now, sir?"

"You will stay here at my desk until we reach the station in Toledo. Then you must disembark."

"But I paid for my ticket all the way to Chicago. I don't have money to buy another one and I don't know a soul in this neck of the woods."

"May I have a word with you, sir?" Rivera took the conductor aside and spoke to him for a moment in hushed tones. The conductor nodded; his fierce expression softened.

Rivera smiled and clapped Hank on the shoulder. "Don't worry, *amigo*. I am an attorney, and I know how to handle these things."

"Sir," said the conductor to Rivera. "You must return to your seat now."

"There are laws which protect veterans," he replied. "You don't wish to provide grounds for a suit, do you?"

The conductor scowled. "Keep an eye on him, then. I need to attend to the mess caused by your friend's outburst."

"No worries, *señor*. If he breaks anything else, I will take responsibility."

After the conductor had left, Hank turned to Miguel. He blinked back the tears as he spoke. "I sure appreciate what you done for me back there. The name's Henry MacMillan. My friends call me Hank." He extended a hand.

The New Mexican shook Hank's hand with a firm grip. "I am pleased to meet you, Hank. There is no need to thank me. I know what war can do to a man. So, from where do you hail?"

"Prescott, in the Arizona Territory."

"Then we are practically neighbors. I thought I heard a hint of the Southwest in your voice. Have you been living here in the East?"

Hank nodded. "For a couple years now, since the war. I was injured in Cuba, and then I came down with cancer, so I went to New York where they got the best doctoring. After I got better I found work and decided to stick around."

"I see. And now where are you headed?"

"Back home. I done had enough of the big city."

Miguel smiled. "Trouble with a *señorita*, perhaps?"

Hank laughed. "You're one sharp fellow." Quickly as it had come, his smile disappeared. "I'm mighty ashamed of what happened back there. I was reading in the paper about the Philippine War. That put some awful things in my head, and I needed to get out to the platform for some air. That's when I ran into that infernal contraption."

"The automated drink cart?" Miguel chuckled. "That 'infernal contraption' serves a fine cup of coffee. I would call it a miracle of modern technology."

Hank nodded. "Yeah, I know. But in Cuba the Spaniards had this thing they called a *carro de combate;* you heard of that?"

"Of course. Our side almost lost the war because of it."

"Right. We was marching up the hill. We lost several men to the Spanish guns, so we really got riled. When Colonel Roosevelt gave the order to advance, we figured we could take them easy. Then that *thing* appeared, shooting left and right, mowing us down like gophers. Our bullets bounced right off the metal plating."

"*Dios mio,* that must have been terrible. Was that when you were wounded?"

"Nope, that happened later. Anyway, the thing shot the Colonel's horse, and when the poor beast fell, it landed on top of him, pinning his leg. My pal Caleb and I were able to get the carcass off of him and pull him to safety."

Miguel's mouth fell open. "That was you? The papers talked about the heroes that saved Roosevelt, but I don't recall seeing your name."

"When the reporters did the interview, I was in a field hospital. Got kicked in the gut by a mule. Poor Caleb had already bought the farm, on San Juan Hill. They gave him the Medal of Honor. They say his folks were proud, but it hardly makes up for him coming home in a box."

Miguel nodded. "A fascinating story. One thing I was wondering. Was it really Roosevelt's idea, how the Rough Riders beat the war machine? Often an officer takes credit for things others have done. I know that from experience."

"Yep. Roosevelt can be a mite too prideful, but he's also smart as a whip. He figured there had to be men inside the machine, so he had us set fire to some branches and throw 'em in front so they couldn't move forwards. When they finally got it turned around – the *carro*'s a real awkward beast – our men had felled some trees so they couldn't retreat. It got mighty hot inside, and the crew had to come out and surrender."

"Amazing," Miguel said. "So the newspaper account was true."

Their conversation was interrupted by the squeal of the brakes; Hank could feel the train slowing as they approached the station.

"Come, *compadre,* let's step out for some air." Hank followed Miguel back into the main part of the train, then out an open door onto the platform. The sign said, 'TOLEDO, OHIO.'

Toledo was not a large city, and its railroad station was appropriately small. Next door to the station was a run-down looking wooden building with the words 'Railroad Grill' painted on the door. Hank and Rivera entered. It was a small place with half a dozen tables and as many patrons. The atmosphere was hazy with tobacco smoke.

"You mentioned coffee," Hank said. "I sure could use a cup. If you'd like to join me it'll be my treat."

"I would prefer tequila. Here in the east, no one knows that drink. But in Arizona..."

"Sure, I've drank my share. But I don't take liquor anymore."

Miguel nodded. "I understand. My eldest brother lost his wife in childbirth, and later became a *borracho*. He would drink beer and wine all day long, but then he met a good woman who was determined to save him. He has been sober for ten years now."

Though he knew it shouldn't matter what Miguel believed of him, Hank bridled at the implication of drunkenness. "It's not that. It's on account of my religion. I've recently been born again, and my church views strong drink as sinful."

"I see," Miguel said. "Though surely you would drink wine for Holy Communion?"

"On that occasion, yes," Hank conceded, "Since the Savior had some himself at the Last Supper." He looked out the window at the train. "Do we even have time for coffee? Maybe we should have stayed on board."

"Don't worry, Hank. Mr. Johnson, the conductor, would have kicked you off anyway. You do still have your ticket stub? We will board a different car and I will talk again with Johnson."

"But what about the damages?"

Miguel laughed. "The railroad has money; they can afford to repair the cart, and to pay for the ruined clothing. That is why they carry insurance, after all. By the way... son, over here!" He called out to a baby-faced waiter who was passing them on his way to the bar. "A tequila for me and my friend, please!"

Hank put up a hand. "Gosh, you don't have to..."

"Nonsense, it's the least I can do. With all you have suffered, you deserve a drink, no?"

Hank nodded. A drink would be good, soothe his nerves a bit. He watched as Miguel pulled a small package from his pocket, and then removed a machine-rolled cigarette.

Miguel held out the pack. "Would you like to join me?"

"No, I gave that up." He watched as Miguel struck a match and lit a cigarette. "On second thought, I'll take one of those. I sure could use it." He reached out and took a cigarette and the match box. "Thank you kindly." He took a deep drag and savored the calming smoke.

At that moment the waiter returned with two oversized shot glasses full of clear liquid. Miguel took one and handed the other to Hank. "Here, my friend. To America! *Salud!*"

"I shouldn't, but..." Miguel was watching him expectantly, so Hank shrugged and said, "Here's mud in your eye!" He raised the drink to his lips and swallowed. The warmth went down his throat to his stomach. *Oh well, the Bible don't say nothing about tequila.*

Miguel drained his glass and placed it upside down on the table. "Waiter! Another round for my friend and me!"

"Thank you kindly, Miguel, but one drink of liquor is plenty for me." Hank's objections went unheeded. He found himself drinking another shot, and then another. Though he had been a veteran drinker in his cow-punching days, he hadn't imbibed more than a few sips of communion wine since his recovery from cancer. His stomach soon rebelled. "Where's the washroom?" he croaked.

Luckily, the place had an indoor water closet. Hank slammed the door behind himself and vomited into the wash basin. The room began to spin and he slumped to the floor. Dimly he heard someone banging on the door and shouting, "Hank! Time to go!"

Abruptly the banging stopped, and Hank realized with a shock what was happening. Quickly he wiped his mouth and stumbled out of the washroom. From outside he heard the puffing of a steam engine and the grinding of wheels as the cars lurched into motion. The train to Chicago had left the station without him, with all his possessions on board.

Chapter 7 – A Fortuitous Meeting

When he first purchased the Stanley Steamer, Fidelio had imagined cruising through the countryside, exploring the vast American continent at an exhilarating forty miles per hour. The reality was not so idyllic. Once he departed the densely populated Eastern seaboard, the quality of the roads declined significantly, as did his average speed.

One could forget about paving; many of them were not even graveled. These were wagon trails, eroded by the elements and years of excessive use. Only by constant vigilance was he able to avoid breaking a wheel or even an axle in the huge pot-shaped holes that he encountered with alarming frequency. In addition he needed to monitor the car's gauges, to ensure the boiler was within safe operational parameters. Another aggravation was the slow-moving horse-drawn wagons in his path. As of yet, there were few other motor carriages on the road.

It took him two full days to make his way through Pennsylvania. Upon reaching Ohio, the landscape leveled out, with a corresponding improvement in the roads. At Akron, he headed north, until he reached Lake Erie. Here the road mostly followed the railway, which in turn hugged the shore of the great lake. Fidelio found it amazing – so much fresh water in one place! After a while, though, it became like the sea coast of his native land; something that receded into the background and was no longer noticed.

As the day wore on, the roads degraded once more. Fidelio had read that this area of northwest Ohio had once been a swamp, now mostly drained to accommodate agriculture. Even so, there were short stretches of the original 'corduroy road' through boggy areas. The rugged surface would have had scant effect on a slow, horse-drawn wagon, but on an automobile it was tooth-jarring.

Around sunset, he entered the city of Toledo. Compared to New York, it was a backwater, but for Ohio, it was a bustling metropolis. As he headed into town on Woodville Street, the volume of traffic – the occasional motorcar as well as people on horseback and the much more common horse-drawn carriage – forced him to slow to a crawl.

He continued west and crossed the bridge over the Maumee River. Freed from the bottleneck of the river crossing, the traffic veered in several directions, and

Fidelio was finally free to accelerate to a respectable fifteen miles per hour. He slowed for the intersection where the two signs pointed toward South Bend and Indianapolis. The former option would take him to Chicago, so he made a sharp right turn at the dry goods store on the next corner.

This route took him past the train station, where he marveled at the number of people coming and going. Momentarily distracted, he did not notice when a man stepped out into the street in front of him. At the last second, Fidelio slammed his foot on the brake pedal. There was a horrible screeching noise and the Steamer skidded to the left but continued forward several yards before stopping.

The man in the street looked up in surprise, just before the rounded nose of Fidelio's car knocked him off his feet. Both driver and pedestrian cried out in alarm. Horses reared and a carriage veered onto the boardwalk, causing pedestrians to scurry. Fidelio could feel scores of eyes upon him.

Fidelio leapt out of his car and ran to where the man lay in the street. The fellow lay unmoving but still breathing. Having learned a bit about trauma medicine during his brief stint in the University's rugby team, Fidelio knelt down for a closer look. If there was any spinal injury, the man could only be moved with the utmost care.

"Sir, are you in pain? Can you feel your extremities?" The man opened his eyes but did not answer. He appeared to be the archetypal cowboy; a square jaw, close-cropped brownish-blond hair, and a chin stubbled with a day's growth of beard. Nearby in the street lay a hat which Fidelio recognized as the 'ten gallon' style.

"Is this..." A man wearing the uniform of a railway detective stared down at Fidelio, but addressed the fallen man. "Is this mulatto giving you trouble?"

Fidelio stood up slowly as he eyed his accuser. "I am Cuban, sir, and you may address me directly. I assure you that this man stepped out in the path of my vehicle."

"Do they allow you people to operate a motorcar?" said another man in a drawling accent. He had a long gray beard one might expect to see in an old war photograph.

"Don't know of any law against it," ventured a third man. "Probably ought to be."

Fidelio struggled to maintain his composure. He'd encountered bigotry before, whether people had assumed him to be Italian, Slavic, or quadroon. Always he'd held his head high and insisted on being treated with respect. Here in the hinterlands, the locals' reaction made him think of the South, which he had read about but never visited. To lose one's temper in this area might be quite dangerous.

"I beg your pardon," Fidelio addressed the detective. "I may have been momentarily distracted. This man, however, has obviously been drinking. Certainly you can smell the liquor on his breath."

The injured man sat up and blinked. "That's the truth, boys. Leave this poor fellow be, it's my fault entirely."

Fidelio held out a hand and helped him to his feet. He had at first assumed the victim was a derelict such as one might encounter on the Bowery. Now he saw that, despite the man's intoxication, he was clean and well-dressed, in a homespun sort of way, though his coat was now torn from the accident.

"Do you need a doctor?" said the gray-bearded man. There's a Doc Hollister down on Third Street."

The victim shook his head. "At this point, you might as well call the undertaker. My life is over."

Fidelio glanced nervously at the self-appointed investigators, and then back at the victim. "I think, sir, you are exaggerating the scope of your injuries. Brush yourself off, get in my car and I will buy you supper as compensation."

"You sure you want to do that?" asked the third man with a sneer. "You might well get your neck broken, driving with this here boy."

"My body's fine," the victim responded. "It's my heart that's hurting." He walked around to the passenger door, twisted the handle, and climbed in.

"Gentlemen, thank you for your concern, but we will be on our way," Fidelio said. The detective nodded and departed, and the two other men followed him.

Fidelio was glad he had left the engine on; warming up the boiler could be time consuming, and he'd already attracted enough unwanted attention. He pulled out the throttle and they were on their way.

As he drove, Fidelio glanced at his passenger, who was staring blankly ahead. He felt responsible for this fellow's well-being, even though the man had brought this mishap upon himself. He appeared to be working class, which evoked in Fidelio a degree of sympathy, but as with many of his kind, strong drink would be his downfall.

Aside from his current condition, Fidelio found the man to be attractive in a rugged sort of way. So far, however, he'd no indication that the stranger shared his atypical carnal appetites.

"You are bleeding." Fidelio half-shouted over the noise of the street. The man's left sleeve was torn, and the entire underside of his arm was skinned and scraped.

"So I am." He held up his arm to examine the wound. "Don't worry; I won't soil your fine leather seat."

Fidelio took a deep breath. "Forgive my asking, but why do you say your life is over?"

"Pardon my melodrama. As the Good Book says, life is a series of tribulations. This latest misfortune is of my own making. I've missed my train, and with it went all my worldly goods."

Fidelio nodded. "That is unfortunate, but the railway company is legally required to return your possessions. Where were you bound?"

"Chicago. From there I meant to switch to the Santa Fe and on to the Arizona Territory."

"Then we will send a telegram to the railway company, instructing them to hold your belongings at Chicago. Do you have sufficient funds for another ticket?"

"Nope. That's why my life is over. At least, it's been seriously derailed."

"There are other ways to reach Chicago. Let us discuss your dilemma over a hot meal, and your situation may not seem so intractable."

The passenger did not answer; he just stared ahead at nothing in particular. Fidelio became concerned he had sustained a concussion. "Are you familiar with this city? Would you know of a good place to dine?"

The man shook his head. "I ain't never been here, and besides, you're not obligated. Just drop me off anywhere."

"Nonsense! It is the least I can do. We shall continue on, and in all likelihood we will encounter a satisfactory eatery in due time."

After driving a few blocks, Fidelio spied a coffee shop. "Aha! That looks like a suitable place for a repast." He turned off the street and pulled up next to the shop.

The man looked Fidelio in the eye for the first time. "I guess I should introduce myself. My name's Henry MacMillan, but you can call me Hank." He held out his hand.

Fidelio took note of the man's firm handshake. "I am most pleased to meet you, Hank. My name is Fidelio Espinoza."

"I'm much obliged for the ride, Mr. Espinoza. As for the meal, I ain't asking for charity, but I can't pay my way, 'cause all my silver was hid at the bottom of my trunk."

"Please, call me Fidelio. Tonight I am paying for us both. I shall be glad for the company. I am certain you would do the same for me if our roles were reversed."

"You're far too kind, friend, but you shouldn't have to pay the price for my folly."

"To err is human. Your situation is but a temporary obstacle. You shall reach Chicago, where your possessions await you."

"Can't possibly see how," Hank said. "Unless I walk the whole way."

"Perish the thought!" Fidelio waved his hand dismissively. "We shall find a solution for your problem, but not on an empty stomach. As my father says, '*El vientre gobierna la mente.*' The belly rules the mind." He turned the key and let the car's steam engine hiss to a stop.

Fidelio was glad to play the Good Samaritan to this hapless fellow. He was already headed for Chicago; he could easily offer him a ride. However, he was undecided about whether to do so. Hank might simply be a working man down on his luck, but he could also be a hopeless dipsomaniac, and Fidelio had no patience for those with self-destructive habits. He decided not to mention it until he decided whether the man's company would be tolerable.

The black, stencil-painted sign read 'Griswold's Cafe.' Light issued from within, though no one sat at any of the tables. It seemed to be almost closing time. Nonetheless, Fidelio strode in and claimed a table at the far corner. Hank followed and sat down beside him.

A bald, frail-looking man wearing a long apron approached them with a barely-audible sigh. When he saw Fidelio he halted, pursed his lips and scanned the man up and down. To his credit, he made no comment on the Cuban's complexion, though he was clearly addressing Hank when he spoke. "What would you gents like to eat?"

Fidelio look at Hank, who was reading the hand-written menu. "All right," he said in his western drawl, "I'll take the roast beef and mashed taters."

Then it was Fidelio's turn. He had an appetite for seafood, but he doubted it would not be available so far inland. "I will have the same, my good man."

"And to drink?"

"Just water, please," Fidelio said.

"Guess I'll have that, too," said Hank.

The bald man shuffled off. Fidelio turned to his dining companion. "Tell me your story, Hank. How did a westerner like you end up in this part of America?"

Hank smiled. "The night may not be long enough to tell the whole tale, but I'll try to tell it short. I was born and raised in the Arizona Territory. My ma and pa died in a stagecoach holdup, so I got raised by my Uncle Malcolm and Aunt Mabel. At fourteen I left school and took a job at Tillman's ranch. It was hard work, but I got to spend my time outdoors, which is where a man ought to be. Now and then I had myself a sweetheart, but I was too much of a rounder, never could stay true to any woman. Too much drinking and carousing, I guess.

Then my dear old grandpa passed away, and I started thinking of my life. Maybe I ought to settle down, get myself my own place. Then I heard tell of the sinking of the Maine. Right away I hit the road for Santa Fe to join up with the Army. I was assigned to Theodore Roosevelt's Rough Riders, and was one of the lucky few who made it to Cuba to fight the Spaniards."

He looked at Fidelio in sudden realization. "Did you say you were Cuban? I hadn't connected the fact that I was in your country."

"I am indeed Cuban. At the time of the outbreak of hostilities, I was a student at the University in Toledo – the original Toledo, in Spain. I was conscripted into the Royal Army but thankfully the war was over before I saw battle."

As he said those words, he noticed Hank's grimace. Had he offended the man? He leaned forward and lowered his voice. "Not to denigrate your service, my friend. I was simply grateful that I was not forced to fight to maintain my country's enslavement." He did not add that he found America's continuing military presence just as onerous.

"No offense taken. I feel way different about the Spanish War now than I did then. I saw a whole bunch of good men die, and came danged close to buying the farm myself. A man stares at Death like that, it changes him."

Fidelio nodded. "However we view the causes and results, war is an ugly business."

The bald man returned with their food, and set down their plates, pointedly serving Hank first. Fidelio shot him an irritated glance. America had many positive aspects; its devotion to freedom and democracy, its inventive spirit, and its nascent labor movement. What a shame such a great land should be corrupted by bigotry.

Hank dug into his food with gusto. Fidelio picked up his utensils and cut a corner from the slab of meat on his plate. It was a bit dry, but the gravy made up for the meat's deficiency in juices. He found himself eating as enthusiastically as his new friend.

The former cowboy took a drink of water from his glass and sighed. "I still feel like I'm taking advantage of your generosity, Fidelio. If you have a postal address I promise I'll make things right at my first opportunity."

Fidelio swallowed his mouthful of potatoes and wiped his face with the napkin. "Do not worry. I have been fortunate to be born into a family of abundant means. I am happy to share my resources with a member of the working class."

Hank narrowed his eyes and gave him a puzzled look, but said nothing. Americans tended to be rather ignorant in their political attitudes. Fidelio decided to return to the previous topic. "So what did you do after the war?"

"Well sir, the Lord must have been watching over me, because I survived the Battle of San Juan Hill without so much as a scratch. But I didn't escape unharmed. A couple days later, I was kicked in the gut by a cantankerous mule. The critter missed my ribs entirely, so I only had to spend a couple of days in the infirmary, but you should have seen the bruise.

"We shipped out to New York City and upon arriving there, I found a job in the docks. It's an amazing place, and it was a welcome change from the heat and bugs in Cuba – no offense, but where I grew up, it's got a dry heat. Anyway, after a few months I took ill with a terrible pain in the gut. The doc said I'd got cancer in the liver."

"How terrible!" Fidelio put down his fork.

"I realized it was the Lord's punishment for the sinful life I'd been leading. So I started reading the Good Book every day and praying for His forgiveness. And what do you know? I got better! Well, having that new-fangled experimental treatment didn't hurt, but even so, the doc said lots of people still die. It was a goldurn real life miracle!"

"I am most gratified to hear that." Fidelio declined to share his skepticism on the matter.

"Since I didn't have no job or sweetheart back home, I decided to stay in New York. I was looking to join a church, 'cause I promised the Lord I'd be a better man. Then, like a sign from on high, I spied a young lady, a sweet angel, standing on a street corner. Her and her group was preaching against the war in the Philippines. Some folks didn't take kindly to that, and I got caught up in a real tussle, and got taken to the hoosegow. When I got out I went right back and joined up with her church, the Society of Friends."

"Ah, the Quakers! I am familiar with them. They are an important group in the history of your country, yes?"

"Yes sir, the Quakers were real important in America. They founded the state of Pennsylvania; also helped get rid of slavery. Though lots of people don't like us on account of us being against war. Like this one fellow in my platoon used to say, 'Quakers is worse than Catholics.'" He looked at Fidelio. "No offense, if that's what you are."

"None taken; I'm certain your opinions are better informed than his."

Fidelio had indeed been raised Catholic, and had never given much thought to church doctrine, until he met Rodrigo at the University. Could the love they had felt really be an abomination, a mortal sin? The question led Fidelio to a study of history which eventually convinced him that, as Marx had said, religion was not a revelation from God but a tool for controlling the masses. Though Fidelio usually kept his views on religion to himself. In this country, his atheism could be as great a liability as his supposedly perverse sexual nature.

"And now, my friend, you are returning to the West. Is it your purpose to evangelize on behalf of your church?"

Hank sighed. "I wish that was the only reason..."

At that moment, the bald little proprietor returned and interrupted Hank's response. "Will there be anything else, gentlemen?"

"I saw your sign for apple pie," Fidelio said, "which is an American delicacy I find irresistible. I'll have a slice of that, please."

He turned to Hank. "And you, sir?"

"Well, I love a good apple pie, but..."

"Then make it two pieces, my good man," Fidelio said.

The bald man flashed them an unconvincing smile, then went to fetch their dessert. Fidelio turned back to Hank and smiled. "You spoke of your motivation for heading west. Was it the advice of Horace Greeley?"

Hank laughed. "Ain't exactly a young man, am I? No, there's things I aim to forget. The lady I mentioned, the one who won me for Christ – she won my heart as well. She was unmarried, so I thought I'd found myself a wife."

"And this young lady did not return your affections?"

"Nope. Sorry to say, she was already sweet on another man. Maybe if I'd met her sooner, or if didn't take so many months to speak my mind." The cowboy's eyes began to get misty.

"Ah, the timeless tragedy of unrequited love. Take heart. There are many unattached women in the world, not just widows and spinsters but young fresh-faced maidens as well. Certainly a God-fearing fellow such as you can find a suitable mate among them."

"You're right, friend. As the Good Book says, the Lord will provide. And how about you? Do you have a sweetheart back in Cuba?"

Fidelio shrugged. "I am a young man, with plenty of time for such pursuits. For the time being I am occupied with my work."

At that moment the waiter returned with their pie and they ate it in silence. On their way out, Fidelio handed the man some silver coins to settle their bill. "Our first order of business is to go to the rail station to arrange for your belongings."

The two men walked back to the Stanley Steamer, which was parked in the dirt lot next to the café. Hank watched in fascination as Fidelio opened the fuel valve and pumped the starter button until the resulting spark ignited the boiler. "You don't need to crank it? That's a major convenience over the cars I've seen."

"You are correct. This model also has a redesigned atomizing oil burner, which cuts the boiler's warm-up time significantly." Hank got in the passenger's seat and waited as Fidelio watched the gauges.

By now Fidelio was certain that Hank was heterosexual. That was to be expected, given that his kind was a small minority, even in urban centers such as New York City. In any case, Fidelio was driven less by his carnal urges and more by the desire for a more spiritual intimacy such as he'd enjoyed with dear Rodrigo.

Regardless of that fact, Fidelio was glad for any sort of agreeable company. Here in the American interior, there would be hazards aplenty, as typified by the cretins they'd encountered in Toledo. Hank might very well be the friend and guide that he needed.

Chapter 8 – A Beneficial Alliance

The rail station was only a few minutes' drive away. Surprisingly, the ticket office was still open, despite it being past 9 o'clock. A handful of passengers, friends, and relatives waited on the benches inside the station.

Hank approached the window. "Beg pardon, ma'am, but I missed my train earlier today. I need to make sure my luggage gets put someplace safe when the train gets to Chicago."

The clerk looked at Hank over her spectacles. "Missed the train? How did that happen?"

"Never mind that. I just don't want my things to get stolen."

"Chicago was your destination?" The clerk took Hank's name and looked at his ticket stub. "All right sir, it should be no problem. When you arrive simply proceed to the baggage agent's office. Will you be buying another ticket? The next rain for Chicago leaves at 8 AM."

Hank sighed and shook his head. "Nope, unless you got a cheaper fare than five dollars."

"Sorry. That is the least expensive ticket we have."

"Well thank you kindly, just the same." Hank tipped his hat and rejoined his new friend.

Fidelio clapped him on the back. " Do not despair, my good fellow. Tomorrow I am driving to Chicago, and you shall accompany me."

"Well don't that beat all! The Lord sure does work in mysterious ways."

"Right." Fidelio gave him a bemused smile. "Now, we must find a place to retire for the night." He spied a colored porter carrying a load of heavy bags. "Young man, can you advise us of the location of a suitable hotel?"

The youth regarded him carefully. "Well sir, there's the Adamson hotel just four blocks west of the station." He paused. "They're exclusive, though, if you know what I mean."

"So it is a reputable establishment, then? Thank you. Here is a quarter for your trouble."

When they reached the Adamson, the front office was dark. After some protracted rapping on the door, a woman appeared, wearing a ragged flannel dressing gown and a flowered night cap. "What do you want?" she snapped.

"Milady, I apologize for disturbing you at this late hour. We wish to rent a room."

She eyed Fidelio suspiciously. "You ain't part Negro, are you? We have a strict policy not to rent to coloreds."

"Madam, I am from an aristocratic Spanish family of Cuba." Fidelio sniffed.

Her eyes opened wide. "I'm very sorry, sir. I'll have your room ready immediately." Fidelio gritted his teeth. If not for the late hour, he would have berated this woman for her bigotry before leaving to spend the night elsewhere.

"Come on, I'll help carry your belongings," Hank said.

The two men went outside. As Fidelio unlocked the luggage compartment at the back of the Steamer, Hank shook his head. "Even before I got religion, I never understood that view. Ain't colored people God's children as well?"

"Indeed. Ignorance and hatred of outsiders is all too common among mankind. Here, would you please carry this for me?" Fidelio handed him a large leather bag, then grabbed the locked metal box that occupied the remainder of the cargo area. He did not wish to lose another prototype to theft.

The woman met them at the door. "My apologies; I forgot we're almost full up. We only have one vacancy, a single. It's a big bed, though. Would you gentlemen be all right with that?"

Fidelio looked at Hank, who shrugged. "Makes no difference to me," the cowboy said.

She led them up the stairs and down a hallway to the room, where she lit the kerosene lamp. "We got clean water in the pitcher on the desk over there, and a chamber pot 'neath the bed. Lavatory's out back if you need to do more than just make water."

"Thank you my good woman." Fidelio handed her a dime. She frowned and made an awkward bow before leaving the room.

"It is strange to smell kerosene again, after residing in East Orange and in New York City, with all the electric lights."

"Someday they'll have those new-fangled lights everywhere," Hank said. He stole a glance at the metal box, but didn't ask the obvious question.

That was just as well. Though Fidelio wasn't ready to trust the man just yet, he preferred not to lie to him, either.

Fidelio opened his leather case and removed his night clothes and toiletries. Hank stood by the bed, wringing his hands. "I'm embarrassed to say I've got no bedclothes."

"I would gladly lend you my spare set, but I doubt they would fit you, since you are more broad-shouldered than I. Sleep in your undergarments; it won't offend me."

The men took turns washing up. Fidelio was about to extinguish the light when he noticed Hank sitting up in bed, eyes closed and hands folded. It brought back memories. It had been many years since he had prayed.

Hank opened his eyes and averted them, having noticed Fidelio's stare. "Good night friend, and thank you. I owe you greatly for your charity."

"You are quite welcome." Fidelio turned off the kerosene lamp and the room was plunged into darkness. As he lay there thinking of the evening's events, he burst out laughing.

Hank sighed. "I was just about asleep, what the heck are you laughing about?"

"My apologies. I was feeling the satisfaction of deceiving that small-minded harpy."

"Who? The hotel clerk?"

"The same. I am one-quarter African on my mother's side, what you Americans would call a quadroon. Since I have European features, I have been able to 'pass,' as the coloreds say."

"Ha! I know Christ said not to call somebody a fool, but her own words do that for her."

Hank's breathing soon became low and regular. Fidelio lay awake in the dark for some time before succumbing to slumber.

As the dawn sun penetrated the lace curtains, Hank lay in bed, half-awake. Yawning, he rolled over and bumped into Fidelio, who mumbled the name 'Rodrigo.' A brother, maybe?

Hank's face turned red. It was lucky Fidelio had not been awake; the man would have figured him for a pervert. He rose quickly and headed down the stairs to use the outdoor facilities. When he returned, Fidelio was already dressed.

"There's breakfast cooking downstairs," Hank said.

"Then let us eat." The men went down to the dining room, where they were greeted by the aroma of eggs and sausage. As there were no other guests present, they sat at the largest of the three tables. The kitchen door opened, and the clerk from the previous evening emerged.

Fidelio tipped his bowler hat, then set it at the edge of the table. "My lady, you look enchanting this morning."

"Why thank you, *señor.* Would you men like a cup of coffee?"

"I sure would." In Hank's opinion, the formless dress she wore was not much of an improvement over last night's flannel nightgown.

"I would like a pot of hot tea, if you please." As the woman retreated, Fidelio muttered in Spanish under his breath. *"Mujer estúpida."*

Hank chuckled. Traveling to Chicago with this fellow was going to be real entertaining.

After they had eaten, Fidelio stood and said, "I shall now pay our bill, then go out and ignite the boiler. Could you please get my bags from upstairs while the engine warms up?"

"Gladly," Hank said. Fidelio's leather case sat by the door of their room, packed and waiting. It was surprisingly light for its size. The metal box was another matter. Hank's labor-hardened muscles complained as he carried it down the stairs. By the time he reached the ground floor, the Stanley Steamer was ready to go.

After a brief stop at the general store, Fidelio refilled the car's fuel tank, and loaded two extra canisters of kerosene into the rear storage area.

They headed west out of Toledo, on the old stagecoach trail that led towards South Bend, and ultimately, Chicago. At the city limits, the hard surfaced macadam gave way to packed gravel. As the distance from the city increased, the road dwindled to a pair of wagon ruts.

Hank was accustomed to the rumbling of iron-rimmed wagon wheels on the trail, yet the motorcar was louder, even out in the open country. Luckily Fidelio had had an extra pair of goggles for him to wear, because the car's tires kicked up a powerful amount of dust.

"So what brought you to America?" Hank asked his traveling companion, raising his voice to be heard over the road noise.

"I am an aspiring inventor. Originally, I came here to apprentice to Thomas Edison."

Hank whistled in appreciation. "The famous inventor? You must be one smart fellow." He thought for a moment. "If you don't mind my asking, why did you leave?"

"Edison is a brilliant man, but he can be a difficult person for whom to work."

"Really? Tell me about it."

The Cuban's story was interesting, even if Hank didn't understand much of it. Fidelio spoke of a device that converted text into Morse-Code-type dots and dashes and stored them on motion-picture film. Fidelio had thought of an improvement to Edison's idea, based on Charles Babbage's mathematical engine, but Edison did not appreciate its value.

"Is that why you quit working for him?"

"No, there was a misunderstanding regarding some work which I was pursuing on my own time. Edison accused me of appropriating his ideas for my own use. However, this was a project I had begun months earlier in my home country."

"I see," Hank nodded. *No wonder he's so all-fired secretive about the box.* "So why Chicago? From what I hear tell, it's mostly railroads and meat packing."

"Chicago is said to be a good place for the entrepreneur, but in truth, I am headed beyond, to the Badlands of North Dakota." He paused to wipe his face with a cloth he kept next to the vehicle's gear shift. "There is a Frenchman living there, the Marquis De Mores, who made his fortune in the cattle business."

"Hmm, the name sounds familiar. Is that what your invention is for, the cattle business?"

"Not exactly. I view the Marquis as a visionary with the resources to fund my endeavor. He is the kind who solves business problems with creative and original thinking."

"How so?"

"His plan was to bypass the Chicago beef cartel by building a slaughterhouse at the source, and shipping the meat to market on refrigerated trains. But the railroads were allied with the cartel, and their predatory pricing drove his business to bankruptcy. A few years later, he returned with a new mission – to ship his product to market using modern airship technology."

"Oh, *that* fellow! The crazy man who shipped meat by dirigible."

"Not so crazy; only the finest cuts, as well as delicacies such as quail and rattlesnake meat. Soon his aerial shipping service was cutting into the profits of the rail companies. Eventually they relented and gave him a more favorable shipping rate for his product."

"You're one brainy hombre, Fidelio. You only deal with the smartest folks around." He laughed. "Present company excluded, of course."

"Do not sell yourself short, Hank. I am sure you are quite capable in your work. As for the Marquis – it is rumored that his foray into the airship business was his wife's idea. She is American, of the Von Hoffman banking family of New York; a most extraordinary woman. The town the Marquis founded is named for her."

"For once it's nice to see the little guys win against the greedy railroads and meat-packers. Though compared to you and me, the Marquis and his wife ain't what you'd call poor."

Fidelio smiled. "I am gratified that you recognize the inherent flaws in the capitalist system. Most Americans are not so open-minded."

Soon their voices tired and the men rode in silence. For a time the road ran parallel to the railway, then it veered off on its own. They passed by countless farms and though a handful of small villages, but encountered few other motorized vehicles. Most of the traffic consisted of riders or horse-drawn wagons. Occasionally a passerby's horse would spook at their approach, but most seemed unimpressed by this new form of transportation.

It was just past midday when Hank's stomach began to rumble. Unfortunately, they had passed through the last village over an hour ago; ahead of them there was nothing but rolling, wooded hills. At least the red, orange and yellow leaves made the scenery enjoyable. He hardly noticed the band of dark clouds on the horizon.

"Dad blast it!" A sudden gust of wind had grabbed Hank's hat and flung it into the trees behind them. To his surprise, Fidelio put the car in reverse and backed up to where it had fallen.

"From the looks of it, we're in for some nasty weather," Hank said as he climbed back in.

"I hope to reach the next village before the storm hits us," Fidelio said.

As they drove on, the clouds darkened, and the wind increased in strength. "We'll never make it!" Hank yelled. "There's a barn up ahead on the right, maybe we can ride it out in there."

Fidelio gripped the wheel tightly and drove on through the blinding, blowing dust. "It is quite difficult to see. Maybe we should stop for a while." As Fidelio said those words, there was a sickening crunch. The Steamer jolted to the right, then abruptly stopped.

Hank grabbed onto the dashboard. If not for his quick reaction, he might have been thrown from the car. "What in blazes just happened?"

Fidelio jumped out of the car without answering. He hurried around the front of the car to inspect the wheel on Hank's side. "The wheel impacted a large stone. The tire is deflated and at least one spoke is broken." At that moment, a drenching rain began.

"Confound this rotten luck!" Hank had been hoping the Lord was done testing him for a while. He got out of the car and huddled beside the car next to Fidelio. "What can I do to help?"

"At this moment, we could use some shelter."

Hank looked over his shoulder. "We're pretty close to that barn I saw. Let's run for it, before we catch our death of cold."

"Agreed!" The men dashed through the field to the barn. Hank slid the door open and they ducked inside.

"Now what? Seems like we're between a rock and a hard spot."

"The obstacle is not insurmountable," Fidelio said. "Once the rain stops, we remove the damaged wheel and replace it with the spare."

Hank nodded. "That was clever of them, to include an extra."

"Unfortunately, my upholstery will be damaged. I regret I did not get the model with the permanent top over the passenger compartment."

"Dang, that's a bitter pill. But like the Good Book says, what does it profit a man to build up riches in this world? Your health, freedom, and loved ones, that stuff's what's important."

Fidelio put a hand on Hank's shoulder. "You are correct. My privileged upbringing has caused me to place too much importance on material things."

"Not saying I'm jealous of your good fortune," Hank said. "But when you grow up poor, you learn to appreciate the little things."

"The two of us are not as different as you suppose. I also lost my mother very early in life. I dreamt of her every night, though I only knew her from photographs."

Hank nodded. "I guess the two of us have got more in common than we thought."

After a few minutes, the downpour ceased and they emerged from their shelter. "I feel just awful about your motorcar," Hank said.

Fidelio walked around and inspected the upholstery. "I believe I can minimize the damage." He opened the trunk and found a towel in his traveling bag.

While Fidelio dried his leather seats, Hank inspected the more significant damages. "We might not be going anywhere soon. That busted wheel has really sunk into the muck."

"That is no problem. The Steamer is equipped with a hydraulic lifting device." Fidelio returned to the trunk and retrieved a metal cylinder with a flat base and a handle on the side.

"Oh, you meant a jack," Hank said. "You got the good kind." He watched

Fidelio insert a handle and pump it up and down. "That ain't gonna work. The jack's sinking into the mud."

Fidelio stepped back for a better view. The jack's piston was pressed against the frame of the car but its base had indeed sunk into the ground. "You are correct. It needs better support."

"I know just the thing." Hank ran back to the barn and returned with a wooden plank. He slipped the board under the Steamer behind the broken wheel.

"Now the jack is too tall to fit under the frame," Fidelio said. "We shall need to excavate the earth on either side of the vehicle to provide more clearance."

"Maybe not," said Hank. He squatted down at the front corner of the car. "I'll lift this little darling while you shove the jack underneath."

With a grunt, Hank lifted the car for a moment as Fidelio placed the jack. Working together, they elevated the car, removed the damaged wheel, and bolted on the spare.

"Now I will need to drive more cautiously for a while," Fidelio said.

Hank returned the board and they were on their way. They did not get far before they encountered a more daunting obstacle. The road led them to a river, where it ended abruptly.

"The rainstorm was more severe than I surmised," Fidelio said. "The river must have risen and swept the bridge from its moorings."

The wooden bridge was just barely intact. The near end had come loose and now floated on the water. Though the swollen river had fallen from its crest, its current still pulled at the bridge's detached end, threatening to wash the entire structure downstream.

"I'm a pretty fair swimmer," Hank said. "I wouldn't mind getting wet to fetch the other end of the bridge, excepting that's a mighty dangerous current."

"Do not risk your life," Fidelio said. "We will head back down the road and find a different crossing. Unless..." He stared at the rushing water. "There is something I want to try, but you must promise me you will not tell others of what you are about to see."

"Sure thing," said Hank. "You've helped me out a lot, so I figure I owe you one."

"Good." Fidelio went back to the trunk and removed the heavy metal box.

Hank watched intently as Fidelio unlocked the case and removed a device that resembled a large metal spider. It was about six inches long, not including its jointed metal legs. There were six of those; the other two were raised and equipped with formidable-looking pincers. Fidelio then got out an eight-inch spool of cabling, one end of which he attached a pair of terminals on the spider's back, and the other to a metal box covered with buttons and switches. "Behold, the Arachno-Automaton. It does not yet have an official name. For now I call it Tarantela."

"This is hardly the time to be playing with toys," Hank said with a grin.

"It is no toy. This is the invention I have worked on for several years."

Hank looked down at the device. "It's an interesting critter, but how's it gonna help us?"

"We need to grab hold of the loose end of the bridge. There is rope in the back of the Steamer, but we have no way to get it there."

"I used to be pretty good at roping calves in my day," Hank said. "Though to lasso a bridge, we'd need something like a hook on the end."

"We could fashion a hook of some sort, but we may not have the time. In addition, I fear that none of the supports individually could support the weight of the bridge."

"You got a better idea?"

Fidelio went back to the trunk and returned with a coil of rope, and fastened one end to Tarantela's body. "If you can throw it onto the bridge, I will do the rest. We must ensure that this wire remains intact, because it is attached to this control." He indicated the metal box. "Next, I must wind it up." He inserted a key in the spider's back and turned it clockwise several rotations.

"I'll give it my best shot. Hand me that thing, please?" Hank held the rope about two feet from the spider and spun it around experimentally. "Is it okay to get it wet?"

"It is somewhat water resistant, but we should attempt to keep it as dry as possible. Hurry, the bridge is about to break free." Fidelio held up the spool on a spindle so it could rotate freely.

"Step back a ways. I don't want to smack you in the face." Hank stared intently at his target as he whirled the spider in a circle above his head, then let it fly. Tarantela hurtled through the air and landed on the deck of the bridge, where it bounced twice and slid down the wet wood toward the water. All at once it awakened and scuttled up the slope, as if alive.

"Well I'll be hog-tied!" Hank held on to the rope as Fidelio worked the controls with a feverish intensity. The spider crawled to the left, then ducked around the nearest support board, out over the turbulent water. "Dang, don't let it fall in."

"Quiet! I must concentrate." The spider clung to the post and came back around, then crawled to the next one. It repeated this procedure, weaving the rope around three more supports on the left side of the bridge. It then crawled to the right and it wrapped the rope around four uprights on that side. Finally it jammed its claws into the floor boards to hold itself fast.

"So far, so good," Fidelio said. "Now, attach the other end of the rope to the front axle of the Steamer. I will use the motorcar to pull the bridge back into place."

"Good idea. I'll make sure the rope don't get hung up on anything. Do you have any gloves? I don't want my hands to get tore up."

"Use my driving gloves." Fidelio tossed them to Hank. "When the engine is ready I will put the Steamer in reverse." Fidelio got in and ignited the boiler. The rope went tight as they waited for the engine to heat up. The force of the current jerked the vehicle's frame, threatening to pull both car and driver into the raging water.

"Brace yourself," shouted Fidelio. The car's rear wheels dug into the wet road and spun wet gravel into the air. Finally the tires made traction and the Steamer crept backwards.

The bridge creaked horribly as the rope twisted and vibrated. Hank held his breath as he clutched it tightly. He wished he'd grabbed the goggles; if the hemp line snapped it might take out an eye. His hands burned beneath the thin cotton gloves, but still he managed to hold on.

Hank was so busy guiding the rope that he jumped in surprise when the bridge rammed into its support posts. "Ho, Fidel, stop! Hold it there while I nail her down!" He dug through the tool box, finding a hammer but no nails – was their effort in vain? Then he saw the screwdrivers.

He grabbed them all and ran down the river, where he pulled with all his might and got it aligned on his support. Then he used the hammer to pound each of the screwdrivers thorough the bridge and into the horizontal frame on top of the pilings.

"What are you doing to my tools?" Fidelio shouted.

"I'll buy you new ones," Hank yelled back. "There, that should hold for a while!" He then used the hammer to bend the screwdriver handles so they would not damage the Steamer's tires.

Fidelio got out of the car to retrieve his creation. "Tarantela is intact. Hank, I am indebted to you." The men gathered up the remaining tools and wound up the rope. The sun was low in the sky when at last they crossed the river and continued on their way.

"Fidelio, I'm mighty impressed by that mechanical critter of yours," Hank shouted over the road noise. "No wonder you quit on Edison; there ain't much the man can teach you."

Fidelio grinned. "You flatter me, but I still have much to learn."

Hank cleared his throat. "I believe things happen for a reason. The Lord sent you to give me a purpose in life, and he also meant for me to help you out of this jam."

The Cuban gave him a cryptic look. "I suppose that is possible. You are certainly quite skilled with mechanical things, not to mention ropes."

Late that evening, they arrived in the village of Elkhart, Indiana. The only open business was a roadside tavern. The two men entered and found seats by a table at the corner. No waiter arrived, so Fidelio went to the bar, and returned momentarily.

"I hope you like chicken soup. That is all they have."

Hank grinned. "I'm a man of simple tastes. Chicken soup it is."

"Tell me," Fidelio asked as he took his seat, "do you have employment waiting for you back in Arizona?"

"Not exactly, but I left on good terms with Mister Tillman, who owns a big spread over in Prescott Valley. I'm pretty sure he'll hire me on if he happens to need a ranch hand."

"So you are committed to returning to the territory?"

Hank shrugged. "Not really. Besides my Uncle Malcolm, I ain't got no kinfolk back in Arizona. If you need any hired help, I'm your man."

Fidelio laughed mightily. "That was what I was about to suggest, though I currently cannot afford to pay you. But you are welcome to accompany me to North Dakota to meet the Marquis. If I can procure financial backing, we will discuss the terms of your employment."

"Hot diggity! I'd like that very much. By the way, I'm looking forward to seeing Chicago. Will we get to spend some time there?"

"Unfortunately not. I was already behind schedule when we hit that accursed pothole. I shall send a telegram to the Marquis, to inform him that our arrival will be delayed. Fortunately I 'ran into' you – quite literally – or I might have been later still."

Hank nodded. "The Lord works in mysterious ways."

"I do not believe in Fate, but it is ironic how we were both in the New York area, then met by chance on the road. By the way, travel by motorcar is more challenging than I anticipated. Although I do not wish to part with the Steamer, I wish I had taken the train to North Dakota."

"There's more than one way to skin a cat," Hank said. "You don't have to get rid of Stanley. Westbound trains always have empty freight cars. It shouldn't cost too much to put her aboard one of them."

"That is a splendid idea, my friend. But first, we must secure lodgings for the evening." Fidelio hailed a passing waitress. "Miss, could you please direct us to the nearest inn or hotel?"

"You're there," answered the petite blonde. "Ma and Pa rent out rooms in the back."

"Then we are fortunate indeed. Now, how about that soup? My companion and I have been on the road all day."

"Right away, sir."

Chapter 9 – A Change of Conveyance

When he and Hank reached Chicago, Fidelio booked passage for both himself and his automobile to Minnesota on the Burlington Route, with a transfer at St. Paul to the Northern Pacific. As Hank did not have sufficient funds to purchase another ticket, Fidelio paid his way once more.

"Thanks Fidel," Hank said. "But I can't keep on accepting charity this way."

"Nonsense. If you are to be my assistant, I shall consider this a business expense."

One of the perks of their first class train tickets was a deluxe sleeping compartment with two bunks. As they had already supped in the Chicago rail station, both men were ready to retire for the night. Fidelio took the upper bunk, leaving the other to Hank. His traveling companion was soon asleep, snoring like the sound of a saw on wood. It reminded him of Rodrigo, whose lungs had been compromised by the pervasive dust of the mine.

Hank was an attractive man, from his sandy hair, graying at the temples, and his perpetually stubbled chin, down to his larger-than-average feet. A lifetime of hard work had given the cow-puncher an enviable musculature, especially on his biceps and pectorals. It was quite obvious, however, that his new friend did not share his sexual proclivities. Even if Hank were to have such desires, which Fidelio believed were inborn, the man's religious strictures would likely preclude acting upon them.

Of course this reminded him of his dear lost Rodrigo. So many memories flooded through Fidelio's mind that his quest for sleep was fruitless. Luckily, the compartment was equipped with two gas lamps mounted in the wall, one for each bunk. Fidelio pushed the button to light his lamp, and then turned down the valve so it was just bright enough to read.

He opened his satchel, withdrew some drawings, and unrolled them on the bunk. They showed the latest version of the automaton. As he looked them over, he felt a familiar sense of frustration. He was stuck on the same problem that had obsessed him during his employment with Edison. How could a device this small take advantage of the latest magnetic technology? For his original conception of a machine that could save men from the risks of underground mining, Tarantela would need to be much greater in size. As the automaton was made larger, its mass would increase exponentially, requiring considerably more power. It was for this reason that Nature had not seen fit to restrict the scale of real-life arachnids.

Fidelio pondered for a while, then got out a tablet and sketched out a few concepts in pencil. No new ideas came to him. He still had no idea how he could miniaturize the cooling system enough to make the use of cryomagnetic power practical.

By his pocket watch he could see it was now well past midnight. There was no use in wasting any more time in this frustrating exercise. Perhaps he could find the answer in a dream, as he had done when the problem of controlling his creation's gait had bedeviled him.

Unfortunately, Fidelio's subconscious mind was not inclined to present him with a solution. Instead he dreamed of the day of that horrible accident in the mine. Fidelio ran in a blind panic to the main tunnel entrance, where he shouted, "Let me through!" but the guards would not let him pass. While the mine owners debated what action to take, Fidelio wanted to grab a shovel and start digging. When rescue crews finally broke through, it was too late. Rodrigo's broken body was just one of scores of corpses removed from the site of the cave-in.

Fidelio awoke with his heart pounding and his nightclothes soaked with sweat. He took a few deep breaths to calm himself, then peered over the edge of his bed. The lower bunk was empty. He hoped he hadn't driven Hank away with all his tossing and turning; these bunks creaked with every little movement. Then Fidelio realized that the sun was shining around the edges of the curtains. Hank was an early riser, so in retrospect, his absence was no surprise.

Fidelio got up, folded his bed into the wall, and dressed quickly. He found Hank in the dining car, which was nearly empty, as it was still quite early. His traveling companion sat alone at a table, reading a newspaper as he drank his coffee and smoked a cigarette. An empty plate lay in front of him. Thankfully, the window beside him was partway open. The smell of smoke reminded him of his father's noxious cigars, which had always made his eyes water.

Hank looked up from his paper and smiled. "Morning, Fidel. If you don't mind me asking, did you sleep okay? Seems like you were muttering half the night."

"I slept for a while but it was not restful. My sincerest apologies if my somniloquy disturbed your sleep."

"Som what? You mean sleep talking? It was no bother. If you spend as much time out on the trail as I have, you get so you can sleep on a pile of rocks in the middle of a thunderstorm."

"That would be a very helpful skill to possess," Fidelio said with a grin. "Tell me, are they still serving breakfast? I don't see any waiters about."

"Oh, they've been around since I got here at the crack of dawn. It's just that they've got a newfangled way of taking your order. You just speak into the whatchamacallit here," he pointed to a metal cone resting on a hook mounted on the wall, "and the cart comes out with your coffee and food and whatnot, all by itself. I hate to admit it, but the first time I saw one, on the Lake Erie Express, I kind of went loco. Reminded me too much of the Spanish *'tanque'* contraptions they used in the war."

"Quite fascinating. I mean the cart, not your unfortunate reaction." Hank had already related that story, and Fidelio did not wish to hear it again. "War does horrible things to a man's mind. As for the other matter, I was reading about 'culinary automata' in one of my scholarly journals, but I haven't yet been served by one."

"Ha! I'm surprised you didn't invent it, smart fellow that you are. Here you go, try it out." Hank removed the cone-shaped device from the hook and handed it to Fidelio. A long rubber tube ran from the point of the cone into the wall.

Fidelio took the cone and spoke into the open end. From the box issued a voice that sounded muffled and mechanical, as on a telephone. His order completed, he handed the device to Hank, who replaced it in its cradle.

Hank took a drag from his cigarette, then stubbed it out in the ashtray. "I got to say again how much I appreciate you taking a chance on a down and out cow-puncher like me. And paying for my ticket, too. I've rode the rails before, but I never been able to travel in style, not like this."

"It was no mere act of charity," Fidelio said. "I expect that ours will be a mutually beneficial partnership. You have the practical experience of the real world, which is important for situations like the one we had back in Ohio."

Hank took a sip of his coffee and laughed. "Now that was a real adventure. But it's probably for the better. It stands to reason a city slicker like yourself would be much more at home traveling the civilized way on the railroad."

Fidelio ignored the jest. "In retrospect, it was the more sensible choice. But I do not regret my attempt, because I also believe that the future of this country is with the motorcar. One does not achieve great things without taking risks, and blazing new trails rather than following those created by others."

"Well, 'twasn't exactly a new trail, but surely the method of locomotion was. Like your eight-legged beasties. The Lord made them first, but your own version is mighty clever."

"Thank you, I'm glad you appreciate my innovation. But as Edison himself says, genius is one percent inspiration..."

"And 99 percent perspiration. Yep, even a rube like me has heard that one."

"Then perhaps you can help me with the perspiration part," Fidelio said. "I'm currently wrestling with the device's source of propulsion." He glanced around the car; there were now diners at two of the other tables. "Though we should keep our voices low."

Hank leaned in conspiratorially. "You can count on me, Fidel. Henry MacMillan is a man who can keep his secrets."

"Excellent. Now, you recall how the device is currently powered by a coiled spring..."

Rail travel was inherently noisy, with the constant clacking of the wheels over the rails, but not nearly so much as travel by motorcar. During their journey to Chicago, conversation had been difficult, and they soon grew hoarse from shouting. Here one could speak at a comfortable volume, particularly when the windows were closed, yet there was enough background noise that they could enjoy some degree of privacy.

Hank listened patiently as Fidelio described his scientific dilemma. Like the stereotypical westerner, he seemed to regard everything he encountered with a kind of bemused indifference. As he took in Fidelio's story, however, a big grin appeared on his face. "The moment I saw that critter of yours, I was powerful interested. I wanted to ask you more about it, but I thought that with everything being hush-hush and all, I'd be wise to keep my mouth shut."

"I appreciate your discretion, my friend. I know you are an honorable man, so I trust you will not reveal the details to the world until my creation is ready to be sent to the patent office."

"You got it," Hank said. "I've been thinking on what you said about the power source. I'm accustomed to dealing with living creatures, and the way they move about is something we all take for granted. As far as your invention goes, though, there's another thing that perplexes me, if it's okay to ask."

"Certainly. At this point I believe we can trust each other."

"How does the dang thing walk? Sure, it looks easy at first glance, but I know for a fact it ain't. You watch a newborn foal struggle to get on its feet and you realize that walking is dreadful complicated, truly one of God's miracles. The way each leg moves in turn, and how the different joints bend this way and that at exactly the right moment."

"For someone with no scientific education, that is a very astute observation. It was indeed a challenge I was also fortunate to have assistance from the faculty of Rutgers University. Even so, I spent several years prior studying the physiology of arachnids. In the prototype version, I encoded the sequences of movement in a series of finely tuned cams located in the spider's legs."

"You don't say! You mean like on a steam locomotive or a sewing machine?"

"Exactly! Then I realized that this same information could be stored as dots on film..."

They discussed the matter for a while, until Hank was satisfied with the explanation, then moved on to the matter of motive power. It was at this point that Fidelio's breakfast finally arrived on a self-powered chromium-plated wheeled cart; a plate of poached eggs and toast, with a pot of tea on the side. *So that explains that metal track in the floor.*

"I was beginning to think they had forgotten me," Fidelio said. He took a bite of egg, which was barely lukewarm, but he was too hungry to send it back.

"I never would have thought it," Hank said. "I mean, that the power source would be a bigger problem than controlling the leg motion. Especially since steam engines have gotten mighty small these days, almost small enough to mount on a bicycle."

Fidelio poured himself a cup of tea, added a cube of sugar, and stirred vigorously. "That much is true. Even so, mounting such an engine on an eight-legged walking device would be a maintenance nightmare, with all the jostling and rattling. Furthermore, it would be a hazardous place for the storage of flammable fuel."

As they finished their breakfast, they heard the squealing of brakes as the train slowed for its arrival in St. Paul, Minnesota. "Isn't this where we get off?" Hank asked.

"Indeed, we shall continue our discussion on the next train."

They found the platform for their connecting train with little difficulty. In the first car they entered, almost every seat was taken. Hank spied two adjacent available spots near the middle, but Fidelio shook his head, and they continued on.

The next car had no empty seats at all. Hank made a disgusted face. "What was wrong with that last one? That young couple wouldn't have paid us no mind. They were too busy making goo-goo eyes at each other."

"We may yet be forced to return to that seat," Fidelio said. "But I am hoping to find one without such close neighbors. I would like to continue our discussion, but I do not wish to be overheard if it can be prevented."

"Fair enough." They walked through two more passenger cars which were all full or nearly so. The next car, surprisingly, was half-empty. Fidelio selected a spot right in the center of the car and sat down.

"Well praise the Lord, we finally found one you like," Hank said with a grin. "Lots of elbow room here, so I reckon it was worth the walk."

"Indeed," Fidelio said. "Now we can continue our discussion undisturbed. I seem to recall that before we left the dining car, there was something you wanted to tell me."

Hank looked puzzled for a moment. "Oh yeah, we were talking about your critters, how the things were put together, and I've got to say the way it all works is powerful clever. Not something I could have thought of myself, not in a million years, but once I saw it, I said, 'Of course, that's how it works.' I might not be good at thinking up new stuff, but once I know how a thing goes, I can figure out how to fix it, sure as shootin.'"

Fidelio smiled. The man's colorful language was a constant source of amusement. "I ascertained as much; that you have much greater practical and mechanical skills than I. It bodes well for our partnership."

"Glad to hear it. The problem is, I'm not quite sure what your automa- um, spiders are *for* exactly. The thing sure saved our bacon when we were stranded back in Ohio, but what about everyday life? The contraption ain't big enough to ride, and it's not little enough to, say, clean out a drainpipe."

Fidelio exhaled and tried to cover his impatience with Hank's lack of imagination. "I have no doubt the automaton will be useful. It can perform a multitude of tasks that are tedious or dangerous for a human being. Remember, this is an early model; I plan to have versions that are both smaller and larger for various purposes."

"Such as?"

Fidelio smiled. "For example, I would particularly wish to employ the automata in an underground mine, where they could drill the rock face or plant explosive charges. Hundreds of lives could be saved each year."

"I can just see 'em with the little metal hat with the lamp on it," Hank chuckled. "But I wonder, how will the miners take to being put out of work? Like the way whalers gripe about those newfangled electric lights, or horse breeders hate the horseless carriage?"

"It may be a cliché to say you cannot stop progress," Fidelio said, "but even if this were possible, should we even try? There would be numerous opportunities for employment outside the mines. In particular, there will be a need for workers to set up and repair the automata. Even if the innovation does put men out of work, can we really say that extracting minerals from tunnels in the ground is worth the risk to life and limb? Think of the husbands that never return home to their wives, the fathers to their children."

Hank regarded him for a moment for answering. "There's a fire in your eyes when you say that. Now I'm starting to understand where you're coming from. Could it be you've lost a loved one to the mines?"

"One should not automatically make that assumption," Fidelio sniffed. "Could I not simply be motivated by the welfare of all mankind?"

"Whoa, sorry, pardner, I didn't mean to stick my nose in your business. But if there's anything you're inclined to talk about it, I'm all ears. Life out on the trail makes a man a mighty good listener."

Fidelio shook his head. "Thank you, but no. At some later time I may wish to do so, but at present I do not wish to relive any painful memories."

"*Comprendo*," Hank said. "You were there for me, *compadre*, and I'll be there for you."

"I appreciate that," Fidelio said, turning his head to hide the moisture in his eye. "In any case there is no need to fret over the fate of the miners. Inventions like this may replace a man's muscle, but not his brains or ingenuity."

"One thing's for sure," Hank said. "They'd need a lot less men to mine a ton of coal."

"That is where capitalist greed comes in. The cheaper its cost, the more will be mined. After all, will Carnegie ever extract enough iron ore? Will Peabody stop mining coal?"

This time, Hank laughed out loud. "I've got to admit, first time I met you I thought, now there's one highfalutin' city-slicker who'll never make it the real world. Was I ever wrong! You're not just book-smart; you're as sly as a riverboat gambler. With an invention like your Tarantela, you'll be as famous as Edison and rich as J.P. Morgan. The sky's the limit, *amigo*."

Fidelio shook his head. "I do not wish to join the ranks of the robber barons! Edison, by the way, is a decent man, but even he has been led astray by the lure of profit."

"My apologies, I didn't mean to cause offense."

"No offense taken. I only meant to convey that my goals are not those of the typical inventor. I see money as a tool for improving the lot of workers. Whatever profits I make beyond what I need for my sustenance and continued research, I will donate to funds on behalf of organizations which promote the welfare of laborers."

Hank nodded. "Good for you. Not to knock your generosity, though, but there's nothing wrong with a man making a buck off his ideas. That's what I aim to do, if I ever come up with an invention of my own. Not that I'm wanting for anything, but I'd sure like to leave something to the young 'uns I hope to have some day."

Fidelio had to smile at Hank's naïve acceptance of the Horatio Alger mythos of 'rags to riches.' He was tempted to make a sarcastic reply, but he stopped himself. *Hank may be uneducated, but he is no fool. I should not risk alienating him.* "Certainly every man desires financial security. But there are two sides to that coin. I have been to slums where the immigrants live, and I have seen the plight of the downtrodden Negroes, in this country and my own. I myself served food to the hungry in the soup kitchens of Havana."

"The Savior commands us to help the poor, and I'll certainly do whatever I can. Of course, the best thing you can do for poor folks is to help 'em get back on their feet. You don't want to encourage idleness." Hank unfolded his jacket, which he had draped over the arm rest, and went through each pocket in turn. Eventually he located a pouch of tobacco, yet he continued searching. "Consarn it, where did I put my papers?"

"Try your shirt pocket," Fidelio said. "And please open the window if you intend to have a cigarette. I realize tobacco smoking is a compelling habit, but I find it quite disagreeable."

Hank nodded. "Sometimes I feel the same way myself, when a saloon gets real smoky. Not that I go to them places anymore." He found the tiny packet, withdrew a paper, and expertly rolled a cigarette. "Fact is, I gave up smoking for a time, though I missed it something awful. Most of the folks in the Society of Friends didn't like the vice any more than drinking, though there was one or two that smoked a pipe. If you ask me, though, the Bible don't say anything about it either way, does it?"

No sooner had Hank lit his cigarette and taken the first drag, that Fidelio noticed a young woman standing behind his traveling companion.

"Excuse me, sir," said a soft feminine voice. "Please, there is no smoking in this car."

"Really?" Hank turned around and smiled when he saw the speaker. Long dark hair framed her face, with smooth skin, a dainty nose, and dark eyes which contrasted with the frown on her full lips. She wore a long blue frock that, unlike so many of the fashions of the day, did not hide the curves of her delicate body.

"No smoking allowed?" Hank continued. "I never heard of such a thing, 'cept in school and church, of course. Well, okay then." He tapped out the offending cigarette in the ashtray built into his armrest. "It won't hurt me none to abstain a while."

"Thank you, sir, we appreciate that."

"Happy to oblige, miss. Is this a new rule of the railroad?"

"Not exactly. It's a special request from Miss Hightower."

At that, Fidelio sat up in his seat to see the rest of the people in the young woman's party. When he and Hank had entered the nearly-empty car, he'd paid no mind to the small group of people at the rear. There sat another young woman with three dark-complected men. "Do you mean Miss Tallulah Hightower the opera singer? Popularly known as the Choctaw Nightingale?"

"The same." Her pretty face showed a hint of a smile. "Good day, sirs."

As soon as she had left, Fidelio leaned over to whisper to his friend. "Can you believe our good fortune, to be honored with the presence of such an exquisite talent? This is the chance of a lifetime. We must speak with her!"

Hank frowned. "I can appreciate how you're all fired up about Miss Hightower. I hear tell she's a real fine singer. But I was raised not to make a nuisance of myself. We'd best leave Miss Hightower and her friends some privacy."

"It is too late for that, my friend," Fidelio said with a gleam in his eye. "You have already displeased the Nightingale with your vile habit. I believe you owe her a personal apology."

Hank's sun-weathered face turned atypically pale. "Gosh, Fidel, that would be powerful bothersome. Maybe it's best we just move to a different car."

"Ha! Are you afraid? A man who has faced outlaws, hostile Indians, the horrors of war, and the ravages of cancer? Have no fear; I shall accompany you on your mission."

"Afraid? Ha! I ain't afraid of nothing!" He glanced back once more. "All right. Let's go." Hank got out of his seat and strode down the aisle, as Fidelio hurried to catch up with him.

Chapter 10 – Unexpected Friends

When Hank reached the back of the car, he stood frozen as if in terror. Five sets of eyes focused on him as he opened his mouth to speak.

"Yes?" said a feminine voice. Unlike the young lady who had approached them, the speaker had the dark complexion and striking facial features of an American Indian. Her long black hair was tied into a braid. She wore a deep burgundy dress in the latest New York fashion.

Hank smiled, nodded and finally found his voice. "Beg your pardon, ma'am. Would you happen to be Miss Tallulah Hightower?"

"Yes, I am. And you are...?" She looked up at the newcomers with deep brown eyes that matched the sandalwood perfection of her skin. Her dark lips held the hint of a bemused smile.

"Well, ah, I'm Henry MacMillan, my friends call me Hank, and um, I'm here to apologize for any discomfort my actions might have caused you."

She raised her eyebrows, as one might regard a precocious child. "Apology accepted, Mister MacMillan. Likely you were not aware, as the railroad posted only one small sign." She pointed to a cardboard placard on the wall near her seat, which read, 'PLEASE NO SMOKING.'

"Furthermore, I'm not one to judge other peoples' vices," she said, casting a pointed look toward the men in her party. "I'm afraid that the smoke irritates my throat, and my voice is, after all, my livelihood."

"You're right, miss; it's a nasty habit. I'm powerful sorry to have bothered you."

Fidelio stepped closer and gave his friend a stern glance.

"Oh, and this is my friend, Fidelio Espinoza, from Havana, Cuba. He doesn't care for my habit, either, surprising as that might be, given where he's from."

Fidelio stepped forward and gave a bow. "It's a great pleasure to meet you, Miss Hightower. I had the immense good fortune of witnessing your performance in Spontini's masterpiece *La Vestale* in Paris three years ago. Since that time, I have been a devoted follower."

"Why thank you. I'm gratified that you enjoyed it."

"Well..." Hank looked more befuddled than Fidelio had ever seen him, "we'll just go back to our seats and let you folks tend to your business."

Once again, Tallulah Hightower smiled. "You gentlemen are welcome to join us for a while. As much as the five of us travel, we never tire of making new friends."

Fidelio arched his eyebrows. "You are certain it would not be an imposition?"

"Of course not. Allow me to introduce the other members of my party. You've already spoken to Isabelle Von Hoffman, my handmaid." The young lady nodded, and Fidelio stepped forward to kiss her hand.

"This dashing gentleman facing me is my vocal coach and accompanist, as well as my cousin: James Hightower. On the right is Fred Seeley, my business manager. Across from him," she motioned to a fellow wearing an unusual headdress, "is Ooche Osceola, my bodyguard." The men shook hands with each other in turn.

Except for Isabelle, they all shared Tallulah's skin color. James and Fred were attired in dark looking suits. On the seat next to James was a bowler hat similar to Fidelio's. Ooche wore traditional native garb: loose-fitting pants, a long, brightly decorated shirt that showcased his muscular physique, and a white turban wrapped around his head. He regarded Hank and Fidelio with a hint of suspicion in his dark eyes.

"*Estonko*," said Ooche as he shook Hank's hand. "In Seminole, it means 'how are you?'"

"Quite well, thank you," Hank said. "That's a real interesting moniker you have."

"Also Seminole. I chose the name to honor the hero of my people, Osceola."

"*Ooche* means 'son'," said Fred with a grin, "which if it was literally true would make our friend at least 60 years old."

Tallulah and exchanged a brief glance with James. He got up and moved across the aisle, leaving room for Hank and Fidelio to sit facing Tallulah and Isabelle.

"Mind if I ask a question?" Hank said as he and Fidelio took their seats. Without waiting for their reply, he continued, "Any of you folks in the Nighthawks? That's your people, right?"

Fidelio shot Hank a shocked glance. There was an awkward silence as Tallulah and her party all looked at each other.

Finally James responded. "Sorry, but we can't answer that, since it *is* a secret society."

Hank grinned sheepishly and slapped himself on the forehead. "Well, of course. Like my uncle used to say, 'Boy, sometimes you ain't got a lick of sense.' I just wanted to say how much I admire you all, how you stick together and fight for your people. And the way they captured that bastard Chivington without firing a shot; that was downright clever."

"Thank you, Mr. MacMillan," Tallulah said. "We were traveling when the incident occurred, but some of our family members were there, and we were with our people in spirit."

Despite his alarm at Hank's outspokenness, Fidelio had been dying to ask the question himself, and was disappointed to hear that no one present had personal knowledge of it. Perhaps he could broach the topic again later, more discreetly. He turned to Tallulah and said, "I must admit I am taken aback to encounter a celebrity of your stature traveling in a coach car."

"The compartments are a bit cramped for my taste," Tallulah said. "I find it more convenient to reserve a portion of a regular passenger car, so we can travel in comfort. So, you are a fan of the opera, Señor Espinoza?"

"Yes, all my life. My father introduced me to classical music at an early age. He started me on violin lessons at the age of seven, but alas, I had no particular talent for the instrument."

"Well I'll be danged!" Hank exclaimed. "I play, too. Of course in Arizona, we call it a fiddle. Gave mine away when I came east to join the Army, and I haven't had one since."

"That's quite interesting, Hank," Fidelio said, "but there is a world of difference between the way the instrument is played in the orchestra and at, for example, a square dance."

"I wouldn't be so dismissive of traditional music, Mr. Espinoza," Tallulah said. "I attended many square dances in my childhood, and enjoyed them immensely. In fact, Fred's father was one of the most celebrated fiddlers in all of Indian Territory."

That led to a discussion of folk music. Fidelio realized that Tallulah and her party, hailing as they did from rural America, had in some respects more in common with Hank than himself.

Fidelio turned to Isabelle, who had so far said little. "What about you, miss? Are you related to the Von Hoffman's of New York City?" The name was well known in financial circles.

"That was my late husband's name," she said. "We met at an opera gala in Manhattan."

"Your late husband?" Hank asked. "I'm awful sorry to hear that. How did he pass away?"

"In the Spanish War. I tried to talk him out of it, but he was determined to volunteer. He was a classically trained pianist; not the sort who was cut out to be a soldier."

"Such foolishness, the white man's war," Ooche said.

Noticing Hank's face going pale at the mention of the war, Fidelio decided to change the subject. "So," he asked, "do you all have some kind of musical talent?"

"I'm the only one who doesn't play an instrument," said Isabelle. "You should hear Fred; he can really play the banjo. Why don't you play something for our new friends?"

"Nah, I'm not that good. Besides, playing for folks I don't know gives me the willies."

"Please, enough of the false modesty," James said. "This man can pick up a storm."

Fred finally relented. He retrieved his instrument from the rack above the seat. "My grandpa came from Carolina," he said as he plucked and adjusted the five strings, "and he taught me a bunch of the old mountain standards. Are y'all familiar with *Wildwood Flower*?"

Fidelio had not heard much banjo music. He was pleasantly surprised by Fred's playing. The man improvised around the simple melody, his fingers practically flying over the strings.

From Fidelio's perspective, the most interesting member of the group was James. The man seemed quite athletic for a musician, and his exotic features and dusky skin reminded him of Rodrigo. Furthermore, he was a lifelong bachelor, and Tallulah's tales of their childhood together made no mention of any sweethearts. Fidelio chided himself for the thoughts that came unbidden. If James had predilections similar to his own, he was the sort Fidelio could easily fall for, but the pain in his heart was still too strong to take that risk.

At least Hank was enjoying himself. The man's shyness had abated, and he laughed and joked with both of the ladies. "Tell me, Hank," Tallulah said, "what do you miss most about your home?"

"Lots of things. Maybe most of all my horse, Jackpot. He was one handsome Appaloosa."

"As you would expect, Hank is an experienced horseman," Fidelio said. "I myself won medals as part of my University's equestrian team, but I suspect he could easily best me."

"That sounds like a challenge," Hank laughed. "I do love horses, but they sure are ornery critters, ain't they? Reminds me of the time my uncle sent me to fetch a mare who'd wandered off. I found her easy enough, but like a fool I'd gone on foot with no saddle or bridle. I tied a rope to her halter for reins, and rode her bareback. It went pretty good until we headed down into a wash, and she stopped real sudden and lowered her head. I went straight over and landed on my back. She just stood there while I coughed and sputtered. I could have swore the beast was laughing at me." The whole group broke into laughter at Hank's story.

Good companionship made the journey pass quickly. Fidelio was amazed that Hank resisted his smoking habit the whole time, except for a brief trip to the bar car. "I'll join you," Fred said, pulling a briar pipe from his jacket pocket. While the two were absent, Fidelio had the chance to converse with James, who told of their meeting with composer Giacomo Puccini in Rome, and how he had accompanied Tallulah as she sang for the Emperor Franz-Josef of Austria.

"Vienna is a beautiful city," James said. "And his Highness is a very gracious audience."

As mid-day drew near, a waiter arrived to take their orders for dinner. Hank and Fidelio stood up to leave, but Tallulah objected. "You may as well stay. Please order whatever you gentlemen would like."

"The Northern Pacific has no speaking tubes or automated serving carts?" asked Fidelio.

"They do," Tallulah said, "but I'm not particularly fond of them."

"Me neither," said Hank, with a knowing glance at Fidelio.

The food was excellent, and the conversation continued long past the meal's end. Soon they found themselves approaching the Fargo rail yard. Fred stood up and stretched.

"Time for another smoke?" Hank asked.

"Sorry, but no. Ooche and I have some business in Sioux Falls. We'll be getting off here and taking a different line south."

"That is unfortunate," Fidelio said. He regarded the two men curiously. It would need to be important business to take Ooche from his duties.

Hank was less circumspect. "So then who'll be protecting Miss Hightower and Miss Von Hoffman?" He looked stricken as he realized what he'd just said. "Beg pardon. It's really none of my business."

"Don't worry," Tallulah said. "We are on our way to visit some dear friends. The three of us will be quite secure until Fred and Ooche return."

"Though it's sweet that you're concerned about us," Isabelle added. "You and Fidelio are welcome to sit with us a while longer and make sure we're protected."

"Are you certain?" Fidelio asked. We do not wish to wear out our welcome."

"Nonsense," Tallulah said. "The three of us will be disembarking this evening, so you can keep us company until then."

"Really? Where are you all headed?" Hank asked her. "We'll be getting off this evening, too, at a town called Medora."

"What a coincidence!" said Isabelle. "We're going there as well, to see my cousin. As it happens, the town is named after her."

"Now don't that beat all?" Hank said. "Your cousin is the Mrs. Marquis De Mores?"

"That's her. Actually, we're not related by blood. She is my husband's cousin."

"Yet another amazing coincidence," Fidelio said. "We have business with the Marquis."

"Then you really must stay," Tallulah said with a smile. "I'm dying to hear how you happen to know our friends."

"Indeed," James said with a smile that to Fidelio, seemed to say more than his actual words. "It appears that Fate may have brought all of us together for a reason."

❀ ⼳ ❀

To Hank, it was one of the best days of his life. To meet by chance with Tallulah Hightower, not only famous but beautiful and charming – the Lord must have decided he'd earned some good times for a change. He'd need to thank Fidelio for forcing him to apologize and making it all possible.

After Fred and Ooche departed, Hank and Fidelio stayed on and visited with Tallulah, Isabelle and James. After a couple of hours had gone by, Fidelio looked at his pocket watch. "My apologies," he said, "but we must make some final preparations for our meeting with the Marquis. Thank you all for a very pleasant time."

"Yes, thank you kindly," Hank said. He put his hat on his head so he could tip it politely.

"The pleasure was ours," said Tallulah. "We will be seeing you at our destination."

To Hank, it seemed silly to leave Tallulah's car, which was still mostly empty, to look for another seat. Fortunately, many people had gotten off at Fargo; there were now plenty of empty seats in the next car.

"I hated to leave, too," Fidelio explained, "but we do not want to overstay our welcome."

"I guess you're right." As much as Hank had enjoyed their visit, he didn't want Tallulah to think he was hopelessly smitten; that kind of attention might scare her off.

"Besides, we need to work on our presentation. We only have one chance to make a first impression, and the presence of pleasant companionship so near may distract us from our work."

"I'll say! That Isabelle is almost as pretty as Tallulah, isn't she?"

"I agree, but unfortunately she is spoken for."

"What do you mean?"

"Did you see the way she kissed Fred when he and Ooche got up to leave? That was more than sisterly affection. The two of them are definitely enamored."

"You mean they're sweethearts? Then why wouldn't they just come out and say it?"

"Most likely it is because Isabelle is recently widowed, and society would view their relationship with disapproval."

"Can't say I blame the poor gal. I'm sure she just needed a shoulder to cry on."

"Now, review these notes, please." He handed a sheaf of notes to Hank. "I will quiz you afterwards until you know the basic points of our presentation as well as I do."

"You got it, boss." Normally he found book learning tedious, but with Tallulah in his thoughts he could have gone to a funeral with a smile.

As the sun sank into the west, Hank and Fidelio put down their work and headed for the dining car. The two men ate their supper in silence.

"You certainly are quiet this afternoon, and you have hardly touched your food. Did you wear out your throat regaling Miss Hightower with your tales of the Wild West?"

Hank chuckled. "No, the pork chops are very tasty. Thanks once again for paying the bill."

"It was my pleasure!" Fidelio chuckled. "If I did not know you are a man of the world, I would suspect you were love sick. I saw the way you kept stealing glances at her, even when someone else was speaking."

Hank shook his head. "I need to watch myself. I've played the fool over a woman one too many times. She's a really wonderful gal, but of course she's way higher class than a working man like me. Still, it makes you wonder – how can such a pretty, smart and charming woman be unmarried, at her age? She's got to be pretty near thirty."

"And why is that so appalling? Tallulah is dedicated to her singing career. To instead choose marriage and a family would rob the world of her considerable talents."

"She could have both," Hank said. "With the right man beside her."

Fidelio, who had been taking a sip of tea at the moment, was overcome by a sudden fit of laughter, which turned into a cough. He wiped the tea off his nose with his handkerchief, still chuckling. "My dear Hank, I had no idea you were smitten so badly."

Hank's face flushed red with embarrassment. "Just because I gave up my life of sin don't mean I'm looking to become a monk."

"Rumor has it that the Nightingale was affianced for a while to a British aristocrat, the young Earl of Swindon, I believe. He broke it off when he realized that he could not change her mind about her career. In all seriousness, would you be willing to accept it?"

"You're dang right I would!" Hank's raised voice earned him stares from the neighboring table, so he lowered his voice. "The Friends may be traditional, but we ain't stodgy, especially where the ladies is concerned."

"Not stodgy? Dressing in gray and black, not daring to show an ankle?"

"*Amigo*, you don't understand Quaker women," Hank said, irritation in his voice. "They dress plain to be humble before God. But they're still our equals, sisters in Christ."

"Point well made. My apologies, I did not mean to malign your religion."

"No offense taken. It's just that I can't always tell when you're serious, or when you're pulling my leg." He leaned in conspiratorially. "It sounds loco now, but I had a mind to ask Tallulah to fix you up with Isabelle. Too bad she's already taken."

"Do not worry about me," Fidelio chuckled. "I am not ready for any romantic commitments."

Hank grinned. "By gosh, I sure had my head up in the clouds today, didn't I?" He became serious again. "I was wondering – do you think maybe Tallulah and James are really cousins?"

"Even if not, they may as well be. Certainly there is nothing of that sort going on between them." He put a hand on Hank's arm. "I can understand your reticence, given that your heart has been broken before. But if you have feelings for Tallulah, there is no shame in wooing her. As my father says, 'La fortuna ayuda las audaces.'"

Fortune favors the bold."

"For a woman like her, I might need some Dutch courage. But I doubt she'd appreciate me smelling like whiskey."

They returned to their seats in the passenger car. Hank sat back, put his hands behind his head, and closed his eyes. Before he knew, he'd dozed off. He awoke to see darkness outside the train windows. Fidelio had turned on the lamp next to his seat, and was studying his notes.

"Good evening, my friend!" Fidelio put his hand on Hank's shoulder. "The day's conversation must have exhausted you. You have slept for over an hour."

"Really? Usually I'm not the kind to take a siesta after my meals. Where are we now?"

"We have passed the town of Dickinson and should be arriving in Medora shortly. I am glad you were able to rest. I hear that the De Mores' have not succumbed to the pedestrian ways of small town life. They have been known to entertain late into the night."

"I appreciate the warning," Hank said with a yawn. "I may need a cup or two of joe."

"Before we arrive, we have a few minutes to rehearse our presentation to the Marquis, to ensure it is both polished and professional. We must not bungle this extraordinary opportunity."

"Right," Hank said. "First you give him the basic idea of the invention, right? Then I tell him how Tarantela kept us from being stranded in Ohio." Even as their conversation went to serious matters, Hank found himself chuckling inside. If Fidelio had noticed that Isabelle was Fred's gal, he must have been interested enough to pay attention.

"What a good idea, to include the anecdote from our journey," Fidelio said. "We must do all we can to pique the man's interest before we let him see the actual device."

Hank looked out the window again. The moon was full, bright enough to let him see the prairie roll by as they rode. "Wish it was still daytime. I'd like a better look at the scenery."

"According to my research, it is subtly different from the rest of the state," Fidelio said. "You recall when we crossed the Missouri River? Beyond that great waterway, the landscape becomes more arid, with rolling hills, and none of those tiny lakes that are so common to the east. As I understand it, those were caused by the great glaciers of the last ice age."

"I have a hard time believing all that," Hank said. "How could the ice come way down here from the North Pole? Maybe those lakes were left over from the Great Flood."

Fidelio opened his mouth to speak, then apparently changed his mind. "I'm sure there are many differing theories about that."

Hank looked out the window again. "Are we slowing down? We must be getting close."

"Indeed. The terrain has become more rugged, and we are entering a curve around the hills. It is fortunate that the moon is giving us some illumination." The train went around the bend, and all at once they saw it.

For a moment, both men were speechless. Hank broke the silence. "Kinda sneaks up on ya, doesn't it?"

"Indeed," Fidelio said. "It is not the kind of landscape where you would expect to find a thriving, bustling community."

The town of Medora was much larger than Fidelio had expected: a jumble of wooden buildings with light-filled windows nestled in a small valley between the barren clay hills. Dominating the town to the north was a tall brick chimney stretching into the dark sky. To the east rose the skeletal towers of the town's airship field. "Look Fidel, there's two of them, and there's a Zeppelin docking right now, at this hour of the night."

"That is surprising. Even the Newark air field had only three towers, and I don't believe they had any evening flights. But cryoelectric technology has revolutionized air travel, like it's done for so many other industries. The new magnetic grapples have automated the docking process, and each tower has an elevator for passengers."

"I envy you and all your travels. Someday I'll get to take a ride in the clouds." Hank turned and pointed excitedly. "Look, up on the hill! That must be the De Mores place." It was a two story house, illuminated by its own pole-mounted electric lights. The building seemed to cover most of the hilltop. "That fellow must be rich enough to buy the whole town."

"Indeed he is," Fidelio said. "And to think that the Vallambrosas were on the edge of bankruptcy just ten short years ago. It was while working on the Indochina railroad that the Marquis encountered the great airship terminal at Haiphong Harbor, where reportedly he – or perhaps the Marquise – got the idea of starting their own transport company in America."

"It sure must be interesting to get to roam the world that way," Hank said. "I wonder how Miss Hightower and the others are they going to get to the Marquis' house."

"It is not just a house," Fidelio chuckled. "As I noted before the locals call it the Chateau. A bit of an exaggeration, unless you compare it to the size of a typical home on the frontier. Before we meet with our friends, though, we must retrieve our luggage." They made their way off of the train, onto the platform and into the station.

Tallulah, James, and Isabelle stood together near the baggage area with a man wearing blue jeans and a long-sleeved checkered shirt in the manner of a cowboy. A porter was already loading the party's bags onto a wheeled cart.

"Mr. Espinoza, Mr. MacMillan," Tallulah said, "this gentleman is Jeff, an employee of our hosts. They have sent him with a horseless carriage to convey us to the Chateau."

"My apologies, but I only have room for three passengers. We weren't expecting you to all get here at the same time," Jeff said with a tip of his hat. "I'll take the ladies first, and also Mr. Hightower, and I'll back for you later, if that's okay."

"That is not a problem," Fidelio said. "I have my own motorcar, which has been shipped here on the train. We will drive to the Chateau, if you will kindly give us directions."

Jeff gave a hearty laugh. "You can hardly get lost. Just look for the highest house in town. There's only one road up the hill."

In a short while they had their things. All Hank's possessions were in his battered metal-sided trunk. Fidelio had his traveling bag, a satchel full of equipment, and the locked box containing Tarantela and enough parts to make one or two more of the mechanized spiders.

"Meeting a real Marquis has got me all nervous," Hank said. "I wish I had the chance to wash up and change my clothes. I ain't exactly wearing my best bib and tucker."

Fidelio raised his eyebrows. "I would not advise it. Your homespun charm is already daunting enough. Miss Hightower can hardly resist you as you are."

"That time I could tell you were funnin' me," Hank grinned.

By this time, the Steamer's boiler was sufficiently warmed up, so the two men were on their way. As they drove through the town, they elicited curious stares from locals riding and walking through town.

"For being past sundown in such a small town," Hank said, "there sure are a lot of folks still out and about. Look at the way they're checking us out. You reckon

107

they ain't seen a motorcar before?"

"Doubtful, since I understand that the Marquis owns three of them. I expect that, like most small town residents, they do not recognize us and are therefore curious about our identity."

As Jeff had said, the De Mores' house was impossible to miss. It stood at the top of a hill, overlooking the town. The only hard part, Hank figured, would be finding the road that went there. Fidelio didn't seem concerned. He drove the Steamer down a cobbled street away from the center of town, past a huge brick building, to which was attached the great chimney they'd seen from the train.

"Is that the Marquis' slaughterhouse? It's every bit as big as the ones back in Chicago."

"It certainly is." Fidelio replied. "It is easy to understand how the Vallambrosas made their fortune." He continued down the street past where the cobbles ended, then crossed the Northern Pacific railroad tracks, whereupon a freshly graveled road led up the hill to the famous Chateau of the Badlands.

Chapter 11 – Badlands Soiree

Though the hill on which the Chateau was situated was not particularly tall, the view from the top was spectacular, with the river below on one side, and the lights of the town on the other.

"So this is the Marquis' *casa*," Hank observed. "It looked smaller in the picture."

"That postcard was almost a decade old. Since then, the Vallambrosas have added on new wings to the east and south."

Fidelio parked the car near the front door and they disembarked.

Hank stopped to examine the large doors on the new addition. "That's mighty strange. Looks like they tacked on a big old barn to their fancy house."

"I believe it is a garage or carriage house, for the Vallambrosas' motorcars," Fidelio said. "Although I have never before seen one attached directly to the house. Once again the Marquis has broken new ground." He smoothed his coat and adjusted his cravat, then knocked on the front door. Hank waited nervously behind him.

In a moment, a short and rather stout colored woman appeared at the door. "Good evening, sir. Were the Vallambrosas expecting you?"

"Certainly. I am Fidelio Ludovico Espinoza Cruz, and this is my associate Henry MacMillan. We arrived today on the same train that brought Miss Hightower and her party."

The woman's face broke into a broad smile. "Oh, that's right. You're the gentleman that had his motorcar shipped all the way from out East. They were just talking about you." She turned and called into the house. "*Monsieur! Madame!* Your guests have arrived."

"Thank you, Corrina," said a female voice from inside. "Tell them to join us in the parlor."

They entered through a narrow doorway. Fidelio was surprised to see that the grand structure had no entry hall. The door led immediately into the parlor, a cozy room with a fireplace in one corner and a piano in the other. It was occupied by several people, including Isabelle and Tallulah, who looked up from their seats and smiled at the newcomers.

A man rose from his chair and strode toward them. "You must be Señor

Espinoza. Welcome to our home!" The Marquis De Mores was of medium height and well-muscled, indicating that his wealth had not precluded him from physical labor. He was a dapper-looking fellow, with dark hair, piercing eyes and an impressive handlebar mustache.

"I have been looking forward to meeting you sir," Fidelio said as they shook hands, "This is my associate, Henry MacMillan."

"Pleased to meet you, your... grace?" Hank stammered.

The Marquis smiled broadly and shook Hank's hand vigorously. "Titles of nobility are of no importance here in the Badlands! Please address me as Antoine." He put an arm around the woman who appeared behind him. "Gentlemen, this is my wife Medora."

The Marquise was a slender, petite woman with dark hair in tight curls. She wore a long blue dress that seemed out of place here on the frontier. "Gentlemen." She extended her hand, which Fidelio brought to his lips and kissed. "How charming!" She turned to the maid. "Corrina, have you set additional places at the table for Mr. Espinoza and Mr. MacMillan?"

"Yes, madame. I had to put the extra leaf in, on account of having so many guests. So there'll be plenty of room." The woman gave a brief curtsey and returned to her duties.

"My cousin Isabelle has informed me how all of you just happened to find yourselves on the same train car. What a delightful happenstance!"

"Indeed," Fidelio replied. "We considered ourselves fortunate, to travel with such pleasant company. We only regret the imposition upon your household of so many guests at the same time."

"Oh, don't be concerned. My husband and I are quite accustomed to entertaining."

"Before meeting Miss Hightower, I did not realize that the two of you were aficionados of the opera. How unfortunate to be so far away from an opera house! My father began taking me to *el Gran Teatro* in Havana at a very early age. Later on, when I was attending the University in Spain, I was fortunate enough to hear Miss Hightower sing in Paris."

"Paris! Isn't it a beautiful city? I have been there a number of times with Antoine, but as you know, he prefers the wide open spaces! Speaking of that, Mr. MacMillan, I understand that you hail from the Arizona Territory."

"That's right, ma'am. We didn't have no luxuries growing up, like city folk do, but we always had enough food to eat and a roof over our heads. The only regretful thing is finding out how much culture and fine music I was missing."

"Then you're in for a treat, because Miss Hightower has promised to sing a song or two for us later this evening."

"I'm sure looking forward to that," Hank said. "If her singing voice is half as pretty as her talking voice, it'll be the cat's meow."

At that, their hostess laughed, evoking a childlike innocence and vitality. "I'm always glad to meet a man who makes an effort to broaden his aesthetic experiences."

"It is unfortunate," the Marquis said, "that the city of Medora is not yet populous enough to support its own opera company. At its current rate of growth, however, it will someday be the largest metropolis in the state, if not a rival to Seattle or Minneapolis."

Fidelio noticed that Tallulah's cousin had appeared in the doorway. "James," he said. "Have you been recuperating from the long ride?"

"Please forgive my absence; I needed to unpack some of my garments," he replied. "How did your motorcar weather the journey? In my experience, the porters can be a bit careless."

"I have no complaints; the Stanley was in perfect condition."

James was now wearing dark slacks, a long-sleeved white shirt and a matching dark vest. The man's fashion sense and attention to his appearance served to further pique Fidelio's interest. "Mrs. Vallambrosa, thank you for allowing me to use your facilities to wash up."

"You are most welcome," Medora said. "It's not every day we have guests of your stature." She turned to her husband, "Antoine, where are the children?"

"I will call them, *mon amour. Enfants, venez vite!*" In a moment, three sets of feet came clambering down the stairway.

"Ah, here they are. *Monsieurs* Espinoza and MacMillan, meet Louis, Paul, and our lovely daughter Athenais." The girl regarded the visitors with an aloof disdain, and the eldest boy seemed only mildly interested, but the youngest was positively jumpy with curiosity.

Corrina appeared at the doorway of the kitchen. "*Monsieur, madame,* honored guests, supper is served."

Everyone took their places around the large table that filled the Chateau's dining room. The Marquis and his wife seated themselves at opposite ends. Fidelio took a place next to the Marquis, and Hank sat next to Fidelio, in the seat directly across from Tallulah. Another maid, a mousy little blonde, appeared with a pitcher and a bottle to fill their water and wine glasses.

"*Monsieur* Vallambrosa," Fidelio continued, "it appears your business is going well. I noticed with interest that there were two docking towers at the Medora airfield."

"Yes, we have a twice-weekly courier, which is on contract with the US Post Office. In addition, we have initiated a passenger service across the state and to St. Paul and Chicago. You gentlemen must experience this conveyance. Like the most luxurious passenger train, only faster, quieter, and a spectacular view. It would have shortened your journey at least a day. However, we could not have carried your motor vehicle."

"I should like to do that some time," Fidelio answered. "Though I'm grateful the railway was able to accommodate my Stanley Steamer. I have grown quite fond of that motorcar."

The Marquis gave a hearty chuckle. "I cannot share your enthusiasm, my friend. True, the Steamer is a well-made car, but the price tag is too steep. Two thousand dollars for a flying teapot? The internal combustion engine is the true future of transportation."

"Antoine," Medora chided, "Mr. Espinoza is our guest. You needn't be quite so frank in your opinions."

Fidelio waved his hand dismissively. "Madame, do not worry; I am familiar with the nickname and find it quite amusing. Indeed, I enjoy discussing the merits of various automobiles. May I ask, sir, what make of motorcar you prefer?"

"I consider myself quite fortunate to own three: a Benz Motorwagon, a Duryea roadster, and a Peugeot Type 19. Of the three, the Peugeot is definitely my favorite. None can surpass the quality of French engineering."

Fidelio bit his lip and smiled. "Admittedly, the Steamer is expensive, but statistically it is more reliable than any vehicle powered by 'infernal' combustion." He was gratified to hear Hank chuckle at his remark. "In addition it is quieter and safer than its gasoline-powered counterpart."

"Safer? I question that assertion. Admittedly, the Steamer has release valves and a number of other safety devices in place, but the internal combustion engine does not need them. It has no boiler threatening to blow its owner to kingdom come."

Fidelio felt his cheeks redden. He knew the Marquis' reputation for outspokenness, but the man's arrogance was beginning to grate on his nerves. "Maybe so, but the Steamer can run on a variety of fuels, something the gasoline engine cannot do. Let us agree to disagree, then."

The Marquis laughed once more. "Please excuse the fervor of my previous remarks. I am a man who enjoys a good debate. You are obviously quite intelligent, so if you prefer the Stanley, that is a point in its favor."

"My husband is a man of strong convictions, but I have heard the Stanley Steamer is a fine automobile," Medora interjected. "I would love to try one someday. Driving a motorcar gives one such a feeling of freedom and power, and it's faster than riding a horse. Eventually I should like to drive the entire breadth of this great country."

Hank, who had probably not noticed the tension of the previous exchange, nonetheless joined the conversation. "I hear tell there's a bunch of merchants in South Dakota that's fixing to pave a highway all the way from Chicago to the Yellowstone Park. Maybe that's something you ought to look into, Mister Marquis, er, I mean, Mister Vallambrosa."

"Please, Hank; remember to call me Antoine." Turning to Fidelio, he said, "Your assistant is an astute fellow. You could learn much from his example."

"Yes, he has already been an invaluable aide." Fidelio took a deep breath. He longed to answer his host's condescension with a stinging retort, but he denied the impulse. Any man who could afford three motorcars was certainly wealthy enough to finance the development of his automaton without a second thought.

As the family and guests sat around the table and conversed, Corrina, assisted by the blonde maid, brought out platters of food on wheeled carts of the kind used in a big-city hotel.

The meal was a simple one, but after their hectic days on the road, it seemed to Fidelio like a gourmet dinner at a fine restaurant in Havana. Venison steak was the main course, served with boiled potatoes, green beans and onions, along with fresh baked bread and fine wine. Rarely did Fidelio imbibe alcohol, but in this case he felt compelled to sample his host's refreshments. The beverage had its expected calming effect, but he resolved to stop at a single glass. His Latin temper had gotten him into trouble in the past. There was no need to add the disinhibiting effects of alcohol to the equation.

Hank, however, had again forgotten his resolution to abandon the sin of intoxicants, and drained half of his glass with his first quaff. "Miss Medora, this wine sure is tasty," he said. "I don't drink much these days, but the Savior Himself turned water into wine, so I suppose I'm allowed the occasional sip." He gave his hostess a toothy smile.

The Vallambrosa children were quiet and well behaved. They did not speak except to request bread, or salt and pepper, and to say "please" and "thank you." The daughter was, like her mother, quite pretty. Tallulah's maidservant bore a resemblance to both of them. If Fidelio had not known better, he would have assumed that Isabelle and Medora were cousins rather than cousins-in-law.

As Fidelio cut into his venison steak, which was surprisingly tender for wild game, he noticed Hank stealing another glance at Tallulah. How amusing heterosexual males were, constantly enamored with every pretty thing they met. Still, Fidelio could understand the frustration engendered by the lack of amorous companionship. Hank, with his crude and homespun manners, was in need of the assistance of a man of a more cultured upbringing.

Fidelio cleared his throat. "I must express my appreciation for the Vallambrosas' kind invitation to visit them here in the Badlands. Not only for the opportunity to present our business proposal, but we have also made new friends on the way. Even my partnership with Hank arose from a chance meeting."

"Really?" asked the Marquise. "That sounds like a fascinating story."

"It's not much to tell," Hank said, irritation in his voice. "I was crossing the street when I got run into by Fidelio's automobile."

There were gasps from the ladies. Tallulah smiled at Hank and said, "I trust you were not seriously injured, or you would not be sitting with us today."

"The car was nearly at a stop when the collision occurred," said Fidelio, "thanks to the Steamer's superior braking system." He looked at his traveling companion. "Hank, perhaps you would like to regale the Marquis with some tales of your native Arizona. The two of you have a common interest in the cattle business."

The glow of the intimate setting, the fine food and wine, seemed to have a softening effect on the Marquis' abrasive demeanor. "Ah, Hank, I thought you had the air of a cowboy about you. I have never visited the Arizona Territory, but I understand that it is even more wild and primitive than the Badlands."

"It must be an exciting place," said young Paul, "fighting outlaws and hostile Indians."

Hank chuckled. "Well, it's rarely as exciting as all that, but it sure is a pretty place. To work in the fresh air in the majesty of the Lord's creation, with just a good buddy or two, that's the life. I can think of a couple times when it got interesting, like when a big rainstorm washed out the bridge to town, or when we lost a dozen head to rustlers. But I'll always remember the day when I met up with a band of renegade Apache, led by the nephew of Geronimo himself."

"Apache?" Paul interjected. "Did they try to scalp you? Did you shoot any of them?"

"No, thank the Lord, to both questions. They had just escaped from the San Carlos reservation and were on the run from the Army. They snuck up behind me and my partner Jim while we was camped in a sheltered valley. When driving cattle, we took turns staying awake to guard against rustlers, but it just so happened, Jim was out answering the call of nature.

"Anyway, when I came to, there was a knife to my throat. The Indian's English weren't much good so we talked in Spanish. I offered him ten head of cattle to leave us be. I knew that'd come out of my pay, but it's better to be a poor and alive than rich and dead.

"Well of course Jim saw all this, but being barely more than a young'un, he was powerful scared. While the Apaches discussed amongst themselves, probably deciding whether to kill me or take me prisoner, I saw Jim, by the light of the moon, poking his head over the hilltop. I gave him a quick bird-call. That was our signal to stay away."

By now, the children were listening with rapt attention. "How did you escape?" Louis asked.

"Jim did as I told him and high-tailed it west. It so happened he ran into a company of Buffalo Soldiers who was pursuing the renegades. Jim told 'em where we were camped, so they came and surrounded us. They got the Apache to surrender with only one of the Indians killed, and none of their own."

"Buffalo soldiers?" asked Athenie. "What are they, soldiers who ride buffalo?" That remark brought laughter from all the adults.

"Colored troops, the sons and grandsons of slaves," Fidelio explained. "The name comes from their shaggy African hair. It reminded the Indians of the dark mane of a bison."

At that point, Tallulah, who had been mostly silent through the discussion, spoke up sharply. "Please excuse my impertinence, but why did you believe the Apaches wished to kill you? And why do you call them renegades? They occupied those lands long before the European conquerors came along."

"Quite true," said the Marquis. "Though the Apache have an unfortunate history of attacking settlements, both in Mexico and the United States."

"That is true," Tallulah said. "But the Apache were justly fearful of losing both their land and their traditions to the invaders. My people learned that lesson only too well. After all of our efforts to adopt the customs and dress of our white neighbors, we were betrayed nonetheless."

"Um, well…" Hank stammered under the stern gaze of the dark-eyed beauty. "I hate what President Jackson did to your people. It was a terrible sin that came out of greed and foolishness.

"In fact, I've got a powerful admiration for your people's cleverness. Take that Sequoyah fellow, for example, actually inventing a new alphabet for the Indian language."

She nodded. "You are kind to say so, Mr. MacMillan. However, I must note that Sequoyah was Cherokee, and that the alphabet he invented was for the Cherokee language."

"Sorry, Miss Tallulah." Hank's face flushed red, giving him a complexion almost as dark as the Nightingale's. "I never got as much book learning as I should have, so I don't always get things right. Actually, I've had good dealings with lots of Indian folk. One of the foremen on Mr. Tillman's ranch where I worked was Navajo; a quiet fellow, but I'd trust the man with my life."

This time, Tallulah smiled, the whiteness of her teeth like a beacon between red lips. "I'm the one who should apologize; my correction was a bit condescending. In my early days, I was employed as a schoolteacher. Even after all these years, it's a rather reflexive response."

"You don't say!" Hank said. "Where did you teach?"

"I taught for two years at Fort Sill, where the US government relocated a band of the Chiricahua Apache. I made many good friends there. That is why I strongly object to any mischaracterization of the Apache people."

"No ma'am, I'd never do that. I've got great sympathy for the Apache. Reminds me of this occasion when I was riding home from town and I spotted this poor fellow passed out on the side of the road…"

Isabelle glanced at Tallulah, her eyes wide with alarm. "Hank," she interrupted. "Thank you for the interesting story. But we should give Fidelio a chance. Maybe he would tell us a tale of his native Cuba."

Fidelio smiled. Despite Hank's obvious interest in Tallulah, the man was determined to put his proverbial foot in his mouth. "One of my favorite stories did not take place in Cuba but in Toledo, Spain, where I attended University." He proceeded to tell how had learned the sport of fencing from his father and honed the art in the college fencing society.

"One evening after a night of fine food and wine, I found myself in a philosophical discussion with the son of an aristocrat from Barcelona. I was advocating the ideal of democracy and women's suffrage. This buffoon, having a dearth of wit with which to defend his position, became angry and challenged me to a duel with swords. He had heard of my skill, but could not believe that an upstart from the colonies could pose any real threat."

"What happened?" Medora asked. She glanced nervously at her husband for a reaction. Fidelio paused for a moment. From his research in the New York Public Library, he knew the Marquis had fought a number of duels, easily winning all of them. This anecdote had seemed like a good way to create a bond with Antoine, but he had not considered the wife's reaction. *I must finish the story, however, or she will assume the worst.*

"I reluctantly accepted the challenge. I managed to dodge his thrusts and parry a few of my own. In retrospect, it was not a fair fight, as he had consumed much more wine than I. We fought for several minutes, and a considerable crowd had gathered, when I was able to make a slash to his belt and drop his trousers to his ankles."

At that the room erupted in laughter. "Did the rascal then slink away in defeat?" the Marquis asked with a smile.

"No, he was even more furious. He charged me with his sword, but the onlookers subdued him. I had no further trouble with him after that." Fidelio did not add that his opponent had also accused him of engaging in 'sodomy' and other 'abominations.' The fact that this was at least partly true did not make it any of the lout's affair.

After dinner, the Vallambrosa family and guests gathered in the parlor. As the group continued their conversation, Fidelio paid close attention to his friend. Although the Nightingale did not seem to harbor any animosity toward Hank, she obviously did not share his romantic interest. Had the man always been this inept with women? Perhaps, in his days as a cowboy, all his sexual experiences had all been with drunken wenches and prostitutes. Since finding Jesus, this avenue was now closed to him.

"Miss Hightower," Fidelio interjected, "I just realized that during our discussions on the train we did not ask about your future performances. I know that you are currently on hiatus, but might you know when you would next be performing?"

Tallulah turned to Fidelio. "Yes, we are currently between seasons. Our performances resume in Chicago next month. Thereafter, we have scheduled a tour of seven cities: Cincinnati, Cleveland, St. Louis, Denver, and so on."

"I admire the hard work you opera singers do," Hank blurted out. "I suppose you must practice every day."

"Of course," sniffed James. "An artist must always keep her voice in peak condition."

Once again Hank's face flushed. "Sorry," he stammered, "I just wondered if maybe a singer needed to rest the throat now and then. Foolish question, I suppose."

"Not at all," Tallulah answered. "In fact, we singers must always guard against overtaxing our vocal chords."

"Miss Hightower," the Marquis said, "would you do us the honor of a song?"

"I'd be delighted, if Medora will oblige me and accompany me on the pianoforte." To the Marquise, she queried, "Do you know any of the arias from the operas of Mozart?"

Their hostess nodded. "I have the piano music for *'Ruhe Sanft, Mein Holdes Leben.'* from *Zaide.* Would that be satisfactory?"

"An outstanding selection," Fidelio said. "It is one of the composer's loveliest compositions."

Medora searched her bookshelf, the top row of which bulged with music books, and selected a well-worn folder. She extracted a thin booklet and sat down at the piano to play.

Though they were a recent invention, Fidelio had acquired an extensive collection of classical recordings on gramophone discs. He regretted that he'd been unable to bring any of them along to America. As he listened to Tallulah's sweet, lyrical voice, he was transported back to that magical night when he had introduced Rodrigo to the opera in Paris.

The Choctaw Nightingale was aptly named. She was as good as or better than any soprano Fidelio had ever heard. Even here, in this intimate setting, with this simple piece, her performance was as inspired as it had been that night at the *Opéra National de Paris.* Had Fidelio possessed any inclination towards the fairer sex, he'd have fallen for her himself.

Hank stared in wonderment as she sang. Fidelio found that surprising, given the limitations of the man's cultural experience. *No, that is unfair.* Hank was himself a musician, and no matter how rustic his training, he was part of a fellowship to which Fidelio did not belong.

As Tallulah finished singing, and the last notes of Medora's piano died away, all the adults, as well as Athenie, applauded enthusiastically. The boys, looking bored, clapped politely.

"Brava!" shouted the Marquis. "Please, sing us another one!"

"I'm sorry sir," James said, "but my cousin is weary from traveling, and the dust and dry air of the railway can be a real irritant. As she said, it is important not to overtax one's voice. He turned to the Vallambrosas' daughter. "Isabelle tells me Athenie has a very lovely voice. Perhaps she could treat us to a performance of her own."

"Oh no," blushed the Vallambrosas' daughter. "I couldn't possibly, not after Miss Hightower's sublime performance."

At this point, young Paul rolled his eyes and Louis let out a barely audible sigh. Medora excused them to go upstairs to attend to their studies.

"Do not belittle your abilities, Athenie," Tallulah said. "Isabelle has been with me for several years and I value her judgment. In any case, I am anxious to hear you for myself."

"And I should like to accompany you," said James, "if your mother would permit me to play her piano. Besides, the opera is always in need of talented young singers. Perhaps you possess the natural talent that, with the proper training and hard work, could propel you to fame."

Finally, with Medora's help, Tallulah coaxed the young girl into singing one of Beethoven's Scottish folk songs, "The Sweetest Lad was Jamie".

The girl cleared her throat and began singing. Her sense of pitch was good, Fidelio decided, and her girlish voice was pleasant. She would make a splendid addition to the local Sunday choir, yet there was none of the passion that would make her another Tallulah Hightower.

Antoine waited until she'd sung the first few stanzas when he turned to Fidelio and Hank. "Music. It's wonderful and beautiful, but you can't ride it, eat it, or make love to it, eh?" His two guests responded with polite chuckles. "Come, gentlemen, to my study. We'll have some more refreshments and perhaps talk a little business on the side."

Chapter 12 – A Demonstration and a Departure

"This is a sizable room," Fidelio commented. Noticing the outdoor-style facing on the interior wall, he asked, "Was it a recent addition?"

"No," the Marquis said, "we had it enclosed some years ago, as storage for our hunting and expeditionary equipment. After the garage was built, this place became my study."

The enclosed porch was filled with hunting trophies: the head of an elk, a stuffed cougar, and a bear made into a rug. To Fidelio, it seemed barbaric, though Hank was impressed. "Look at the size of this fella! Black bear, isn't he? I'd bet he put up quite a struggle."

"My wife shot the creature on a hunting trip to Wyoming. She was accompanied by two experienced guides, of course, but she downed the beast herself."

Hank let out a long whistle.

"Medora is an extraordinary woman," Fidelio said.

"It has been a good marriage – not only is she an exemplary companion, but the business contacts of her family in New York have been quite lucrative. Corrina!" he called. "It's a bit chilly in here; we'll need the Franklin stove lit."

As the maid complied, the Marquis opened a cabinet on the back wall. "May I interest you men in a taste of brandy, or a smoke, perhaps?"

"Much obliged," Hank said as he accepted the long cigar. "Lately, I've been reduced to rolling my own cigs."

"Not for me, thanks," Fidelio said, trying not to show his distaste at the odor of tobacco as the other two men lit up. He refused the brandy at first – a glass of wine was his strict limit, and even that he drank rarely – but his host prevailed, and the Cuban was soon holding a snifter of a potent and expensive draught.

The Marquis took a deep drag on his cigar and exhaled a perfect smoke ring. "Gentlemen, I realize you are probably weary from your journey, but I am most enthusiastic to see the invention Fidelio has written to me about."

"Certainly," Fidelio said, taking a sip of brandy. Unaccustomed to imbibing, he fought not to cough as it went down. "Are you familiar with the design and operation of automata?"

"Only slightly, though as of late I have had the chance to become better acquainted with the operation of complex machinery. Kindly enlighten me further."

"Typically we start with nature as a model," Fidelio began, "and consider what animal best fits our needs." Surprisingly, considering the man's earlier arrogance, the Marquis listened intently to his explanation, nodding and asking questions that showed a keen insight.

Fidelio suddenly realized that in his nervous, distracted state he had finished the glass of brandy and that their host had poured him another. *No more,* he told himself. *I must keep my wits about me.* He discreetly pushed the glass a few inches away, and continued his dissertation.

"I can wait no longer," the Marquis declared. "I must see this wondrous device!"

"It is in my automobile," Fidelio looked around. "Does this door lead to the outside?"

"I'll fetch it for you, friend," Hank said. In a moment he returned with a heavy metal box, which he set at Fidelio's feet.

Fidelio inserted a key into the lock on the box. "As you recall from our correspondence, I must request you sign my standard agreement, which states that this interchange remain confidential, until this innovation is ready for submission to the patent office."

The Marquis waved his hand dismissively. "Not necessary, *mon ami!* You have my reputation and my word as a gentleman!"

Fidelio snapped the box closed. "I am sorry, but if the contract is not signed, this demonstration cannot proceed."

The Marquis flushed. "You impugn my honor as a gentleman? I am deeply offended!"

"It is not a matter of honor, but common sense; such an agreement protects us both."

"You would enter my home, partake of my hospitality, and waste my time in such a fashion?" The Marquis got up from his seat and approached Fidelio, fists clenched at his side.

Hank got up and stood between them. "Now fellows, no need to get riled. Sir," he addressed the Marquis, "you got to understand, Fidelio's first invention got pinched by a low-down varmint on his first day in America, so he's naturally a mite sensitive about it."

Fidelio nodded. "Sir, I apologize for my brusque behavior."

"Apology accepted." The Marquis exhaled loudly. After a moment's reflection, he said, "All right, I will sign your paper." He fetched a pen from his desk and wrote the name on the contract with a flourish.

Fidelio opened the case and gingerly removed the multi-legged mechanism. "Sir, I give you the Arachno-automaton!"

"Hmm," said the Marquis, "most interesting. May I examine it more closely?" He accepted the device from Fidelio and turned it over in his hands. "Frankly I expected this would be larger. This looks rather more like a toy than a useful invention."

This time, Fidelio was careful not to show his irritation. *Foolish man,* he thought to himself. *He does not realize this invention's limitless potential.* "This is a prototype," he explained, "which can be enlarged as required. Though small size is sometimes an advantage. Imagine a day when automata might perform delicate tasks such as surgery..."

"Ha! Not likely any sane person would allow a mechanical contraption near their insides!" The Marquis laughed. "No offense intended. Let's see what your creation can do."

"Keep in mind," Fidelio said as turned the key on the back of the device, "that this model is powered by a windable spring. I hope to replace that with some form of electrochemical power, such as a battery." He set it on the floor and flipped a lever on its back. The creature walked as if alive, easily navigating around a spittoon obstructing its way. It halted in front of a leather boot, extended its claws, and grasped the footwear, lifting it off of the floor. The automaton returned with the boot, which towered over it like the oversized burden of an ant.

"Amazing!" exclaimed the Marquis. "I can definitely foresee the applications in a factory environment, though my particular business would require something much larger."

Hank took a swallow of brandy; Fidelio shot him a sharp glance. Was that his third glass?

"You bet," Hank said, his speech a bit slurred, "it could come in real handy in the slaughterhouse, doing detail work, like cutting up a side of beef."

"Exactly! But transportation is the part of the De Mores Company that is growing the most rapidly. If it could only provide my dirigible transport business a competitive advantage, I would be quite eager to invest in the further development of this device."

"Hmm, perhaps in maintenance of the gas bag. We could incorporate a sensor to detect hydrogen leaks." As Fidelio struggled to restrain his excitement, he wondered if he was saying too much. The Marquis was a capitalist, motivated mainly by profit. The man might be tempted to use his ideas, in violation of the spirit, if not the letter of their confidentiality agreement.

"If you don't mind my asking," Fidelio began carefully, "I am interested to hear what motivated your foray into the construction and utilization of airships."

"That is an astute question, from a man who drives a steam-powered motorcar." The Marquis grinned briefly to underscore his jest. "You may be aware of my work on the railroad in French Indochina. During that time, I occasionally traveled by Zeppelin between Hanoi and Saigon. I realized that if I could replicate this service in North America, I could divert commerce from the railroads, thus breaking their monopolistic arrangement with the Chicago beef trust."

"Most impressive," said Fidelio. "Such an undertaking must have required a significant outlay of capital."

"My wife was instrumental in overcoming this obstacle. She suggested that we establish our own airship factory, which we did, on the Missouri River just south of Bismarck. Perhaps you saw it on your train journey here. In addition, to reduce the cost of the Duralumin required for the frame, we acquired our own bauxite mine in Arkansas."

"That must've cost a pretty penny." Hank took a long draw on his cigar.

"Indeed. We were forced to seek funding from the financial sector. The rate of interest on the loan was just short of exorbitant." The Marquis lowered his voice and spoke in a conspiratorial fashion. "Fortunately, we were able to bypass the miner's union and import workers from Nicaragua whose labor was considerably less expensive."

Fidelio's eyes widened at the man's backward attitude. He knew any business partnership required compromise, but was there enough common ground here for any sort of relationship? He tried to hold his tongue, but couldn't help himself. "I understand the costs of doing business. But can you blame the union for desiring a working wage?"

He had expected the Marquis to erupt in anger. The man simply shrugged. "You have a valid argument. I am not without compassion for the common people. But I have a business to run, and must bend to the realities of the market."

Fidelio was about to answer him when Hank interrupted. "Both of you got a good point," Hank glanced pointedly at Fidelio as he spoke. "The Good Book says we should be charitable and not seek riches in this world. But you know," he paused for a hiccup, "some of the heroes of the Old Testament were wealthy, like Solomon for example. It's the hankering to be rich that's helped this country to grow and be great."

"Exactly!" The Marquis clapped Hank on the back. "My friend, you are a very practical man. Your common sense is a helpful counterpoint to the brilliant intellect of your associate."

The unexpected compliment deflated Fidelio's temper. "Thank you, sir, for that vote of confidence. Hank and I have only been together for a few days, and already I am impressed by his dedication and sense of integrity."

The Marquis nodded, then sat quietly for a while stroking his beard. "An idea has occurred to me. Fidelio, have you ever considered enlarging your automaton and mounting a gun or some other weaponry on it? Certainly the United States Army would be very interested in such an invention."

Fidelio sighed. "It certainly is feasible, but I prefer to dedicate my invention to peaceful and productive purposes." He wondered whether he could possibly have a satisfactory partnership with this man. He and Edison had clashed on occasion, but the inventor at least shared his abhorrence for warfare.

"A man of principle, eh?" Their host smiled. "Such ideals are admirable, even if they do run counter to the way of the world." He waved his hand dismissively. "It was only a suggestion. It is not my desire to run your business for you, rather to make a profitable investment. Toward that end, I can provide facilities for your work. The town's blacksmith recently passed without an heir, and I have purchased his shop. It has plenty of space for you to pursue your work."

"That is most generous," Fidelio said. "It would be an excellent place for us to continue our work." In reality, his feelings were in conflict. Here in the hinterlands, there would be none of the distractions of the city, but sadly, none of the intriguing 'men's clubs' of Manhattan.

"Do you have an investment contract?" the Marquis asked. "If not, I could have my barrister draw one up."

"I have already done that, sir." Fidelio reached into the automaton's case and withdrew a leather satchel. Inside was a document consisting of three typewritten pages, bound with a staple.

The Marquis smiled. "I expected you would." He briefly scanned each page. "It appears to be reasonable. I must have Bjornsen review it, though I expect he will require no major changes. In any case, I am greatly impressed with you and the potential of your invention. Even if it never progresses beyond the size of a child's toy, it could still be profitable."

"Thank you, sir. I look forward to a productive partnership."

Fidelio shook hands with the Marquis once again, as did Hank.

"Good, that is settled. Now let us rejoin the ladies – and James – in the parlor. Perhaps we can persuade Miss Hightower to sing for us one more time."

The 'Chateau De Mores,' as the locals called the Vallambrosas' house on the hilltop, had numerous bedrooms on the second story, enough to accommodate several guests. Tallulah and Isabelle volunteered to share a room, so each of the male visitors had his own. Hank was relieved to have a bed to himself. He fell asleep quickly, and dreamt of a brown-skinned lady with the voice of an angel, enticingly close but untouchable.

On the following day, Antoine had several pressing issues which required his attention at the slaughterhouse, thus it was up to Medora to entertain their guests. At the breakfast table, she said, "We are experiencing a bit of an Indian summer. As the weather is so beautiful, I suggest we take a drive in the country."

"The scenery in the canyons of the Little Missouri River is breathtaking," Medora explained. "The hills are adorned in multiple colors, as if painted by the Almighty himself. Also the area is rich in wildlife. We may see wild horses, or even a herd of bison. Among our properties in the area is a lovely little meadow, which we should be able to reach by midday. It's a perfect spot for a picnic. I could have Corrina prepare lunches for us."

"That sounds like a splendid idea," Tallulah replied. "I've noticed that the leaves are turning, which will make the view all the more beautiful."

"That's one humdinger of an idea," Hank said. "I'm an outdoorsman myself, and I love good scenery." Though with the lovely ladies in the group, the painted hills would not be his first priority.

They left town in a procession of three horseless carriages. Medora drove the first with Isabelle and the two youngest children. The second of the Vallambrosas' vehicles was driven by Louis with Tallulah, Isabelle and James as passengers. Fidelio and Hank followed behind in the Steamer. The rutted trail jarred their teeth as they drove.

It was, however, well worth the journey. They disembarked in a wide grassy meadow, bordered by the river to the west and surrounded on by colorful hills. During the drive everyone had worked up an appetite, so they immediately lay down some blankets and set out the food. Corrina had prepared a chicken dinner with homemade bread and a fruit salad.

After the meal, there was time for relaxation. The Vallambrosa boys headed out to explore the hills. Fidelio followed along with Hank and James, which gave him a chance to expound on the geology of the area. Hank smiled to himself; it was just like Fidelio to read up on that stuff beforehand.

A few yards down the trail, Hank stopped. "Sorry, gents, I've decided to head back. Hiking right after eating is kind of tough on the digestion." He felt guilty about the white lie, but it was for a good cause. Hank returned to where the ladies were busy packing up the baskets. "Is there anything I can do to help?"

"How gracious of you to offer," Medora said, "but all we need to do is gather up the dirty dishes and such, and that's almost done."

"It's such a nice sunny day," Tallulah said. "I would like to go for a walk. Isabelle," she called to her attendant, who was helping Athenie load the baskets in the car, "would you be a dear and fetch my parasol?"

Isabelle brought it to her. "I think I'll stay here in the shade. It's a bit warm for my taste."

"Mr. MacMillan, would you care to join me?"

"Uh... it'd be my pleasure," Hank stammered. "And like I said back on the train, it's Hank, remember?"

"All right, Hank it is."

As they strolled through the tall grass, Hank kept an eye out for wild animals. Having grown up in Arizona, he was mindful of venomous critters. Then again, it was getting towards winter, so it was unlikely anything would bother them.

"I'm accustomed to spending my time out of doors," Hank said, "and I miss that life. Before I got sick, I used to take all this beauty for granted. When I got better, I promised myself not to be in such an all-fired hurry. I aim to slow down and appreciate my life."

"That's an admirable philosophy. When my mother passed away last year, I arrived at a similar conclusion. Though it's not easy for a person in my position. I love my music, but it is a very demanding vocation."

"Yep," Hank said. "Now and then the good Lord sends us a message, reminds us to focus on what's most important."

Tallulah smiled. "And what, if I may ask, is most important to you, Hank?"

"Number one, my relationship with the Lord. And second, I'm looking to settle down, raise a family, if I can find me the right woman."

"I see," Tallulah nodded. "I recall that you spoke of a young lady in New

York. When she married, it must have been devastating for you."

"It was a like being thrown from a bucking bronco, but it was really my own darn fault. I never did know how to court a lady proper," Hank sighed. "And how about you, Tallulah? Is there anything you ever wanted real bad, but you just couldn't have?" The second he'd uttered the words, he regretted them. "Sorry, ma'am, none of my business. Feel free to tell me so."

She stopped walking and looked him in the eye. "No need to apologize. You have every right to ask that question, even if I choose not to answer." A sly smile crossed her face. "But I will. There is one thing I want, if the good Lord is willing. I want to make a difference in the world, especially for my people."

"That's a mighty admirable thing to want. Most folks would say something selfish, which is kind of what my wish is, isn't it?"

"Again, you have no reason to apologize. What would happen to the human race if no one were to marry and have families? Certainly I would love to have children someday, if the situation arose, but for the moment my career takes priority."

"For a fine, cultured woman like yourself, who travels all over the world and meets fancy people, I'm surprised you haven't had some handsome fellow sweep you off your feet."

"Thank you," Tallulah smiled. "I have met many interesting men over the years." She shrugged. "One would not think so, but being in the public eye can be quite lonely. It's difficult to get to know anyone well. There *was* a gentleman in the orchestra who courted me – a dear, sweet fellow. He will make some lucky woman a fine husband. But I was committed to finding a match among my own people."

Hank swallowed hard. "I can understand that."

Tallulah laughed. "Now, however, I realize that love is not something you can order, like dinner at a restaurant. The heart has a mind of its own, if you'll excuse the mixed metaphor."

They walked on in silence for a while. Hank kept a smile on his face, though his heart ached. She was so close, so beautiful, and she smelled so sweet.

All at once Hank grabbed her around the waist.

Tallulah shrieked. "What is the meaning of this?"

"Rattler," Hank breathed, pointing into the brush. There was a good-sized rock hidden in the yellowing vegetation, where a snake reared up and rattled.

"My goodness," Tallulah stepped away, smoothing her ruffled clothing. "There are many of these snakes on the Choctaw lands. I don't understand why it didn't warn us."

"I think this Indian summer's got the snakes all discombobulated."

"I was just about to step there. I owe you my life, Hank MacMillan."

"Aw, shucks, ma'am. I'm sure you'd do the same for me."

With a coy smile, she looked into his eyes. Hank took a step closer, with every intention of kissing her, but stopped himself. Would a gentleman take advantage of the situation?

They headed back to join the others. The ladies made a great fuss over his "heroic actions." Hank savored the attention, but deep inside, knew a woman of Tallulah's caliber would never fall for an uneducated old cowpoke like him. Some dreams just weren't meant to be.

A few days after that splendid picnic, Tallulah and her party boarded the train, headed east. After all the farewells, the Nightingale placed a chaste kiss on Hank's cheek. As the train pulled out of the station, Hank felt his eyes burning. Not wanting the others to see such an unmanly display, he walked to the far end of the platform. To his dismay, Fidelio followed him.

"No need to be so melancholy, my friend. Tallulah is a wonderful and cultured woman; her fondness for you testifies to your merit as a man. Even if your paths never again cross, you will know this in your heart."

"You sure have a way with fancy words," Hank said. "Though I wonder if she was just being kind. I'm just a dumb old cowboy."

"She thinks very highly of you. She told me so herself. But why would she want to marry? To give up the music she loves cook, clean, and have babies?"

"Not on my account," Hank argued. "I'd be happy to travel along and help out. It would be a sin to deprive the world of Tallulah's voice; she's like an angel who fell to earth."

"Would it be wise to raise a child in such a situation, traveling from town to town?"

"Well..." Hank paused. "I don't know. But with the money from her singing we could hire a nanny."

Fidelio shook his head. "Hank, you never cease to amaze me. Such progressive attitudes in an old-fashioned package! Come, let us join the others."

At that moment a familiar figure emerged from the station. "Did I miss their departure?" The Marquis gave his wife a quick peck on the lips. "My apologies, *mon amour*, it has been a busy day."

"No matter," Medora said with a shrug. "Your work is most important."

"Fidelio, my good man," said the Marquis. "I'm glad to see you here. I have consulted with my attorney and we have decided to accept your contract without modification."

"That is excellent news! But what about my friend Hank? Have you given thought to employing him in De Mores Enterprises?"

The Marquis shook his head. "There are no open positions at the slaughterhouse. Though as you recall, the town currently has no blacksmith. Hank, you've done some smithing, no?"

"You bet. I've shod many a horse in my day."

"My company was the late Mr. Jensen's biggest customer. If you are interested, you could work for me in that capacity. The pay would be twelve dollars a week, with the potential for an increase later on."

Hank swallowed hard. "That's more than fair, sir." The Marquis shook hands with both of them.

So it happened that Hank and Fidelio came to reside in Medora, North Dakota. The blacksmith's widow headed to Fargo to live with her children, and the two men moved into the Jensens' former house behind the shop.

Of course Antoine Vallambrosa never did anything halfway. The day he took possession of the shop, a huge sign went up: 'De Mores Machining and Metalwork.' He ordered the most modern machine tools, including a lathe, drill press and welder, from Chicago. This would not only serve the needs of Fidelio's project, but support the metalworking needs of the townspeople, at a fraction of the late smith's time and effort.

Luckily, Hank had already done plenty of metal work in New York. He was already skilled on the lathe and drill. The welder was a bit more difficult, and Fidelio, who had learned the art while working for Edison, offered to teach him. He was not a patient instructor. The man's Cuban temper often seemed on the verge of erupting. "Keep the bead straight and clean," he would scold. "Not only does it look better, it will be stronger."

At times, Hank got red-faced at Fidelio's criticism. In the past, he might have offered to step outside and settle the matter with a good old-fashioned fistfight. That was the old Hank MacMillan. Nowadays he'd take a deep breath, recite the Beatitudes, or maybe take a cigarette break, and he'd feel better in no time.

Hank's biggest frustration was that he was actually employed by both Fidelio and the Marquis. Of course, Vallambrosa's 'requests' always took priority. Usually these tasks involved the slaughterhouse. The chains and pulleys which supported the carcasses of the beasts being butchered required frequent repair. Another of Hank's chores was to sharpen and repair the saws used for cutting the meat.

If Fidelio could be a bit temperamental at times, the Marquis made him seem patient as a saint. If someone in his employ messed up big time, or caused an accident, that man was out the door. On several occasions, Vallambrosa bawled out Hank for minor mistakes, and he didn't alternate his criticisms with words of encouragement, as did Fidelio. But one thing Hank could say for the man, he was a perfectionist. His slaughterhouse was the cleanest and best run he'd ever seen. Even the cattle benefited, in a way. They were killed quickly and painlessly by a metal ball propelled into the head by a small magnetic cannon mounted above the entry chute. That beat the heck out of knocking them dead with a hammer!

Fidelio spent most of his time in the shop, making steady progress on the automaton. Hank divided his time between the shop and the slaughterhouse. As the latter wasn't a pleasant place to work, he brought the equipment to the shop for repairs whenever possible.

Even after those busy days, Hank often lay awake in bed, thinking of Tallulah. After her departure in the fall, she and Hank exchanged several letters. Her letters were filled with news of the opera, as they prepared for their upcoming national tour. Hank wondered, did she have feelings for him, or were the letters an obligation? Did she just need a sympathetic ear? He was glad for his work; it kept such questions off his mind.

Now and then the Marquis dropped in to check on Fidelio's progress. "It still moves too slowly," he commented as he watched the automaton. "Perhaps you could decrease its weight."

"That is a good idea," Fidelio replied, "but difficult, since the lead-acid battery is massive."

"There's your problem. Why do you not use the cryomagnetic energy storage everyone's talking about?"

"It would be even more unwieldy," Fidelio explained, "because of the cooling apparatus required. If we could reduce both size and cost by about 50%, it may become feasible."

"Perhaps De Mores Industries shall research this technology," the Marquis said.

Fidelio nodded, though he regarded these proclamations skeptically. The Marquis was far too busy to entertain all his whims. "I have been investigating it, but it is as yet quite expensive to implement. I will keep you informed of anything I discover."

After Vallambrosa departed, Fidelio turned to Hank. "Antoine can be a bit overbearing. I do not envy you for working with him each day. Does he still force his employees to work fourteen-hour shifts? Considering all the sharp-edged equipment, it does not seem safe."

"Yep. But it's one of the better slaughterhouses I've seen, cleaner than most. With the price of beef so high, he's trying to make up for last year's losses. I did mention the problem to him, but he brushed me off. 'MacMillan,' Hank quoted in a French accent, 'you are a practical fellow, but stick to what you know.'"

Fidelio had to smile despite himself. "An excellent impression. Still," he shook his head, "this is why I support the labor movement, to counter this kind of exploitation. I fear that the Marquis' negligence shall someday lead to tragedy."

Chapter 13 – A Welcome Diversion

As the weeks passed, the weather got colder. Snow fell on the Badlands, making the eroded hills look like oddly-shaped powdered-sugar pastries. Meanwhile, the automaton seemed more and more like a real-life creature. With Hank as his assistant, Fidelio tested its ability to carry things in its hand-like claws. In the beginning, it would sometimes damage a piece of scrap metal. As its control became more precise, it could carry raw eggs without damaging them.

Early Monday morning, the Vallambrosas arrived at the shop. Fidelio had invited them for another demonstration. "Behold," he announced. "The improved Tarantela." Fidelio flipped the 'on' switch on the creature's back, then raised a tin whistle to his lips and blew a few short notes. Tarantela's electric motor hummed as it crept across the floor like a giant spider.

"Its gait has become much smoother," said Medora.

"Beware that pole," said her husband, "Any repair costs shall come out of your funding."

Medora put a hand on her husband's arm. "Antoine," she chided, "have faith in the young man. We have, after all, invested our money in his idea."

They watched intently as Tarantela headed for the pillar, and then circled around without touching it.

"I have studied the physiology of the bat," Fidelio said. "Like that creature, the automaton uses sound to sense obstacles in its path."

"Sound?" said the Marquis. "I hear nothing, not even a squeak."

"Its frequency is beyond the range of human hearing."

When it reached the table by the opposite wall, the automaton stopped and waited. On Fidelio's auditory signal, it extended a forelimb and clamped a claw on the handle of the coffee pot atop the table. Hank went over to the supply closet, ready to fetch the mop. Yet the creature managed to lift and carry the pot without mishap.

The machine stopped in front of the chair where the Marquis sat. "Please hold your cup under the pot," Fidelio said.

The Marquis hesitated for a moment, then did so. Tarantela swiveled its claw and poured, stopping just before the cup was full. He looked at Fidelio in amazement. "Not a drop spilled!" He took a sip and frowned. "We must get you some better beans."

"Corrina has spoiled you with her excellent coffee," Medora said as she held out her cup for the mechanical waiter.

Fidelio shrugged. "How you can drink that bitter beverage is beyond me." With a smile he added, "No offense; I am sure it is an acquired taste. In any case, we are progressing steadily."

The Marquis set down his cup. "I am impressed. Have you also increased the operational range?"

"That comes next," said Hank. "Soon as we can squeeze in a chill-o-netic battery." He looked over at Fidelio and smiled.

Fidelio grimaced and corrected him. "Say cryomagnetic; I find the slang term quite irritating. That task is on hold until we receive the equipment from Germany. At that point Tarantela should be able to operate autonomously for several hours without recharging."

"If not for the wonders you have already shown me, I would not believe it," said the Marquis. "By all means, proceed. Oh, and Hank, are you done constructing the new railings? Yesterday we had another incident where cattle broke through. No one was injured, thank God."

"I hope to finish up this afternoon."

"See that you do." He turned to his wife. "*Mon amour,* we must be going."

After the Vallambrosas had left, Fidelio shook his head. "That man is as arrogant as ever. I worry about the safety of the workers, especially you, when you've been up half the night drinking and playing cards."

"You sound like my Aunt Mabel," Hank laughed. "Don't worry, it's just a friendly game, and I don't take more than a shot or two of whiskey for my throat. Besides, you and August sit up playing chess 'til the cock crows."

"True, but August's work does not involve huge animals and life-threatening machinery." August was a rancher's son in his early twenties. He worked as a clerk at the post office.

"You two fellas, scrawny as you are, no wonder you stick to mental activities."

"One can be slender and still physically fit," Fidelio said through clenched teeth.

"Don't take everything so seriously, *amigo.* It's just a bit of good-natured ribbing." Hank was glad Fidelio had found a companion who shared his interests, since he himself didn't have the knack for that brainy stuff.

He glanced at his pocket watch. "Holy Moses, I've got to work on those busted railings." He carried the metal piping to the far side of the shop and donned his mask and gloves. Soon the shop was filled with flickering shadows from the brilliant flame of the oxy-acetylene torch.

Early the next morning, there was a knock on the shop door. Fidelio switched off Tarantela and went to answer. "Madame Vallambrosa! To what do we owe the pleasure?"

"I have news that may interest both you and Hank."

Hearing his name, Hank extinguished his torch, pushed up his mask, and ambled over. "Morning, ma'am."

"Good morning. I assume you know Tallulah's company will be in St. Paul next month."

"Of course," Fidelio said. "As much as we would love to see *La Bohème,* we do not have time to travel all that distance."

"It so happens that Antoine and I are traveling by Zeppelin to St. Paul to negotiate on some mining interests. I convinced him to reschedule his meeting to the fifth of the month."

The Cuban narrowed his eyes and stroked his goatee. "The fifth? That is the weekend of the performance."

"Exactly. We can arrange air passage for you both at a substantial discount."

Fidelio beamed and took both of Medora's hands in his. "*¡Qué fantástico!* Did you hear that, Hank? We are going to see the Nightingale."

Hank gave a whoop and reached up to toss his hat, but found the welding mask in its place. "I'm happier'n a pig in mud. Haven't been so tickled since I went to my first rodeo."

"Wonderful!" Medora gently freed herself from Fidelio's grasp. "My secretary will contact you to confirm the details. *Adieu,* gentlemen." She smiled and left the shop.

"We are most fortunate," Fidelio said. "To see Tallulah's performance and to ride on the *Prairie Zephyr.* In the meantime, we must get you some better clothes. You cannot attend the opera looking like you are going to a barn dance."

Hank looked down at himself. "You think I'm fixin' on wearin' this? Of course I'll get new duds, and you're welcome to help me pick 'em out. I'm sure you won't steer me wrong."

⚙ ⌜⩑ ⚙

Fidelio and Hank arrived at the airfield before dawn. There was snow on the ground and a chill in the air. The *Prairie Zephyr,* tinted golden by the sodium-vapor spotlights, loomed over the South Tower.

Fidelio was draped in a long cloak with a fur-lined collar; while Hank wore the same battered leather coat he'd had for many a trail ride. He had kept it over his friend's objections, but at least he'd had the leather reconditioned, and all loose seams repaired.

They stepped into the elevator. "Where are the other passengers?" asked Hank.

"I prefer to arrive early. As they say, '*A quien madruga, Dios le ayuda.*'"

Hank chuckled. "Hedging your bets with the Lord, eh?"

"I sometimes forget you understand Spanish," Fidelio sighed. "It is only an expression."

On reaching the top, they headed down the gangway. Halfway to their destination, Fidelio stopped and gazed at the hills. Hank waited in the center of the walk, staring at his feet.

"Does the height make you uncomfortable?" Fidelio asked. "My apologies; I cannot get enough of this glorious view."

The walkway took them past the ship's gondola. "Do we all have to crowd into that little thing?" Hank asked.

"No, no. That is the control car. It contains the bridge from where the pilot and the rest of the crew direct the airship. The passenger area is incorporated in the airship's hull."

"Good morning, sirs." A steward in a dark blue uniform met them at the entrance to the craft. "Tickets?" With a plier-like device he punched a hole in each, then handed them back.

They entered a door-sized opening in the hull which, surfaced with shiny aluminum plating, had appeared from the ground to be an extension of the airbag. The passageway, lit by electric lamps, led to a T-shaped intersection. Another steward met them halfway. He checked their tickets, then allowed them to proceed.

At the passage's end, a sign labeled 'Passenger Cabin' pointed left with a red arrow. As they turned the corner, the steward called back to them.

"Excuse me, sirs. Your seats are the other way, in the executive compartment."

With a bemused grin, Fidelio led Hank in the other direction. At a door marked 'Authorized Personnel Only,' a steward checked their ticket yet again. "Welcome, sirs."

"Holy cats," Hank said as they stepped inside. "I ain't never seen a view like this." The entire forward wall of the compartment was a window, mounted at a 45-degree angle. They could see the sun rising over the painted hills, and people tiny as insects entering the tower elevator.

"It does not make you nervous?" Fidelio asked.

"Not when there's glass betwixt me and the ground." Hank thought a moment. "We are at the front of the ship, right? What do they call that again?"

"The bow," Fidelio said. "Currently we are above and forward of the bridge."

"Gentlemen, good morning," said a familiar French-accented voice.

"Good morning *monsieur, madame*." Fidelio said. "Athenie, I did not know you were accompanying us."

The girl brightened at his acknowledgment. "Is this your first time on an airship, Mr. Espinoza?"

"I have flown before, but for Hank this is his first."

"You are in for a treat, Hank" said Medora. She turned to an older couple sitting next to them in broad, leather-upholstered chairs. "This is Charles Wagner, manager of Billings County Bank, and his wife Edna. Charles and Edna, meet Fidelio Espinoza of Cuba and Hank MacMillan of Arizona."

The men shook hands. Fidelio kissed the ladies' hands. Hank tipped his hat.

"Fidelio's invention is simply brilliant," the Marquis said. "I believe my investment will pay me back many-fold."

"Fascinating!" said the banker. "Tell me about your creation, Mr. Espinoza."

"It is a type of automaton which will revolutionize industrial processes around the world. I cannot go into detail at this time, as it is not quite ready for the patent office."

Antoine put his hand on Fidelio's shoulder. "Let us just say that I have seen a demonstration and was greatly impressed."

"Please, have a seat." Medora motioned to the empty chairs next to her.

"I never thought traveling by airship would be so all-fired fancy," said Hank.

"We are fortunate to be riding in the lounge," Fidelio said. "In the main passenger cabin, the seating is more akin to that of a railroad car."

A voice issued from a trumpet-shaped device on the back wall. "This is

Captain Zimmerman. We are about to begin our journey, so sit back, relax and enjoy your time with De Mores Airship Lines. We will arrive in St. Paul in approximately six hours."

There was a loud clank that caused Hank to jump to his feet.

"Do not be alarmed," Fidelio said. "It is merely the sound of the magnetic grapples releasing the airship from the tower."

The craft vibrated and the engines started with a throaty growl that turned into a high-pitched hum. The tower quickly receded into the distance.

Hank soon tired of the talk of stocks, bonds, and commodities. He excused himself and found an empty seat to starboard by the view port and rolled himself a cigarette. As he was about to light up, a steward appeared. "Sir, that's not allowed!"

"Huh? I thought the De Mores Company didn't do hydrogen."

"You are partly correct. Could I have those matches, please?"

Hank reluctantly handed them over.

"Smoking *is* permitted, but you must procure a light from the staff. A safety precaution, sir." The steward produced a metal lighter and flicked on the flame to ignite Hank's cigarette.

"Thank you kindly. It'd be a long flight without a smoke."

"Eugene, over here," the Marquis called. He puffed on his cigar as the steward applied the lighter. To Hank, he said, "The prohibition on matches is a standard rule of airship travel."

Hank shrugged. "Powerful sorry. I thought you were using that new helion stuff."

"Helium. Almost light as hydrogen but non-combustible. Someday we may use it exclusively, but it is quite costly. Currently the hydrogen is confined to the inner envelope. The helium is between that and the outer skin. Thus the hydrogen is isolated from the atmosphere."

"We also use the hydrogen for fuel," added Medora.

"What about the change in lift," Wagner asked, "as the gas is consumed?"

"We use water ballast, which is gradually released as we travel," the Marquis explained.

"Interesting." Hank exhaled a stream of smoke. "Where's Fidelio?"

"To port, with Athenie." The Marquis' daughter was listening to Fidelio with rapt attention. "She is smitten with your friend, but fortunately he does not return her interest."

Hank frowned. "Why'd you say that? I thought you liked Fidelio."

The Marquis laughed. "Ah, Hank, so direct. Your friend is a fine young man, but when the time comes, we shall arrange for her a husband of an appropriate social standing." He drew a deck of cards from his jacket pocket and turned to his companions. "How about a game of Bridge? Charles, I recall we promised you and Edna a chance to avenge your earlier defeat."

"We accept your challenge," said the banker.

Hank sat by himself, smoking and watching the scenery. It was downright amazing, seeing America from above.

At first they flew over barren hills with scattered herds of buffalo. Abruptly the landscape changed to rolling plains, white with snow. There was the occasional homestead, with its red barn, cattle and rows of sheltering trees. It was a desolate area, devoid of any towns or villages. As the airship continued its eastbound path, they encountered a railway, a ribbon of steel spanning the prairie from horizon to horizon. Was that the Northern Pacific?

A female voice answered his unspoken question. "That's the Milwaukee Road. We shall follow it for much of our journey. May I have a seat?"

Hank looked up at Medora and smiled broadly. What man could refuse such a pretty lady? "Yes, ma'am, please do. I thought you and Antoine was playing cards."

"Fidelio expressed an interest in learning the game, so I allowed him to play in my stead. My, what a splendid view! The winters here are bitterly cold, but the snow is lovely."

"The Lord always gives us something to be thankful for."

After some polite conversation, Medora broached a more personal topic. "I hear that you and Tallulah have been corresponding faithfully. You've taken a fancy to her, haven't you?"

"Shucks, ma'am, I'm sorry..." In his embarrassment, he was at a loss for words.

Medora put her hand on his. "Do not apologize, Hank. Tallulah thinks the world of you. However, being an honorable woman, and since her situation does not allow for courtship, I am certain she would not wish to lead you on."

"I understand." Hank swallowed hard. Where the Nightingale was concerned, it was tough to keep his head on straight. Probably she'd asked Medora to have a talk with him, let him down easy. "She'd make some lucky man one heck of a wife." His voice cracked as he spoke.

"Yes, I expect she'll marry someday. Even the most adventurous tire of constant travel."

Hank nodded. Medora's reassurances failed to cheer him.

"This is your first opera, yes? Perhaps I should give you a bit of background. It is the tale of young bohemians living in Paris. It is a love story, with elements of comedy and tragedy."

"Thanks, ma'am. Fidelio's filled me in on all that, since they won't be singing in English."

As if summoned, his friend appeared behind Medora. "Bridge is a surprisingly complex game," Fidelio said. "Might I have a word of advice on how to bid this hand?"

"Certainly." Medora rose from her seat. "It was pleasant speaking with you, Hank."

"Likewise." He tipped his hat, then gestured to a waiter.

"Sir?"

"Kentucky bourbon whiskey, water back, and make it a double, please."

When the waiter reappeared to take dinner orders, Hank was feeling no pain. He was delighted to discover buffalo steak on the menu, as well as some excellent beer to wash it down.

⊗ ᚱᚨ ⊗

Though Hank and Fidelio had passed through St. Paul and Minneapolis before, they had seen nothing beyond the passenger stations, grain elevators and freight depots that lined the railway. Now they had a view from above. The Twin Cities were ensconced by trees and dotted with lakes, frozen white. Through their midst flowed the great Mississippi.

"Quite amazing, this country," Fidelio said. "One could travel a lifetime and barely see a small portion."

Hank nodded. "I can scarce wrap my head around it." He took a drag and exhaled smoke toward the viewport, making it look like fog had descended on Minnesota.

"The Vallambrosas have business in Minneapolis. The afternoon is ours to see the sights. Tonight we shall join them at the Metropolitan Opera, in the De Mores Company's private box."

Hank stubbed out his smoke and finished his drink. "Oughtn't we get flowers for Miss Tallulah? She said in her letter she'd like to see us after the show."

Fidelio nodded. "We certainly shall. As for the visit, though, do not be too hopeful. Our time with Miss Hightower will be brief, assuming we get to see her at all." He looked at Hank's empty glass. "And please do not celebrate too much."

139

Hank laughed. "Don't worry, my friend. I may have lost a piece of my liver but I still know how to pace myself."

The St. Paul Aerodrome was located south of the Twin Cities, near the town of Bloomington. Like the De Mores Airfield, it had two towers, yet it was much busier. It took several minutes for Fidelio to flag down a taxi. "I have directions to a continental restaurant near the Capitol," he said as they rode. "Medora says it is the only place in the Upper Midwest that serves *duck a l'orange*."

"Orange duck?" Hank laughed. "I've shot many a duck, but never an orange one."

They disembarked near the river. "Let us walk for a while," Fidelio said. "I am told the city's historic district is quite charming."

"Yep, it's real pretty." Hank didn't mind walking, but wished he'd brought a heavier coat. After an hour in the cold, they stepped into the restaurant, all toasty warm with its blazing fireplace. The dark wood paneling and fragrant pipe smoke marked it as an upper-class eatery.

"By jiminy, this is one uptown place," Hank said. "Linen table cloths and waiters in their Sunday best."

"Fortunately it is midday," Fidelio said, "or you would not be allowed in without a necktie." He adjusted his elegant black cravat and picked a speck of lint off of his coat.

"What do you mean?" Hank said indignantly. "I got my finest bolo on." Affecting an air of grandiosity, he adjusted the silver eagle insignia fastened around his neck with a leather cord.

The maître d' arrived to seat them. Hank ordered the porterhouse steak and Fidelio the duck. Afterwards Hank treated himself to a brandy. His wallet was almost empty, but it was a special occasion. "I could get used to the rich folks' life."

"There are many advantages," Fidelio said. "But even the life of a millionaire is empty without companionship."

"Darn tootin'." Hank felt a pang of longing. Why did he have to fall for a society woman? The moment she stepped on stage, he'd be lovesick again. Still, he wouldn't miss it for the world.

That evening at the opera house was a real high-class shindig, with motorcars and horse-drawn carriages everywhere. The opera had procured an empty lot for the vehicles. Hank and Fidelio took their place in line at the door with men and women in fur coats, suits and dresses.

Hank let out a whistle. "Get a load of all the fancy-dressed society folks."

"As always, you have a way with words," Fidelio chuckled. "I was not aware there was so much wealth in Minnesota."

"This place looks brand spankin' new."

"The original opera house burned down ten years ago," Fidelio said. "So they erected a new, better facility. Of course, it is not nearly as grand as the Metropolitan in New York City."

"Miss Nola used to talk about that place. If I'd known about highbrow music back then, I could have took her to the opera and maybe won her over." Hank sighed. "But then I'd have never met you or Miss Tallulah."

They entered the hall with the rest of the crowd. Fidelio found an usher, who led them up the stairs to the Marquis' box.

The Vallambrosas and Wagners were already seated and conversing among themselves. Hank suffered a moment of vertigo as he looked over the railing. Quickly he took his seat. "Don't think I've heard that song before."

"The orchestra is tuning up," Fidelio said with a grin.

"So they are. Downright clever, how they put 'em in a hole in front of the stage."

The conductor tapped his baton, and the music began. It was like Fidelio's gramophone records, but rich and full, with no scratches or pops.

When the curtain lifted, it was like nothing Hank had ever seen, with the costumes, music, and singing. He strained his eyes to read the program in the dim light.

Tallulah appeared, in a simple peasant dress, and her lovely voice filled the hall. To Hank, seeing her again felt like an arrow to the heart. How could a lowly cowboy ever hope to woo a lady like her?

Hank followed the story as best he could. Occasionally Fidelio would lean over and whisper a few words of explanation, such as, "Those two are in love," or "she has taken ill."

Eventually Hank politely shook his head to Fidelio's commentary. He preferred to simply enjoy the music and the sight of Tallulah on stage.

When the curtain fell, and the singers returned for their bows, Hank was not ready for it to end. Tallulah entered last. The crowd rose from their seats, cheered and threw roses at her feet.

Hank leaned over to Fidelio, "Gosh dang, we forgot the flowers."

"Do not worry; the bouquet will be delivered to her dressing room, bearing our note."

"Thanks for handlin' that, Fidel," Hank said with a frown. "But I would've liked to see what we were sendin' her, or at least signed my own name on the note."

The lights came up and the audience began moving for the exits. "We're gathering for drinks at *L'Étoile du Nord*," said Medora. "Would you care to join us?"

"Thank you, no," Fidelio replied, then said to Hank. "We shall now go to see Tallulah."

They headed toward the stage, against the flow of the crowd. By a door with a sign marked 'No Admittance,' a large man stood guard in an ill-fitting tuxedo. Fidelio showed him a note from his coat pocket. He nodded and let them pass. Hank gave his friend a questioning look.

"The note is from the Vallambrosas," Fidelio explained. "They are significant patrons of this opera."

They proceeded down a hallway to a door bearing a cardboard sign that read 'Miss Hightower.' Fidelio knocked and a feminine voice said, "Enter."

Hank felt so light-headed, he almost stumbled at the threshold. There she was, wearing a maroon dressing gown that barely concealed her delightful figure. She held a china teacup in her hand. Isabelle, dressed modestly in a blue frock, sat beside her.

"Welcome! Please have a seat." The Nightingale motioned to a pair of empty chairs. "Would you like some tea? Normally I don't have visitors after a performance, but it was our only chance to see you." Her smile was lovely as ever, but her face betrayed her weariness.

"That is our good fortune." Fidelio kissed her hand, and then Isabelle's. "It is wonderful to see you."

Hank kissed their hands also, feeling awkward. "That was the prettiest singing I ever did hear."

"Hank, you are most kind. Thank you both for the beautiful roses."

"You're welcome." The room was packed with bouquets of all descriptions. The place smelled sweeter than his Aunt Mabel's garden. "Looks like you've got no shortage of admirers."

"These are from people who fancy themselves patrons of the arts and the local culture. The gifts are to satisfy their egos. When they come from a friend, it means so much more."

At those words, Tallulah's deep brown eyes met Hank's, and he felt like a feather could have knocked him over.

"How is your cousin James?" Fidelio asked. "And Fred and Ooche? Do they still travel with you?"

"James is with us as always. At the moment he is meeting with patrons on behalf of the opera. Fred and Ooche are assisting the stage crew."

"With all the costumes, sets, and props, that must be a daunting task," Fidelio said.

"I envy how you get to travel," Hank said. "I've been all over the Southwest but I've got a hankering to see New Orleans and San Francisco. Maybe even London or Paris someday."

"Speaking of travel," Isabelle said, "Tell them where we're going next autumn."

Tallulah's face brightened. "I almost forgot! The Chicago Opera has been invited to perform at the Manila Opera House in the Philippine Islands."

"How interesting!" Fidelio said. "But I hear there are hostilities. Will it be safe?"

"I'm told that the island of Luzon, where Manila is located, is secure."

"It's Roosevelt's idea," said Isabelle with a grimace. "He wants to show how confident America is of winning the war, by bringing our culture to the *savages*."

Hank was dumbfounded. "Miss Tallulah, I thought you were opposed to war."

Tallulah nodded. "My going to Manila doesn't mean I approve. It's a chance to see the situation for myself. As a public figure, if I advocate for peace, people may pay attention."

"An admirable goal," Fidelio said. "I have been following the situation in the islands, and I too am opposed to McKinley's imperialism."

"Have you heard the rumors about the Army's new secret weapon?" Isabelle said. "A fearsome machine, like a giant insect with a Gatling gun under its belly. They say it strides into a village and destroys everything in its path. When I first heard this I thought of your Tarantela – though I would be very surprised if you had sold your invention to the Army."

Fidelio's dark complexion turned pale as if someone had just struck him. "This is the first I have heard of it. Please tell me, who told you this story?"

"Isabelle, you know the Duke is prone to telling fantastic tales," Tallulah said. "He is merely vying for your attention. What would Fred say if he heard you were flirting?"

The Nightingale's cousin-in-law regarded her darkly. "That's part of our..." She stopped in mid-sentence. "Fred's not the jealous type. He's flattered when other men are interested in me."

"You should not be so quick to dismiss these rumors," Fidelio said. "I have heard talk of a secret weapon, but I never dreamed it would be an automaton. Please, tell me everything you know about this."

"Sorry." Isabelle shook her head. "That's all."

"I don't see how they could've done that so quick," Hank said. "You've been working on your spider for years, and it's just now getting up to snuff."

"Speaking of Tarantela, how is your work progressing, Fidelio?" Tallulah inquired. "Have you succeeded in operating it without the cable?"

"We have made substantial progress. It now responds to auditory signals."

By Fidelio's tight-lipped smile, Hank could tell he was upset.

Someone knocked on the door. "Miss Hightower? We're closing in fifteen minutes."

"My goodness, is it that late? I must change quickly. Gentlemen, it's been lovely."

Isabelle stepped forward and took each of their hands in turn. "I'll write you if I hear anything more," she said to Fidelio.

Tallulah stood, embraced the Cuban, and kissed him on his cheek. "Godspeed, Fidelio. I'll give your regards to James." Hank felt a pang of envy, until she embraced him in turn. "Hank, my sweet cowboy. Take good care of Fidelio, and please keep writing. I treasure your letters." She gave him a quick peck on the lips.

Hank was so surprised, his knees almost buckled under him. It took him the entire long walk from backstage and through the opera house to get his head out of the clouds.

As he and Fidelio stood at the curb, Hank said," Something's got you rattled, *amigo*."

"You are perceptive," Fidelio answered. "Once again I am chastising myself for losing Tarantela's prototype. But let us not ruin this happy occasion. Have you enjoyed our excursion?"

"It's been one heck of a day, one I won't never forget. Now that it's over, I'm sadder than dry biscuits without a speck of gravy."

"I noticed the kiss Miss Hightower gave you. It makes me wonder if her feelings for you go beyond friendship."

Hank shook his head. "I ain't gonna fool myself no more about that. Still, I wish we didn't have to go home tomorrow." He turned away, worried that his eyes might start to water. "Hey, a taxi!" He put two fingers in his mouth and emitted a loud whistle.

"Good work, Hank," Fidelio said as the horse-drawn coach pulled up. "You are more of a city-dweller than I thought."

Hank grinned. "I did spend over a year in New York City, you know."

They clambered in, and Fidelio said, "To the Selby Hotel, my good man."

The driver jerked the reins and they were off clip-clopping down the street.

"What Isabelle told us," Hank said, "sounds to me like a tall tale. What do you think?"

"It is impossible to say. Normally I regard everything I hear with a degree of skepticism. I would be doubtful, had my creation not been stolen. It is too much of a coincidence."

Hank rubbed his chin as he pondered. "Have you read the *War of the Worlds*, by H.G. Wells? The Martians had a giant walking war machine. Maybe that's where they got the idea."

Fidelio shrugged. "I have been so busy; I have scarcely had time to read. If this book is as popular as *The Time Machine,* the idea is sure to enter the popular consciousness." He sighed loudly. "I have procrastinated far too long. The moment we return to Medora, I shall begin work on my patent application."

Fidelio made good on his promise. He set about collecting all his papers and technical drawings, summarizing the major points of his invention. Its primary description was "A multi-legged self-powered industrial automaton with arachnid-style locomotion."

The work was not easy for Hank, with his eighth-grade education. Luckily Fidelio's friend August had studied a bit of law in college. "You must begin with a search of existing patents, to avoid duplicating anyone else's work," he told Fidelio. They spent hours in the public library, which due to a grant from the Marquis, had an impressive collection of scientific books. Included was a set of volumes from the US Patent Office listing all patents issued to date.

This process took several weeks, during which time Fidelio halted his work on Tarantela. Hank took the opportunity to earn extra money by working more hours at the slaughterhouse. It was unpleasant, bad-smelling work. Not that he couldn't handle it; he'd done a lot of that sort of work on his uncle's ranch.

The problem was, he couldn't shake this feeling of doom, the same feeling he'd had just before the Spaniards rolled in with their *tanques*. That had to be it, he decided; all the stench and bellowing and cow blood was re-awakening his shell shock. He prayed the Lord would help him overcome his problem.

Chapter 14 – Cataclysm and Controversy

It was a frantic day in the abattoir. Hank entered the west side of the building, which was devoted to meat processing. Each of the six butchering stations had a freshly skinned side of beef hanging by a chain from the ceiling. Six workers used steam-powered reciprocating saws to butcher the carcasses. The red hunks of flesh fell into a clean metal tub below.

Hank was thankful that the exhaust from the steam engines was sent outdoors through a metal pipe. The atmosphere in this place was oppressive enough already. *This would be a perfect job for Fidel's automaton,* he thought as he walked on. *We could attach the saw in place of one of the spider's limbs.* Not only would it be less messy for the workers, but also a lot safer. They wouldn't be standing so close to all those sharp moving blades.

He was jarred from his thoughts by a horrific scream. Hank's first instinct was to run, as he'd done on several occasions since the war. *No!* Instead, he began reciting the Twenty-Third Psalm in his head. *Yea, though I walk through the valley of the shadow of death...*

The panic subsided, and he turned around to behold a gruesome scene. One of the saw operators clutched his blood-soaked arm, which had been amputated halfway between the elbow and wrist. The automatic saw lay on the floor, still going back and forth, but with half its blade missing. No one came to shut it off; instead they stared horror-stricken at the injured man.

Hank dashed to the scene of the carnage. He doffed his shirt and tore off a sleeve. The poor man hollered in pain. Two of his co-workers held him still as Hank tied the cloth tightly around the stump of his arm. "Where's the danged medic?" Hank asked them.

"He's out sick, but there's morphine in the infirmary," one of the other saw-operators said. The victim had now fallen silent. *Shock.* Hank had seen that in his injured comrades in the war. This poor guy needed doctoring quick or he was going to die.

"Let's get him outside." Hank and one of the other men carried the unfortunate worker through the crowded floor of the plant. All activity around them was now at a halt. Several men left their stations and followed, offering help and advice.

"Keep his head up," one said.

"Is the tourniquet on his arm tight enough?" said another.

"Cover him up with this jacket, 'cause he's bound to go into shock," said a third.

As they reached the door, they heard an ear-piercing, whistling shriek followed by a rumbling blast. Hank looked back and saw the cloud of steam and fire. It was all he could do to keep from dropping the man and fleeing. He prayed *Lord, give me strength!*

"An engine!" a man shouted. "Somebody forgot to shut theirs off!"

"Fire crew, assemble!" snapped the supervisor. A cadre of men responded instantly. They uncoiled a long hose while others started the engine that ran the water pump.

While everyone rushed around, an automobile pulled up and the Marquis jumped out. "What on earth is happening?"

Hank told him about the amputation and the ensuing explosion, as the doctor had just arrived to tend to the injured man. Vallambrosa did not hesitate. He stripped off his jacket and vest and joined Hank to work with the fire crew. Within a few minutes, the town's volunteer fire department arrived to help, as well as the county sheriff and his deputy.

By the time the fire was extinguished, it had destroyed a third of the slaughterhouse. Five men were unaccounted for. Pieces of charred body parts protruded from the broken brick and twisted metal at the site of the steam engine explosion.

"Sweet mother Mary." The sheriff shook his head and wiped his hands on his soot stained shirt. "It breaks my heart to think of those widows and fatherless kids."

"I will do whatever I can to help," the Marquis said.

"You won't like this," the sheriff said, "but we'll need to shut down the slaughterhouse for a few days to perform an investigation."

"Do what you must, but please remember that every day this business is shuttered, it costs this town many hundreds of dollars in wages."

As it turned out, the investigation took only two days. The sheriff's official ruling was 'carelessness.' He laid the blame on the worker who had lost his arm, saying that he had neglected the maintenance of his saw. The man was doing surprisingly well considering the circumstances of the amputation, but only time would tell when he would be able to work again.

The rebuilding of the slaughterhouse began at once, and proceeded at a frenzied pace. Hank had all the work he could handle, though he hoped the Marquis would make safety a higher priority this time. In any case, the facility was soon operational again.

By its nature, it had always been a noisy, smelly, unpleasant place to work, but most of the men had seemed to appreciate their jobs. Lately, though, Hank noticed a shift in attitude. His newest duty was safety inspector. He was tasked with checking things like electrical wiring, steam engine pressure values, and the chains that supported the sides of beef. As he made his rounds just before the early shift began, he overheard the men grumbling.

"The problems didn't get fixed," one of butchers said. He had worked in the station next to the injured man.

His coworker nodded. "Putting in a couple extra fire extinguishers ain't gonna do it. That rich Frenchman has got to replace this old, unsafe equipment. Like the power saws, for example. We're still using the same kind that sliced poor Otto's arm off."

When Hank mentioned this to Fidelio, the Cuban replied, "The workers need to organize and form a union. That is the only way to ensure that their demands will be met."

"I don't think the Marquis would be too keen on that idea."

"I, too, was born of privilege, but with wealth comes responsibility. My father taught me this lesson by example, through his work to feed the poor of Havana."

"I don't have a strong opinion on unions, either way," Hank said, "Lots of the workers in New York City got treated terrible, and I can't say I blame them for going on strike. But one thing I'm sure of – you and I ought not to get involved. That's a matter for the Marquis' regular employees to sort out."

Fidelio shook his head. "I understand your desire that we keep quiet for the sake of our project, but sometimes a man must take a stand. All I can promise is that I will be discreet."

Hank soon discovered that there were others in the workforce who had the same idea as Fidelio. That next day at the slaughterhouse, a fellow named Jim pressed a piece of paper into his hand. "Don't read it 'til you leave the plant," he said. "By the way, the other guys didn't want me to tell you. They thought you might be in management's pocket. But I think you're a straight-up guy, and you'll at least give it a chance, okay?"

Later on, as he was headed back to Fidelio's shop, Hank read the notice. In crude hand lettering it read, 'Workers meeting Saturday night, 7PM, basement of Catholic church."

Hank decided not to show it to Fidelio. The man could get into enough trouble on his own. As the week went by, he heard no more mention of it. He spent the morning of the following Saturday checking the pipes that drained the animals' offal into the Little Missouri River. As he did so, he noticed numerous fish floating on the surface downstream.

"Well, I'll be damned," he muttered to himself. He'd seen a few dead fish there a few weeks ago, but now it was worse. At the time, he'd gone straight to the company offices.

"I know you care a lot about this town," he'd told the Marquis. "So I think if we dug a catch pond, and put the waste in there, it'd keep the river clean. Maybe once the stuff dries up, we can sell it as fertilizer."

"Hank, thank you for bringing this to my attention," Vallambrosa had said. "I will personally make sure this matter is addressed as soon as possible."

To Hank, the Marquis had always been a good man at heart, but he was beginning to doubt that judgment. Of course the company was busy repairing the slaughterhouse, but with many of the workers idle, there would have been plenty hands to dig out a pond. Besides, nothing at all had been done in the weeks before the fire.

⊗ ﬁ⅄ ⊗

The more Hank thought about it, the angrier he became. There were people who depended on those fish for food. What right did one rich guy have to ruin it for everybody? Suddenly the union meeting didn't seem like such a bad idea.

The church basement was packed with people, mostly the men who performed the distasteful labor of the slaughterhouse, but several ladies from the front office as well. Fidelio was surprised to see Hank in the doorway, looking for a place to sit. "Hank, over here."

Hank made his way through the crowd. "Fidel, Augie. Didn't expect to see you guys here."

"We're here as concerned citizens," Fidelio said. "Did you change your mind about the union?"

Hank shrugged. "I wanted to see what all the fuss was about. Besides, I actually do work for De Mores, unlike the two of you."

"I told him he would be jeopardizing his business relationship with Vallambrosa," August said. "I came along to make sure he stays out of trouble."

"You're horning in on my job," Hank grinned. "But you're welcome to have it."

"Quiet," snapped Fidelio. "The meeting is about to begin."

A man walked up to the podium and the room fell silent. "Good evening everyone. I'm sure most of you know me, but for the benefit of any newcomers, my name is Jim Novak. I was at the butcher station next to Otto Froehlich, the unfortunate fellow who lost his arm. I witnessed the incident that led to the tragic fire, for which he has been made a scapegoat."

"Hear, hear!" someone shouted.

"I asked Otto to come and tell his side of the story, but he's too ashamed to show his face in town. It's downright evil, the way the company put blame for its hazardous working conditions on that poor man. If De Mores doesn't start getting us better equipment, that sort of tragedy is bound to happen again. That's why we need to get together and form a union!"

The resulting outbreak of yelling and shouting took Jim a minute or two to bring to order. Fidelio leaned over to Hank, and said, "This is a good sign. Hopefully these strong emotions will lead to a sense of solidarity."

A gray-haired fellow stood up; Fidelio recalled he had moved to Medora from the East. "Sam Larsen, packaging. I move we form a union, the Dakota Slaughterhouse Workers."

"Be specific," someone shouted. "*North* Dakota Slaughterhouse Workers."

"You are out of order, Tom," Jim said. "You know the drill. Stand up and ask the chairman to be recognized."

"Chairman?" Another man stood up. "I move we ask these outsiders to leave." He looked directly at Fidelio and his companions. "I know for a fact that the Spaniard sitting there is a business partner of De Mores. He's probably a company spy."

"Charlie, we already have a motion on the floor. We'll vote on yours when it's your turn."

The first motion passed unanimously, not counting a few abstentions such as Hank's.

Hank stood up, "Sir? May I have a few words about the next motion?"

"Yes, Hank, make it brief. We have much to discuss."

"I've known Fidelio a few months now and sure as I'm standing here, this man is no spy. In fact, he's got personal experience working with unions from back when he was in Europe."

"I call the motion!" someone shouted.

Fidelio watched nervously as Jim counted raised hands for the yeas and nays. It was a close vote, but Fidelio and August were permitted to stay.

People began shouting suggestions out of turn. Eventually Jim regained sufficient order to put the various motions to a vote. They rejected the addition of 'North' to the name, in hopes of possible future chapters in South Dakota. The group would apply for recognition from the American Federation of Labor. They formed a committee to draft a list of demands for De Mores, which the organization would debate and vote upon at the next meeting.

"Is management unwelcome here?" said a French-accented voice from the doorway. The crowd fell silent. Hank slunk down in his chair, but it was no use hiding. Fidelio's dark complexion and expensive clothing made their presence impossible to miss.

"That may not be a good idea, sir," said Jim. "But we can put it to a vote."

"Do not trouble yourself. I will be brief," the Marquis said. "I wish to go on record that I have no problem with you people associating with anyone you like outside of working hours. But if you decide to call a 'strike' or some such foolishness, the De Mores Company will consider your jobs abandoned, and will replace you at once." With that, the Frenchman turned and strode out of the hall.

Once again, the room broke out in turmoil. "He can't tell us what to do!"

"We have our rights!" shouted another man.

"Who does he think he is? I move we call a strike." Without even completing their list of demands, the motion passed, 75-32.

As they left the church, Fidelio turned to Hank. "You seem upset, my friend."

"Well, Fidel, it's a dilemma. I need the work, and I also think the men were a bit hasty to walk out before trying to talk things out a bit more."

"I noticed you abstained from voting," August said. "Does that mean you'll cross the picket line?"

Hank stopped for a moment to ponder. "I'm not convinced a strike would be a good idea right now. But I'm a man of my word. I'll stand by my friends, thick or thin."

Though his sympathies were with the union, Fidelio continued his work as best he could. Though he had marched, along with his leftist classmates, in solidarity with the miners during their strike in Spain, it was not wise to do so now. Still, his thoughts turned frequently to that time, and of course to Rodrigo, dark-haired and beautiful, with the muscles of a Greek statue, skin pale from all that time spent underground.

Without his job in the slaughterhouse, Hank assisted Fidelio full time. Technically, their work might have been considered contrary to the union, since the Marquis was a significant investor in Fidelio's automata. Happily, no angry men with signs appeared to picket the shop.

Yet Fidelio's work on Tarantela had reached an impasse. The batteries he had installed only provided motive power for a few more minutes of activity. Consequently he spent much of his time in research and calculation, which left Hank to find his own tasks. By the time two weeks had passed, the cowboy had cleaned the entire shop and calibrated all electrical meters.

The drawback was that Fidelio no longer had the place to himself in the afternoons, when August finished his early shift. That was probably just as well. In a small town like this people were bound to gossip and Fidelio did not want to see the man ostracized for their relations.

At the beginning of the third week of the strike, the Marquis showed up at the workshop. "Fidelio, I have a request."

From the tone of the man's voice, Fidelio expected the request would be a demand, but he simply said, "Certainly, Antoine, let us hear it."

"As a result of this infernal strike, I have had great difficulty staffing my business. The De Mores Company is operating at a fraction of its capacity, and we are losing hundreds of dollars each day. When I invested in this venture, you spoke of using the automata to handle the more hazardous aspects of meat production. I could use that kind of assistance now."

Fidelio exhaled, and hoped it hadn't sounded like a sigh. "I am sorry sir. Although we have made considerable progress, it is still not ready. The new battery-powered automaton only operates slightly longer than the previous model. I am researching more powerful batteries and more efficient motors, but this effort will require several weeks at the least."

"I hear that the Edison Company has introduced a more effective direct current motor. Could you perhaps adapt the automaton to use it instead? At this point, money is no object."

"I will consider it, but the redesign would take until the end of the month at least. And frankly, I would rather not deploy my invention in your plant under these circumstances." As soon as Fidelio said those words, he realized his error, but there was no taking them back.

The Marquis knitted his brow. "What do you mean by that?"

"I would prefer you reach an agreement with the workers first. I created the automaton with the goal of improving their lot, not worsening it. I hope to see the existing workers retrained in maintenance and operation of these devices. That way you can keep everyone employed, and increase productivity while simultaneously lowering your costs."

"*Merde!* Not *those* workers. By refusing to perform their duties, they have abandoned their employment. It will be a cold day in hell before I rehire any of those troublemakers."

"You may have no choice. The town seems to be mostly behind the workers."

The Marquis' face reddened as his voice got louder. "I will not be coerced or blackmailed in any aspect of my business. The slaughterhouse is of my own design and is much safer than others in this country; you and Hank have both said as much. These workers are a gang of lazy good-for-nothings who do not appreciate how well the De Mores Company has treated them!"

Hank had been listening quietly in the corner while rewinding the core for an electric motor. "Sir, would you be open to a compromise? You got the right to run your business, but from what you said at the meeting, the men got the idea you don't care about their well-being. I think they were too quick to judge you. If we all sit down and talk, I'm sure we can work it out."

"I would have been willing to talk," the Marquis snapped, "if you had not all gone on strike like a bunch of hooligans. I will not tolerate employees who do not respect my authority."

At that remark, Fidelio felt his temper rising. "Antoine, you do not understand the American way, nor do you understand the plight of the working class."

The Marquis snorted. "What do you know of America? I have been here far longer than you! I'm beginning to regret our association. I was not aware of your Marxist sympathies."

"When did I claim to be a Marxist?" Fidelio stepped closer to Vallambrosa. He realized he was courting disaster, but could not stop himself. "You may pretend to be a friend of the working man, but you only care for yourself. You represent the most loathsome form of capitalism, that which will doom itself by its greed and lust for profit."

The Marquis poked a finger in Fidelio's chest. He lowered his voice to barely above a whisper, but his anger was evident. "You forget, *sir*, whose property you are standing in at this very moment. I have charged you a reasonable rent. I have invested a considerable sum in your invention. How dare you insult me in such an uncouth fashion! Would you back up your evil words with swords or pistols? You call yourselves reds. I say your color is yellow!"

At once Hank stepped in between them. "Gentlemen, please there's no need to duel for goodness sakes! Please, let's all calm down before someone does something he regrets!"

The Marquis stepped back and turned away from Fidelio. He said nothing for several moments. "You are correct, Hank. I promised Medora I would fight no more duels. But if I speak with this communistic oaf for one more minute, I shall not be responsible for my actions!"

Fidel stood up with clenched fists and red face. "Your wife is correct; dueling is uncivilized. Perhaps a round of fisticuffs can settle this argument."

"Fidel, no!" Hank said. "I've been in many a tussle in my day, and it don't fix anything; it only leads to more trouble."

The Frenchman and the Cuban glared at each other for a few moments. Finally the Marquis broke the silence. "Considering our irreconcilable differences," he huffed, "I think it would be best to sever our business relationship."

"Let's not be too hasty. People with different ideas can still get along," Hank said, pointedly looking at Fidelio.

Fidelio nodded. "That is true. But not when one of them persists in behaving like an ass."

"I am gratified you can recognize your own shortcomings," said the Marquis without a trace of humor. "Hank, despite your humble upbringing you are twice the gentleman as this Cuban fop. You may keep your job with the De Mores Company, if you agree to forswear this union nonsense."

Hank shook his head. "Sorry, sir, I got to be loyal to my friends."

"Then it's settled." The Marquis checked his pocket watch. "The two of you have forty-eight hours to get yourselves and your possessions out of this facility. Espinoza, I shall sell all my shares in your venture – as soon I can locate the fool who wishes to buy them." With those words, he stormed out the door of the shop, got into his motorcar, and drove off.

Hank plopped down into a chair, rolled a cigarette, lit up, and took a sullen drag.

"You are angry with me," Fidelio said.

"You bet I'm angry!" Hank exhaled a stream of smoke. "This was a good job, and a nice place to live. It was beginning to feel like home."

"Do not despair, my friend. From each crisis comes opportunity. You will recall I have been corresponding with Nikola Tesla. He is currently experimenting with electricity and magnetism in the town of Colorado Springs. This is, I believe, the kind of knowledge I need to make Tarantela a practical reality. It is time we paid Mr. Tesla a visit."

It did not take long for them to vacate the De Mores machine shop. They began the next day at the crack of dawn. Fidelio was like a man possessed; he refused to stop for dinner. Though Hank's stomach was growling, he kept on working. By sundown they had it all in crates and boxes piled up at the front door.

"Sorry, Fidel," Hank said. "I can't work no longer without some grub. I aim to go to the general store and get some food for the both of us. Maybe some ham, cheese and bread."

Fidelio soon relented. The two men sat in the empty building and ate their meager supper without speaking. It was now too dark to clean, so they decided to turn in.

The next morning Fidelio arose early and went to work loading the trailer. It was basically a wooden box on wheels that was hitched behind the Steamer. He had paid a local man to build it, for hauling supplies from the train station.

Soon Fidelio smelled the familiar odor of burning tobacco. Hank appeared at the door of the workshop, eyes half closed and a cigarette in his hand.

"Good morning, my friend!" Fidelio said. "Please gather your belongings. There is plenty of room remaining in the trailer."

Hank yawned, "By gosh, that thing is going to come in handy."

Their packing and cleaning was interrupted several times during the day. Around mid-morning, Jim Novak showed up with three other members of the union. "Morning, Fidelio, Hank," he said. "Just stopped by to see if the rumor was true. You're really leaving us?"

"That is correct. We are relocating to Colorado."

"We wanted to thank you for sticking your neck out for us." Jim said. "We're sorry it turned out this way. Best of luck to you both!" He and his companions shook hands with Fidelio and Hank and were on their way.

"Doggone, it's nice to be appreciated," Hank said. "Makes me feel real sorry to go."

At around noon, as Hank and Fidelio were loading up their personal belongings, a familiar horseless carriage pulled up in front of the shop. It was not, as it first appeared, the Marquis, but his wife Medora. She got out and approached the two men.

"I wanted to give the two of you the news. Antoine has decided to meet with the strikers."

"I am pleased to hear that," Fidelio said. "I hope they can reach a mutually beneficial agreement."

"I see you have already vacated the premises," she said. "Since the principal reason for your argument will soon be resolved, I was hoping that Antoine might have a talk with you gentlemen, and perhaps reconcile. Alas, once he has made up his mind, he can be very stubborn."

"You're mighty kind to worry about us, Mrs. Vallambrosa," Hank said. "Do you really think you can talk him into it?"

Medora smiled. "The two of us are equal partners. As the daughter of a New York banker, I have a thorough understanding of the world of business. Fidelio, I believe your invention has great promise. As such, I have talked Charles Wagner, our banker friend whom you met in the *Zephyr*, into purchasing our shares."

"Thank you, madam; you have done us a great service! I am loathe to admit that I had not given much thought to how I could possibly buy them back. Please, come in and join us for a cup of tea. We won't be leaving until tomorrow morning."

"I'm sorry, but I cannot stay. I wish you both the best of luck! Charles will send a courier this afternoon with papers for you to sign. You are welcome to have an attorney review them, but it's a fairly straightforward agreement." She shook hands with both of them and departed.

"That is one extraordinary lady," Hank said.

Shortly after two o'clock, a velocipede came down the gravel street. Though popular in the East, they had yet to catch on in remote areas like the Badlands, with their dearth of paved roads. Fidelio only knew one person in town who had one.

"Good afternoon," said August as he stuck out a foot to stop the two-wheeled contraption. I heard from Mrs. Vallambrosa that you and the Marquis had a parting of the ways."

"That is correct, unfortunately," said Fidelio.

August frowned. "Were you planning to leave without bidding me farewell?"

"Of course not. I was about ready to go to the post office to retrieve my mail, and to leave a forwarding address."

"What if I had not been at work today?"

Apparently sensing an impending argument, Hank ceased his work tying down the cargo on the trailer. "Need to find some more rope." He disappeared into the shop.

"I apologize," Fidelio said. "I am not good with emotional situations."

"I realize that, but still... How can you behave so coldly to a... close friend? I've barely seen you at all these last two weeks."

"Again I am sorry. Unfortunately, there was no privacy at the shop, with Hank there every day."

"I see. In any case, it's all for the best. It has afforded me the opportunity to reacquaint myself with the church. By the way, here is your mail." He handed Fidelio a bundle of letters tied with string.

Fidelio's eyes widened in surprise. "The church?" Though August had not been an atheist like himself, he had often expressed a derisive skepticism about Christian doctrine.

"I've had many long talks with Father Dietrich, and he helped me to see the right path. I've decided to renew my engagement to Sarah Johnson."

Fidelio stared, open-mouthed, for a moment. "If that is what you want to do."

"It's what God wants," August said. "Best of luck on your journey. I'll pray for you."

"Thank you." Fidelio watched him ride away, feeling angry with himself, the Church, and mankind in general. He hoped August would find happiness.

As Fidelio had planned, he and Hank arose early, fueled up the Steamer, and headed south on the old stagecoach route that connected Medora with Deadwood, South Dakota. The sky was clear and the weather brisk, an ideal day for travel.

After a few hours' ride, the men left the Badlands behind and entered an area of lonely bluffs and empty arid prairies. As they traveled south, the settlements became fewer and further between. By the angle of the sun, Fidelio calculated they had entered the state of South Dakota, though there was no sign to mark the border. They broke for a quick meal, and then rode on.

As night fell they found themselves far from any settlement, and were forced to pitch the tent Fidelio had acquired at the mercantile in Medora. Hank, outdoorsman that he was, had also brought along a spare bedroll.

Fidelio was grateful for Hank's companionship. He felt terribly exposed in this desolate place. The howls of the coyote made his skin prickle. Hank looked up from the Bible he was reading by lamplight. "Don't worry. I'm sure they're just celebrating a kill."

"Oh." Fidelio loaded a cartridge of lead shot into his Mercier pistol.

"Just joshin' you," Hank said. "I hope you know how to use that thing."

"I studied marksmanship in my university days in Spain, and I have hunted pheasant on more than one occasion. I don't see any reason to take unnecessary chances. I'm not certain that the Sioux have been entirely pacified."

"I don't think you've got nothing to worry about them poor Indians. They're lucky if they have anything to eat."

"Which would make them all the more dangerous, I presume." Not consoled by Hank's arguments, Fidelio slept with his pistol in hand that night.

Chapter 15 – An Alarming Revelation

Fortunately, they had no trouble from man or beast. The next morning, Hank cooked up the bacon and eggs they'd bought the day before in the village of Bowman, then they continued south through the desolate countryside. Fidelio finally relented and let Hank drive the motorcar for a while. His worries about Hank's competence had been unfounded. The cowboy had no problem keeping his eyes on the gauges and steering clear of dangerous rocks and ruts.

"You're been mighty quiet lately," Hank shouted over the noise of the road.

"I have had many issues on my mind," Fidelio replied.

"Your friend August seemed to be worked up about something," Hank said.

"It was nothing," Fidelio said. "No, that is not true. I was not a very good friend to him."

"Don't kick yourself, *amigo,* I've been in that same boat. I reckon lots of folks have a tough time saying *adios.* When I left New York, I didn't say nothing to nobody. I did send a letter to the Friends Hall to tell 'em I was gone, just so they wouldn't worry."

"That was understandable. You left with a broken heart."

"True, but I hate to make people think I don't care. The Friends were mighty kind to me; made me feel like part of the family." He glanced at Fidelio and grinned. "But let's not waste our time bellyachin'. I know the good Lord forgives me for my sins. And I have faith that I'll find myself another good woman someday, someone who actually wants to marry me."

"I have no doubt that you will," Fidelio said.

"Maybe we'll even find a girl for you, huh?"

Fidelio laughed. "Now that would be a real achievement."

Hank paused at the entrance of the hotel dining room. His eyes took a moment to adjust to the dim gas lighting, a bit longer to adapt to the smoky haze. Where was Fidelio? He shouldn't be hard to spot. Most likely he'd be the only one wearing a bowler instead of a cowboy hat.

"May I help you, sir?" A waitress appeared behind Hank, startling him so badly he almost threw a punch at her. She was a pretty little thing, probably in her late teens, with curly blonde hair and a slight figure that barely filled the bustier of her lacy blue gown. Though he usually preferred a more mature woman, he wasn't about to complain.

"Help? Um, well...," he stammered, "I was aimin' to meet my traveling companion for supper."

She suppressed a giggle, and then glanced to the corner of the murkily-lit room. "Was he kind of dark and spoke with an accent, maybe Mexican? Dressed real dapper like?"

"That would be him, miss. He's from Cuba, though, not Mexico."

The young lady's smile brightened. "Cuba? I've never met anyone from there before. Your friend is over in yonder corner. Have a seat and I'll be right over to take your orders."

No wonder he had not seen his friend; he was halfway hidden by a pillar. Hank approached the table, pulled out a chair, and sat down. "Howdy, Fidel."

"Good afternoon, my friend." Fidelio smiled. "I trust you found the mercantile."

"Yep, I got enough tabacky to last me to Colorado Springs. Oh, and by the way," he dug into his pocket and produced two shiny silver dollars. "Here's what I owe you for the room."

"Thank you, my good man. Unfortunately, there was only a single vacancy, which is surprising, considering the exorbitant cost of lodging at this establishment."

"That's a mining town for you. Gold has a way of bringing out the deadly sins, and not just greed. On my way back I passed two saloons, a house of ill repute, and an opium den."

"Yes. I hear Deadwood has its share of violent crime as well. I am grateful I did not arrive in this place alone."

Hank laughed. "I'm sure you'd manage with that crazy buckshot pistol. And as for company, between Belle Fourche and here, I thought you'd lost the power of speech."

The Cuban nodded. "I apologize for my reticence. I was mulling over my argument with the Marquis. He is a stubborn man, but not unreasonable. If only I could have kept my temper!"

Hank shrugged. "Who's to say your arguing ain't the reason he caved in and decided to deal with the union? True, it cost us a bit of trouble, but you just might have done some good for the working folk."

Fidelio nodded. "You may be correct. Perhaps our time in the Badlands was not wasted."

"I'm gratified the Marquis saw the light," Hank said, "whatever the reason. He's got plenty riches for any man, with a big house, a beautiful wife and three healthy young'uns. His orneriness almost cost him the respect of the whole town."

"Indeed. Still, I regret leaving. I found Medora to be quite charming, the woman and the community both. Speaking of charming ladies, did you reply to Tallulah's most recent letter?"

"I had one ready to mail, but I've got to add a PS now. I'm sure Medora will tell her what happened, but I want her to hear our side of the story, too." Hank looked down and noticed a big metal box next to Fidelio's chair. "Pardon my asking, but why'd you drag that in here? You mean for Tarantela to try its hand – or should I say its claw – at bartending?"

"An interesting idea," Fidelio said. "In all seriousness, though, I am concerned about the criminal element in this community. You recall that my original prototype was stolen. I do not wish to repeat the incident."

"Can't say I blame you." Hank pulled the tobacco pouch from his pocket and rolled a cigarette. The long drive had given him a powerful thirst, and there were at least a dozen bottles of Kentucky whiskey behind the bar. He supposed one drink wouldn't hurt, but he didn't like to drink alone, and Fidelio was not about to join him, so he put it out of his mind. "No offense, but I never did understand why you partnered up with the Marquis. Ain't he one of those robber barons you're always going on about?"

Fidelio sniffed. "I may be opposed to capitalist exploitation, but I am also a realist. In order to improve the world, I must deal with society as it is."

The blond waitress reappeared. "Good evening, gentlemen," she drawled. "Are you all ready to order?"

Fidelio craned his neck to look at the blackboard next to the bar, where items and prices were posted. "I notice you serve bison steak. During my time working with the Marquis De Mores, I developed an appreciation of that delicacy."

The girl's eyes went wide. "You know the Marquis? That guy's downright famous. Is he as charming as they say he is?"

"He is a gentleman, though a bit mercurial at times." He paused to stroke his goatee with one finger. "I would like the porterhouse cut, cooked moderately with baked potato and butter beans. Do you have bottled mineral water?"

"You bet. We have the finest artesian water from the Pacific Northwest. And you, sir?"

"The same," Hank said, "Without the beans, or the water. I'm in the mood for something sweet." He looked up from his menu and winked. "How is your sarsaparilla?"

"I'm partial to it myself," she said, "though we don't get much call for it, excepting for the children."

"Well, that suits me just fine, because tonight I feel young at heart." Hank gave her a sly grin. The girl blushed, then jotted their orders on a paper tablet and headed for the kitchen.

"You surprise me," Fidelio said. "I expected you would order a whiskey or beer."

Hank laughed. "I ain't exactly been practicing temperance, but that don't mean I've gone back to my old ways. I'll have a drink now and again, but only to be sociable."

"I did not mean to imply disapproval. You know that I have no affinity for strong drink; it dulls the faculties. It is your prerogative, of course, but does not your religion frown on alcohol?"

"You got me there," Hank said. "But I figure, as long as a man can just have a glass or two without getting pickled, most likely the Lord is okay with it. I can still be a Quaker, long as I practice moderation."

"I have great respect for the Society of Friends, even if I do not share their beliefs. Their commitment to egalitarianism, as well as their opposition to war and violence, is quite commendable. In addition, they were among the first churches to take a stand against slavery."

"You're a lot like a Quaker in many ways, Fidel. Money don't mean that much to you, and you really care about the poor and downtrodden. You don't run around with wild women, neither. Far as I know, you don't indulge in any of the seven sins, 'cept maybe a little bit of pride."

"Thank you. Do you mean to once again proselytize for your religion?" Fidelio smiled. Hank's attempts to preach the Word of God seemed to amuse him more than anything.

"According to the Good Book, I'm obliged to," Hank said, "so I got to remind you that, no matter how good a life you live, you can't be saved without faith in Jesus."

Fidelio's smile disappeared. "You know my stance on this matter."

At that moment, the young lady returned with their drinks. "Here you are.

Your supper will be out shortly."

"Ah, at last." Fidelio took a sip, and made a face. "This does not taste right. I think it may contain alcohol. I shall have a word with the bartender." Before the girl could respond, he got up with glass in hand and strode to the bar.

"Don't mind him, miss," Hank said to the waitress. "He can be a mite ornery at times. Here, something for your trouble." He handed her a silver half dollar.

"Why, thank you!" She grinned as she dropped the coin into her cleavage. Hank's eyes followed the coin as it fell, and admired her backside as she sashayed over to another table.

Hank drank his sarsaparilla, enjoying the tangy sweetness. Most of the tables in the room were now occupied, and the conversation was too loud for him to hear what Fidelio was saying to the man behind the bar. The fellow was young, barely out of his teens, with the thick dark hair and brown complexion of a Mexican. Surprisingly, Fidelio did not look angry. Maybe it was his natural sympathy for a fellow working man.

The man on the stool to Fidelio's right, however, was another matter. He was big and muscular, with short-cropped brownish hair with a beard to match. His flushed, sun-weathered face was flushed from the effects of strong drink. The man glared at Fidelio the entire time.

The Cuban paid the big man no attention. He accepted a new glass from the Mexican barkeep and returned to the table.

"It was a simple misunderstanding. The young fellow recently migrated here from New Mexico, where he had scant opportunity to achieve proficiency in English."

"I see," Hank nodded. "By the way, did you notice that big fellow on the bar stool giving you the stink eye?"

Fidelio shrugged. "The man said nothing, though he was clearly inebriated. Some become belligerent under the influence of alcohol."

As if on cue, they heard raised voices and turned to look. The big man was having a loud conversation with a mature attractive woman with bright red hair who stood behind the bar next to the young Mexican.

"I won't stand for it, Margie!" The big man's speech was rather slurred. "I didn't come way out west to have to drink in the same room with a goddamn half-breed!"

"Keep your britches on, Zeke. It's none of your business who we serve. Anyhow, Jess spoke to the man. He's a Spaniard from Cuba."

"What a jackass!" Hank growled. "In my younger days, I'd have knocked that son of a bitch off his stool. But I'm a man of the Lord now, and I believe in turning the other cheek."

"There is a third alternative." Fidelio unlocked his box and removed the latest incarnation of his creation. "I have been meaning to test Tarantela in a more challenging environment."

"Are you sure you want to do that, Fidel? I thought you said you didn't want outsiders to see your invention yet."

"It is probably too late for caution, if Isabelle's story was true."

"Not sure I'd believe those rumors," Hank said. "Men see some pretty crazy things in the terror of battle. And they also tell tall tales when they're trying to impress a lady."

Fidelio just shook his head. He moved some levers on the metal arachnid's back, and then set the creature on the floor. He removed a tin whistle from his pocket and blew a few barely audible notes. The machine scuttled across the room toward the ranting drunkard.

Margie looked in their direction; her eyes widened in alarm. She nodded when she saw Fidelio put his finger to his lips.

The automaton reached the big man and climbed directly up a leg of his trousers. When it reached the man's buttocks, it deployed the claws at the end of its mechanical arms.

"Awk! Who did that? I'll kill the bastard!" The man sprang to his feet and saw the machine hanging on to the seat of his dungarees. "Help! Get this demon off me!"

"What thing?" Margie said calmly. "I told you, Zeke, if you don't lay off the hard stuff, you'll start seeing things what ain't there."

Zeke spun around frantically. "You old witch, I can feel it pinch my backside! Is this some kind of black magic?" He managed to shake off the automaton, then ran out the door.

Everyone in the place broke out laughing, except Fidelio. When the noise died down, he blew some more notes on his whistle. The spider righted itself and scampered back to their table. He picked it up and inspected it carefully. "I was foolish to let my anger get the best of me. Fortunately it was not damaged." He switched the device off and returned it to its case.

Hank slapped his companion on the back. "I'll be doggoned. All this time, I thought you had no sense of humor. Mark my words, even if you never get them things to mine coal, people will buy the little ones just to mess around with. You'll be rich as Rockefeller."

"It is no toy," Fidelio sniffed. "And I plan to use the profits for the benefit of mankind."

In a moment the blond waitress arrived with two tumblers full of golden brown liquid. "Margie sent these, they're on the house."

"That's most hospitable of you, but we don't..."

"Oh shush, it would be rude to refuse the lady's hospitality." Hank slid both glasses in front of himself. "Bring my friend another mineral water, please. I'm buying."

"Right away, sir." She went immediately to the bar to fetch it.

Hank took a sip from the first glass – smooth! He looked up to see Fidelio smiling.

"A toast," his companion said, "to the Society of Friends."

Hank clinked his glass with Fidelio's. "Don't let this humor thing go to your head, *amigo*."

"I should say the same about you and liquor. Wine, at least, has a pleasant taste, but how you can drink that poison is beyond me."

"You get used to it. And don't worry; I'm bound to moderation anyway, because when I was sick they took out a piece of my liver. I can't put it down like I used to."

"Perhaps that was the silver lining to the dark cloud of your illness." Fidelio raised his glass. "May you live to be 100."

As they toasted again, the red-headed woman appeared. "Good evening, gents, I'm Margaret Jameson, proprietress of this establishment. I trust you're enjoying your evening?"

"Certainly," Fidelio said. "Your hospitality has been outstanding."

"Darn tootin'." Hank grinned. "You and your husband run a real fine establishment."

"My poor husband is six feet under. He left me his share of the hotel, which consists of this watering hole. Ain't much, but it's a living." She studied the two men carefully. "I don't know what that thing-a-ma-bob was, but it sure scared the hell out of old Ezekiel."

"It is a prototype of an invention I am working on," Fidelio said. "It is not yet patented, so I hope I can count on your discretion."

"Can't speak for old Zeke, but nobody's going to believe him. The rest of the drunks in this place, probably the same. As for me and Julio," she looked at the bartender, "we'll keep our traps shut, won't we?" She laughed. "Anything you fellows want, give me a holler, okay?"

As she left, Hank finished the last sip of his first whiskey. "You realize she's going to tell every single person she knows, don't you? It's too good a story to pass up."

"Yes, I suppose you are correct. My impulsiveness can be a problem at times."

"It was worth it to scare the holy hell out of that horse's ass."

The steaks arrived; they were rare, exactly how Hank liked them. Fidelio, however, called the waitress back over. "I specified medium. Please cook this more thoroughly." To Hank, he added, "One can contract a nasty bacterial infection from raw meat."

"I'll take that chance." By the time Hank had finished his steak and downed the second glass of whiskey, he was feeling light-headed.

"Is something amiss, friend?" Fidelio asked.

"Nope, just a mite dizzy. Like I said, I can't quite handle my liquor the way I used to." Hank got up and promptly tripped over the leg of the neighboring chair, almost landing in the lap of an elderly lady seated at the next table. To make things worse, Hank reached out a hand and tried to smooth the woman's rumpled dress.

She was not amused. "Goodness gracious! This is not a place for drunkards!"

"Please excuse my friend; he has recently been ill. He should not have been celebrating. Come friend; let us go to our room."

Fidelio helped Hank to his feet, then put his arm around the man's shoulder. He walked the inebriated would-be Quaker down the hallway and up the stairs. As they went, Hank sang, "I am a pilgrim and a stranger," at the top of his lungs.

Sometime later Hank awoke to a pounding headache and an eerie yellow light. "Who's there?" he mumbled.

"I am sorry I woke you," Fidelio said. "I must wash my face before retiring."

"What's that light? Is that one of them newfangled battery lanterns?"

"Better than that. This lamp utilizes the improved battery I designed for the next incarnation of Tarantela. It can provide a light source for as long as thirty minutes."

Hank let out a long whistle. "I saw one of them new *flash-lights* at the World's Fair in Buffalo, you know, where the President got shot. It could only stay on for a couple of seconds. Yours is better, but I'm not fixing to replace my trusty hurricane lamp any time soon."

Vaughn L. Treude

"Do not dismiss this technology. In a few years, kerosene and gas lighting will be a thing of the past."

"Most likely you're right. These are amazing times we live in. By the bye, sorry about my scene in the restaurant. Proves I need to watch myself with the firewater. Where were you all this time? I hope you weren't setting here nursemaiding me."

Fidelio hung his jacket over the straight-backed wooden chair, removed his boots, and sat down on the end of the bed. "No, I paid a visit to a recent acquaintance," he paused, as if considering his words carefully, "And I am rather fatigued."

Hank laughed and then grimaced. "Fidel, you sly devil. I was a bit of a Lothario myself in my younger days. Was it the sweet little blond filly? She had her eye on you."

"No, it was not our waitress."

"I see. So was it Mrs. Jameson, then? Nothing wrong with enjoying the company of a mature lady – except for the sinning part, I guess. An older woman learns to do many a thing that a younger woman ain't never heard of."

Fidelio shook his head. "It is best I say no more. I fear you would not understand, and I am loathe to jeopardize our friendship."

"Try me, *amigo*. Believe me, I can't be shocked."

"Do not be so certain. I will probably regret this, but you have become a fast friend, and the keeping of secrets is a very lonely business. If you swear you will not become judgmental, or share this very personal information with anyone else, I will tell you."

"I promise, on my honor as a gentleman," Hank said.

"Very well. I spent the evening with Julio, the bartender."

Hank was puzzled. "But you ain't even a drinker. I did hear you speaking Spanish with the fellow, so you got that in common, but..." At once the realization hit him. He got up so quickly he slipped off the sagging mattress and hit the floor with a crash.

"Hank! Are you injured?" Fidelio rushed around the bed to help him to his feet.

"I'm good, I just... you know, bonked my noggin. Don't need no help, I'm not a cripple." He stared at Fidelio. "So you're saying you're a – a –"

"Homosexual," Fidelio replied. "Do you believe I should be stoned, as in the Old Testament? Or tossed in a dungeon like Oscar Wilde? Or do you practice the

168

love and forgiveness espoused by your Savior, but so seldom practiced by your fellow Christians?"

"Uh no, er, um yes. It's nothing personal, I swear it. It's just, I'm a mite taken aback. All this time and I didn't realize, makes me feel pretty darn stupid."

"Do not be harsh on yourself. Men of my kind take great pains to keep our natures hidden. Even in a cosmopolitan city such as New York, where a man might live openly with another man, one must not admit it is more than friendship. In most jurisdictions, the activity is punishable by law." He paused. "Maybe I should never have burdened you with this."

"No, it's all right, really. It's just those times we were on the road, when we..."

"Shared a bed?" Fidelio laughed. "Pardon my amusement, but your fears are unfounded. My condition is not a disease you can contract by proximity. Besides, I prefer a younger man with shapely buttocks. You hardly even have a derrière."

"Doggone it, man, spare me the unnecessary detail!"

"My apologies," Fidelio continued, speaking just above a whisper. "Please lower your voice. You cannot comprehend how difficult it is to keep one's nature a secret, day after day, and no one with whom to confide."

"But if you've got a... what would you call him... a sweetheart, then at least you and him could talk freely, I mean..."

"True, but that is more the exception than the rule. I have known love; my first perished in a tragic accident. The most recent was a dear companion I was forced to leave behind – though the relationship was doomed anyway, because he could not bear the disapproval of society."

Hank sat with mouth agape. "You mean August? But... didn't he just get hitched to Sarah Johnson?"

"Only because he was convinced that hell-fire awaited him if he did not mend his ways. Thus he must forsake happiness in life for the promise of an illusory paradise."

"That's right, you don't believe in the hereafter, do you?" Hank sighed. "Please don't take this wrong, but maybe I should go." He rubbed his forehead with his right hand. "Ohh, my head is actin' up something fierce."

Fidelio showed him no sympathy. "And where shall you go? This hotel has no unoccupied rooms."

"Well..." Hank eyed the wooden chair over by the desk. "I've slept sitting up many a time on the trail, I can do it again." He pulled his leather jacket from the hook on the wall where it hung. The chair creaked as he sat down and covered himself up.

Fidelio removed his shirt and pants, then pulled on his nightshirt, and settled into bed. "If you prefer the chair, so be it."

When Hank awoke, his headache was gone. The pain had relocated to every other part of his body. To his surprise, he was covered with a quilt. The bed was empty, with the sheets tucked neatly in place. Had Fidelio abandoned him?

He could hardly blame the man; he probably felt insulted by his friend's lack of trust, after opening up about his terrible secret. Hank thought of all the gambling, drinking and carousing he'd done in his life, in particular all the women he'd paid for. He felt a pang of guilt as he remembered the Savior's words: "Let he who is without sin cast the first stone."

Hank walked around the bed and threw open the dusty curtains. The window overlooked the courtyard behind the hotel. The sun was just barely up; the neighboring buildings cast long shadows on the brown grass, still dotted with patches of frost.

A slender man bent over the open hood of the Stanley Steamer, tinkering with its engine.

Maybe Providence had brought the two of them together. If any other man had made that confession, Hank would have considered him a moral degenerate. Fidelio, on the other hand, was a genius, and also kind and generous. He truly wanted to make the world a better place. Hank wondered what the others in his prayer group would say about him traveling with such a person. Yet in his heart, Henry MacMillan knew he was not a man who should be casting stones.

Hank quickly dressed and headed downstairs to the hotel dining room. Just as he got there, Fidelio entered from the other door. "I checked all the seals and hoses on the Steamer," he said. "I hear Wyoming is even more desolate than South Dakota. I would hate to be stranded."

"You're right about that," said Hank. "Suppose we should go get us some food."

The hotel staff had the food all laid out on a long table like a Sunday family dinner. Nothing looked very appetizing but Hank realized he had to eat. He scooped some steak and eggs onto his plate, and filled a cup with coffee from the blue enameled pot. Hank sat down, took a sip of coffee, ate a few bites of meat, and then poked around with his fork.

"I appreciate your understanding," Fidelio said between sips of tea. "And the fact that you have not attempted to 'convert' me from my inclinations. Not that such a conversion is possible. I believe that these tendencies are innate; they are either present or not."

Hank looked around to make sure no one else was listening. Their hostess was busy serving other guests, and the room was loud with conversation. He was glad the young blonde was not working this morning. It would have been embarrassing to see her after the scene he'd made the night before.

He looked back at Fidelio. "So you're saying you were born this way?"

"Exactly."

"Just because a fellow has..." Hank chose his words carefully, "unnatural desires, don't mean he has to succumb. The Lord made us imperfect but also gave us a chance for redemption."

"I understand the concepts of sin and penance. I was raised as a Catholic, after all. But let us consider. Would you be happy as a Christian if you were forbidden to be with a woman?"

"I haven't been, since I left my sinnin' days behind. I aim to find myself a wife."

"Very well. Now suppose that option was also taken from you? Would you agree that perhaps your Deity's strictures were unreasonable?"

"Well..." Now it was Hank's term to ponder for a while. "The Bible tells how Sodom and Gomorrah were destroyed on account of that sort of wickedness." Hank regretted those words the moment he said them. Fidelio's situation, he realized, was much more complicated.

"You do not allow that such stories may have been embellished as they were passed down over the ages?"

"No!" Hank exploded. He noticed the couple at the next table staring, so he lowered his voice. "My apologies for the outburst. I'm a Christian and this is what I know. My belief in God, and in the Bible as the Word of God, has gotten me through many a hard time." He looked at Fidelio's stony expression, then continued, "That's the way I was taught, anyhow."

"And the people who recorded the Word of God could not have erred?"

"Not in my view." Hank flushed in anger for a moment, but reminded himself that his friend was sincere, and did not intend to provoke him. "Fidelio, I'm a simple man. I don't have lots of book learnin' like you. I know how the Savior preaches love and forgiveness, but I also know what the Bible says about your kind. I guess I'm just a trifle confused."

"I respect your dedication to your principles. If you no longer wish to associate with me, I understand. However, I propose a compromise. I will listen respectfully to your opinions, and you will agree to do the same with mine. I promise I will attempt to maintain an open mind."

Hank sighed, and leaned back in his chair. "I reckon that's a fair compromise."

"Shall we shake hands on it, then?" Fidelio extended a hand across the table.

"You've got a deal."

Chapter 16 – The Wizard of Colorado Springs

"This should get us a ways," Hank said as he emptied the can of kerosene into the motorcar's fuel tank. "We'll stick these four other cans in the trailer for spare. We may need 'em. There's a whole lot of nothing between here and Cheyenne."

"Compared to yesterdays' drive? Wyoming must be very desolate indeed."

"Yup. Too dry for cattle country, good for nothing but sheep."

"I expect it will be an interesting journey then."

Hank laughed. "Fidel, you're full of surprises." Realizing what he'd just said, he quickly added, "Jokes, I mean, sense of humor. Miles of scrub land's got to be anything but interesting."

"I did not intend to be humorous," Fidelio smiled. "What I meant was, we will have ample time for conversation, assuming our voices hold out. If we can manage 100 to 120 miles between sunrise and sunset, we should reach Colorado Springs four days hence."

"You got a way of seeing the sunny side of everything," Hank said as he climbed into the passenger seat. "After our troubles in Ohio, though, I'm glad we fancied up the Steamer. Maybe I won't lose my hat this time." He extended a hand and knocked on the detachable roof they had added at the Marquis' shop. "By the bye, do you think you might let me take the reins again?"

"Perhaps, if all goes well." Fidelio said as he started the engine. "Until then, you may serve as navigator." He handed Hank a map of the area he had bought at the hotel.

As they rumbled down the dirt street westward out of Deadwood, Hank shouted, "It's going to be one heck of a ride! Let's hope we don't need that second spare wheel."

The trail took them into the fragrant pines of the Black Hills. Hank studied the map as Fidelio drove. "I see we're going the same way as the old Cheyenne-Black Hills Stage. Darn shame that outfit folded up."

"How true. The railroad is a powerful competitor. Now there is no satisfactory connection to the west. Hopefully someone will take over the maintenance of this road."

It seemed that Hank had overcome his discomfort with Fidelio's revelation, though there was a subtle change in his behavior. Formerly, Hank had spoken frequently of his past sexual liaisons, usually adding, "But I'm a changed man now." Today, Hank avoided the topic, for which Fidelio was grateful. He was tired of feigning interest in his stories of romantic conquest.

The Black Hills were a welcome respite from the arid grasslands between Medora and Deadwood. Fidelio found the scent of the pine forest exhilarating. It was not, however, an easy drive. The trail was strewn with rocks the size of a man's fist.

They soon tired of conversing. Fidelio's mood slipped into melancholy. He missed his native Cuba, his dear Rodrigo and even his overbearing father. Regrets, however, would get him nowhere. Instead, he pondered Isabelle's story about the Army's testing of 'fighting insects.' If this was so, the Patent Office might see this as 'prior art,' causing serious problems with his recent application. Again he cursed the naiveté that had cost him Tarantela's first prototype.

Finally they emerged from the forest into open country. "Tell me, Hank," Fidelio said, "Will we encounter a town or village soon? I could certainly use a repast."

"You mean grub, right? Well..." he unfolded the map, "we're heading south. The village of Newcastle should be over yonder hill, but I wouldn't recommend stopping there."

"Why not?"

"Bad outbreak of the smallpox, back in double-aught," Hank explained.

As they crested the hill they saw it. The town, a cluster of buildings at a crossroads, seemed eerily quiet, with a lone old man standing on the corner. Fidelio drove on without stopping. He wished the Steamer had an enclosed cab like the newer models.

Soon they entered a green valley in the midst of an interesting rock formation. It was an idyllic scene, with a herd of deer grazing on the green grass below. "This would be a good place to stop," Fidelio said. "All this sitting has given me leg cramps."

"Good idea," Hank said. "'Cause I got to see a man about a horse."

"What are you talking about? Is that some sort of euphemism?"

"Yoo-what? You got me with that one. Anyhow, don't forget, we got ham and bread with us. While we're stopped we may as well have ourselves a picnic."

"An excellent suggestion. We shall dine *al fresco*." He pulled off the trail and parked the car under the tree. After Hank returned from a quick trip to the bushes, the two men sat on the grass and ate their sandwiches. The deer, a few dozen yards down the road, continued their grazing. "This would be a splendid place for some photographs," Fidelio commented.

"You got that right. This place is darn pretty, and I don't think I've ever got so close to deer in the wild. You could use your new-fangled box camera. Too bad we can't get closer."

"Perhaps we can. You have not seen my latest idea for Tarantela." He went over to retrieve Tarantela's metal box from the Steamer's trunk. Additionally he brought a leather case containing the camera. He removed both from their enclosures, and then attached the camera to one of the spider's claws.

"I didn't know you had it set up for photography," Hank said. "The little feller never fails to amaze me."

"I have not had time to test this mode of operation," Fidelio said, "but now is a perfect opportunity." He pulled the well-used tin whistle from his pocket. "One day I shall control Tarantela by radio waves, but for now we must rely upon auditory signals."

"Yep. I hope the noise don't spook the deer."

Hank watched as Fidelio guided the automaton down the trail. Sometimes it got snagged in twigs or brush, which its 'bat hearing' had failed to detect. Fidelio simply blew his whistle and ordered it to back up, away from the obstacle. The deer took no notice of the sounds, regarding them perhaps as the calls of a songbird. Soon the machine was in the midst of the herd. The animals regarded it curiously but did not flee.

Fidelio made a few more notes on the whistle and waited. "It is near the limit of its range. Perhaps we cannot..." As he spoke, a metallic chime issued from the spider, causing several deer to look its way. "Ah, it is functioning after all!"

By tooting the whistle, he took several photographs, including one of a great stag that approached to sniff the metal visitor. "I sure hope that one turns out," Hank said with a chuckle.

Once the spider had returned and Fidelio had put it and the camera away, he said, "Hank, would you like to take the wheel once more? I am in need of a rest."

"Lord a-mighty! I was hoping I'd get another crack at it." Hank got behind the wheel and started up the Steamer as he'd seen Fidelio do so many times. "Now how do I work this gear thingie again?" After several jerks, he got it into gear and pulled hesitantly onto the road.

"Perhaps this was a mistake," Fidelio said. "This hilly terrain will require much shifting."

"For a young *hombre,* you're sure a fussy old codger. Don't fret. This ain't my first rodeo, you know."

Hank soon mastered the art of shifting down to climb hills and to a higher gear for the flat parts. It was confusing, though. "You mean I got to shift *up* to go downhill as well?"

"The transmission helps to slow the car. If you rely on brakes alone, they will overheat."

Despite his stern lectures, Fidelio was impressed. Hank was a quick learner. Soon they passed through a village where they stopped to purchase deer jerky and fill their water jugs. Afterwards, Hank got behind the wheel again as if he had been doing it for years.

Around sunset they found themselves in an open meadow. "Guess we're sleeping under the stars again," Hank said.

Fidelio had expected his friend to place his bedroll much farther away than he had previously. To his surprise, he did not. Fidelio had to admit that Hank was surprisingly accepting of his homosexuality. 'Judge not, lest ye be judged,' perhaps?

On the third day, the two travelers reached Denver. Colorado's capital sprang out from the high plains like a surprise birthday party, nestled against snow-capped mountains to the west. Its stately brick buildings stood young and proud, rebuilt since the city's devastating fire. Here there were Zeppelins in the sky, and the streets were lined with new-fangled electric light poles.

The road into the city was choked with traffic, mostly horse-drawn wagons, a few velocipedes and a number of horseless carriages. To the east, the Capitol's golden dome shone in rays of the setting sun. This city had literally emerged from the riches of the earth.

Near the center of town, Fidelio and Hank stopped at the fancy new Oxford Hotel, where they booked a room and enjoyed a hot cooked meal, which was especially comforting on such a brisk spring evening. Afterwards, they sat in the dining room, Fidelio enjoying a cup of tea while Hank smoked a cigarette. Two women approached them, a blonde and a brunette in low-cut velvety dresses. "Would you gentlemen like some company?"

"Certainly," Fidelio said, "I have a question for you."

"Okay," the blonde said. "What would you big, strong, men like to know?"

"Regarding the local industries, which is more dominant, gold or silver mining?"

"I think we could find something a lot more interesting to talk about," said the brunette, "unless you're fixing to buy us jewelry." She leaned over and pressed her ample breasts against Fidelio's body as she stroked his goatee.

"If you asked my druthers, I'd like to talk about the Bible," Hank said.

"My goodness it's getting late. All of a sudden I'm mighty tired," the blonde said. "Come along, Jessie Belle."

After they'd left, Fidelio said, "You frightened them off. I would have liked to ask another question or two."

"There ain't nothin' in those pretty heads but sin and temptation."

The rooms were an exorbitant five dollars per night, so once again they shared, but fortunately there were two separate cots. After Hank had put on his bedclothes, he watched Fidelio as he washed his face in the basin. "You ain't fixin' to go and meet anybody, are you?"

Fidelio dropped the towel he'd been using to dry off. "Perish the thought! I do not know a soul in this place. But if you would like to go visit Jessie Belle, be my guest."

Hank's faced reddened. "Beg pardon. Guess I got a lot to learn about... you know."

"No apologies required, my friend. Let us get some sleep. Tomorrow we rise early."

⚙ ʃ⅄ ⚙

The last leg of their journey turned out to be the most eventful. A few miles south of Denver, an encounter with a large stone dispatched the Steamer's left front tire. Near the halfway point, an enormous rut claimed another wheel. With both spares gone, Fidelio became quite cautious, slowing to an agonizing 15 miles per hour.

"Praise the Lord, we made it!" Hank exclaimed as he saw the sign that said 'Colorado Springs, Population 21,000.' "I thought for sure we'd be sleeping under the stars again."

"I am gratified as well," Fidelio said. "Tomorrow morning, our first order of business will be to find a repair shop..." A thunderous boom interrupted him. He slammed on the brakes, causing the vehicle to skid to the left. "Hank?" The passenger seat was empty.

He looked back and saw his friend behind the car, on the right side of the road. Hank was breathing in ragged gasps, crouched in a patch of late-spring snow like a frightened rabbit. Fidelio got out of the car and approached him. "Are you all

177

right, my friend?"

"Yep," Hank said, his eyes downcast as he got up from the ground and brushed himself off. "Lord a-mighty! That gave me one heck of a start. It sounded like a cannon going off."

"Are you certain you are not injured?" Fidelio put a hand on Hank's arm.

"I told you, I'm fine!" Hank jerked his arm free. "I learned how to fall proper when I was busting broncos."

"You must deal with your condition, my friend," Fidelio said as he opened the car door for Hank. "Jumping from a moving vehicle could be fatal. Have you tried psychoanalysis?"

"My doc in New York sent me to a headshrinker; what a load of bull pucky! I hardly even remember my ma, much less wanting to get cozy with her." Hank shuddered. "I'll stick with the power of prayer." He examined his crushed cowboy hat, and popped out the crown as best he could. "Maybe I need to tie myself to the seat. What was that ruckus, anyhow?"

"The sound emanated from the direction we are traveling. Oddly enough, the passersby did not seem to notice."

Hank laughed. "Could they all be hard of hearing?"

As the dusk deepened, flickering lights appeared in the houses on either side of the street. The town had no street lamps, and the sky deepened to black. Fidelio turned the car onto a side street that soon narrowed to a dirt trail with a moderate up-slope.

"Holy cats!" Hank exclaimed. "Can you feel that? All the hairs on my body are standing on end. And look! My hands are glowing. What in tarnation is going on?"

"We shall soon find out," Fidelio said. "I believe we have reached our destination."

They had arrived at a wooden barn-like structure. Protruding from the roof was a ten foot metal-framed tower, with a central pole that extended into the sky. A blue glow emanated from the uncurtained windows. Suddenly the air was torn by a thunderclap.

This time, Hank remained in his seat, crouched down with his arms over his head. "Confound it; I'm as skittish as a jackrabbit drinking coffee."

"Quickly, let us greet our host before the next explosion."

Fidelio knocked on the door, but there was no response.

"Let me try." Hank stepped forward and pounded the wood with well-scarred fists.

The door swung open. A lanky man, taller even than Fidelio, appeared before them. His hair was dark and tousled, and tinted goggles obscured his eyes. Muff-like ear protectors hung around his neck. He wore denim coveralls with dark scorch marks in several places. In a Slavic accent he said, "May I help you gentlemen?"

"Mr. Tesla, I believe you are expecting us. I am Fidelio Espinoza of Havana, Cuba. This is my associate, Hank MacMillan."

"Of course! Come in, gentlemen! I shall give you a tour of my laboratory." When Hank extended his hand, Tesla shook his head. "I do not shake hands. It is a prime factor in the spread of disease."

Hank shrugged and glanced at his own hands. He and Fidelio followed their host inside.

"This is my resonant transformer." Tesla waved his hand at a cylindrical device that stood taller than a man inside a metal cage. "It produces an electrical tension of over one million volts, enough to simulate lightning. You may have heard the discharge as you approached."

Hank nodded. "We sure did."

On the fringes of the huge open room were shelves and tables piled with equipment. "Here are various volt-meters and magnetometers," Tesla said. "Pardon the disarray; I have recently returned from my other facility at Wardenclyffe in Long Island."

"I heard how J. P. Morgan withdrew funding for your wireless telegraphy research," Fidelio said. "That is a great misfortune."

"Mr. Morgan encountered financial difficulties," Tesla said, "so I will complete that work at a later date." He looked at Hank, who was stifling a yawn. "Forgive me, I am a poor host. Please join me in my humble supper. I have a loaf of bread, and some fruit and vegetables."

"Thank you, that is very kind of you," said Fidelio.

"Yeah, thanks," Hank added.

Tesla led them to a bench obscured by papers covered in theoretical calculations. He moved the papers to one side, and continued to talk as he lay out mismatched plates and silver. He set the food in the middle, and gestured for his guests to sit.

On taking his seat, Hank folded his hands, bowed his head and closed his eyes for a quick silent prayer. When he opened them again, he found Tesla staring at him, so he felt obliged to say something. "It sure is an honor to meet you, sir. I've heard a whole bunch about you."

"Probably most of it bad, no?" Tesla laughed. "Since, if I understand correctly, Señor Espinoza also worked for my previous employer in New Jersey."

"Yes," Fidelio said. "I believe you and Edison are both geniuses in your own right."

Tesla waved his hand. "I prefer not to speak about that man. Though I have been looking forward to seeing your automaton. Tell me, where did you get the idea?"

"Please, call me Fidelio." He paused from spreading butter on his bread. "I was lying in a meadow one sunny afternoon in Spain, when I noticed a spider climbing a stalk of grass, and thought, could I make a machine to mimic that creature's wondrous abilities?" He chose not to mention what he had been doing in the grass, and with whom.

After they finished eating, Fidelio retrieved Tarantela's box from the car. As he inserted the key into the lock, Tesla held up his hand. He opened a drawer in a wooden filing cabinet and withdrew a piece of paper.

"Before we begin any working relationship, here is an agreement which details the rights of each of us as inventors. I always specify these arrangements in writing. That is a lesson I have learned the hard way."

He handed the paper to Fidelio, who read it quickly. The two men signed, and Hank added his signature as a witness.

Fidelio opened the case and removed the automaton. He set it on the floor, flipped the switch on its back, and whistled a few notes. The spider skittered across the laboratory floor.

"I call it Tarantela," Fidelio explained, "for obvious reasons."

"Incredible mobility," Tesla said, wide-eyed. "But I have seen toys that can walk almost as well. What else does it do?"

"Observe." Fidelio put some broccoli on a plate and set it upon the floor in Tarantela's path. When the creature encountered the obstruction, it halted and extended a metal arm. With the vegetable grasped in its claw, it continued across the lab and stopped at Tesla's feet.

"What an amazing degree of control," Tesla said, picking up Tarantela to examine it closely. "What is the power source?"

"It is an electrical battery," Fidelio said, "but the range is rather limited."

Tesla's angular face beamed with enthusiasm. "I'm certain we could find a better alternative. Have you investigated cryomagnetics?"

"Yes, though the cooling apparatus is at present too cumbersome. Tarantela must be mobile, as my goal is to utilize it in mining and industry, to save workers from hazardous labor."

"Ingenious," Tesla nodded. "Obviously, there would also be military applications."

"Military!" Fidelio cried. He felt his stomach turn as he thought of Isabelle's rumor. "Pardon my outburst, but surely you do not condone warfare, wanton killing and destruction."

Tesla shrugged. "Of course not, but at times it is a regrettable necessity. Allow me to show you something." He led Hank and Fidelio to a cabinet on the other side of the giant transformer. He unlocked it and removed something that looked like a metallic wine bottle mounted horizontally on a steel tripod.

"This is my concept for an electrically powered particle weapon. Or as my assistant Mario in New York called it, the 'death ray.'"

"Does it... *function?*" Perhaps, Fidelio thought, an alliance with Tesla was not a good idea. He glanced at Hank, whose face had gone pale.

"Do not be alarmed," Tesla said. "Its power output can be varied for each purpose. It can stop an enemy's infantry and cavalry by producing intense discomfort, yet also sink hostile ships and drop airships from the sky. These defensive capabilities may someday make war obsolete."

"I hope you're right," said Hank. "I was in the war in Cuba, and I can't say a single good thing about it."

"Cuba? Is that where the two of you met?"

"No. I was conscripted by the Spanish crown," Fidelio said, "but happily the war was over before I would have been forced to participate."

Tesla led them out of the storeroom. As he locked the door, he said. "Did you favor the American side of the conflict?"

Fidelio shook his head. "I oppose colonialism by any nation."

"I agree. My homeland only recently won its freedom from the Ottoman Empire."

The men continued their discussion well into the night, not just about science but also current events. Though Tesla was not particularly well-informed on the latter, he was able to discuss politics with a complete lack of acrimony. "Goodness, look at the time," Tesla said, consulting his pocket watch. "I have a spare room in back, if you need a place to stay."

"Thank you," Fidelio said. "Tomorrow we shall seek lodging in the city."

"It was right kind of Mr. Tesla to put us up for the night," Hank said as they carried their luggage to the room. He stared at the single bed. "Jumpin' Jiminy, that's a bit too cozy."

"Do not worry, the divan looks comfortable." Fidelio lay down; his legs hung off the end.

"Would you like to trade, *amigo?*" Hank chuckled. "I'm not as tall as you are."

"Thank you, I will be fine," He paused. "Hank, what is your opinion of our host?"

"He's a brilliant fellow, a bit of an odd fish, but seems basically good at heart."

"I have heard he has no interest in women."

"Like you?" Hank sat up in bed and looked at Fidelio. "You'd be a better judge of that than me. In his case, though, I'd wager it's more like a sailor being married to the sea, 'cepting that Tesla's wife is science."

"That is an astute observation." Fidelio, however, was not convinced.

The next day, the men rented rooms in a boarding house a half mile away. The owner, a widow named Mrs. Johnson, did not share the suspicion with which much of the town viewed the Serbian inventor. "Such a sweet man," she said. "It seems I've introduced him to every single lady in Colorado, and he still can't find a wife!"

Tesla was every bit as eccentric and impulsive as their first meeting had indicated. He put aside his research into lightning in favor of evaluating Fidelio's invention. "I have been thinking about your Tarantela," he said, "and I have some ideas on that power problem you mentioned."

"That is good, because the charge on the batteries is spent far too quickly. And as I said before, cryomagnetic technology has significant disadvantages as well."

"Have you thought about storing energy externally?"

"Of course, but a cable thick enough to carry sufficient power would restrict its mobility."

"Hmm, I see your point," Tesla said, nodding thoughtfully.

Hank listened to their discussion as he wound a coil of copper wire; it seemed like he'd done hundreds already. Since their arrival he had rarely spoken, intimidated by the brilliance of his companions. Yet Tesla's inquisitive nature was contagious. Hank looked up from his work and said, "If only we could send power through the air, like messages from a wireless telegraph."

"An excellent suggestion!" Tesla said. "I was about to propose the very same thing. By utilizing magnetic induction, your automaton would need no internal power source. It could receive the power it requires on specially designed coils."

Fidelio brightened. "That would work well in a factory environment, or anywhere Tarantela has a limited range of movement. It would lower the device's overall cost as well."

"We should test this idea at once!" Tesla said. "Hank, I'm sorry to interrupt you, but please put that aside. For this application we need a different sort of coil."

"Yes, sir." Hank's normally impassive face bore a contented smile.

Tesla worked even longer hours than Edison, having no family to vie for his attention. Though Fidelio found the man attractive, he saw no clear signs of romantic interest. At times he held Fidelio's gaze a moment too long, but he would catch himself and look away. Perhaps it was only social awkwardness, but he had to know for certain. Fidelio did not dare pose the question directly, so he tried to obtain the information by stealth. "Your maid Maria," he began, "would you say she is a comely woman?"

"I suppose," Tesla replied. As he worked on the automaton's wiring, he wore magnifying spectacles, which made his eyes look huge, like some monstrous insect. "Could you fetch me some more solder from the drawer, please?"

"Certainly." Fidelio found a roll of the tin and lead alloy wire and handed it to Tesla. "Have you ever considered marriage and a family?"

Tesla kept his eyes focused on his work. "What? Marriage? No, not really." He turned to Fidelio and smiled. "Oh, I understand. If you're interested in Maria, I have no objection. Take her to dinner. She is particularly fond of food. Or so I would suppose; most people like to eat."

"I am sure she is a nice lady, but no," Fidelio felt himself flush. "Forgive my curiosity."

"Then you may tell your friend Hank she is available," Tesla said as he returned to his work. "I've noticed him stealing glances at the señorita. They would make a handsome couple. Or allow Mrs. Johnson to introduce them. Perhaps then she would leave me be for a while."

"Quite possibly they would," Fidelio said. "Sadly he loves another, someone far away."

Tesla sighed. "I understand. I, too, have felt the sting of unrequited love."

"Who was the... person?"

"I should not say, as it was not appropriate."

Fidelio nodded. "I do not fault your reticence. If you ever wish to talk, however, I assure you that I am not one to spread the secrets of others."

"You certainly are an inquisitive fellow. All right, I will tell you." Tesla straightened up, and looked Fidelio in the eye. "It was the wife of my best friend. As much as I tried, I could not conceal my feelings for her. She was one of the reasons I left Washington."

Fidelio's eyes widened in surprise, having expected a different sort of confession. "That is unfortunate, but Colorado has many fine women."

"No," Tesla snapped. "There will be no other for me. Why do you harangue me about this? Are you and Mrs. Johnson in league?"

"No, no," Fidelio said. "I was merely making conversation. My apologies for the intrusion."

This is a waste of time, Fidelio berated himself. He vowed to focus on his work with Tarantela; that was the most important thing. No matter how enticing he found the Serbian inventor's exotic looks and brilliant mind, he would let the matter rest.

Chapter 17 – Ominous News from Afar

Despite the inherent frustration, Fidelio found work with Tesla to be fascinating. The man's knowledge was incredibly broad. His current fascination was the science of cryonics.

"When I heard of the amazing properties of materials under extreme cold," Tesla said, "I realized that this discovery would revolutionize life for all mankind."

Fidelio smiled at Tesla's dramatic language. "I understand its benefits for large-scale power generation. However, the need for refrigeration seems to eliminate its application in ambulatory devices such as Tarantela."

Tesla laughed. "It is obvious you have worked with Edison. You have absorbed the man's limited, unimaginative viewpoint."

"I agree he can be difficult, but he has created some amazing inventions."

"Do not be offended by my jest. Truly, Edison's stubbornness will be his downfall. He refuses to acknowledge the superiority of alternating current for transmission of power."

"AC is indeed superior in that respect. I remain skeptical about cryomagnetics, however."

"Allow me to show you something. Hank!" he called across the lab. "You must see this."

"Yes, sir." Hank put down the motor he'd been repairing and joined them.

Tesla opened a nearby metal cabinet. "As you recall, cryoelectric materials require temperatures below that of liquefied nitrogen for their unique properties to manifest."

"Yes. I have seen Edison's cryonics lab. It has a compressor that allows him to liquefy as much air as he needs for his experiments."

"I have discovered materials that enter the cryoelectric state at much higher temperatures. Hank, please fetch a block of dry ice from the freezer. Remember to use the tongs."

"Right," Hank said. He returned with a large white chunk, trailing vapor as he walked. Tesla directed him to set the dry ice in a large ceramic pan in the center of the table.

Tesla placed a flat grayish piece of metal on top of the dry ice. "Let's give this a minute to reach the desired temperature."

"This dry ice stuff is solid," Hank said. "Is it colder than that liquid air Edison uses?"

"Not at all," Tesla explained. "This is carbon dioxide, the gas we exhale from our lungs. It freezes at about the temperature of the coldest winter at the South Pole. Now observe." He picked up a magnet from the table and placed it on top of the chilled metal. The magnet sprang up, and floated in the air an inch above the surface.

"I'll be hornswoggled!" Hank exclaimed. "I know magnets can pull on iron and steel with a powerful force, but push them away? How in blazes does it do that?"

"I have read of this phenomenon but never seen it for myself," Fidelio said, grinning with avid interest. "If I understand correctly, when in the cryoelectric state, a material rejects all magnetic fields. The effect is so strong that a magnet cannot even make physical contact."

"Correct! You are not as ignorant of electromagnetic theory as I assumed."

"I am interested in all fields of knowledge." Fidelio reminded himself that Tesla was not being condescending; the man was above such petty concerns.

"I am working on a composite which will maintain the cryoelectric state at a temperature as high as 25 degrees Centigrade. Just imagine, a train that floats above its tracks."

"The implications are revolutionary," Fidelio said. "Perhaps this technology is appropriate for Tarantela after all."

"Indeed. Your automaton is brilliant. Once we have corrected its minor deficiencies, it will be far greater than any of Edison's creations."

Tesla placed a hand on Fidelio's shoulder – he was wearing gloves of course – but the sensation, even through all those layers of fabric, was enough to give Fidelio goose-flesh.

That was how Tesla worked, jumping from one idea to the next. It was not that the man lacked discipline. Rather, he was wise enough to put a project aside when he was not making progress, and return to it later. It was another way he was unlike Edison, who would work ceaselessly on a single invention until he virtually willed it into existence.

Fidelio, however, grew more disheartened by the day. Just when it seemed they were on the verge of a breakthrough with cryomagnetics, Tesla moved back to magnetic induction, and then to batteries. The man himself was a distraction, with his wild hair and soulful eyes. Each day there were incidents that reinforced Fidelio's obsession; not just eye contact, but also the accidental brush of a hand. Of course, the germ-fearing Tesla would immediately wash after such incidents, yet he told Fidelio, "For someone who works so hard, you have very soft hands."

For once Fidelio was at a loss for words. "Thank you," was all he could manage.

⊗ ᚦᚯ ⊗

Working on Tarantela had once been Fidelio's refuge from the world. Now it reminded him of his failures – the loss of its early prototype, the unnecessary delay in filing the patent, and his inability to verify rumors of the 'war machine.' He spent several hours per week on that last problem, reading periodicals at the public library and writing to his contacts in other cities.

Tesla continued to be a distraction. The man's eccentric personality made it difficult to discern the significance of his mannerisms. Though Fidelio was reluctant to take up the matter with Hank, there was no one else with whom he could confide. He decided to mention it one sunny day as he and Hank ate their noon meal under a tree. Here their conversation would be private, because Tesla did not believe in eating outdoors.

"I can detect the subtle signs," Fidelio said. "The way he stares at me bit too long – even at you sometimes."

Hank began coughing, choking on his sandwich. "Bull-lony! If that was a joke it ain't funny!" He wiped the spilled mustard from his shirt. "Anyhow, it don't prove a thing. Nick is one odd duck. He won't shake hands or eat outdoors. He don't even drink coffee or tea."

"His emphasis on health is not strange, it is admirable."

"I don't know. You seen how he puts ice in his water? That can't be good for a person."

"A glass of cold water is refreshing on a hot day. If more people could make their own ice, the practice would become popular."

"Not for me," Hank said. "But don't jump to no conclusions. Maybe it's normal for men from his country to stare."

"Perhaps." Clearly this discussion made Hank uncomfortable, so Fidelio changed the subject. "By the way, how was your Bible study meeting? Were there any interesting ladies?"

"Nope. The Widow Frey is pert' near eighty, and the parson's daughter is around sixteen."

187

"I believe that would be a marriageable age in Arizona," Fidelio said with a smile.

"Maybe for Mormons and Mexicans. I like a lady with a few years under her belt."

"You prefer a mature woman, then."

"You bet. It takes time for a woman to learn her way around a kitchen. I'm too old to wait for some young filly to learn to make the perfect baking powder biscuits and pecan pie."

⊕ ⼮⅄ ⊕

One evening shortly thereafter, Hank and Fidelio arrived home late from Tesla's lab to find Mrs. Johnson cleaning up in the kitchen. "Good evening, gentlemen," she said.

Her daughter Irene, a tall skinny girl in her early teens, was drying the dishes. "Good evening, Señor Espinoza, Mr. MacMillan."

"Good evening," Fidelio said. "How are you lovely ladies tonight?"

Irene blushed and looked away.

"I'm sorry, but we just finished supper," said Mrs. Johnson. "If you like, I'll put some stew on the stove to warm up."

"Thanks ma'am, that's right kind of you," Hank said. "I got some quick business to attend to. Mind if I use your writing desk?"

"Be my guest. There's paper in the drawer, and a bottle of ink in the well."

The men went to the living room, where the desk was located. "I have purchased some stationery," Fidelio said, pulling a package from his satchel, "to replenish our landlady's supply."

"You're like the little angel feller on my shoulder," Hank grinned. He sat down at the desk, dipped his pen in ink, and began writing.

"You are quite an epistolarian," Fidelio said. "You wrote a letter two nights ago."

"Fidel, you know I'm a Quaker."

"No, as in epistles – oh, never mind," Fidelio leaned over Hank's shoulder for a closer look. "Is it your uncle this time?"

"You know darn well who I'm writing to."

"Miss Hightower again? You said you were no longer smitten with her."

"Nothin' wrong with a man and woman in – what's it called? – a philharmonic friendship." He looked at Fidelio. "I told you the opera's coming to

188

Denver next month, didn't I?"

"You mentioned it several times. I have posted our order for tickets. And the word is *platonic,* by the way."

Hank continued writing. "Much obliged for the grammar lesson. Oh, and you can take the cost of the tickets out of my next week's pay."

"I will." Fidelio took a seat on the divan and watched as his friend wrote. He was glad Hank was being exposed to culture, and his handwriting had improved markedly. Still, his obsession was becoming a problem for both of them. If Tallulah did not respond within a few days, Hank became irritable, like the week after New Year's when he'd tried to give up smoking.

Fidelio decided to act on Tesla's advice. "Speaking of the fairer sex, I have noticed your interest in Maria. Nikola said he would not object if you were to woo her."

"Nick's housekeeper? I admit she's easy on the eye, but she's just a kid. What is she, eighteen, nineteen? Next thing you'll be fixing me up with Irene."

"Do not be ridiculous. Maria does seem fond of you. As you have said, Latin girls marry young. In your search for a wife, you should not ignore any potential candidates."

"Fidel," Hank snapped, "'T'ain't none of your business." He noticed Fidelio's smile and his anger faded. "I can never tell when you're joshin'." He stuffed the letter into an envelope. "I'm going out for a quick puff."

Mrs. Johnson's finicky views on smoking irritated Hank, but gratified Fidelio. He did not mind tobacco smoke so much when fresh, but the stale odor it left behind disgusted him.

⊗ ᛒᚨ ⊗

The following Saturday, Fidelio returned to the boarding house late in the afternoon. He found Hank out back with a hammer and a bucket of nails. He was replacing the broken planks that had fallen off of Mrs. Johnson's back fence.

"*Hola,* Fidel! I was just finishing up." Hank lit a newly-rolled cigarette and inhaled. "How was your trip to the library? Any luck this time?"

Fidelio shrugged. "I found nothing to corroborate the war machine rumors. The American newspapers say nothing at all. However, in the Mexican periodical *La Casera* there was a story about the US Army testing a secret weapon near the border. At the moment it is my only lead."

"You're a regular Sherlock Holmes," Hank laughed. "Which is good, 'cause it

189

ain't gonna be easy. The Army has all kinds of secrets, and the papers are in cahoots with them. Like how they don't report on any of the terrible cruel things the U.S. of A. is doing in the Philippines."

"That is true," Fidelio said. "I approach all news with skepticism. Unfortunately, I have so little information. I have contacted several people, including my professor friends at Rutgers. No one has heard anything new."

"Did you check with Fred Seeley? That feller's a writer. He's got his ear to the ground."

"Yes. He told the same story as Isabelle, with slightly more detail."

"Makes sense, since those two are sweethearts. I mentioned it to Tallulah in my last letter but she didn't know nothing either."

"What about that woman from the Quakers? Did she not travel to Asia as a missionary?"

"Hmm... Suppose she could be in the Philippines. I could write the group and ask."

"Please be discreet. We do not want to attract too much attention."

Fidelio continued his search. He sent a telegram to Doctor Laplace at Rutgers, who had contacts in Washington. Fidelio had been loathe to employ that medium, fearing the scrutiny of the authorities, but he could no longer afford the time it took for a letter to traverse the country.

Each morning, he drove to the Western Union office to check for Laplace's reply. It came in only three days. "NO COMMENT FROM WAR DEPT STOP SPRINGFIELD ARMS FILED PATENT ON SPIDER LIKE DEVICE TWO MONTHS AGO STOP"

Fidelio's heart sank. The thief had added insult to injury by selling his creation to a gun manufacturer. How could he prove the idea was his? Springfield could afford the best attorneys to protect its reputation. Nonetheless, he would hire an attorney to write an inquiry to the Patent Office. He was by no means an expert on the laws governing intellectual property.

On his return to Tesla's laboratory, the sight that greeted Fidelio drove those troubles from his mind. The latest version of Tarantela – nicknamed Octavo, since it was the eighth – walked across the room with a huge piece of metal strapped to its back. "You must see this!" Tesla exclaimed. "It's from an idea that came to me in a dream last night."

"¡Increíble!" Fidelio stared, wide-eyed. "How much does the payload weigh?"

"Thirty pounds, give or take an ounce," Hank said, beaming.

"How is that possible?" He looked again at Tarantela. On the side of its torso were three cylindrical protrusions. "Wait, the coils! You moved them! It made that much of a difference?"

Tesla nodded. "I reworked my calculations; you were right all along. The body of the spider was absorbing too much energy. We simply moved the antennae."

"We also redid the power circuit with bigger cap-a-whatsits," Hank said.

"*Qué fantástico!*" Fidelio exclaimed. "I thought we were months away from a solution."

Tesla straightened his shoulders, an effect that, combined with his impressive height, Fidelio found breathtaking. "I had no doubt we would succeed," he said. "By the way, did you receive a response from your telegram?"

"We can discuss that later. For now, let us bask in the glow of my – um, that is, *our* accomplishment."

"This calls for a toast!" Hank said. "Nick, do you have any hooch on hand?"

"I have Scotch whiskey for a special occasion." He retrieved a bottle from a cabinet by the icebox and the cistern where he kept his drinking water. On the table he set three small glasses and poured a generous amount of liquor into each.

"Thank you no," Fidelio said.

"Just a sip, for luck," Tesla handed him a glass. He raised his own and cried, "*Ziveli!*"

"Cheers!" Hank clinked his glass against both of theirs.

"*Salud!*" Fidelio raised his glass to his lips. The powerful smell took him by surprise; what he had intended as a sip became a gulp. He coughed violently, and could not stop. On the table he spied a glass of water; he grabbed it and swallowed. As he did so, something hard and cold became lodged in his throat. The glass hit the floor with a crash as he gasped for air.

"He's choking!" Hank struck him on his back.

"Step away!" Tesla wrapped his arms around Fidelio and gave him a bear hug.

The hug made Fidelio cough and spit the ice across the room, freeing his air passage. His panic subsided, but the giddiness remained. Tesla set him down gently, then bent over him with a look of grave concern. As Fidelio gazed up at the man he idolized, an overwhelming desire overcame him. He grabbed the back of Tesla's neck, pulled him in, and kissed him on the lips.

Tesla jumped back, eyes wide in astonishment. "*Dodjavola!* Have you gone mad? Do you wish to kill me with a microbial infection?"

Again, Fidelio felt faint. "Beg pardon; in my country men are quite open with their affection." He looked over at Hank, who was staring open-mouthed, at a loss for words.

Tesla soaked a napkin is whiskey, and wiped his face. "The alcohol should kill the worst of the bacteria." He looked at the shards on the floor, then at Fidelio. "You drank from my water glass! Even if you have no concern for your health, you have no right to jeopardize mine."

"Your health?" Fidelio croaked. "I was the one choking."

"It was only ice! Which proves you should not take other peoples' drinks." Tesla turned away from them. "This incident has upset me greatly. Both of you, please leave! Before I can continue working, I must sterilize everything!"

"But we were celebrating," Hank said weakly.

"I need time alone," Tesla said. "Go!"

A short time later, Hank and Fidelio sat in Deirdre's Tea Room, a charming place that Fidelio had recently discovered. Hank puffed his third consecutive cigarette. Luckily they were sitting next to an open window. Fidelio sipped his tea and grimaced; his head was pounding.

The cafe's namesake, a curly-haired matronly woman approached them. "Problem with your tea, sir? Would you fancy more sugar?"

Fidelio, who had been holding his head in his hands, looked up at their hostess. "It is fine as always, madam. I am suffering from a bit of a headache."

"Sorry to hear that, dearie. Might I bring you anything else?"

He smiled weakly. "All right, I would like a scone with butter, please."

Deirdre nodded. "Right away, good sir."

"You okay?" Hank asked. "And what the heck's a scone?"

"It is an English pastry. As for my mental state, I am deeply embarrassed."

"Don't kick yourself. You weren't in your right mind."

Fidelio sighed. "The alcohol, combined with asphyxia, caused me to act rashly. I allowed myself to believe Nikola might someday return my affection. What I desire is never to be."

"Uh, well..." Hank looked as if he wanted to console his friend, but could not find the words.

"I brought you gents an extra." Deirdre said, setting down two plates, each with a scone and a large pat of butter. "Seemed like you might be needing it."

"You are most kind, madam." He turned back to Hank. "I will apologize again and hope he can overlook my indiscretion."

"Don't worry, he won't give us the boot," Hank said, "But even if he does, we already made a heap of progress." He smeared some butter on his scone and took a bite. "Not bad. Definitely needs the butter, though."

"Besides this unfortunate incident," Fidelio said. "I am also upset about what I just discovered." He related to Hank what the professor had said in his letter.

"Holy cats," Hank said. "I was starting to think the fighting spider story was just a tall tale. But it makes sense; Springfield makes tons of weapons for the government."

When they returned to the laboratory, Tesla was working on his magnetic levitation project. "Fidelio," he said, "would you kindly get the meter and measure the field strength?"

"Certainly," Fidelio said. After that, the situation at the laboratory was back to normal, and Tesla did not mention the incident again.

"As you know," Tesla said one morning a few days later, "I have been corresponding with J. P. Morgan."

Fidelio looked up from the mass of melted wiring in the Tarantela he had tested the day before. Tesla's wondrous energy source was tricky to control. It would need some sort of circuitry to prevent excessive current flow. "Did Mr. Morgan agree to provide funding?"

"Not yet. He has, however, put forward an interesting proposition."

"Proposition?" Hank entered the lab, the smoke of his recent cigarette clinging to him.

"J. P. Morgan," Tesla said, "has connections among the mine owners of this state. Aldous Bunker, the proprietor of the largest gold mine in Cripple Creek, has inquired about machinery that could be used to automate the mining process."

Fidelio looked at Tesla. "How much did you tell him?"

"Don't worry, I respect our agreement. I merely stated that a colleague of mine had a revolutionary invention. Mr. Bunker is very interested to see it."

"That's powerful good news," Hank said. He gave Fidelio a congratulatory slap on the shoulder. Ignoring Tesla's dismayed stare, he continued, "With money like that behind you, you could have a laboratory and workshop all your own."

"I would not get excited yet," Fidelio said. "Although we have made some amazing breakthroughs, it will take time to make Tarantela robust enough for hard-rock mining."

Fidelio had other reservations. At the union meetings he had recently been attending, the miners had complained bitterly about conditions at Bunker's mine. The man had extended their workday without any increase in pay, and fired anyone he suspected of being a union organizer. Fidelio feared that Bunker was the kind who would use Tarantela to eliminate jobs rather than improve safety. Yet it was useless to object; Tesla was naïve enough to think his friendship with Morgan would overrule the man's robber-baron instincts.

"Like Columbus," Tesla said, "Our voyage of discovery requires sponsors. Fidelio, would you meet with Mr. Bunker, if Mr. Morgan can set it up?"

"Perhaps, if he would agree to a non-disclosure agreement," Fidelio said. On the other hand, he wondered if that would give him any protection against a man like Bunker.

⚙ ᚱᛉ ⚙

"Fidel, you almost ready?" Hank knocked on the bedroom door. "I swear," he muttered to himself, "that feller takes longer to pretty himself up than a woman."

The door opened. Fidelio's face was covered in shaving cream. "Just one moment."

Hank laughed. "You're shaving the beard? I thought it made you look all dapper-like. Every time I stop shaving I look like an old grizzled prospector."

"It was time for a change." Fidelio peered into the mirror as he scraped his chin with a straight razor. "I wish to look my best for our meeting."

Hank shrugged. "Okay, *amigo*. Tesla is waiting; let's not dawdle."

Tesla was already seated behind the wheel of his four-seat Electrobat wagon. As one might have expected, he was decked out in the latest driving gear, including a duster and goggles, driving gloves and a tweed cap. Hank opened the door and climbed into the back. Fidelio took the passenger seat in front.

"You are in for a treat, gentlemen," Tesla said. "Aldous Bunker is one of the wealthiest men in Colorado Springs. His house was designed by a noted Philadelphia architect and incorporates elements of the Italian Renaissance."

Tesla drove westward down a gravel road that took them out of the city limits to the foothills of the Front Range of the Rockies. Pike's Peak loomed in the

194

distance. He turned right onto a cobblestone trail flanked by stone pillars, past a sign that read 'BUNKER.'

They drove uphill at a steep incline. Around a corner, the mansion came into view. Its facade was spanned by more pillars. A wide oblate dome topped it all.

"Gosh a-mighty!" Hank exclaimed. "This place makes the Chateau De Mores look like the shack I grew up in."

Fidelio turned around and gave Hank a stern look.

They followed Tesla up the long cobblestone walk. Fidelio carried the metal box containing Tarantela, having refused Hank's offer of assistance. At the enormous front door, Tesla rang the bell, and it opened immediately. There stood a diminutive Oriental man who greeted them in broken English. "Welcome. Mr. Bunker expecting you."

They followed him under a huge chandelier and down a hallway floored with coral-pink tiles. As they passed the parlor, a woman sat there reading in a well-padded armchair. Hank could not resist glancing back for a look at her strawberry blonde hair, milky skin, and the rust-colored dress with its plunging neckline. She looked up from her book; he quickly turned his head.

At the end of the hall, they entered a dining room dominated by a long oak table. A stout man sat at one end, puffing a cigar. "Welcome, gentlemen!" He stood up to greet them.

Bunker, who was a bit shorter than Hank, craned his neck to look up at the lanky Serb. "Mr. Tesla, it's an honor to finally meet the man who can call down the thunder like Zeus."

"I am pleased to meet you as well, Mr. Bunker," Tesla shook the man's hand, causing Hank to stare in shock, until he realized that Tesla was still wearing his driving gloves. "These are the gentlemen I told you about." He introduced Fidelio and Hank.

"Please, have a seat. Messrs. Espinoza and MacMillan," he gestured to the two chairs on his right, and "Mr. Tesla," he indicated the one to his left.

My wife is at a charity function, so our dinner will be a modest one." To the butler he said, "Huang, fetch some coffee. And kindly ask my niece to get her nose out of that book and join us."

Chapter 18 – A Demonstration in Vain

Moments after Bunker and his guests had sat down, two petite Mexican girls appeared with trays of food. Shortly thereafter, the young woman from the parlor entered and claimed a seat directly across from Hank.

Bunker glared at her. "Gentleman, this is my niece, Wilhelmina Hill."

"Sorry Uncle," she smiled. "I'm afraid I lost track of time." She looked across the table. "Is this the famous inventor, Mr. Tesla?"

"Yes," Bunker said. "And his associates, Mr. MacMillan and Mr. Espinoza." He cleared his throat. "Now, let's get down to brass tacks. As you can see, business is good. The only fly in the ointment is those damned uppity miners." He looked at Hank. "About your invention..."

"Mr. Espinoza is the inventor, sir," Hank said.

"Yes, sir, the invention is mine," Fidelio said, "though Hank has given me invaluable assistance."

Bunker appraised Fidelio carefully. "Are you Spanish? I see a trace of the Moor in your complexion. Interesting. My sources tell me a mysterious Spaniard has been attending those infernal union meetings. That fellow had a beard, though, and wore tiny wire-rimmed glasses."

"I see," said Fidelio, clearing his throat. "However, I am not Spanish but Cuban."

Hank realized what seemed amiss about Fidelio, besides his new clean-shaven look: he had left his spectacles at home.

The 'modest' meal was actually quite sumptuous, with roast pheasant as the main course. It was difficult for Hank to keep his mind on the food with the young lady sitting so close.

When they had finished eating, Bunker lit another cigar. "So, this wondrous machine, do you have it with you?"

"Yes. I wish to thank you for signing the non-disclosure agreement we sent. We inventors cannot be too careful." Fidelio opened his case, removed the mechanical creature, and set it on the table. "It is called Tarantela, which is a Spanish word for spider. Would you like a demonstration?"

"Please do. Those feet will not scratch the table, will they?"

196

"Do not worry; their soles are padded with felt," Fidelio said.

Bunker looked at his niece. "The non-disclosure agreement includes you, young lady. I do not wish the details of this confidential meeting to end up in one of your gossip articles."

Fidelio's eyes widened at the mention of the word 'gossip.'

The girl smiled sweetly. "No, Uncle, I won't. Besides it isn't *gossip,* it's a society column, and the *Gazette* hasn't even published any of mine yet," she said, pouting.

Bunker shook his head and muttered something under his breath.

Hank looked at her again. She was not just a pretty face, but one smart lady. When she noticed him staring, she smiled. This time, he smiled and nodded in return.

"Observe." Fidelio threw a switch on Tarantela's back. It crawled down the table and stopped at the centerpiece. Fidelio raised a tin whistle to his lips and blew a barely audible note.

Bunker's niece watched indifferently at first, but with increasing interest as the automaton, in response to Fidelio's auditory commands, extended a claw around a crystal candlestick.

The machine continued on to Bunker. Fidelio blew the whistle again. Tarantela stopped and set the candle down gently in front of their host. "Bravo!" cried Bunker. His niece laughed and clapped enthusiastically.

"What else can it do?" Bunker demanded. "Let us see more!"

"You have seen how it utilizes its forelimbs for grasping," Tesla said. "Its main purpose is to perform hazardous or unpleasant tasks. In a mine, it could plant charges and widen tunnels, thereby protecting the workers from accidents."

"But it is controlled by sound," Bunker said. "The mine is a very noisy environment."

"This is an early model," Fidelio answered. "We are currently adapting the device's control system to use Mr. Tesla's wireless telegraphy."

"Ingenious! However, my priority is security. Could you add on some sort of weapon?"

"I would not recommend it," Fidelio said with a grimace, "We could not guarantee that a bullet would not hit an innocent bystander."

"Oh, no guns, of course, too dangerous inside a mine." He puffed his cigar and grinned. "Just a thought, in case the workers get out of hand. But it won't be necessary, especially if you make it man-sized. By its looks alone, it'll scare the hell out

197

of all those Chinks and Micks."

Fidelio winced. Even Hank grimaced at Bunker's remark.

"If you simply need to keep order," Tesla said, "why not hire more guards?"

"I have, but since the cave-in at the Eldorado, they're too scared to go into the mines. Blasted cowards!"

Fidelio exhaled loudly, barely concealing his distaste. "Please bear in mind, sir, that at present the automata are several months away from being ready for industrial use."

Bunker set his cigar in a marble ashtray. "I appreciate your honesty, but it's not too early to begin thinking about applications for your invention. Of course, the sooner you could deliver me a dozen or so man-sized spiders, the happier I'd be."

"Of course," Tesla said, glancing over at Fidelio. "We thank you for your time, sir."

They got up from their seats. As Fidelio and Tesla headed for the hallway, Hank lingered behind to speak to Bunker's niece. "Pardon, miss, what book were you reading?"

She gave him an amused smile. "*Pride and Prejudice*, by Jane Austen. Are you familiar with her work?"

"Why yes. They had us read one in school. Something about a girl named Emily."

"That's *Emma*. I am impressed, sir. In this town there is a distressing dearth of interest in culture. It took me considerable time to find a literary discussion group. We meet every Tuesday evening, at Councilman Tyler's house on Nevada Avenue."

"Is that so? I'm down-right fascinated with cultural things."

Wilhelmina smiled and nodded. "I believe I jotted down the information on the back of one of my calling cards." She opened a tiny purse. "Ah here, it is."

Hank took the card in both hands and read it. The name 'Wilhelmina Charlotte Hill' was embossed in bold lettering. "Thank you, miss. Ah, it says 'journalist.' That's right, you were talking about working for the *Gazette,* weren't you?"

"It is something I'm working on. Up to now my work has all been freelance, but I hope to someday be employed in a more permanent capacity."

Aldous Bunker gave a snort of derision as he passed by. She responded with an evil glare, then turned back to Hank. "Well, Mr. MacMillan, it has been a real pleasure meeting you."

"For me as well. Until next time, Miss Hill."

Fidelio said nothing until they were back in Tesla's automobile. "Hank, I applaud your boldness. She is beautiful, intelligent, and apparently unmarried."

"Yep, but I'm not counting my chickens yet. How can such a fine lady not have a beau?"

"Perhaps she is waiting for the right man to come along," Tesla said.

"As for her uncle," Fidelio said, "I am repulsed by the man's attitude. I would never want to see Tarantela employed in support of his anti-labor agenda."

"That is your decision," said Tesla. "I would advise you to remain neutral. In any case, I hear there has been plenty of name-calling and thuggery on the part of both the owners and the workers."

"Sure is a coincidence," Hank said with a chuckle, "about that Spanish union rabble rouser. I never knew you had yourself a twin."

"Yes, that is quite amazing," said Fidelio, scowling at Hank's attempt at humor.

"Don't be discouraged, pardner," Hank said. "There's got to be mine owners who treat their workers better. We'll do a deal with them, and drive that old devil Bunker out of business."

"That would please me greatly," said Fidelio.

After the meeting with Bunker, Fidelio contacted an attorney to draft a complaint letter for the Patent Office. Then he threw himself into his work.

"My first priority," he said, "is to produce a larger version which can operate on Tesla's magnetic induction power, and a more portable and efficient coil for the broadcast."

"Don't worry about the second one," Hank said. "Nick's already got me building a new coil, half the size of the first."

Fidelio nodded. "We are fortunate to have his assistance. Still, there is much to be done. Regretfully, I will no longer have time to attend union meetings."

"Cripple Creek's a long drive," Hank said, "and it sounds like Bunker's got eyes everywhere. Best you lay low for a spell."

"I am gratified by your concern," Fidelio smiled slyly, "Or perhaps are you worried about the disapproval of a certain young lady?"

Hank laughed. "I don't know what the heck you're talkin' about. Though I might just go to her book club on Tuesday. 'Cause I like to read."

At that, Fidelio laughed out loud.

That next morning, Fidelio awoke from a terrible dream. He was at a meeting of the Western Federation of Miners. The one-eyed union leader 'Big Bill' Haywood, was at the podium. There was a gunshot, and Bill fell to the floor. In the hall's doorway stood a petite red-blonde woman with a revolver. She pointed the gun at Fidelio, a satisfied smirk on her face.

What on earth did it mean? Fidelio knew better than to interpret dreams literally. Freud would probably say that he had deep-seated anger against women, from growing up without a mother. More likely it was envy. After losing both Rodrigo and August, Fidelio was forced to endure his loneliness as Hank enjoyed the intoxicating initial stages of a new relationship.

Fidelio quickly shaved and got dressed. Hank was at the breakfast table with their fellow boarder, a traveling salesman called Mahoney, who was completely absorbed in his newspaper. Mrs. Johnson was busy serving eggs, biscuits and gravy. "Morning, boys," she said.

"*Buenos días, señora.*"

When he saw Fidelio, Hank's smile faded. "Looks like you had a rough night."

Without a word, Fidelio poured himself a cup of coffee from the pot on the table.

Hank smiled sympathetically. "You must be mighty upset to drink coffee."

Fidelio took a sip and grimaced. "I have been thinking about what Aldous Bunker said. I fear that he is plotting to shortchange the working men of this state."

"That's as plain as the nose on his face," Hank said. "But what can we do about it?"

Fidelio shrugged. "There is someone I need to see. Kindly inform Nikola that I will be out for the morning. I will drive you to the laboratory and be on my way."

"I'd be happy to tag along, if I can be of any help."

"I would appreciate that," Fidelio said. "It could be hazardous, however. When I last went there, I believe I was being followed."

Hank shrugged. "What's a little danger between friends?"

The two men got into the Steamer. After a brief stop at Tesla's lab to inform him of their plans, they were off to a village called Divide at the edge of the mining district.

"Where we headed?"

"The Gold Dust Saloon. It is frequented by miners, both current and retired."

Hank laughed, "It's a tad early for me, and you don't even drink."

"They do serve breakfast. Although, seeing as we have already eaten, I am going there only to meet with someone."

When they entered the hazy atmosphere of the tavern, Hank was surprised at the number of patrons. He was even more surprised when several men greeted Fidelio, calling him Ludovico, which as Hank recalled, was his middle name.

"We looking for anyone in particular?" Hank asked.

"There she is, at the end of the bar."

"She?" Hank had noticed her without realizing it was a woman. She was tall for a lady and sturdily built, wearing dungarees and a man's checkered shirt. Her short brown hair was mostly covered by a Confederate Army cap. Between her teeth was a long-stemmed clay pipe.

"Lil, this is my friend Hank," Fidelio said. "Hank, this is Lillian Hutmacher, the only woman to work at both the Chaparral and Bunker Hill mines."

Lil set down her pipe and shook Hank's hand, nearly crushing his fingers. "Folks call me Dainty," she grinned, showing a gold tooth, "'cause I ain't. There's not a man alive I can't match in drinkin', cussin' or fightin.'" In front of her was an enormous plate of fried potatoes and eggs and a huge mug of coffee. "It's been a while, Ludo. I thought you'd got too fancy for this dump."

Fidelio chuckled. "Not at all. In fact, I missed the intellectual stimulation."

"Ha!" She took a swallow of coffee. "You've got something up your sleeve, don't ya?"

"Indeed, I have a question. Is Big Bill still in the area?"

"Of course. Why you asking me? I thought you went to all the WFM meetings."

"I need to speak to him," Fidelio repeated. At this point the bartender, a curvaceous but tough-looking woman with wild blond hair, interrupted him to ask for his order. "Black tea, please." He turned back to Lil and lowered his voice. "Recently we spoke with Aldous Bunker."

"That money-grubbing son of a bitch?"

"The same. It appears that he has spies at the union meetings. He made a point of saying that 'a Spanish fellow,' as he put it, had been stirring up trouble."

"Oh." She smiled as she refilled her pipe. "Your twin brother, right? He didn't see any family resemblance?"

"The description was of a bearded man with glasses. I had left my spectacles at home."

"Oh, you shaved! No wonder you looked different!" She sighed, "We figured they was sending infiltrators; there's our proof. I'll tell Bill you need to see him. You still work for that crazy Russian?"

"Serbian," he corrected. "Some may think him crazy, because his genius is beyond their comprehension."

"Okay. I'll have him send a messenger to that guy's lab. And now I got to get to work." She got off her stool, went behind the bar and began washing the piled up dishes. The blonde whispered something in her ear and giggled. In response, Lil gave her a slap on the butt and then kissed her on the lips, lingering for a moment too long for any sort of friendly greeting.

Hank glanced at Fidelio, who just smiled and nodded. Once more, the cowboy was dumbfounded.

The next day, a lad on a velocipede arrived at Tesla's door with a sealed envelope. Fidelio tore it open. "It is from Bill. He wants me to meet him at Julio's Restaurant at 7 PM."

"You don't look happy about it," Hank said.

"He is a great man, but as a legend in the labor community, I find him intimidating." He folded the note and put it in his pocket. "Would you care to accompany me?"

"You bet. I'm there for you, *amigo*."

Hank and Fidelio arrived at the restaurant at the prearranged time. Big Bill Haywood sat at a table in the back. He was a tall dark-haired fellow wearing brown trousers and a black jacket. As the man stood up to shake their hands, Fidelio was once again jarred by his missing right eye. The story was that Big Bill had lost it as a boy and never bothered to get a glass replacement, nor did he wear an eye patch.

"Evening, Ludo," he said, using Fidelio's 'radical' alias. "Who's your friend?"

"The name's Hank. Pleased to meet you, sir."

"Likewise. Have a seat." He waved a hand toward the empty chairs. "Lil said you had something important to tell me, but she wouldn't say what it was."

"I did not want to speak of it at the Gold Dust," Fidelio replied. "When I tell you the story, you will understand why."

Haywood sipped his beer as he listened to Fidelio's story. When it was finished he said, "Mechanical critters? Sounds like you've been plotting with the capitalists to eliminate our jobs."

"Not at all," said Fidelio. "If it is done correctly, nobody need lose his job. We can accomplish greater efficiency with far less risk to life and limb."

"But greater efficiency means they wouldn't need to hire as many of us, doesn't it?"

"Not necessarily. Automation could be coupled with a shorter working day. Productivity would remain constant or even increase, so your wages need not suffer."

"More time to spend fishin', or with your families," Hank said.

"I'll have to give that some thought," Haywood said. "I appreciate, though, that you advocate it for the sake of labor and not for the capitalists."

"I consider myself a syndicalist," Fidelio said, "and I believe that workers will someday be the owners of all the factories, mills, and mines."

"That's what the Industrial Workers of the World is about," Haywood replied. "The WFM is just one brigade in the war. And this will be a major battle. First, we must eliminate the spies. And second, we need to stop reactionaries like Bunker from replacing us with machines."

Hank grimaced. "You wouldn't hurt anybody, would you? I agree the owners can be too greedy, but the good Lord don't want us fighting evil with more evil."

Haywood laughed and slapped Hank on the shoulder. "Don't worry; we won't hurt those guys – least not *too* bad. Mostly we'll make sure they're *unwelcome* at our meetings."

Hank appeared at the door of Fidelio's room with a worried look on his face. "How do I look, Fidel? I don't want to go to the book club looking like a tramp."

Fidelio looked at his friend and smiled. "You look *maravilloso* – splendid. The blue shirt matches your eyes. I have never seen you part your hair in the middle like that, but it suits you."

"Honest? The kids at school used to say my hair was the color of mud."

"Nonsense. It is the rich hue of Mediterranean sand."

Hank laughed. "Thank you kindly. And a whole bunch for letting me drive the Steamer."

"You are welcome. When you arrive, you are sure to impress your lady friend."

Hank was nervous about driving the Steamer by himself. Without Fidelio to help him keep an eye on the gauges, would he be able to focus on the road? But it was actually a cakewalk. He smiled as the passersby stared at him going down the street. Finding the councilman's house was also easy, as it was on a main thoroughfare.

He parked the car on the street and headed up the long walkway with his copy of *Pride and Prejudice* in hand. The house was huge. He stood at the door and took a deep breath. Then he grabbed the antique lion-face door knocker and rapped it three times.

A tiny woman in a black dress and white apron answered the door. "May I help you?"

"Good evening, I'm Hank MacMillan. I'm here for the lit-er-ary society."

"One moment." The maid gave him a puzzled look and disappeared, closing the door behind her.

The door reopened, this time by a chestnut-haired lady in a long blue dress. "I am Mrs. Ida Tyler. Please come in, Mr. MacMillan. I apologize that we were not expecting you. Are you from the college?"

He stepped inside. "No ma'am, I'm not any kind of professor, though I do aim to broaden my mind. Pleased to make your acquaintance. I heard about this from Miss Wilhelmina Hill."

As Hank spoke her name, she entered the hallway with a sphinx-like smile. Her gown was deep green, more modest than the previous one. "Mr. MacMillan, what a pleasant surprise."

"Well, I was curious what your group might be like, so I came to have a look-see. And please, call me Hank."

She arched her eyebrows. "Perhaps next time. For now we'd best stay somewhat formal." She motioned down the hallway. "Come along, I'll introduce you to the group."

As they entered the parlor, Hank was shocked to discover he was the only man there. When would he learn to think things out before acting? For a moment, he considered leaving, but Wilhelmina had already begun introducing him to the five other ladies. They ranged in age from twenties to sixties. Four were "Mrs.", though their hostess noted that one was a widow. Besides Wilhelmina, the only other "Miss" was a retired schoolteacher who was getting on in years.

"Please have a seat, Mr. MacMillan." Mrs. Tyler directed him to a settee in the center of the room, next to Wilhelmina. "Would you care for some tea?"

"Why, sure." Hank felt like a giant as he accepted the tiny china cup. He'd always thought tea was a ladies' drink, but with a bit of sugar, it wasn't so bad. As he struggled to balance the book, cup and saucer, he wished there was something stronger in there. Hopefully the ladies would chat among themselves and ignore him.

"Mr. MacMillan," said the schoolmarm, almost startling him into dropping his cup, "I see you have a copy of *Pride and Prejudice*, the book we have been discussing. Please share with us, what is your favorite part?"

"Well I...," he cleared his throat. He had a moment of panic, since he hadn't gotten past Chapter Two. "I like it a lot. I got a chuckle when the father said he wouldn't go see the new neighbor, and then surprised them by visiting the feller without telling any of the girls."

That earned him a laugh from the ladies, except for Wilhelmina, who regarded him quizzically. Despite his best efforts, Hank blushed. Hopefully he was off the hook now.

The ladies, however, were not done with him. They plied him with questions and discreetly mentioned their unmarried daughters, which seemed too obvious even to Hank. After what seemed like an hour of interrogation, they returned to discussing the book.

Later on, as they finished their discussion of Chapter 8, Wilhelmina suddenly said, "Goodness look at the time. I hate to desert this lovely gathering but I promised Uncle I would be home by nine PM." She glanced at Miss Spinster; apparently they'd arrived together.

"My dear, I was not quite ready to depart," she said.

Hank jumped to his feet, nearly spilling his tea. "I'd be happy to take you, Miss Hill."

Wilhelmina smiled. "If it would not be too much trouble."

"No trouble at all." Finally he could make his escape from this nerve-racking little soiree. Hank grinned as they headed out the door together. "Evening, ladies, and thank you kindly!"

Wilhelmina brightened when she saw the Steamer. "Good gracious, is this yours?"

"Nope. It belongs to Fidelio, but I'm saving up for one of my own."

He helped her into the car. "I apologize if this evening was awkward for you," she said.

"Nope, not at all," he said with a cough. He started the car and pulled into the street. They rode in uncomfortable silence. As they approached the Bunker mansion, Hank summoned all his courage. "Have you been to Deirdre's Tea Room? Fidel loves the place. They have this dessert thing called a scone. I could meet you there, or my friend and me both, if that'd be more proper."

She smiled. "I *am* familiar with scones. If you wish to bring your friend, I shall bring a friend as well. I believe I'm free next week Friday evening."

Hank suppressed a chuckle at the thought of her bringing a girl for Fidelio. Then he remembered Tallulah's performance in Denver – but no, that was Saturday. He smiled and tried to act calm and confident. "That'd be just dandy, Miss Wilhelmina."

⚙ ⼓⼈ ⚙

"I still can't believe it," Hank said as they entered the lab. "You, a regular at a saloon! And all the fellers knew you by name – well, sort of. So you going back to talk to Lil again?"

"No, not today. I never said I was going to the Gold Dust. My plans for today are completely different."

Tesla was already at work, testing ceramics for cryomagnetic properties. Without looking up at his coworkers, he continued immersing each sample in a fuming bath of liquid nitrogen.

"Good morning Nikola," Fidelio said. "How are the experiments proceeding?"

"About as expected. I have seen small improvements in the rare earth blends, but nothing yet of practical value."

"Do you require assistance?" Fidelio asked him.

"Why do you ask? I overheard you saying something about having other plans."

Fidelio and Hank looked at each other in surprise. Tesla would often miss things that people said to him directly.

"As a matter of fact," Fidelio said, "There is something I need to do this morning."

"Then by all means, go." Tesla waved them away and immediately looked back at his experiment. "Don't worry, I will manage."

Shortly thereafter, Fidelio and Hank were on the road.

"I appreciate your company," Fidelio said. "I realize I have said it before, but this journey could be particularly dangerous."

"You talk like I'm some kind of greenhorn. I've been in plenty of dangerous situations before. I'm sure I can handle whatever you're throwin' at me."

"I do not follow that argument. I would think your experiences would make you want to avoid such risks all the more, especially after the psychological trauma of warfare."

"You know what they say about getting back on the horse," Hank said. "If

I'm gonna get over my problem, I've got to get out there and take some chances. Besides, this must be darn important, to get you out of the lab. Now can you tell me where we're going?"

"I apologize for being secretive. Sometimes knowledge can put people at risk. I heard a rumor that the Blue Mountain Mine, which is owned by an associate of our friend Bunker, had received a shipment of automata from the East."

"You don't say! But how will we know for sure? They ain't about to shout it from the mountaintop."

"I concur. We shall perform surveillance of the facility from afar. If these machines are indeed my stolen design, I intend to take possession of one."

Hank was aghast. "I'm in enough trouble with the Lord as it is. I don't aim to break no commandments."

"The law might call it theft, but I would only be taking what has been stolen from me."

"You got a point," said Hank. "But no judge is gonna say, 'Poor feller, you got the shaft from the evil companies. Case dismissed.' No, he'll say, 'Grand theft, five years in the hoosegow.'"

"Only if they catch us," Fidelio said. "Do not worry. I doubt we shall get close enough to be detected on this first mission."

Chapter 19 – A Grave Injustice

"*First* mission?" Hank exhaled loudly. "You're sayin' you mean to go more than once?"

"Only if it is necessary," Fidelio said.

"All right, but I ain't going to steal nothin'. At most I might agree to distract 'em while you do the stealing."

"I see." Fidelio resisted the urge to point out the flaws in that reasoning, lest he risk Hank changing his mind.

When they had almost reached the town of Cripple Creek, Fidelio turned onto a dirt trail leading up a hill. He could feel Hank's eyes on him as he drove right past a 'No Trespassing' sign.

"The problem with this plan," Hank said, his voice quavering with the jarring of the vehicle, "is that somebody's almost sure to see us."

"Do you think I would not consider that? This is an alternate route, not heavily traveled. Big Bill says the workers typically follow the rail spur that carries the ore, about a mile north of here."

They ascended the hill slowly. Fidelio had expected a forest, but it was mostly scrub, with rocky areas between. Hank looked around nervously as they went. Though the Steamer was quieter than most automobiles, it was still too large for easy concealment. Finally they found a good place behind a rock outcropping topped with scraggly junipers.

Fidelio reached into the car's storage compartment and withdrew a map, which he unfolded and studied. "We are approximately a hundred yards from the crest of the hill. From there, we shall observe the mine entrance."

"Okay," Hank said. "But won't the spiders all be down below?"

"Space within the mine is at a premium. They will not store them underground, so hopefully we will see one." Fidelio got out of the car, and opened the trunk. "Take this, please." He handed Hank a small satchel.

"Ah, you've got a Tarantela in here, don't you? I'll bet it's got the camera attachment like you was using when we drove through Wyoming."

"But of course," Fidelio said with a smug smile. He picked up a leather case containing a pair of binoculars. "Let us be on our way. While the sky remains overcast, it will be more difficult for someone to spot us."

They walked up the hill as quietly as they could manage. Hank put a cigarette in his mouth and then put it back in his pocket before Fidelio could chastise him. "Sorry, *amigo*," he said with a sigh. "Force of habit."

At the summit they paused behind a large boulder. The mine entrance was completely visible from their vantage point. They took turns using the binoculars. The mine was a flurry of activity, with workers milling about, and a train of empty ore cars being pulled in.

"No sign of any mechanical critters," Hank said. He handed the binoculars to Fidelio.

"It may be a long wait." He took another look. "*Dios mio!* There it is!" It was at least eight feet tall. Fidelio shuddered; this was how he had first envisioned his creation. The multi-legged machine emerged from a fenced storage area, followed by a worker carrying a metal box.

"Let me see," Hank accepted the binoculars from Fidelio. "By golly, it's the spitting image of Tarantela, only ten times larger."

"*Esos bastardos diabólicos. Hijos de putas, malditos ladrones!*" He continued with a string of muttered oaths that could have made a sailor blush, provided he understood Spanish.

"Settle down, *amigo*," Hank warned. "They might just hear you from all the way down there. Tell me, was I seeing things or was there a cable coming out of the spider's back?"

"Yes, it is exactly like Tarantela's prototype. The automaton must be tethered to an operator."

Hank lowered the field glasses and looked at Hank. "Those dirty bastards, they stole your baby. I'd be hoppin' mad too if I was you."

"Believe me, I am not happy about this, not in the least."

"At least it ain't as good as yours is," Hank said, taking another look. "This danged thing walks like a newborn foal. Plus that cable means they can't work it by radio waves."

"Hand me the glass, please." As Fidelio watched the spider, he bit his lip in frustration. "This is exactly what I feared. *Puta madre!* I am sickened to my very soul."

"Land o' Goshen, you got to be upset to cuss like that," Hank said. "We got to do something. We could take a picture, but it's going to look damn tiny from here.

Should we try and send Tarantela down there?"

Fidelio exhaled, now regaining control of his emotions. "That was my plan. With the new battery, its range is several hundred yards. Our primary limitation is time. If only we could use Tesla's coil, but the distance is too great. Hand me the satchel, please."

Fidelio opened the case, set the miniature spider on the ground and adjusted its settings.

Hank watched over his shoulder. "Holy cow, you painted it!"

"The French call it *camouflage*. The mottled brown coloring will help it to avoid being seen. If someone does catch a glimpse of it, they will assume it to be a small mammal."

"I learned about that camo stuff in the Army. Still, that's mighty clever, pardner."

They sent the automaton scuttling into the brush. Hank watched it through the binoculars, while Fidelio worked the remote control.

Getting Tarantela to the mine was a slow process. Fidelio walked it between patches of brush and scrub for concealment. Near the mine entrance, the plant life dwindled, so he guided it between piles of rock, outbuildings, and unused mine cars.

"I wish I knew what it's seeing," Hank said. "Too bad it can't send pictures by wireless."

"Someday that may be possible." Fidelio took a peek above the big rock that concealed them. "Say, is that another one?"

Hank swung the binoculars over. "Yep, it's another spider. By the way, how will Tarantela know what to look at? You said it was blind as a bat."

"Bats are not blind. Remember, besides sound, Tarantela can now sense heat and motion, as does the pit viper."

"Viper? You mean like a rattler?"

"Exactly." Fidelio stared into the valley. "I can see very little at this distance. Could you please hold the binoculars so I can see?"

"You got it, pardner." Hank held the spyglass up to Fidelio's face, leaving his friends' hands free to work the controls.

The oversized spider walked across the mine yard with its operator close behind. Tarantela followed them both a few yards back. Each time Fidelio pressed the 'shutter' button, the spider responded with an electrical pulse that caused the controller to emit a 'beep' sound. Still, they would not know if any of the photographs were good until they were developed.

"I have seen enough." Fidelio pulled back a lever on the control box. The small spider turned and headed back up the hill. "I was hoping the activity outside the mine would subside around this time of day. We will need to return late at night if we wish to obtain one of their counterfeit machines."

Tarantela came to a halt ten yards away from them, its battery power exhausted. Fidelio went to retrieve it, removed the camera, then packed the device back in its case.

They hurried back to the Steamer, once again trying to go as silently as possible. The sun was setting by the time they reached the base of the hill and were on their way back to Colorado Springs.

"This really gets my dander up," Hank said. "It's obvious they stole your invention. If we get a chance to take one, I'll sure help you pinch it."

"Thank you, my friend. Your support means the world to me."

A full moon was rising into the darkening sky when Hank spoke up. "You know, Fidel, that car has been following us since we turned off the mine road."

"Perhaps it is just a coincidence. To be on the safe side, I shall go faster." As Fidelio accelerated, the other car matched his speed.

"He's following us for sure."

"Hold on," Fidelio shouted over the wind as he accelerated again. "We are moving at an unsafe speed."

The other car's engine roared. It pulled passed them on the left, skirting the edge of the road. In the twilight, Fidelio could not see the occupants. The mysterious vehicle was well ahead of them when it suddenly stopped in the middle of the road. The rear of the Steamer skidded to the side as Fidelio slammed on the brakes. "*Idiota!*"

"Is that joker tryin' to kill us?" Hank shouted.

The Steamer's headlights shone on the other vehicle, which stood at an angle in the middle of the road. It was a large car, a four-seater. The front door flew open and a short stocky man emerged, wearing dark pants and a sport coat.

"He does not look very threatening," Fidelio said.

"Look at his jacket," Hank said, "He's packing a pistol."

Next the rear door opened and a huge bald-headed man got out, dressed in worker's gray coveralls. A third man, even bigger than the previous one, emerged from the far side of the vehicle. Both carried large wooden clubs.

"Let's get the hell out of here!" Hank cried.

"I concur." Fidelio pulled back the gear shift and pulled out the throttle. The wheels threw gravel as the car lurched backward.

"Stop!" Hank yelled. "Another car! What is this horse shit?"

The Steamer stopped again, hemmed in by the two interlopers. Fidelio turned and looked behind, then reached into the glove compartment for his pistol.

"Drop it," a voice shouted, "or we'll fill you fill of lead. Hands up, both of you!"

Fidelio's gun clunked to the floorboard. Two more men disembarked from the second car, and there was now a shotgun in addition to the revolver pointed at their heads.

The club-wielding ruffians from the first car approached and flanked the Steamer, one on each side. The small man came to the driver's side door. "Get out of the car."

"By whose authority?" Fidelio demanded.

"Mine, you God-damned Mexican dandy." He nodded at his bald henchman, who yanked open the door, grabbed Fidelio by his shoulders, and pulled him out of the car.

"Hey!" Hank yelled. "Get your mitts off my friend!"

"Shut up, hayseed, or we'll shoot you both!"

The man dragged Fidelio by his arm, stopping in the road between the Steamer and the first car. The other goon stood behind and pinned back both of the Cuban's arms. Fidelio felt as if they might be wrenched from their sockets.

The short man glared at him. "Where is it? Where's the spider?"

"What?" Fidelio was too surprised to attempt an answer. The short man stepped forward and punched him in the stomach. *"Hijo de puta!"*

"No!" Hank jumped out of the Steamer, heedless of the guns pointed his way.

There was a dull thud as a henchman's club connected with Hank's head. He collapsed to the ground. Three men descended on him, kicking him savagely.

"Stop!" Fidelio cried. "I will answer you."

"That's enough, boys." He turned back to Fidelio. "You know what I mean. The thing you stole from the mine. Johnson, search the car."

"I stole nothing!"

Ignoring Fidelio's objection, one of the thugs broke open the Steamer's trunk with a crowbar. He and another ruffian tossed Fidelio's belongings on the ground until one of them found and opened the satchel. "Here it is, boss!"

"Don't forget the camera. They said they was taking pictures. Help him look for it, Joe!"

There was the sound of another engine and a honking horn. Yet another vehicle had arrived. An unfamiliar voice yelled, "What's going on here?" Three men strode up in khaki uniforms. "Jack, I told you to stay out of this county."

"I'm not the lawbreaker," the short man said. "We caught these scoundrels trespassing on private land and stealing company property. It was in Teller County, outside your jurisdiction."

"Well, you're in El Paso County now, and I won't have vigilantes operating on my turf. Get the hell out before I arrest the lot of you."

"We got him out-numbered, boss," one of the henchmen said.

"You got a death wish, jackass? My deputies got my back, and they're all crack shots. And put down that mechanical thing, that's evidence!"

"Drop 'em," Jack ordered. The man holding Tarantela and the camera hurled them at the ground with full force. The camera bounced a foot in the air and a claw flew off the spider.

"No!" Fidelio croaked.

"Sheriff," Jack said, "You'll be hearing from our employers, and they won't be happy."

"They can go screw themselves." Doors and engines roared as the ruffians drove away. "Hey fancy boy," the sheriff addressed Fidelio. "You need help getting up, or you just like laying in the road like a horse turd?"

"I am fine." Fidelio struggled to his feet. "But my friend there..."

"Check on the cowboy," the sheriff ordered one of his deputies, a scrawny buck-toothed fellow. "Make sure they didn't kill him."

The deputy knelt down by Hank. "Nah, he's still breathing."

"Thank you, Sheriff," Fidelio said. "I believe those ruffians meant to murder us."

"Don't thank me just yet." He grabbed Fidelio's arms as one of the deputies fastened metal cuffs over his wrists. "'Cause you're under arrest."

"Why? What on earth is the charge?"

"Theft, and causing a disturbance."

"They were lying. The equipment they tried to steal," he pointed to the spider, "belongs to me. It is they who are the thieves."

"You can tell it to the judge. Clem, help Jenkins load that other guy in the wagon."

"What about my automobile?"

"We'll drive it in. It'll be safe in the impound yard. Don't worry, you'll get a trial. We believe in law and order in these parts."

A short time later, Fidelio found himself sharing a jail cell with Hank. He had once been beaten by the police at a labor march in Spain, but his current bleak mood was worse than the pain he had endured back then.

Hank lay quietly on the wooden bench, bruised and bloodied. He opened his eyes and looked at Fidelio. "What the heck are you taking off your clothes for?"

"It is only my shirt," Fidelio replied. "Since the deputies refused to provide you with dressing for your wound, I am forced to improvise." He grabbed the shirt in both hands, gritted his teeth, and tore off the left sleeve.

"Hey! You don't have to wreck your fancy togs on my account."

"It shall be easily replaced," he said as he turned to the right sleeve and ripped it free as well. "Much more easily than your bodily tissues if they succumb to infection." He donned the ruined shirt and set to work dressing the worst of Hank's wounds.

"Much obliged, amigo," Hank said. "Sorry you had to ruin your shirt."

" It is I who should apologize. I should not have gotten you into this predicament."

"It's not that. I've been in the clink before. It's just that my gut hurts like hell. Those sons of bitches – pardon my French."

"French?" Fidelio rolled his eyes. "It is a terrible injustice, but we are alive and well."

"Well? I feel like I've been rode hard and put away wet." Hank doubled over and coughed violently, spitting blood all over his face and shirt.

"Hank!" Fidelio pulled out his handkerchief and wiped his friend's face. "You are injured. Lie still!"

Hank groaned. "Feel horrible. Wilhelmina... Tallulah... Denver."

"Yes, you are quite the ladies' man." Fidelio's attempt at levity fell flat, as he realized what Hank meant. Tomorrow was their appointment to meet Bunker's niece at the tea house. The day after that was Tallulah's performance in Denver. It seemed likely they would miss both.

"Do not worry, Hank. There will be other operas." Hearing no answer, he became alarmed. "Hank! Stay with me! You should not sleep after a head injury!" Fearful of hurting his friend further, he gave his face a light slap. Again, there was no response.

He put his ear on Hank's chest. "Hank, wake up!" Fidelio had not felt so helpless since the mine collapse that had taken Rodrigo's life. His eyes began to water; he could feel his throat closing up as he fought the urge to weep.

Fidelio stood and grabbed the bars of the cell. Attempting to shake them made no noise. "Guard! This man needs a doctor!"

"Shut up, Paco," came a voice from around the corner. "We don't pay no mind to no-account agitators around here."

"I insist on my right to contact an attorney!"

"We ain't got no telephone, you stupid greaser." laughed the deputy.

Fidelio huffed in exasperation. "That is not true! I saw one on the way in!"

The deputy ignored all his subsequent entreaties. Fidelio slouched down on his bunk and fought back tears. The night passed like an eternity. Hank lay perfectly still, breathing regularly, but just barely. Finally, out of sheer exhaustion, Fidelio fell asleep on the hard bunk.

The following days were hellish; not so much from the confinement and the runny gruel they fed him, but seeing his friend lying injured and unconscious. Periodically Fidelio checked under Hank's bandages for signs of infection. At times Hank awakened briefly and Fidelio tried to get him to sip some water. Most alarming was the blood that sometimes dribbled from Hank's mouth. Fidelio called out to demand a doctor, but the deputies ignored his pleas.

Fidelio barely slept at all, until the third night of their incarceration, when exhaustion overtook him. Normally in times of stress he dreamed of Rodrigo, but this time he was at the St. Paul opera house, watching Tallulah. In the midst of the song she stopped singing, and turned to address the audience.

"I have legal representation," she huffed. 'I will not tolerate this miscarriage of justice."

One of the male singers responded in a whiny, backwoods accent. "The Sheriff said nobody was to see the prisoner."

Fidelio opened his eyes, and realized that the dream conversation was really happening.

"Fine," said the female voice. "My attorney will require your name for the lawsuit."

"Okay, okay." A wooden chair creaked as the deputy got to his feet. "C'mon, follow me."

"I'm not going into your filthy jail. I have the bail money. I demand they be released."

"All right, no need to make a stink." There were footsteps in the hall, and Deputy Clem appeared at the cell door, inserting a key in the lock. "It's your lucky day, Paco."

The deputy took him out front, where Tallulah and Isabelle waited with a short well-dressed stranger with thick spectacles. Conscious of his hygiene, Fidelio resisted the urge to hug his friends. "Ladies, I shall be eternally grateful! But I fear for Hank. He has lost consciousness and they have refused my pleas for medical attention."

Tallulah glared at the jailer. "You didn't send for a doctor?"

"He looked fine to me." The deputy sighed. "All right, I'll get the stretcher." He walked away muttering to himself. "Damned uppity Injuns and Hebes."

Clem and another deputy returned with Hank suspended between them on a filthy canvas stretcher. "He's all yours." Abruptly they set him down, almost dropping him to the hard floor.

"Are you trying to kill him?" Fidelio snarled. Clem just shrugged in response.

"Mister Gellman," Tallulah addressed the well-dressed man, "could you please help us get him to the hospital?"

"Certainly, madam." He gave the deputy a sharp look. "When I return I shall have a court order for you and Sheriff Jones to explain yourselves."

Gellman's automobile, one of the new four-door Stanleys, was parked out front. He and Fidelio carried Hank out in the stretcher with the ladies leading the way. As they were lifting Hank into the back seat he muttered, "Tallulah... love you... always."

Isabelle, eyes wide, looked at her companion. Neither woman said a word.

"Mr. Gellman," Fidelio said. "I must retrieve my own vehicle from the impound yard. Where are you taking him? Give me the directions and I shall meet you there."

"St. Francis," said Gellman, "on Woodmen Road. They'll take good care of your friend."

Fidelio was relieved to see Tarantela – or rather, its component pieces – on the front seat of the Steamer. At least there was fuel in the tank. He drove to the hospital, where he joined Tallulah and Isabelle in the waiting room. Gellman had brought them there and gone on his way.

"Did you speak to the doctor?" Fidelio asked.

"Not directly," Isabelle said. "But his prognosis is good." She looked at Fidelio.

"And what about you? Would you like to see a doctor?"

Fidelio shook his head. "Besides being treated roughly at the time of the arrest, my main problem is a lack of sleep."

"I was concerned when you two did not visit me after the show," Tallulah said. "I couldn't shake the feeling something was terribly wrong. The next day I placed a telephone call to Mr. Tesla, who said the two of you had not returned home when expected."

"Funny thing, he wasn't sure how much time had passed since he'd last seen you," Isabelle said.

"Mr. Tesla becomes occupied with his work," Fidelio said, "to the exclusion of all else."

"We were worried about you," Tallulah said, "and besides Mr. Tesla, there are few people with telephones in the city. Fortunately, the sheriff's office has one. The deputy informed us that two men matching your description had been taken into custody."

"If Hank suffers any permanent harm," Fidelio said, "I shall seek punitive damages through the courts."

"I'd hoped to stay until he awakened," Tallulah said, "but we must rejoin the company."

A slender blonde nurse approached them. "Are you Mr. MacMillan's people?"

Fidelio jumped to his feet. "How is he?"

"Your friend is just fine. He had lots of internal bleeding, so the doctor recommends he stay here for the night."

"*Gracias a Dios!*" Fidelio said, feeling immediately embarrassed by the religious outburst. He took the Choctaw Nightingale's hand in his. "Tallulah, Isabelle, Hank and I both owe you a great debt. I do not know how we will ever repay you."

"There is no need," Tallulah said, and kissed him on the cheek, as did Isabelle. She called to the nurse. "Miss? Is Mr. MacMillan awake? May we speak to him?"

"I'm sorry. He is still under anesthesia. The doctor left strict instructions that he must not be disturbed for at least two hours."

"Very well then, we must be going. Take good care of Hank, Fidelio. Give him our best wishes for a speedy recovery. And give our regards to Mr. Tesla as well."

217

"I most definitely shall."

"Three days?" Despite his friend's efforts to calm him, Hank was red in the face with anger. "Consarn it, I'm not a cripple! I'll go loco laying idle for so long!"

"Those are your doctor's orders," Fidelio sniffed, "and I intend to see them carried out. Do not worry; there will be plenty to do for you when you return to work. To alleviate any boredom, I bought you this." He handed Hank a brand new book.

"*The First Men in the Moon?* Is this one of them crazy scientific fantasy books?" Hank studied the dust jacket. "H. G. Wells. That fellow can spin one heck of a tale. Thanks, Fidel."

Fidelio spent the first day at the house, waiting on Hank like a nursemaid, and working on plans for the next Tarantela in his spare time. "Here is your dinner," he said as he carried in the tray. "Hot vegetable soup and bread, gentle on the digestion."

Hank sat up and stretched, then tucked into his meal with enthusiasm. "I still can't hardly believe Tallulah came to bail me – us – out of the clink," he said between bites. "You say she don't have feelings for me, but if that's so, why'd she do it?"

Fidelio sighed. Tallulah's feelings were likely more complex than Hank wanted to believe. As he attempted to compose a tactful answer, there was a knock on the bedroom door. The landlady's daughter stood in the doorway. "Mr. MacMillan? There's a lady to see you."

"Send her in," Fidelio said, without waiting for Hank to answer.

Wilhelmina appeared before the girl could fetch her. "Oh, Hank!" she cried. "I had no idea what happened! I thought you'd forgotten our appointment." She rushed to the bed and embraced the astonished cowboy.

"No need to fret about it," Hank laughed. "I did forget, being conked out and in jail."

"You brave man," Wilhelmina cooed. She glanced at Fidelio. "Has your friend been taking care of you?"

"I told him I'd be fine," Hank said. "He should be at work, helping Mr. Tesla."

"You're a wonderful friend, Fillipio, but you can go back to work. I'll take care of Hank."

"The name is Fidelio. And remember, Hank, Mrs. Johnson does not allow us lady visitors."

Wilhelmina smiled sweetly. "I've already spoken to your landlady. We'll keep the door open. Nothing improper will happen."

"Then I shall leave Hank in your capable hands." He paused at the doorway for a look back. Wilhelmina was busy checking Hank's bandages. Fidelio could not help feeling envious of his friend. Though he had met a few intriguing 'confirmed bachelors' at the union meetings, he currently had no time for any romantic entanglements.

⚘ 🏴 ⚘

Nikola Tesla was not a sentimental man. He did not visit Hank at the boarding house, but he did send a basket of fruit and cakes – as if the fellow did not have enough to eat, with Mrs. Johnson and Wilhelmina doting on him. Though he seldom spoke of political matters, Tesla was outraged over the sheriff's treatment of his colleagues.

"You should sue for false arrest," he said. "Hire that Jewish attorney fellow."

Fidelio shook his head. "I thought so initially, but I have changed my mind. If I sue anyone, it will be the companies that are profiting from the theft of my creation."

That evening, young Irene brought Hank a letter that had arrived during their absence. "I'm sorry, Mr. MacMillan. In all the excitement I forgot about it."

"No problem, darlin'. It's from Aunt Mabel," Hank tore the envelope eagerly. "Oh my..." As he read the letter, his eyes welled up with tears. In a choked voice, he said, "Uncle Malcolm passed away. Real sudden-like, but then, he was 77 and all. Funeral was last Sunday." Hank began to sob. "I missed his funeral! I should've been there for my aunt!"

"Oh, poor dear!" Wilhelmina hugged him as he wept. "There, there, I'm here for you."

"My deepest condolences," said Fidelio. "Your uncle must have been a remarkable man." He deeply wished he could comfort his friend, but suddenly he felt like an intruder. Without another word, he went to his room. He had recently bought a new Conan Doyle book which he had barely started reading.

Chapter 20 – Infernal Machines

A few days later, Hank returned to work. As they entered the lab, Tesla looked up from his experiment, his face obscured in fog from the dry ice. "Ah, Hank," he said. "Now that you are back, let's have a look at Fidelio's damaged automaton. I'm curious to see if any of the film from the camera can be developed."

"Yes, sir!" Hank was all smiles. "I was wondering about that myself."

It was soon apparent that the spider was beyond repair. Though camera seemed intact, a visit to Tesla's dark room confirmed the film had been exposed. Fidelio was sorely disappointed.

For the next few weeks, Fidelio focused on his work, with no contact with the union. The newspaper said little about the mines, being more concerned about international affairs, such as the war in the Philippines. He decided to make a pilgrimage to the Gold Dust to see Dainty Lil.

"Ludovico, good to see you! And Hank!" She shook both their hands. By now she knew Fidelio's real name, but the alias had stuck. "I'm grateful to see you two are among the living, especially you, Hank. How the hell are you? Weren't you laid up a spell?"

"Yep, but I'm not the sort to be down for long," Hank said with a grin.

"We have been busy with our scientific pursuits," Fidelio said. "Still, we do not want to lose touch with our friends."

"Just glad to see you're okay. We've missed you at the WFM meetings. We haven't had one good philosophical discussion since you left."

Daisy appeared from behind the bar. "What can I get you gentlemen?" Hank ordered a beer, and Fidelio requested his usual tea.

"I still support the workers," Fidelio said, "though I was concerned about what Aldous Bunker told us. His spies seem to have taken an interest in me."

"That may be so," Lil said. "But the gossip I hear says a certain friend of ours has been courting Bunker's niece." With that remark she winked at Hank.

Hank looked embarrassed. "Don't you worry. I'm seeing the lady, not her uncle."

"'Just joshin' ya!" Lil laughed and slapped Hank on the shoulder. "But if you happen to hear anything that'd help our cause, you'll let us know, right?"

"Well..." Hank was saved from answering when Daisy set their drinks in front of them. He didn't want to make any promises he couldn't keep.

"Thank you." Fidelio took a sip from his cup, then grimaced and blew on the hot liquid. "Tell me, what is new in Cripple Creek?"

"It wasn't in the paper," Lil said, "but the dirigible from Denver paid us two surprise visits last week. Bunker's people picked up two big crates each time. Must've been six foot square, each box. Oh, and the owner's association had a powwow at the Rocky Springs Hotel."

"What was the topic of discussion?"

Lil shrugged. "We had a man working as a waiter at the hotel, but the bosses must have got suspicious, 'cause they fired him. They had themselves a private room. Lord only knows what they talked about."

"Something's up," Hank observed. "Them big crates must've cost a pretty penny to ship."

Fidelio exhaled and shook his head. "It is as I suspected."

"What?" Lil looked concerned. "Tell me, what do you know about this?"

"Those crates are no doubt filled with machines, automata, intended to replace human workers with mechanical ones."

"I heard the stories; thought they was crazy. And how do you know?"

"Because," Fidelio said with a scowl, "the machines are based on a stolen invention, one that I developed."

At this point, there was a lull in the conversation of the patrons nearby. Even Daisy stopped waiting on customers and was now standing next to them, listening.

Fidelio looked around nervously and lowered his voice. "Well, I..."

Lil looked over at Daisy and the two exchanged a knowing glance.

"Hey Luke!" Daisy called to a big man several stools down. She leaned over the bar, showing off her décolletage. "Why don't you tell us again how you kicked McNalley's ass last week?"

Fidelio lowered his voice, leaned toward Lil and continued. "Years ago, a dear friend of mine died in a mine collapse. I decided to invent something to prevent such tragedies in the future." He went on to tell of his creation of Tarantela, the theft of the prototype, and his suspicion that the stolen invention had ended up at Bunker's company. When he got to the part about being attacked on their return from Teller County, Lil interrupted him.

"Wait a minute! We was told you guys was in a motorcar accident! So that's why you've been a 'no show' at the last few meetings?"

"They were trying to scare us off," Hank said. "We ain't chicken; we just let 'em think that way."

"Can't say I'd blame you," Lil said. "Tell me, Ludo, what're you gonna do about your invention? I'd be all pissed if that were my baby they pinched."

"First, we need to get our hands on one of the counterfeit automata. We will take it apart in the lab, so I can verify it is my design. Then I shall file a complaint with the Patent Office."

Lil sighed. "Lifting one of them things from the mine? That's a tall order. Security around them places is tighter than a mosquito's ass stretched over a rain barrel." She paused and rubbed her chin. "I know a man who can help, but it'll cost you."

"I will pay whatever it takes," Fidelio said. As he said this, he mentally computed his available funds. It pained him to think he might be forced to approach his father again for help.

⚙ ᚠᚪ ⚙

The sun had just set, and dusk was fast turning to night. Fidelio wrinkled his nose as he stood waiting beside Hank. "Where is he? And why did we have to meet him in such a vile-smelling location?"

Hank grinned at his friend's distress. "Out here by the stockyards is kind of off the beaten path. There's the cows bellering to keep folks from listenin', and the stink to keep 'em away."

Lil's contact was a wiry fellow with a grizzled gray beard carrying a burlap sack. "We could only get a little one. Sorry about the dings. One of the legs is broke. Our man dropped it when he was running from the dogs."

"Even damaged, it will help us immeasurably. It was a heroic effort on your part." Fidelio took the sack from the bearded miner. "*Que pesado!* Are there bricks in this bag?"

The miner laughed. "She's a heavy one, ain't she?"

"Indeed. Here is an extra silver dollar for your trouble." Fidelio put the spider in the trunk of the Steamer, then he and Hank were on their way. As they drove, he kept glancing in the rear-view mirror. "Is that motorcar following us?"

"Keep your eyes on the road, *amigo*," Hank said. "I'll keep a lookout for bad guys."

Fidelio had intended to drop the spider off and examine it in the morning, but as they neared Tesla's laboratory there was a crackle of electricity in the air.

"Nick must still be at work," Hank said.

Inside the lab, Tesla was in rapt concentration, watching the lightning arc between electrodes. His hair stood on end, and he seemed unfazed by his proximity to 100,000 volts.

"Gentlemen!" he called. He threw open the breaker and the lighting ceased. "Pardon me. You are just in time."

"Burning the midnight oil, Nick?" Though Hank's nickname for him seemed disrespectful to Fidelio, Tesla did not seem to mind.

"You will recall my 'free energy' project. I feel I am on the verge of a breakthrough. Here, I'll show you..."

"Please do," said Fidelio, "But just one moment. Do you remember how we tried to photograph the automata at the Bunker Hill mine?"

"Certainly. It was unfortunate that those thugs destroyed your camera."

"We now have conclusive evidence," Fidelio said. He took the burlap sack from Hank. "Last Tuesday a crate filled with these arrived at the Cripple Creek Airfield." With some difficulty, he pulled the heavy machine from the bag and handed it to Tesla.

"Astonishing! It is almost an exact copy – superficially at least." He picked up the device in as if weighing it. "It's quite heavy. A terrible design; the extra mass will limit its mobility."

"It appears to be powered by a chemical battery," Fidelio said, "probably an older technology like the one invented by Edison. His design contained a significant amount of lead."

"That's amusing, because the trend is for lighter metals, such as cadmium. It would be just like Edison to do the opposite." Tesla smiled and set the device on a nearby workbench. "No matter; batteries will be obsolete when man can draw power from the earth's magnetic field."

"First thing tomorrow morning, I wish to analyze this automaton," Fidelio said, "as a means of proving that the design of this device was stolen from my own."

"Why wait?" Tesla grinned. "I am curious to see what lies inside this heavy little fellow."

"I quite agree." Fidelio had already begun disassembling the counterfeit Tarantela. It was Hank's job to make sketches, take notes, and attach a tag to each of the parts. Since the injury, they'd given him less strenuous tasks than before.

Every now and again, Tesla would cluck his tongue in disapproval. "I cannot believe what they've done to your creation. Even Edison – or a child – could have

223

done this better."

"I'll bet it walks like a broken-down nag on its way to the glue factory," Hank said.

"I do enjoy your colorful language," Tesla said with a chuckle. "As for the extra mass, Fidelio, you were correct about the lead-acid battery. An effective solution, but hardly elegant."

"Indeed, they have made many changes," Fidelio said. "Would you agree, however, that it is fundamentally derived from the same design as my own?"

"I have little doubt," Tesla said. "I would gladly sign an affidavit to that effect."

Hank was now seeing Wilhelmina on a regular basis. He did not return to the literary society, but he did escort her to dances and parties around town. He also accompanied her to services at Grace Episcopal Church. It reminded him of going to Catholic Mass with Aunt Mabel. Wilhelmina tried Hank's Quaker prayer meeting one time, but she was not impressed. "Where's the pipe organ, the candles, the recitations? What kind of religion is this?"

Still, Hank enjoyed spending time with her. He loved to be seen in public with the pretty strawberry blonde on his arm. So he overlooked her critical remarks, like "Please comb that hair," and "Don't slouch, dear." Though she did not insist he abandon his tobacco habit, she wrinkled her nose with such distaste when he smoked, that he lit up far less frequently.

Courting 'Willie' was as tricky as roping a gopher. Because of her uncle's anti-union stance, Fidelio insisted they keep the details of their work on the automata from her. That wasn't easy, since she was the curious sort. Having no job besides community volunteer work, and her would-be 'society column,' she could stop by at any time, and often did.

Fidelio, Hank, and Tesla were busy studying the control mechanisms on the legs of the counterfeit spider when there was a rapping at the door.

Tesla exhaled in frustration. "Hank, could you see who's there?"

When Hank opened the door, there stood Wilhelmina. He stepped out to join her, shutting the door behind him.

"Good day, sweet Henry. Am I interrupting?" Wilhelmina squeezed his hand and gave him a peck on the cheek. She looked fetching in her light gray riding skirt with a matching coat and hat. Her horse Chestnut was tied to a nearby post. Her usual riding partner was missing.

"No, no. It's always mighty fine to see you, Willie! Where's Mrs. Tyler?"

"She's feeling out of sorts, poor thing." Wilhelmina peered through the window in the front door. "May I come in and see what mad experiments you gentlemen are up to?"

"Let me ask Mr. Tesla first. Some of that electrical equipment can be real dangerous." Before she could object, he slipped inside and closed the door again. "Willie's here."

"So?" Tesla said. "Bring her in."

"She must not see this spider." Fidelio threw a sheet over the workbench. "If she realizes that it came from the mine, she might inform her uncle."

"Inform my uncle of what?" Wilhelmina swept past Hank into the lab, a frown on her pretty face.

"Th-that he's real sweet on you," Hank stammered.

Wilhelmina laughed mirthlessly at Fidelio's open-mouthed expression. "Filippio finds that joke as funny as I do. Seriously, what is so important that you need to hide it from me?"

"Sweetie," Hank said, "it's just that Fidelio is a shy feller."

"Yes, I am known to be quite suspicious and unreasonable," Fidelio agreed.

"What in blazes are you people going on about?" Tesla huffed.

"I can tell when I'm not welcome." Wilhelmina stormed out and was in the saddle before Hank could stop her. The next day, it took thirty minutes of apologizing to get back in her good graces. Were all women this ornery? He wondered how Tallulah would have reacted in this situation, then immediately chastised himself for the thought. *Ain't gonna happen, let it go.*

Meanwhile, the mechanical spiders appeared at practically every mine, and were soon doing tasks previously reserved for humans. Big Bill called an emergency union meeting. Hank and Fidelio drove out to attend. The two of them elicited some suspicious stares from the rank and file members, until Haywood greeted them both with a smile and a handshake.

One after another, the speakers rose to denounce the "infernal machines" that would "take our jobs and leave our families to starve." Fidelio looked more crestfallen with each tirade.

"Don't take it personal, Fidel," Hank whispered. "It's not your invention's fault, it's the owners. They only care about money, and the workers be damned."

"I know," Fidelio said. "It is discouraging, because when the time comes to convince the workers to support this innovation, it will be all the more difficult. The companies will have ruined our chance to make mining a safer and less strenuous occupation."

After a few more testimonials, a man named Marco rose to speak. "I move we issue a statement on how we're opposed to oughta-may-tons in the mines, and how we'll call a strike against any owner who uses these machines either to replace workers or reduce their hours."

The motion was seconded and put to a vote, and passed 93-9. The next business was to choose a committee to write the statement. "Looks like it's all over but the shouting," Hank said, noticing Fidelio's hang-dog expression. "Let's get the heck out of Dodge."

The two men got up and walked out, drawing more suspicious looks from the miners.

The union's statement was printed in the *Daily Gazette*, along with an opposing view from the president of the Mine Owner's Association. "Each mine is a privately held company," wrote Aldous Bunker, "and as such, we will employ any and all machinery we see fit."

Two days later, the *Gazette* had a one word headline: "Strike!" Below the article read, "The Western Federation of Miners has declared a strike, commencing immediately against all mines that employ mechanical automata in excavation work. A spokesman for the Mine Owners' Association replied that, 'Mechanization is being done solely for the benefit of the workers. No illegal actions or threats of violence will deter this progress.'"

At all the mines in the area, excluding "Solidarity" (which was owned by a former miner,) work ground to a halt. Picketers marched at every site. At the union hall in Cripple Creek, the wives cooked meals so the strikers could man the picket line in shifts.

Two days later, the trucks arrived bearing replacement miners from the East. The strikers surrounded the vehicles, slowing their pace to a crawl. "Scabs!", "Traitors!" and "Sons of bitches!" they shouted, waving shovels, bats, and axe handles in the air.

To Fidelio, who had seen protests turn violent in Spain, this behavior seemed unwise. "We should confront the strike-breakers with leaflets and non-violent persuasion." Though the union ignored his proposal, some of the new arrivals walked off their jobs in sympathy. One barrel-chested man marched out and proclaimed, in a thick German accent, "I came all this way not to be a scab." He joined the picket line, with several of his fellows.

In nearby Colorado Springs, pro-labor groups picketed the First National Bank, which had financed many of the mines in the area. The sheriff and his deputies arrived to arrest them for trespassing, and the county jail was soon full.

It seemed that everyone in the streets was talking about the strike, either for or against. Fist-fights became common. Hank ducked for cover every time a car backfired, which was especially embarrassing in Wilhelmina's presence. "You're a grown man, get a hold of yourself," she said, a frown on her luscious red lips.

"You can't know what it's like unless you been in a war," Hank said, after which he refused to discuss it further.

It was difficult for Hank to focus on his work, especially with Fidelio's frequent tirades against the 'capitalist exploiters.' "There is talk of calling out the militia to force the strikers to return to work," he said. "Did not this nation fight a war to end slavery?"

"It's more complicated than that," Hank answered. His father and both his uncles had fought for the Confederacy. "Though slavery is wrong, of course."

Only Tesla remained aloof from the controversy. "I am on the verge of a breakthrough," he kept saying, "a revolution in technology that will render these economic disputes obsolete."

Though Hank was sympathetic to the strikers, he did not join the picket line with Fidelio. He was careful not to discuss the issue with Wilhelmina, whose views on the labor movement were appallingly similar to her uncle's.

At first Fidelio had been happy about his friend's new relationship, and appreciated the great improvement in Hank's mood. Wilhelmina had seemed, in some ways, to be a godsend. She was strong-willed and independent, a cut above the average female. It soon became apparent, however, that her will did not just apply to her own life, but to Hank's as well.

Though he hated to eavesdrop, Fidelio overheard them one evening as he returned from a meeting. The two were sitting together in the parlor of the boarding house.

"I wish you wouldn't associate with those union people," Wilhelmina said, a petulant tone in her voice. "Uncle Aldous says they're all Red agitators."

Hank laughed. "You said you didn't care what 'that grumpy old man' thought."

"This time he happens to be right."

"Maybe, maybe not. I reckon he's got his reasons to go against the union, 'cause if they get their way, it'll hit him right in the bank book."

Wilhelmina did not reply; she simply crossed her arms and scowled at him. Hank was greatly relieved to see that his friend had arrived. "Oh hey, Fidel, didn't realize you were back."

"Good evening, Fil – Fidelio," said Wilhelmina, a frown on her rosy lips. "Tell me, do you support the strike?"

"The union approved the strike by a unanimous vote," Fidelio answered, "and I believe it is their right to do so."

"I don't understand what you see in those people. You're an inventor, from a good family, and you're making something of yourself. Those lazy miners would rather strike than work."

"Quite the opposite. They want to work, and the bosses are trying to replace them."

"My uncle is a responsible businessman, not a villain. Have you ever talked to him or the other owners to get their side of the story?"

"I am too weary to discuss these issues now," Fidelio sighed. "Good night to you both. Hank, I shall see you in the morning." He turned and strode out of the parlor.

As he was entering his bedroom, he heard Wilhelmina say, "I wish you'd reconsider going to work for Uncle." Curious, Fidelio held the door open and listened.

"Willie, I've got a job. I can't just leave my friends in a lurch. Fidelio's done so much for me, and besides, this work is powerful interestin.'"

"It's very nice you get to play with toys," she said, "but it's time to grow up. If we're going to have a life together, you'll need a better-paying job. Or would you rather have me giving piano lessons to all our friends' children just to pay the bills?" Her words were pleading, almost seductive.

Fidelio did not wait to hear Hank's reply.

As the strike continued, more crates arrived, filled with more clockwork spiders. By now, almost every mine in the county had bought some of the machines. The shipments became a target for sabotage. Many of the wooden crates containing them were set ablaze in the warehouse, though the culprits were never caught.

Two additional spiders found their way to Tesla's lab, where Fidelio and Hank could dissect them. Fidelio began to worry that he would bring the sheriff to his host's doorstep. "Nikola," he said. "I would like one more week to finish my research on the mining spiders, after which I promise they will be off your property."

"Really? I was hoping to have more time. These appear to be somewhat more advanced."

The self-imposed deadline forced Fidelio and Hank to work into the wee hours of the morning. Willie complained bitterly, but Hank stood his ground.

"It is disappointing," said Fidelio early one morning "that they have managed to incorporate the cryomagnetic power source in the stolen design, before I had the opportunity."

"Doesn't make 'em smarter," Hank said. "They just got more money and people to work on it."

These new spiders had two specialized designs, which incorporated extra features – the 'driller,' which sported a rock-boring bit in the front, and the 'placer,' with an extendable claw to plant dynamite for blasting tunnels. Underneath, their frameworks were identical.

As the strike continued, vandalism and sabotage became more frequent. The mine owners hired additional guards from the Pinkerton Detective Agency. Several were stationed at every mine entrance, and they prowled the streets of Cripple Creek like ill-tempered guard dogs. Now and then they would provoke a dust-up and then drag a few miners to jail. If they dared to resist, or insist on their rights, likely as not they'd be gunned down in the street.

Fidelio wished he could be there to support the workers. Analyzing the counterfeit spiders, however, had given him some ideas. He began planning a new, larger Tarantela that would incorporate some special features of his own.

Late one evening, Fidelio returned to the boarding house, having been out late with Big Bill. He was surprised to see Hank's door ajar. His friend sat in bed, reading his Bible to the light of the kerosene lamp.

"You are up late, my friend. Is something bothering you?"

"Not exactly. Just got a lot of stuff on my mind."

"Very well; I shall retire It has been an exhausting day." He turned to go.

All at once, Hank blurted out, "Willie thinks – I mean, I think – we should get hitched."

Fidelio turned back. "Do you mean married? Who should get married?"

"Willie and me, of course," Hank replied.

Really? That is a major step in a man's life."

Hank gave an embarrassed laugh. "You don't sound real tickled about it."

Fidelio grimaced for an instant. "I do not interfere in the affairs of others."

"You're against it," Hank said, "'Cause you don't like Willie."

"That does not matter," Fidelio admitted. "My concern is that you not act rashly."

"Not sirree, it's not rash at all. I've been looking for a wife, and I've found one. By the bye, I want you to be my best man."

"I would be honored. I wish only the best for you." Fidelio wondered if Willie had really driven Tallulah from Hank's mind. That development, at least, would be for the best.

⊕ ⼏ ⊕

At the end of the week, it was time to move the spiders. As Fidelio was off someplace on union business, the task fell to Hank, who borrowed Tesla's car to transport them. Hank had suggested taking them apart to reuse the pieces, but Fidelio would not hear of it. "We may still need them. They will be secure in Mrs. Johnson's barn." Hank hid them behind some hay bales.

Back in the boarding house, he found a letter from Tallulah waiting for him on the desk.

"Dearest Hank," it began, "How are you feeling? I certainly hope you are well. I have been praying for your speedy recovery.

"Please forgive my tardy response. Our tour of the East is going splendidly. I was briefly afflicted with a sore throat, so I tried your aunt's raw egg remedy. My voice was restored, and I didn't miss a single performance. Please convey my thanks to her."

"I hope your work is going well in Colorado. The newspapers have stories of the strike, which cause me concern. I know you are a man of peace, but others are not. Please be careful.

"I miss our conversations. I often think of our picnic in the Badlands, when you saved me from the snake. As I told you then, I have little choice but to follow my Muse wherever it leads, but if I could be two places at once, I would choose the company of friends like you.

"Give Fidelio my regards. Both of you are forever in my thoughts."

On the back of the last page was one more paragraph: "P.S. My people have taken an interest in the events in Colorado. Some of our friends shall be contacting you soon."

That was mysterious. Was she referring to her friends James, Fred and Ooche? And why would they come here? Hank remembered a conversation he'd had with Fidelio after they'd last seen her. Fidelio had said, "Have you ever wondered why Tallulah travels with so many people?"

Hank shrugged. "It does seem a bit much to have four people working for her. But she's an important lady, I reckon that's why."

"It goes deeper. She keeps close contact with her clan in Oklahoma. This is more than familial loyalty. Tallulah does not simply represent her people; she is a nexus of information."

"Like a spy?" Hank shook his head. "I can't believe such a thing."

"It is just a guess, but if it were so, would you blame her? The Indians are outnumbered in their own country, not even allowed to vote in your elections. Your forefathers fought a war of independence over far less."

Hank was startled from his memories by the sound of someone at the door. He stashed the letter in his coat pocket.

Fidelio stood there, winded, as if he'd run up a few flights of stairs. "Have you heard the news? Governor Peabody, that *hijo de una puta*, is sending troops to end the strike!"

"Peabody?" Hank looked puzzled. "What happened to Governor Orman?"

"He was sent to Washington months ago, to replace Senator Bowen, after he died in that airship mishap. Do you not read the newspaper?"

"Yes, but..." Mostly Hank followed the reports from the Philippine War, and in the last few months, the sections that dealt with music and literature. "Are you sure, Fidel? Maybe the Governor just wants to keep the peace."

"Mark my words – Peabody masquerades as a man of the people but he is in fact a tool of the wealthy. Nothing good can come of this intervention."

"I'm praying you're wrong." Hank glanced at his pocket watch. "Lordy, I got to go. Take a deep breath, Fidel. Don't panic." Outside was Tesla's car. Hank felt guilty for borrowing it yet again. Since his uncle had willed him a whole 640 acres of his big Arizona ranch, he could certainly afford his own, but he hated to part with his family legacy.

Chapter 21 - The Scourge of Cripple Creek

Hank drove straight to Bunker's mansion. Chang, the butler, greeted him with a formal bow as he let him in. Wilhelmina came down the hall, looking flawlessly lovely as usual, and greeted him with a peck on the lips.

Her lips were so rosy and soft, Hank almost forgot why he was there. "You ready to go, Sugar Muffin? I'm anxious to try that Chinese cooking you've been talking about."

"What's that in your jacket pocket?"

"My pocket?" He hadn't realized the envelope was sticking out. "Letter from a friend."

"Let me see it." Before Hank could open his mouth to object, she snatched it from his pocket, and quickly read the return address.

"You're corresponding with a woman?" her face reddened, "Behind my back?"

"It's not like that, Willie. We're just friends, me and her."

"Hightower – is this the opera singer? You're friends with the Choctaw Nightingale?"

Hank nodded, not sure whether to be proud or evasive. "Yep. Met her at the Marquis' digs in North Dakota." Would this get him a pass? He knew how Willie loved the opera.

"I agree she is quite talented," Wilhelmina sniffed. "And I suppose it's okay, because surely you cannot be romantically interested in an *Indian*. But you still should have told me."

"I must've not heard you right," Hank asked, irritated. "I have to say it ain't very Christian to think less of folks on account of the color of their skin."

"Well, no, of course I don't," Wilhelmina snapped. "But everybody knows it's best when people associate with their own kind."

"Maybe so," Hank said. "But it ain't nobody else's business if they do or they don't."

The ride to the restaurant passed in icy silence. When they arrived, Hank asked, "You ain't still upset, are you?"

She sighed. "Are you carrying a torch for this... *woman?* Don't try to deny it."

"Sweetie, it ain't – I mean it isn't – like that."

The waiter took them to their table. Willie ordered for the both of them, then sat there in silence. Hank was relieved when the food arrived. It was tasty but different than he was used to; all chopped up and served on rice. Wilhelmina ate hers with a pair of wooden sticks. Hank tried briefly, then gave up and used a fork. Willie glared at him, as if he'd disappointed her once again.

As they ate, Hank pondered. Why did Willie, who was such a strong-minded woman, have to be so touchy about everything? Still, he hated to think how life would be without her. Finally, he made up his mind. He'd intended to wait until he'd saved enough for a car of his own, but now was as good a time as any.

When the waiter brought the bill, Hank said, "Can you come back in just a bit?" Hank got down on his knees and took Wilhelmina's hand in his.

Her mouth fell open. "What on earth are you doing?"

"Wilhelmina Hill, I'd like you to be my wife."

She sputtered and blushed. "Henry, this is not fair. I was really angry with you. What am I supposed to say when you do something like this?"

"How 'bout sayin' yes?" Hank grinned and reached into his pocket. "A classy lady like you deserves a ring of your own, but for now we'll have to make do with my mama's." He slipped the gold band over her finger. It was a bit large, but at least it fit.

"Oh Hank, this is really sweet and... I was thinking maybe we should wait until you're a bit more established... and of course my uncle will be *furious*," she smiled at that thought, "but all right, Henry MacMillan, I'll marry you."

"Willie, you've made me a very happy man." She touched her lips to his, and for once she kept them there a while. Hank felt all warm and cozy inside.

"First thing we've got to do," Wilhelmina began excitedly, "is go ring shopping. I mean, your mother's gold band is all very nice for a rancher's wife, but it is quite a bit too large, and with its sentimental value, surely you wouldn't want me to risk losing it. In any case, these days a woman needs a pretty diamond to show off to all of her friends, don't you think?"

Suddenly Hank's throat went dry. "Sure, Willie," he said, forcing a smile. "I just want you to be happy."

Between Tesla's projects and their own, Fidelio and Hank worked around the clock. There was barely time to eat and sleep. Only rarely did Hank see Wilhelmina, which upset her greatly.

"Hank, I haven't seen you in days." Her pout made him feel like a real scalawag. "If I didn't know better, I'd suspect there was someone else."

"Of course not, darlin'." He gave her a hug and a peck on her rosy lips. "You're the only girl for me, and anyway," he chuckled, "how could I find the time?"

Wilhelmina was not amused, and cut their date short. As a consequence, Hank was in a vile mood the next day. After half the morning had passed, Fidelio took him aside.

"Perhaps I have been unreasonable," Fidelio said. "Since we have removed the mine company's spiders from this facility, I withdraw my objection to Wilhelmina's presence." He looked at Tesla. "With your permission of course."

"Huh, what? Oh, certainly," Tesla said. "An attractive woman brightens up any place."

The following day, when Wilhelmina and Mrs. Tyler dropped by on their daily ride, Tesla gave them a tour, showing them his many inventions, most of which they could scarcely understand. "What happened to that cute spider you demonstrated for Uncle?" Wilhelmina asked.

"It has been greatly improved," Tesla said. "Would you like to see it?"

"Yes," Wilhelmina nodded. "Don't worry, Ida," she explained to Mrs. Tyler, "It is not nearly so intimidating as a real spider."

"I'll get it, Fidel." Hank opened a storage closet and retrieved a mid-sized model and its wireless controller. He set the spider on the floor on handed the controller box to Fidelio.

"All right, I will show you," said Fidelio through clenched teeth. He switched on the controller and began pushing buttons and turning dials. The machine came to life, moving across the floor. "As you can see, the automaton walks on its own power, much like a living spider."

"How precious!" Mrs. Tyler said. "It would be a wonderful gift for my grand-nephew."

"It is not a toy," Fidelio sniffed. "Like an actual spider, it can bear an object many times its own weight. Observe." He pushed a lever, and the spider crawled to the other side of the lab. Using both claws, it picked up a 50-pound electrical transformer and carried it back to Fidelio.

"I see," Mrs. Tyler said. "It would be quite useful around the house, when I needed something heavy to be moved."

"It is far more flexible than that." Fidelio began pressing buttons in a long,

234

complicated sequence. The spider walked to a table, extended a claw upward, and withdrew a single chrysanthemum from a delicate crystal vase. It then brought the flower to Mrs. Tyler.

"How sweet!" she cried as she took the blossom from Tarantela's claw. "If it can hold down a job, perhaps it could even replace my husband." Both women laughed at her joke.

"These are much like the spiders they use in my uncle's mine, though much smaller," Wilhelmina said. "Are these based upon those?"

Fidelio cast her an evil glare.

"Oh no, Fidelio got the idea first," Hank said. "His version is lots better. It don't even need a wire to control it. It gets its orders from that little box, right through the air."

"I see," Wilhelmina said. "And what is this?" She pointed to the giant coil which dominated the room. "'High Tension,'" she read, "That means danger, doesn't it?"

"Indeed it does," Tesla said. "I was saving that for last. Now stand back, ladies. I will demonstrate how man can steal lightning from the heavens."

"Thoroughly amazing, Mr. Tesla," Wilhelmina said when he had finished. Both ladies enthusiastically clapped their gloved hands. "Hank, honey, let's go outside and sit for a while. The electrical smell is giving me a headache."

"Actually, I believe that ozone, in low concentrations, has health benefits," Tesla said.

"Thanks anyway, Nick," Hank said with a smile. The couple went out and sat on the bench in front of the lab, while Mrs. Tyler chatted with Tesla and Fidelio. As Hank rolled a cigarette, Wilhelmina pulled a pencil and tablet from her purse and began writing.

"What're you doing, sweetie?"

She gave him an amused smile. "Hank, dear, you know I'm a journalist."

"Really? They hired you on? Ya-hoo!" He leaned in and gave her a smack on the lips.

The surprise kiss made Wilhelmina jump, breaking the lead of her pencil. She slammed her notebook on the bench with an exasperated sigh. "What do you mean by that? That I can't be a journalist unless some man with a newspaper decides to pay me?"

"No, I... confound it, you know what I meant!"

"Oh? Then what is the problem? Am I not allowed to write about Mr.

235

Tesla's projects?"

"Uh... of course you can. Though maybe you ought to ask Nick and Fidelio first. Inventors are always worried about folks stealing their ideas."

She furrowed her brow. "Once again I've failed to get the proper permission from a man."

Hank opened his mouth, trying to decide whether to explain himself further or attempt an apology. It was too late for either; Wilhelmina was already at the door of the lab.

"Ida!" she called to Mrs. Tyler. "We ought to be going." She looked at Hank. "Or do I need permission for that as well?"

As the ladies rode away, Fidelio smiled at Hank in amusement.

Hank sighed. "Doggone it. I wonder how long she'll stay mad at me this time."

"I am certain she will be back soon," Fidelio said, "Now, let us get back to work."

Wilhelmina returned the next morning, her anger forgotten. Her visits were by now a daily occurrence, and she often brought a picnic lunch to share with Hank. Tesla was not bound by the clock, however. He would often force her to wait as they finished an experiment. To Fidelio's surprise, she did not sigh or complain, but instead sat quietly reading her book. Perhaps Hank's relaxed, lackadaisical manner was influencing her for the better.

Their next project was to remove Tarantela's chemical battery and install Tesla's geomagnetic energy receiver in its place. This produced a dramatic improvement in the automaton's range, as well as increasing its speed. Its metal legs were a blur as they clicked across the floor. "Let us try increasing the gain," Tesla said, pushing the lever forward on the controller. There was a loud 'pop' and a plume of smoke rose from the box.

"¡Maldita sea!" Fidelio cried. "I should have warned you not to do that."

"Ouch!" Tesla said, holding up his burned fingers. We shall need to add a safety fuse, or the operator may be injured."

"I do have a spare controller," Fidelio said. "Hank, could you retrieve it, please?"

"Yep. I know right where it's at." Hank opened a cabinet door and rummaged around for a while. Then he looked through the neighboring cabinets. "Don't that just beat all? It's not here."

"What do you mean it's not there?" snapped Fidelio.

"One of us probably misplaced it," said Tesla. "These things happen when men are deprived of sleep. I propose that Hank build another while Fidelio and I diagnose the problem with this one. I expect we will find the missing controller as soon as we stop searching."

⊛ ⼸ ⼸ ⊛

Meanwhile in the mining district, the standoff continued. The owners steadfastly refused to come to the bargaining table. Frequent scuffles broke out between the striking miners and their replacements. Despite the presence of the Pinkertons, one of these brawls escalated into a gunfight, and a number of people were killed.

The next day, Governor Peabody met with the press for an important announcement. Fidelio might have missed this news, had he not sent Hank into town to run some errands. Hank returned with a copy of the *Gazette* under his arm. He lit up a smoke and sat down on the front step to read the paper. Fidelio took a seat beside him. "What news do we have today?"

"Your old pal Peabody's sending in the Guard, under a guy named Sherman Bell. Holy Moses, I know him! I served with him in the war! He weren't no *general* back then, though."

"You have met that man?" Fidelio exclaimed. "Perhaps you know something about him that could be of use to the workers' cause."

"What, like vices, skeletons in the closet? None I know of, 'cept that I've never met a man who was so full of himself. When the Bible talks about the sin of pride, I think of him."

"Then I dread to see what this man will do," Fidelio said.

If General Bell had faults, hesitation and indecision were not among them. He declared Teller County to be "under martial law, until civil order and respect for the law is restored."

Bell's actions stirred a great deal of controversy. Many business leaders supported him, though most working people were opposed. As much as the situation infuriated Fidelio, he tried not to discuss it around Wilhelmina. This was not easy, as she and Hank often spoke of it in the parlor of the boarding house.

"I wish no harm to the miners," Wilhelmina said, "but we've got to have law and order."

"What about fairness?" Hank said. "Bell is one cantankerous old billy goat."

"You should meet with him," she suggested. "Perhaps you could serve as negotiator."

Hank shook his head. "No thanks. I got too many folks egging me on from both sides."

It took great effort for Fidelio to hold his tongue.

The editor of the *Gazette* echoed Wilhelmina's sentiment when he wrote, "Martial law is at this time a necessary evil, lest the union foment anarchy."

Bell soon surpassed Fidelio's worst expectations. He shut down the weekly Cripple Creek newspaper after it editorialized against him. His soldiers occupied the union hall and imprisoned the WFM leadership, including Haywood, without charge or evidence. Many of the replacement miners had arrived without knowledge of the situation and were reluctant to be strike-breakers. Nonetheless, Bell threatened them with arrest if they did not continue working.

A few days later, a train arrived from the east carrying cars filled with a new kind of 'security.' Dainty Lil, who had so far avoided the fate of her comrades, rode her horse to Tesla's laboratory, agitated and breathless.

"It's like something out of a nightmare!" she said. "They come walking out of the train cars on six metal legs, just like those infernal mining machines, only twice the size."

"Now that's queer," Hank said. "What'd they need 'em that big for?"

"It ain't for the mines. They got to be for the Guard, or maybe the Pinkertons. They done took off the drill and shovel attachments, and now each of those devils has a Gatling gun under its belly. Bell's got half our folks locked up, now he wants to shoot us?"

"*Madre de Dios!*" exclaimed Fidelio. "Has my creation been corrupted yet again?"

"What Bell is doing just ain't right," Hank said. "We've got to do something!"

"Damn right," Lil said. "But what the holy hell can we do?"

"We must see those machines," Fidelio said, raising his voice. "We cannot fight this abomination without more knowledge."

"Do you think that would be wise?" asked Tesla. "Remember what happened last time you went to the mining district?"

At the mention of the incident, Hank crossed his arms as if protecting his stomach.

Fidelio exhaled loudly. "You have a point. But I cannot sit on my hands and do nothing."

"It's your decision," Tesla said, turning back to his work.

The problem was that there were only one motorcar road to Cripple Creek. According to Lil, Bell's men had erected a roadblock at the county line and were only letting people in for 'legitimate business.'

Fortunately, Tesla had a map of the area. "There are many abandoned mines, and roads and trails all over," he said. "I have thoroughly explored the area looking for minerals to use in my cryomagnetic experiments." He took a roll of paper from his bookshelf and spread it out on his work table. "Here!" He pointed at a faint line. "You can bypass the roadblock by taking this trail, which runs a mile south of the road."

"Is it passable by motorcar?" Fidelio asked. "That'd be a long walk."

"You could go on horseback, I suppose," Tesla said, "though I would not recommend riding those vile creatures."

Hank began to say something, but Fidelio gestured for silence. Later that evening, Fidelio told Hank that Tesla's brother had died in a horse-riding accident.

"Poor Nick," Hank said. "As if being all terrified of germs ain't enough."

They set out the next morning, finding the trail head at a bend in the road. This time, the 'No Trespassing' sign was not on the post, but lying on the ground nearby. "Obviously, the owners do not maintain their property," Fidelio observed.

Without a word of argument, Hank got out of the car, opened the wire-and-post gate, and dragged it out of the way. He closed it once Fidelio had driven through.

They followed the trail up a gradual slope, though it was impossible to see much because of all the trees. After two or three miles, Fidelio pulled off the trail. "We should be near the summit." They walked to a rocky outcropping that provided a good vantage point.

Fidelio pulled out his field glasses and surveyed the surrounding countryside. The main road to Cripple Creek was visible below. "Curse it all! There is another roadblock past the first one. You have been studying the map. Did you see any possible ways around?"

"Something's coming!" Hank half-whispered as he grabbed Fidelio's arm.

Hearing the crack of breaking branches from within the trees, both men turned around.

Fidelio's mouth dropped open. "*¡Ay diablo!*"

Standing before them was a machine that looked much like one of the mine spiders, but with the Gatling guns that Lil had described. Its metal joints creaked as it swiveled its body to the left and right on its long metal legs. From its top a plume of

239

steam or gas escaped with a hiss.

"D– does it see us?" Hank stammered.

Fidelio held a finger to his lips. "No," he whispered, "But there must be an operator nearby. We must retreat while the machine hides us from his sight." He gestured toward the car.

The two men backed away, keeping an eye on the monstrosity which was slowly turning its body in a broad arc. Fidelio couldn't help wondering if it could 'see' by echolocation, like Tarantela. It gave no sign that it had 'noticed' them. In any case, they were soon out of its 'sight' behind trees, rocks and brush.

"F– Fidel, did we lose it?" Hank's eyes were wide with terror.

As Fidelio was about to answer, they heard the screeching crunch of a shattering tree, followed by the humming of hydraulic pistons and the slam of heavy metal feet on the earth. Hank let out a wordless shriek and took off at a run, crashing through the brush. Fidelio took off in pursuit, but soon lost sight of him. The car was to the east, but Hank had gone north in his blind panic, and the metal footfalls behind Fidelio were getting closer.

He had to return to the Steamer, or they would both die. Fidelio turned and ran back toward the ridge where he had left the motorcar. The noise of the spider receded in the distance. He was shocked to see Hank in the passenger seat, red-faced and sweaty. "How did you...?"

"Never mind," Hank wheezed, "Boiler's all warmed up, let's go!"

Fidelio jumped in and threw the car into gear. The trees were thick around them, and it took several agonizing seconds to get the car turned around. "You found your way back," he said to Hank as they bounced down the trail. "If you had not been here to light the boiler...."

For a moment Hank stared at Fidelio uncomprehendingly. "There was a light, and a voice in my head that said, 'Be still, I am with thee.' And my terrible fright was gone."

"Then I thank your God, or whomever was responsible," Fidelio said, "Had you not found your way, I do not know what I would done."

"Oh no!" Hank cried. "I can hear that thing! It's right on our tail."

Fidelio strained his ears to hear over the rushing wind and the creaking of the Steamer's springs on the rugged trail. There were definitely heavy steps, getting nearer by the second. "Where is the spider's operator? The man would need to be on horseback to keep up."

"Damn it man, I don't know!" Hank said, trying to squeeze himself down as low in his seat as he could. "But it's coming for us!"

"Hmm, still not visible," Fidelio said. "Could they have the wireless controllers?" He shook his head in answer to his own question. "It cannot be, only Tesla has that technology."

The noise got louder. "I can see it!" Hank yelled. "Son of a bitch! *Mas rápido!* Or we're done for! That there gun's gonna blow our goddamn heads off!"

"This is fast as I dare go," Fidelio shouted back, "lest I kill the both of us."

As they bounced down the rocky trail, the spider opened fire, sending bullets whizzing past them. Fidelio pushed the Steamer to the limit, and they managed to pull ahead.

"The gate!" Hank was out of the car before Fidelio had come to a full stop.

Hank opened it and jumped back in. Fidelio breathed a sigh of relief as he pulled onto the road back to Colorado Springs. The mechanical monster was nowhere to be seen. Momentarily they passed a parked Ford Roadster emblazoned with the Pinkerton Agency's seal. It pulled out behind them, honking its horn wildly. Fidelio shoved the accelerator lever all the way forward.

"They must've seen us trespassing!" Hank yelled.

"I am not obliged to stop. They will not catch us in that inferior car."

Hank looked back. "That inferior car's gaining on us! And the passenger's got a gun."

"That is an outrage!" Fidelio reached over and opened the compartment in front of Hank. "Take my pistol, in case they fire at us!"

"No way, no how! I just can't! I promised the Lord." Hank sat in the passenger seat with had his arms folded resolutely.

A shot whistled past Fidelio's ear, and a second ricocheted off a rock. Hank crouched low in his seat, muttering, "Our Father, who art in Heaven, hallowed be thy name..."

Fidelio's heart pounded. He struggled to control his breathing. Besides the gunshots, he was driving the Steamer at top speed down a twisty gravel road. Just beyond a curve, where the pursuers could not see them, he saw his chance. "Hank, hold on!"

He turned the steering wheel so sharply that two of the Steamer's wheels left the road for a moment. What he had thought was a trail was instead a rocky creek bed running down the hillside. The water sprayed in all directions as they went.

Hank let out a scream of terror.

"Shut up!" Without slowing down, Fidelio turned again, sideswiping a tree

241

and dropping the right front wheel into a huge hole. As they stopped abruptly, Hank smacked his face on the windshield. Up above on the hillside they could hear a gasoline-powered vehicle roaring past.

Hank pulled a handkerchief from his pocket to stop the blood flowing from his nose. "What the hell? Was that a creek we just drove through?"

"We are fortunate I am a skillful driver. Come, help me change this wheel."

It took several attempts to get the hydraulic jack seated in a spot where it would not sink into the muddy earth. With a mighty effort they raised the car and replaced the wheel, then pushed the vehicle forward, out of the hole.

Through all of this Fidelio maintained his composure. He lit the engine's burner and watched the pressure gauge. The needle refused to budge. In a minute there was a whistling noise. Fidelio jumped out, unlatched the seat, and pulled it forward to expose the car's boiler. "There is a bullet hole in the tank! *¡Esos cabrónes detestables!*" He continued with a string of curses so vile that Hank broke out laughing.

"Whose mother is a what and does what to who?" he guffawed. It took him a while to stop, despite Fidelio's angry stare. "Well, I guess we're hoofin' it."

The walk took several hours. When they arrived at the lab, there was a horse tied at the post, and a young woman pacing back and forth in front of the door. "Hank!" she cried when she saw them. "You missed our dinner. Mr. Tesla didn't know where you were. I was worried sick!"

"I'm fine, sweetheart," he said as she embraced him. "Little mishap with the Steamer."

Fidelio went directly into the lab. "Good evening, Nikola. I am sorry we are so late."

"That is a moot point, since I didn't know when to expect you. Hank's fiancée insisted I call the hospital and the county jail, but you were not at either place."

"We were fortunate to escape injury," Fidelio said. "Now, may I request a favor?"

Though the sun was setting, Tesla grudgingly agreed to drive them to the accident site in his Electrobat. They brought lanterns, tools and a torch, with which Hank made a temporary patch to the boiler. At long last it was able to hold a moderate pressure.

"Nikola," Fidelio said. "I am most grateful for your help."

"It was not a problem," said Tesla as he got into his car. "You are the first assistants I have ever had who were not completely inept."

They rode into town at a 10 mile per hour crawl. "I cannot risk the boiler," Fidelio explained. His heart jumped as he drove past a Pinkerton vehicle, yet it did not take pursuit.

When they reached the boarding house, they found Wilhelmina in the parlor, dozing sitting up in the easy chair. The men tried to tiptoe past, but at that moment she awoke.

"Henry MacMillan," she said. "I'll have a word with you."

"Willie darlin'," he said. "It was sweet of you to wait, but I'm beat. It's time to turn in."

She ignored his plea. "What happened today? You're involved with those union people again, aren't you? Didn't I tell you to stay away from them?"

"It was not the union, but the Pinkerton thugs who pursued us and caused me to crash my motorcar," Fidelio said. "You should ask your uncle if they were acting under his direction."

Wilhelmina flushed. "What are you implying? Uncle Aldous does not consort with ruffians! You take that back!"

Fidelio grimaced. "Excuse me." He turned and left, despite Hank's pleading expression.

Wilhelmina was still talking. "And as for you, Mr. MacMillan..."

Several weeks passed. Every day as Fidelio read the *Gazette* he was infuriated by General Bell's latest outrage, as well as the support the newspaper gave him. They even featured his picture on the front page, standing in a pose that made him look arrogant and cocksure. Bell was a handsome man, bearing a strong physical resemblance to Fidelio's lost Rodrigo. Like Bell, he had been a confident man, but he was also kind, with a quiet and introspective nature.

Fidelio was greatly concerned about the military spiders. He asked around at the Gold Dust, and several patrons confirmed that the spiders were now operated without any connection, nor with an audible signal, as Fidelio's earlier models had used. How could this have been achieved so quickly? He remembered the spare remote control, which had never been found. "Do you think the missing wireless controller could have been stolen?" he asked Tesla.

"Impossible!" Tesla declared. "There was no opportunity. No one has been in this laboratory that we don't know."

Later that week they were working late, gathered around one of the earlier models of Tarantela, which had ceased functioning. Fidelio was certain it was a short circuit, but Tesla was not convinced. A banging noise caused them all to jump.

"What was that?" Fidelio said. "Nikola, did you leave the coil on?" When left powered on, it would sometimes make a spontaneous discharge.

"Of course not," Tesla snapped. "And it has a shutoff timer, just to be safe."

"It was the door," Hank said. The men all looked at each other. "Okay, I'll get it."

"Hank, wait." Fidelio lowered his voice to a whisper. "Do you think it might be the authorities? You know how Bell has been arresting his critics in Cripple Creek. I hear he is closely allied with the sheriff of this county, and that there have been arrests here as well."

"It's not the Sheriff I'm worried about," Hank whispered back. "It's them Pinkerton goons. They're like a law all to themselves."

"You are both being ridiculous," Tesla sighed. "Never mind, I will answer the door."

In less than a minute, Tesla returned from the door. "Your fears were groundless," he smiled. "It was just two Indians. One was dressed like a white person; the other looked like some kind of Hindu fakir. I told them they had the wrong address."

"What?" Fidelio cried. "Hank, come along!" The two men ran out the door, leaving Tesla perplexed behind them. A gas-powered coupe was pulling away from the front gate.

Hank ran on ahead. "Whoa there! Fred! Ooche!"

The car halted. Hank caught up and stood by the passenger side, panting. "I think them cigs are starting to get to me."

"That's what you white men get for misusing the sacred tobacco," said Ooche Osceola in exaggerated indignation. Beside him, Fred Seeley sat in the driver's seat, grinning.

"Was that the famous Tesla?" Fred asked. "He seemed kind of puzzled."

"None of us were expecting you," Fidelio said. "But you are quite welcome."

"That's good," Fred said. "Because we just drove all the way from Muscogee and we'd hate to turn back around."

244

Chapter 22 – A New Alliance

Sometime later, they sat over an impromptu meal of ham, potatoes, and baked beans in Tesla's residence a half-mile from the workshop. "Normally I have a housekeeper who cooks for me," Tesla explained. "But Hank's cooking is certainly edible."

"It's fine," Fred said. "Thank you, Hank, and to you Mr. Tesla, for providing the food."

"I hear you people like liquor," Tesla continued, "though I don't have much on hand."

Fidelio and Hank looked at each other, aghast, though the remark elicited a chuckle from Fred. Fidelio quickly changed the subject. "To what do we owe the pleasure of your visit?"

"We apologize for arriving unannounced," Fred said, "But we were concerned that the authorities might intercept your mail."

"In America?" said Tesla. "God forbid!"

Ooche finished the last of his potatoes and pushed back his plate. "Our mission here is of a confidential nature." He looked over at Tesla.

"You can trust Nick," Hank said.

"I appreciate the vote of confidence," Tesla said. "However, I have much to do, and I prefer not to be involved in any schemes of a possibly unlawful nature."

The other four men all looked at each other.

"I must return to the workshop," he continued. "You are welcome to stay here and continue your discussion." Tesla got up and left.

"Peculiar fellow, isn't he?" said Fred.

"Most geniuses are a mite on the odd side," said Hank with a glance at Fidelio.

Fidelio laughed. "If eccentricity is a prerequisite for genius, I am well qualified. I am, however, surprised Tallulah has not written Hank recently, perhaps hinting about your visit."

"She did, actually," Hank said. "Sorry. I caught some heat from Willie about it, and then it slipped my mind."

"Willie?" Ooche asked, with arched eyebrows.

245

"Hank is affianced," Fidelio explained, "to a very headstrong young lady."

Fred's eyes went wide and he broke out in a grin. "Congratulations, Hank!"

"May the Spirits bless your upcoming union," Ooche added.

"Uh, thanks," Hank mumbled, embarrassed by the attention.

Ooche said, "As I was saying, this is more than a friendly visit. In fact, we do not normally discuss these things with outsiders, but the Elders gave us special permission."

"The Elders?" Hank asked.

"The leaders of the Five Tribes," Fred said. He lowered his voice and glanced briefly out the window. "The Nighthawk uprising gave us all hope for the future of our people. But we know the leaders in Washington will not give up easily. At some point there will be another confrontation, and we want to know what we're up against."

"Not that we mind giving a black eye to the white man," Ooche said. "Present company excluded. Though I have my suspicions about this fellow." He slapped Fidelio on the shoulder.

Fidelio winced. "You would be correct; I am one quarter African, though I have been advised to keep that information to myself. In any case, your arrival is most fortuitous. We are struggling to find a way to fight General Bell, and we could use the help."

"He's an *eenahduh*," Fred said. "A snake. But why is it your responsibility to stop him?"

"You remember Fidel's Tarantela?" said Hank. "His first one got swiped in New Jersey, and they sold it to somebody else who made a whole mess of copies."

Their guests gave him a puzzled look. "Someone stole your what?" Fred asked.

"They were not with us in Medora, so they did not see it, remember?" Fidelio said. To Fred and Ooche, he explained, "Some time ago I created an automaton, a multi-legged machine resembling a spider."

"Tallulah and Isabelle have spoken of this invention," said Ooche. "To me it sounded like dark magic, to make a copy of one of the Great Spirit's creatures. But what does that have to do with the miner's strike?"

"It's not magic, I can vouch for that," said Hank. "Though it is pretty darn clever."

"The thief sold my invention to the Springfield Company, which has made a much larger version," Fidelio explained. "It is a mechanical laborer intended to replace the miners."

"Wasn't that the whole point of your invention?" asked Fred. "To do folks' work for them?"

"No! I never meant to eliminate jobs, simply to take over the most dangerous tasks."

"To top it all off," said Hank. "The National Guard's got 'em too, and they put Gatling guns on 'em. We've just got to find a way to stop that."

"It sounds monstrous," said Ooche. "But also like an interesting challenge. Our strategy is to use the white man's technology against him. That's how we beat the Dawes Act."

"You all were pretty smart to use the magnets like that," Hank said. "And you know, Tesla is big on magnetism. The worrisome thing though, is that Nick's a good friend of ours, and he's pretty well-known around these parts. We don't want to bring any trouble to his door."

Fred nodded. "We may have a solution. Do you know the Miller Bicycle Repair Shop?"

"I have driven by it," Fidelio said.

"The proprietor, Oscar Miller, is one of us; he's a quarter Chickasaw," Fred explained. "Like you, he gets by as white. We'll be staying with him. I'm sure he'd love to see your spiders."

"About this Bell person..." Ooche said. "Is he as vile a skunk as the rumors say? And could we scout out his camp? Surely we could find some weakness."

"It will not be easy," Fidelio said. "He has guards on all the roads into the mine country."

They continued their discussion of the mine, the strike, and the spiders, until Tesla returned at about midnight, at which time Hank and Fidelio returned to the boarding house, and Fred and Ooche went to Miller's residence.

⚙ 𝍐 ⚙

The next day, Fidelio and Hank drove to the Gold Dust to meet with Lil. Fred and Ooche stayed behind. The place did not welcome Indians, and in any case, Ooche had no desire to enter "the white man's den of iniquity." When they arrived, Lil was not at her usual seat. Daisy was behind the bar, with her hair unwashed, and dark circles under her eyes.

"I ain't seen my Lil in three whole days," Daisy told them. "She said she was going to the mercantile and she never came back. I'm half-crazy with worry."

"That's awful," Hank said, "Why didn't you come to us?"

247

"I'm not the kind to impose," she said. "I checked with the Sheriff Jones, and he hadn't heard nothin'."

Fidelio winced at the name. "Is there anything else you can tell us?"

"The union folks are still in jail. The mines're being worked by scabs. And there was an accident. The elevator at the Lewis mine fell and eight men died. Bell called it sabotage, which is loco, since he's got most of the union locked up. That gave him the excuse he was waiting for."

"To do what?" Hank asked.

"He seized all the union's provisions, the food they set aside for the wives and kids during the strike. Now the militia's got control, and they've been damn stingy. Folks say Bell aims to break the union by starving their families. The women have taken to stealin' food or *worse* to support their men in jail."

Hank shook his head. "I wouldn't have thought even old Swaggering Sherman would sink that low. The man is a lower'n a rattlesnake's belly."

"Last time we tried to go to Cripple Creek, we were arrested," Fidelio said. "There must be a way we can bypass Bell's gauntlet."

"Well..." she thought a moment. "The main road goes around Pike's Peak to the north, but there's another way to the south, where the other railway goes. 'Course, we'd have to stay out of sight, and it's pretty rough country. You fellows know how to ride, don't you?"

"Does a frog have a water-tight butt?" laughed Hank. "Damn right we can ride. Fidelio claims to be quite the horseman; though I haven't seen it for myself."

"You shall see," Fidelio said. "The cowboy was not the first to domesticate the horse."

The two men bid farewell to Daisy and left the saloon. "Speaking of loco," Hank said as they got into the Steamer, "Are you really fixing to go to Cripple Creek? Sounds like a good way to get killed."

"There is no good way to die," Fidelio said. "But sometimes a man must take chances if he is truly to live."

"'Maybe you're right,'" Hank said. "'For whosoever will save his life shall lose it.'"

Fidelio gave him a puzzled smile. "I have heard that Bible verse before, and I never was certain what Jesus meant when he said it. I sincerely hope it is not a portent of things to come."

Later that evening, after returning from the Gold Dust, Fidelio and Hank paid a visit to the cycle shop. Oscar Miller was a short little fellow with a sun-weathered face. "So you've been working with the famous Tesla?" he said. "I'd sure like to meet that man."

"Come by the lab and we'll introduce you," said Hank.

"I'd also like to see these marvelous spiders for myself."

"You are welcome," Fidelio said, "providing you agree to tell no one about it, because I do not want the scoundrels who are misusing my creation to steal any more of my ideas."

Miller held up his hand. "You have my word."

"Hank," Fidelio said, "Would you take the Steamer and get a Tarantela from Tesla's lab? In the meantime, I shall see if we can utilize this cycle repair equipment for our purposes."

"You got it, boss." Hank was already headed for the door.

Although it was well past dark, Tesla was working late as usual. As Hank approached the building, he saw electricity flickering in the windows.

"Evening, Nick," he said as he entered. "Burning the midnight oil again?"

"Indeed." He looked around. "Where is your young lady? I had begun to think she was your shadow."

"She's fine," Hank replied. Wilhelmina had once again complained of a headache the previous night, though Hank had his doubts. Probably she was angry at him for some reason.

"While you're here, could you assist me with this wiring? You have a very deft touch."

"Okay, Nick. Fidel's expectin' me back, though, so we'll have to make it quick." As Hank picked up the soldering iron, there was a pounding at the door.

Tesla exhaled loudly and got up from his chair. "Who could it be at this hour?" When he opened the door, a group of uniformed men shouldered their way past him into the lab.

"This is National Guard business," announced a sturdy red-headed man with a misshapen nose. "We've been informed this facility contains stolen property from the Bunker Hill Mine."

"That is a lie!" Tesla cried. "And where is your search warrant? I know my rights!"

"All rights have been suspended for the duration of the state of emergency. Hey you!" he called to Hank. "Drop that thing and put up your hands! Culver," he said to a man who looked barely more than a boy, "keep 'em both covered. Don't either of you move a muscle."

Hank stood with hands raised, completely flabbergasted. He stared as the men scattered through the lab, opening drawers and cabinets. "I heard that Bell had took charge only in the mine country, not Colorado Springs."

"Shut your trap, hayseed!" said the man with the crooked nose.

"Hopkins!" Tesla exclaimed. "Lloyd Hopkins from Edison's lab! I knew I remembered you from somewhere. What happened to your nose?"

"None of your damn business," Hopkins said. "I hope for your sake you've got no contraband in this lab."

Tesla flushed with anger as the men rifled through his drawers and cabinets and opened closets. They scattered papers, tossed glass bottles to shatter on the floor, and threw delicate instruments around like hay bales. "I hope you're prepared for a lawsuit, Lloyd." He kept his hands up as ordered, but his hands were clenched into fists. "You! Stay away from the big coil! It has a dangerously high electrical tension!'" He started to move, but the boy with the gun pointed it at him menacingly.

"Huh," the man grunted. "I bet you're hiding something behind it." He laughed as he opened the metal gate. "Don't worry, I ain't gonna kiss it or nothin'."

"There's nothing in there but 'lectricity!" Hank shouted. "It's dangerous!"

As the guardsman entered the cage, he tripped over the threshold, brushing the gun on his hip against the coil. The resulting explosion threw him across the room, where he lay twitching.

"For God's sake, let me help him!" pleaded Tesla.

Hopkins nodded in response. Tesla ran over and put his ear to the man's chest, then grabbed his wrist. Then he used both hands to push on the man's chest. Hank was shocked to see that Tesla was touching him with his bare hands.

"What the hell are you doing?" Hopkins barked.

"I am trying to restart his breathing." Tesla pushed a few more times. "He has a very faint heartbeat. If you get him to a doctor immediately he may survive."

"You bastard!" Hopkins put his gun to Tesla's head. "Are you helping or killing him?"

Tesla ceased his work and exhaled loudly. "If you would keep abreast of technology instead of acting as a hired thug, you would know that."

"Damn you all!" Hopkins put his gun back in its holster. "Costello! Don't just stand there gawking. Pick up those papers; they might be evidence. Culver, McCafferty, pick up Walker and get him in the car. Tesla, you'll be hearing from the sheriff."

"I welcome any investigation. I have done nothing wrong."

When they were gone, Hank shook his head. "Powerful sorry that happened. That feller just wouldn't listen. As the Good Book says, 'He that hath ears to hear, let him hear.'"

"I could use a drink," Tesla said. "And you?"

Hank nodded.

Tesla retrieved a bottle from the cabinet, and poured two generous glasses. He sat down, took a drink, and sighed. "My American citizenship is one of my proudest possessions. I love this land, in part because of her tradition of human rights and freedom."

"You got that right," Hank said. He tilted his head back and swallowed a big gulp.

"I have tried to stay neutral in this struggle. But General Bell, with his despotic ways, has forced my hand. I must join the fight to preserve my country's freedom."

"Amen," Hank said. "So, that red-haired fellow, you know him from before, right?"

"That is correct. He worked for Edison," Tesla said.

"I wonder if Fidelio knows him," Hank said. "And how the heck did he end up out here?"

"Who knows? It seems he has fallen on hard times."

"Yep," Hank said. "Life has a way of messing things up for people."

"The best-laid plans of mice and men," quoted Tesla.

Hank nodded. "I have the feeling we're gonna envy the mice by the time this is all over."

Back at the cycle shop, Hank gave them a quick summary of what had transpired. "Him and his men just barged in without so much as a 'please' or a 'thank you.' He was barking orders like a drill sergeant at boot camp. His men were just as bad, destroying the lab like a bunch of apes. If they'd just listened to us, that poor fellow wouldn't've ended up cooking himself."

Fidelio nodded briskly. "The whole affair is an outrage. I am certainly glad that we moved the mining spiders."

"You say the man in charge knew Tesla from before?" asked Fred.

Hank nodded. "They both worked for Edison. Fidel, you know a man named Hopkins?"

Fidelio's face went pale. "Hopkins? With red hair, fair skin and a broken nose?"

"Yep, that's him."

"I do know him. We were friends for a while, but he betrayed my trust." In response to Hank's quizzical look, Fidelio said, "That is a story for another time."

Hank glanced at his pocket watch. "Good gracious! I'm late to meet Willie at the house. Mind giving me a ride?"

Fidelio nodded. "Not at all, let us be going. Mr. Miller, I apologize for not giving the demonstration I promised you. Shall we make it another time?"

"Yes, certainly," Miller responded, "and please call me Oscar, okay?"

During the ride to the boarding house, Fidelio said, "There is something I must tell you. When Hopkins and I had our falling out, we decided to settle our differences in the boxing ring."

"Really?" Hank said. "I wouldn't figure you for a fighter."

"There is much you do not know about me," Fidelio smiled. "I prevailed in three rounds, but he could not accept defeat. Later he broke into my quarters and found photographs of my dear friend Rodrigo. Thus he realized who I am. I thought myself safe, as he had no real proof and lived many hundreds of miles away. His arrival in Colorado does not bode well for me."

"I see," Hank nodded. "Do you think he'll make trouble for you? I know there's laws against... well, what you folks practice. Not that I think it's anybody's business."

"I am grateful for your tolerance and understanding," Fidelio said. "I shall be watchful from now on."

"Me, too," Hank said, putting a hand on his friend's shoulder. "I got yer back, pardner."

Wilhelmina was waiting for Hank in the kitchen, talking animatedly with Mrs. Johnson. Hank felt an immense relief, until she saw him and her face darkened. "You're over an hour late."

"Powerful sorry, Willie; we had some trouble at the lab." Again he told the story of the raid by Hopkins and his men, though he left out some of the more violent details.

"Why, that's outrageous!" said Mrs. Miller. "To be so rude to a sweet man like Mr. Tesla."

"Indeed," Wilhelmina said. "They should have gone through proper legal channels."

"Now you see why I say Bell is trouble?" Hank said.

"I shall reserve judgment until I've heard from all sides," Wilhelmina sniffed. "Uncle will be wondering where I am since I've been kept waiting for so long. I shall see you tomorrow."

Outside the house a carriage waited to take her home. Hank sighed; he'd gotten off easy this time.

The next day, Fred and Ooche brought Oscar to Tesla's lab. The Serbian inventor was mopping the floor. There was a pile of broken equipment on a table and a strong smell of disinfectant in the air.

"I'm honored to meet you, Mr. Tesla," Oscar said.

"Thank you." Tesla put down his mop. "Welcome to my laboratory. Please forgive the mess." He proceeded to give them a tour with his usual flourish, though Fidelio and Hank had to persuade him to demonstrate the artificial lightning. The recent tragedy had diminished Tesla's enthusiasm for his creation.

Next Fidelio brought out a small Tarantela, and put it through its usual paces. Their guests were all quite impressed, though it was difficult to compete with Tesla's pyrotechnics.

"Oh, I almost forgot," said Tesla. "You Indians may be interested in this." He unlocked a closet and retrieved a device that looked like a rifle with no hole in the barrel, attached by a thick cable to a battery on wheels. Fred and Ooche both took a few steps back. "Its principal drawback is that it requires considerable current, far too much for a geomagnetic power source."

He pointed the device at a nearby workbench and squeezed the trigger. With a loud clatter that made everyone jump, a cluster of tools and metal parts flew off the bench and attached themselves to the barrel. Tesla staggered under the weight of all the heavy objects.

"Hoo doggies!" cried Hank. "Why didn't you show this to me and Fidel before?"

Tesla shrugged. "I had thought it impractical, and put it aside. But then I recalled last year's incident in the Indian Territory."

"Most white folks would like to forget it," Fred laughed. "Your magnet gun is impressive. Much smaller than the giant magnets our people used. But you might be right about it being impractical. The other guy could easily shoot you before you disarmed him."

"I disagree," Oscar said. "All you need is the element of surprise."

"Speaking of adversaries," Fidelio said. "Governor Peabody is coming to Cripple Creek next week for a meeting with the mine owners. Rumor has it he will announce his plans to have the strikers tried for conspiracy. Of course we will not be welcome, but we need to know what transpires. My thought is that Tarantela could get into places where we cannot."

"To do what, take pictures?" asked Ooche. "I say we abduct that devil, and hold him until they release the captives."

"Easy, chief," Fred said, drawing an angry glare from his friend. "Remember, we can't win a direct confrontation with the white man."

"Would you have had the Nighthawks do nothing?" Ooche sneered.

"They were backed into a corner," Fred said. "Best to not get ourselves in that position."

"How do you know the Governor's plans?" asked Tesla. "I've seen nothing in the papers."

Fidelio stepped closer and lowered his voice. "I have a contact among the mine owners."

"Would that be old Jeb Jackson?" Hank grinned. For once, Fidelio was speechless.

"Sorry," Hank said, "but it ain't hard to guess. Jeb struck it rich and ended up with his own mine. He never forgot where he came from, and he always treated his workers fair."

"What I need to know is," said Fidelio, "are the rest of you interested?"

"Darn tootin'," Hank said, "Remember, we promised Daisy we'd help her find Lil."

"Who's Lil?" asked Oscar.

"She is a friend of ours," explained Fidelio, "who disappeared recently. Although retired, she worked with the miners' union; therefore we suspect she is imprisoned in Cripple Creek with the strikers and other opponents of Sherman Bell. And yes, Ooche, I hope to do more than take pictures. Ideally I would like to free the strikers and make a citizen's arrest of the General."

Hank laughed. "Might as well snatch the Governor too, while you're at it."

"Though I am still angry about the illegal raid," Tesla said, "that line of thinking is dangerous. We would all end up in prison, or dead."

"What do you propose, then?" asked Ooche with a scowl. "Shall we do

254

nothing, until the powers that be back *us* into a corner?" He looked pointedly at Fred.

"I like Fidelio's first idea," Hank said. "People around the country ain't up in arms 'cause they don't know what's goin' on. Pictures would really help, and we could get 'em in the Denver paper, and all over. Nick, weren't you working on a small version of Edison's sound machine? We could hide that in the hotel where the governor aims to meet with the mine owners."

"Sadly, I fear the wax cylinder would not survive the transit. But it is a good idea."

Fidelio smiled and nodded. Hank was thinking more and more like a scientist. Still, the cowboy looked worried. No doubt he realized this would be more than a fact-finding mission.

"I'm willing to help with any preparations," said Oscar, "but I'm afraid I can't come along with you. I'm a widower, remember. I've got three kids who depend on me."

"We understand," Hank said, patting him on the shoulder, "and thanks."

The following days were very busy. Tesla, Fidelio, Hank and Oscar worked to prepare two small Tarantelas for the mission. Fidelio also insisted on a backup plan. "Bell's men have adapted their automata for wireless control. We recently lost a transmitter box and its matching receiver. I believe their technology, like the spider design itself, was stolen from us."

"Who could have possibly done that?" Hank asked, irritation in his voice.

"It is possible, albeit unlikely," Tesla said. "Still, I am in favor of testing Fidelio's hypothesis. My wireless receivers each use a different frequency. If we equip the control box with a frequency selector, perhaps we can turn our adversary's spiders against him."

"I thought you didn't want to do anything unlawful," Ooche said.

"It is merely an experiment," Tesla replied. "If the military spiders are not secured against electromagnetic interference that is not our fault."

Though Fred and Ooche were not as technically adept as the others, there was plenty for them to do. To get to Cripple Creek they would need to pass through the back country. That would require horses, feed and tack. Fortunately, Tesla's lab was situated on a large property, with plenty of room for livestock. They set to work building a fence to hold the animals.

"What beautiful creatures!" said Wilhelmina as she stood by the fence. "I thought Mr. Tesla hated horses."

"Ahem," Hank coughed. "No, he doesn't *hate* 'em, he just don't like to ride 'em. But he's always looking for a good investment, and horse racing's an up and coming sport in these parts."

"Really?" Wilhelmina asked. "Is he planning on racing the mule, too?"

"Oh no," Hank said. "That one's mine. When we went to the stock sale I couldn't resist her." That much was true. Hank had insisted they buy a pack animal to carry the extra gear.

"Is that so?" Wilhelmina narrowed her eyes as if unconvinced. Hank hated lying to her, and promised himself he'd come clean when this business was over.

A few days before the Governor's visit, they met at Oscar's shop to plan their journey. Fidelio spread a map out on a table. "Daisy suggests we take this route," he traced a line with his finger, "south of the mountains."

"Will it be difficult going?" Tesla asked.

"'Course not, long as we go on horseback," Daisy said.

"I see," said Tesla with a sigh.

"There's a rail line through there, so we won't have no trouble finding our way," Daisy continued. "We just got to stay out of sight, in case the train goes by."

"We need protection," said Ooche. "I say we each carry a sidearm, in case of trouble."

"Oh no," said Hank. "I don't do that no more."

"We are not asking you to shoot anyone," Fidelio said. "However, a gun will have a deterrent effect on anyone who might wish us harm."

"And you never know, we might come across a grizzly," Fred added.

"All right then," Hank said, "but only for bears or whatnot."

That evening, Hank took Wilhelmina to her favorite Chinese restaurant. He poked at his sweet and sour pork with his fork as she ate her lemon chicken with those crazy sticks. He cleared his throat. "Willie, I got to go out of town for a few days."

"I see." She looked at him quizzically. "May I ask when and where?"

"Starting tomorrow." Hank said. "And it's not far."

She pursed her lips in a frown. "You're not going to tell me what this is about?"

"Well, sweetie..." Hank hesitated. "It's business for Fidelio and Nick. Electrical stuff."

Wilhelmina sighed. "If you feel you must keep secrets from your future wife..." She slapped the wooden sticks down on the table and wiped her mouth with a napkin. "Suddenly I've lost my appetite. I'd like to go home."

"Sure, Willie." He pulled the napkin out of his collar and called the waiter for the bill.

They rode in silence all the way to the Bunker mansion. Hank felt a gnawing pain in his stomach, not just because she was angry, but because he feared she might have a right to be.

Chapter 23 – A Hazardous Mission

Fidelio and Hank arose the next morning before dawn, and went directly to the lab. Tesla was out back, holding the saddle in his hands and staring at the black mare. She was the oldest of the horses, thus he had judged her the safest to ride. Hank was about to lend a hand when Fidelio said, "Allow me."

Hank had claimed a dappled gray stallion and named him Jackpot, after his horse back in Arizona. After all this time, getting Jackpot set up was still automatic. As Hank finished, he was surprised to see that Fidelio had already saddled Tesla's horse and was almost done with his own. Tesla was fastening a big, bulky pack to the mule. He had christened her 'Radmila,' which in Serbian meant 'sweet happiness.'

"I fear I may have made an error," Tesla said. "I was irrationally angry when I decided to go along on this mission."

"There is nothing irrational about standing for one's principles," said Fidelio. "If we let Bell's people get away with searching your lab illegally, who knows where it will end?"

"You're right," Tesla agreed, though the look in his eyes said he was not convinced.

Fidelio swung into the saddle and grinned. "Are we ready?"

"You bet," Hank said, "though that hat ain't exactly standard issue. Maybe we ought to get you something more traditional." He put a hand on his battered cowboy hat.

Fidelio tapped the brim of his derby. "It *is* traditional – for a man of taste and breeding."

"That reminds me." Tesla disappeared into the lab. In a moment he emerged, wearing an outfit that made Fidelio's dandy duds look positively manly.

He had fastened an explorer's pith helmet to his head with a leather strap. On his torso was a padded vest covered with something that looked like chain mail.

Hank could hardly keep from laughing. "If you're planning an African safari, you ought to wear a shirt that won't get rusty in the rain."

Fidelio gave Hank a stern glance.

"Laugh if you wish," Tesla said, "but horses are dangerous beasts, and it is only out of necessity that I agree to ride one at all. Now, on which side do I embark?"

Hank helped Tesla into the saddle, then hitched Radmila to Jackpot with a length of rope, and they were off. At first Tesla seemed terrified, but he soon calmed down enough to carry on a conversation. The old nag had been a good choice; she was a gentle, plodding creature.

In short order they passed the farmer's market, where they saw Fred, Ooche, and Daisy browsing the vegetable stands. Hank waved to them and soon the other three had mounted their horses and caught up with them.

"Mornin', fellers," Daisy said. "Beautiful day for a ride, ain't it?" She smiled half-heartedly, then her face returned to the haggard look she'd had since Lil's disappearance.

"Do not worry," Fidelio said. "We will do everything humanly possible to find her."

"You bet!" Hank said. "Good gosh, it's been a long time. I forgot how much I enjoyed riding."

"Good day, everyone!" Fred called. He saw Tesla, and could barely suppress his laughter. "I thought we weren't supposed to attract attention. It's strange enough, two Indians riding with four, I mean three, white folks."

Tesla scowled at him. "As I was saying before, horses are dangerous."

"Other than that old mare, yes," Fred nodded. "Try riding next to Fidelio. Maybe folks will just think you're wearing the latest fashions from out east."

"I know some of us are a bit green at this," Daisy said, "but let's pick up the pace. We got lots of ground to cover."

They headed southwest out of town until their path intersected the railway.

"I thought we weren't going to be following the tracks," Ooche said.

"Unfortunately, we got to, for a mile or so," Daisy said. "Later there's a trail that runs along to the north. There's lots of claims up there that didn't pan out."

As they rode, they reviewed their plans. Fidelio tried to talk quietly at first, but to be heard over the noise of the horses' hooves on the trail he almost had to shout. "Group one will be Daisy, Ooche, and me. We shall use our Tarantela for a photographic survey of the area. If we encounter military spiders, we shall test the new wireless control, and if possible, disable them.

"Group two is of course Nikola, Fred and Hank. They will provide a disturbance to divert the attention of the Guard and interrupt the Governor's speech. They will also provide support for us if anything goes awry."

"Don't forget Radmila," Tesla said. He had developed a fondness for the mule, perhaps because he would not be required to ride her.

"Radmila will go with Group Two, since she carries your equipment."

"I'm looking forward to it," Ooche said. "I brought my own spyglass, so I won't miss the look on that bastard Bell's face when he finds out we've snuck in right under his nose."

Ooche's enthusiasm was contagious. Even Tesla joined in the jesting and laughter. Hank, however, remained quiet.

Fidelio rode up alongside him. "What is wrong, my friend?"

"You don't miss nothing," Hank said. "Last night Willie and I had a real spat. She wanted to know where I was going, and I lied to her. The thing that grates on my gizzard is, what if I don't come back? I'd hate the last words we said to each other to be angry ones."

Daisy approached as they were conversing. "Just be glad your fiancée is safe."

"She is right," Fidelio said. "Wilhelmina is a mercurial woman, but I believe she loves you in her own way. It is unfortunate that her uncle is such a reactionary."

Fred nodded. "From what I hear, old Aldous is a son of a bitch. But Fidelio, didn't you almost go into business with him?"

"That was before I met him," Fidelio sniffed. "All capitalists exploit their workers, but some are worse than others."

"Seems to me," Fred interjected, "you're angry about how Bunker buys from the people who stole your invention. They're taking your profits. If you were really against capitalism and all, would that matter?" He looked at Fidelio and grinned.

Fidelio's Spanish complexion darkened with anger. "It is a difference of intent. I have no plans to enrich myself, but to better humanity."

"Don't let him get to you," said Ooche with a laugh. "I always said Fred should've been a white man, the way he loves making money."

Fred laughed in return. "And what's wrong with making money? If the Elders hadn't gone into business with Wilson Magnetics, we'd have never beaten that dirty skunk Chivington."

This led to a spirited discussion of politics, and how an ideal society might be structured. Hank was grateful, as it took his mind off Willie. He just wanted to get through this alive, so he and Willie could get hitched and start having young'uns. It wasn't that he was all that fond of children – he could take 'em or leave 'em – but he did want a son to carry on his father's name.

Daisy kept them right on track. Though she kept them out of sight of the railroad, they heard the train whistle as the ore cars rumbled through the mountains.

They rode on until sunset.

"Here's a good spot," Daisy said. "Nice and sheltered, plenty of firewood and a clean mountain stream. Lil and I used to come here often," she added with a crack in her voice.

At her remark, Fred and Ooche looked at each other, but said nothing.

"We should forgo the fire," Fidelio said. "We must be as inconspicuous as possible."

It was a chilly night, with no moon and the stars all around. They laid out their bedrolls on a bed of soft pine needles, fed the animals, and dined on salted meat and bread. Fred broke out a bottle of whiskey, which he shared with Hank, Daisy and Tesla.

"We'd best not get too lit up," Daisy said. "We've got a big day ahead of us."

"That's why I brought just a small bottle," said Fred. "Sometimes it's so good going down you forget to stop."

⊗ ᚠᚥ ⊗

In the morning they lit a small fire to make coffee, after which they saddled up, and the groups went their separate ways. Hank had studied Tesla's map carefully, so he didn't expect to get lost. Still he felt apprehensive as he watched the other group disappear into the trees.

Fidelio was surprised how close they were to Cripple Creek. After only two hours of riding, the town became visible in the distance.

He and his companions took their place on the mountainside overlooking the town. They tied the horses in a clearing and gave each a bag of oats. Then they walked a few yards down the slope. Through the binoculars and spyglass, they could see armed guards in front of the public buildings, and big mechanical spiders patrolling the streets.

"Lil told me about them things," Daisy said, "but I could scarce believe it 'til I saw 'em with my own eyes."

Ooche just shook his head and muttered something in his language, probably a prayer.

A small number of regular citizens were out walking, but it was eerily quiet for the time of day. Likewise, the rail depot was empty except for a pair of passenger cars parked on a siding.

"Do you see those rail cars?" Fidelio remarked. "I have heard that the Governor has his own conveyance."

"That's right," said Daisy. "They say it's real fancy-like. Us taxpayers ought to get a free tour, since we done paid for it."

Fidelio opened his saddle bag and removed a Tarantela. "*Buena suerte, niño.*" He planted a quick kiss on its metal shell, then sent it down the hill. Using the wireless control box, he directed it to the nearest of the patrolling spiders. As the big machine clomped along, the tiny one grabbed onto one of its legs and climbed up.

"What's it doing?" asked Daisy.

"The big spiders have a cryomagnetic power system," Fidelio explained. "It depends on a heat pump which keeps its circuitry well below the freezing point of carbon dioxide. If Tarantela can disable that pump, the circuits will warm up and stop working."

"Holy Jesus, that's clever."

Fidelio watched through his binoculars as the tiny spider extended a drill bit and bored a hole into the big spider, right above the left shoulder. Soon it was surrounded by a cloud of white vapor. The big spider's steps slowed until it stopped entirely.

"One down," Ooche said. "How many do they have?"

"I counted seven," Fidelio said. "Most of which are beyond our current range."

They watched as the tiny spider scuttled down the big arachnid's leg and went in pursuit of another. The second spider met the same fate as the first. Someone must have noticed, because a pair of soldiers rode up on horseback. Fidelio thrust forward the lever on the controller, saying, "*Aprisa, pequeño.*" As the small spider scuttled through the brush, one of the soldiers drew his gun and fired. Fidelio winced as Tarantela flew into the air and landed motionless on its back.

"Those sneaky slithering *chitta-micco,*" Ooche spat, pulling out his revolver. "Let me take care of their spiders. I'm a crack shot, even at this distance."

"No!" Fidelio held up a hand. "It is noisy, it endangers innocent people, and the outcome is not nearly so reliable as with employing Tarantela."

"What now?" asked Daisy.

"We shall try the modified controller," Fidelio said. "Luckily, they are sending another of the spiders over our way." He removed another metal box from his pack and fiddled with the controls. Down below them, the spider hesitated, then made a sharp left turn. Its operator ran after it, pressing frantically on his own controller. As he got closer it halted and resumed its original path. After that, the operator stayed close behind.

Fidelio raised the controller box as if to throw it, then stopped himself. He exhaled in disgust.

"What's wrong?" Ooche asked. "It seems you've proved that your idea is workable."

"That is true," Fidelio said, "But they will now be vigilant for intruders, so I doubt I will be able to accomplish much. Where is Tesla? He should have begun the diversion by now."

"The best-laid plans," Daisy said, "often get shot to shit."

Fidelio was momentarily taken aback to hear a woman using coarse language. Then he laughed "True, but we have come too far to give up now. If I get closer, I should be able to overpower their signal with mine and take control of the spiders again."

"I'll come with you," Ooche said, "and keep an eye out for soldiers."

"No! Two people will be more easily seen. You and Daisy stay here. Someone should keep an eye on the horses, and also watch for mirror signals from Hank's party."

Ooche nodded and took out his gun. "All right. I'll cover you from here."

With that, Fidelio headed down the hill. With his gun in a holster on his belt, he felt like he was in a dime novel western. His heart pounded as he dashed from one clump of brush or pile of rocks to another. Halfway down the slope he stopped to catch his breath.

Nearby, the two soldiers had opened the service hatch of a disabled spider, and were apparently having a heated discussion about how to repair it. It was a perfect opportunity. As Fidelio reached for the controller in his pocket, he heard a voice from behind.

"Get your hands above your head, or you're a dead man!"

Hank and the others waited in their designated place, on a hillside on the other end of town. "Fred, could I have the spyglass, please?"

"Sure." Fred handed it over. "I saw Ooche and Daisy, but I don't know where Fidel is."

"I bet he got impatient and tried to get closer in." Hank scanned down the hill. "There he is, behind the big rock. Gol durn it, if I can see him, so can the others – oh shit, damn it all to hell and back, they got him!"

"Is he okay?" asked Fred. "Let me see!"

"He's got his hands up. They got a gun on him," Hank said. He handed Fred the telescope and went to check on Tesla. "Nick, what in tarnation are you doing?" He glanced at his pocket watch. "You should have had that thing ready fifteen minutes ago."

"I am sorry Hank, but geomagnetic energy is still in its infancy. Something about our location is causing it to charge more slowly than I anticipated." He looked back at the meter. "Aha!" Tesla said triumphantly. "It's ready. Shall I unleash the lightning?"

"No, wait a moment," Hank said. "They got a gun on Fidelio. I'm a-feared of what they might do if something startles 'em."

As they marched him down the hill in handcuffs, Fidelio cursed his impulsiveness. Once again he was captured. Worse still, they had taken his prized Mercier pistol, which he had not even had a chance to draw. Would they now send him to prison as a saboteur? Or would his life and his dreams end here? He wondered if the others in his party were still all right.

Cripple Creek was a small settlement, and it was not a long walk from the outskirts to the center of town. They walked at a brisk pace, but not fast enough for his captors. Every so often they would shove him or stick the gun barrel in his back. Finally they reached the courthouse. The soldiers took him around back to the sheriff's office, where an unpleasant surprise met him.

"Christ on a crutch!" said a mocking voice. "Never thought I'd see your sissy face again!"

"Lloyd Hopkins," Fidelio said, staring at his former friend. "Time has not been kind to you." Hopkins' nose, misshapen since their boxing match, was now crisscrossed by dozens of tiny blood vessels.

"So many times I've dreamed of revenge," said Hopkins, "and my prayers have been answered. Hopefully you'll go to the pen for a long time. But that's not good enough for me."

"What do you mean?" Fidelio asked, his stomach clenching in fear.

"I know what you are," Hopkins said, leaning in closer. His breath was foul with the odor of rum. "A sick, disgusting pervert. And guess what? The boys in my squad hate queers as much as I do. What do you say I introduce you? Now don't go getting all excited; this ain't the kind of party you're accustomed to. No, these boys are gonna teach you a lesson."

"You have not changed," Fidelio said, "You are a contemptible little man, a hopeless, pathetic *borracho*."

"Sticks and stones, Espinoza." Hopkins' laugh was cruel and mirthless. "Boys!" he called to the next room. "I got someone for you to meet."

"Damn, they took Fidel inside somewhere!" Hank lowered the binoculars. "We shouldn't have waited! Nick, you ready?"

" Indeed. I have been ready for some time now. Shall I aim at that pile of rocks over there?"

"They'd hear it," Fred said, "but they might just think somebody's blasting."

Hank scratched his head. "Maybe if you try a bit closer to town..."

"How about those trees by the railroad track?" Tesla peered into the eyepiece. He flipped some stronger lenses in place for a better view and turned the crank to adjust the antenna's direction.

"Do you think it's safe?" Fred said. "It's been real dry this year."

Tesla pushed his tinted goggles over his eyes and squeezed the trigger. A jagged bolt rent the air with a deafening crack. The boom caused Hank to yelp in surprise. Momentarily blinded by the flash, he tripped over a rock. Instinctively he rolled to one side and sprang back to his feet.

"A direct hit!" cried Tesla.

When Hank's eyes had recovered, he saw that the biggest tree was split wide open, its trunk blackened, leaves and branches burning. As they watched, the fire spread to the other trees.

"Oh no!" cried Fred. "We have to put that out!"

"Let Bell's people do it," Hank said. "Keep 'em out of our hair while we rescue Fidel."

Fidelio winced and braced himself for yet another blow to the gut.

"Hopkins, what's this commotion?" called a baritone voice from the entryway.

"Just a moment, sir!" To his men, Hopkins snarled "Okay, stop!" then left the room.

The private standing in front of Fidelio halted mid-punch. The two men who had been holding him in place released him, and he collapsed, coughing bloody spittle onto the floor. He could see the soldiers' boots at eye level and braced himself for a possible kick.

"I heard some distressing news from Private Luedtke," the deep voice continued.

"About what, sir?" Hopkins replied.

Fidelio's tormentors eyed each other nervously. One grabbed him under the arms and shoved him into a chair.

Blood trickled down Fidelio's face from his nose and the lacerations on his scalp. His body was a mass of aches and pains. The room swayed. He felt he might pass out at any moment. He turned and vomited on the floor.

"Get the mop, Sculley," somebody said. "You're the lowest rank here."

Over the muttered curses of Private Sculley as he cleaned, Fidelio heard a new voice. "General! We had a lighting strike north of town. The trees are on fire and it's spreading."

"Lightning? For Pete's sake, there's not a cloud in the sky! Hopkins, you and your men get your asses over there and put out that fire!"

Hopkins' face appeared in the doorway. "You heard the General. There's axes and shovels at the fire station. Clancey, you're in charge of the tanker wagon. Now move it, on the double!"

Hopkins and his underlings disappeared, and a dark-haired man entered the room.

Fidelio gasped. In a moment of confusion he reached out a hand, then quickly withdrew it. The illustrations in the *Gazette* had not done him justice. Sherman Bell's resemblance to Rodrigo was quite striking.

"Tsk, tsk, you're a mess. I shall need to discipline those hooligans." Bell pulled up a chair and sat facing him. "What is your name, and what were you doing in a restricted area?"

Fidelio sat up straight and winced at the pain. Possibly they had cracked one of his ribs. "I am not required to answer any questions."

"Ah, a foreigner. Spain, am I right? Your English is quite good. Tell me, Spaniard, who sent you? Are you one of those anarchist provocateurs?"

"That is a tendentious question," Fidelio said. He knew he should stay silent, but the throbbing in his head made it difficult to think straight.

"Then I'll ask another. I heard Hopkins call you a 'queer.' Are you a homosexual?"

"That is none of your concern."

Bell nodded. "I see. I do not approve of Hopkins' actions in this matter. He's enthusiastic, but he's always been a loose cannon."

"I am grateful for your intercession," Fidelio said.

The General laughed drily. "I detest vigilantism. Don't take that to mean I condone your sickness. If you have violated our state's laws against sodomy, I hope to see you punished. After all, public morality must be maintained."

"Dang it, we've got to go get him!" Hank said. "I know what those people are like. They'll beat the hell out of an unarmed man soon as look at him."

"You were right about the fire," Fred said as he stared through the spyglass. "They've sent a whole platoon to put it out."

Tesla paused from his work on a long metallic instrument, which lay in pieces on the ground. "You should remain here, Hank. Getting yourself captured will not help our friend."

"I can't just sit on my hind end and do nothing! Fred, are you with me?"

"Sorry, Hank. I agree with Mr. Tesla."

"To Hell with the both of you!" Hank ignored Fred calling him back and took off down the thickly wooded slope, creeping from one tree to the next. From below he could hear the shouts from the men fighting the fire. Silently he prayed none of them would be hurt.

It was a farther trek down the hill than Hank had expected. When he finally reached Cripple Creek, the place looked deserted. Hank skirted the storefronts of the main thoroughfare, now mostly closed and locked. Bell's martial law had turned it into a ghost town.

Hank rounded a corner and found himself staring at an eight-foot-tall spider. His hand went reflexively to his revolver. As he slowly backed away, he considered whether he could hit the vulnerable spot just above the coolant tank.

He drew and fired. The bullet ricocheted off steel plate. The monster plodded toward him. Despite being winded from the long walk down the mountain, Hank ran in a blind panic. His lungs burned and his leg muscles screamed in protest. Suddenly he felt a much sharper pain in the behind, as a gunshot knocked him off his feet.

As he lay in the street, two uniformed men looked down at him. "Christ, what an idiot. What you go and shoot at the spider for?"

Hank just gritted his teeth and hissed, "Oh shit it hurts."

"Lay still, cowboy. Get a stretcher and we'll take him in. And get his gun."

As they carried him to a horse-drawn wagon, Hank gritted his teeth from the pain. Every bump they went over hurt like hell. What hurt worse was the fact that he had failed Fidelio.

The soldiers brought him through the side door of a church, then continued downstairs to the basement. Hank was surprised to see a dozen empty cots. "The doc will be here soon," one of his escorts said. They dumped him on a cot and left.

"Gentlemen!" scolded a female voice. "Do not treat an injured man like a rag doll."

"Why are there so many beds?" asked a second female voice.

"We had to do this on account of the elevator accident," answered the first woman. "We left it set up in case there was trouble during the Governor's visit."

"I read about the incident in the *Gazette*," said the second woman. "Such a tragedy!"

The second lady's voice sounded exactly like Wilhelmina, but how could she be here? Lying on his stomach, Hank could not see them. He propped himself on his elbows for a look.

"Sir," said the first woman, an elderly lady in a nurse's uniform, "do not get up. I am coming to help you. What is your injury?"

Hank stared at Wilhelmina, who was wide-eyed with surprise, but the nurse reminded him of his strict schoolmarm, and he had to answer her first. "It's a mite embarrassing to share with a lady. I took a bullet in the seat. Suppose it ain't too serious, but it hurts like the devil."

"The doctor may be a while," the nurse said. "But I can give you a shot for the pain."

"I know this man," Wilhelmina said. "Hank, why in goodness' name are you here?"

"I was fixin' to ask you the same thing, Willie."

Fidelio took a deep breath and closed his eyes. The general continued to shout questions in his ear. "You expect me to believe that? Tell me who you're really working for!"

The interrogation was cut short by an interruption. "General, sir! The fire is worsening."

"Those incompetent fools..." Bell turned back to Fidelio. "Spaniard, can you walk?"

"I believe so," Fidelio said.

"Good. Because I'm not about to leave you unguarded."

Fidelio stood, feeling pain in his head, stomach and chest. He followed the messenger and the general outside and stood with them on the courthouse steps. From the hillside to the north rose a thick plume of smoke. Bell said, "Did your people start the fire?"

Fidelio shook his head. "I know nothing of that. What about the spider automata?"

Bell looked puzzled. "Are you saying those iron insects started the fire?"

"No. You could use them to fight the fire. Attach shovels and cover it with earth."

"An interesting idea, but I understand those things can't stand heat."

"They may last for a time," Fidelio said. "Better to sacrifice them than a human life."

Bell eyed him suspiciously. "You seem to know a lot about these things." To the soldier he said, "Private, are all the battle spiders are operational?"

"Five of them, sir."

"Two of them broke down again already? Never mind; round up two of them, install the shovel attachments and bring them to the fire. We'll see how they do as firemen."

"Yes, sir!"

Fidelio limped on ahead with Bell aiming a pistol at his back. As they walked, Bell barked out orders. "McDonald, bring my wagon around. Bauer, where's the Governor? Is he with those damned reporters?"

"Sir, he's scheduled to deliver his speech in less than an hour."

"Not if half his audience is out fighting the fire. I will direct the fire suppression effort. Tell the Governor he's welcome to join me."

Fidelio looked back at Bell. "Will the Governor be willing to take that risk?"

Bell laughed. "A politician never misses an opportunity for publicity."

When they reached their destination, the Governor was already there, sleeves rolled up, holding a fire hose and posing for a photograph. The spiders were hard at work, filling their shovels and flinging the dirt onto the blaze.

"It seems to be working," Bell said.

"Yes," said Fidelio. "I expect their cooling systems will hold out for an hour or two."

All at once, shots rang out. Peabody's aides pushed the Governor to the ground as the soldiers returned fire. A man clutching a rifle fell from a nearby tree.

Fidelio stopped and turned his head to look. Did he know that man? Before he could see, Bell grabbed him by the collar.

"You bastard! You set that fire as a distraction so you could assassinate the Governor."

"No!" Fidelio said, "we – I mean I – would never employ violence."

The General took Fidelio by the arm and dragged him to the carriage. "Get in," he snarled. Bell got into the driver's seat and jerked the reins. "Giddap!"

"Where are we going?" Fidelio asked.

"I'm going to lock you up with your rabble-rousing friends."

Chapter 24 – Battle of the Mechanical Monsters

They soon arrived at the camp Fidelio had seen from the hillside. A huge Civil-War-era tent loomed behind an eight-foot barbed-wire fence, with guards stationed all around. In places the fence had been bolstered by wooden planks, further isolating the prisoners.

The soldier at the gate saluted the General.

"At ease, corporal. I have here a genuine anarchist agitator."

"We'll take care of him. Private!" A scrawny young guardsman opened the wooden gate, which rolled out on a cast-iron wheel. They shoved Fidelio inside and shut the gate behind him.

The stench inside reminded Fidelio of the cattle pens by the Marquis' slaughterhouse. He shuddered when he saw the reason; an open latrine. The enclosure was packed with over a hundred men, standing, sitting or lying down. Over by the fence, an Army mess tent provided shade from the hot summer sun for a lucky few.

Inside the tent, near the corner, three inmates sat on overturned buckets around a wooden supply crate, playing cards. Fidelio recognized Big Bill Haywood and Dainty Lil. The third was former Teller County Sheriff Henry Robertson. The *Gazette* had noted his 'resignation' from office and subsequent disappearance.

Lil looked up in surprise and said something to Haywood.

"Fidelio!" Haywood waved him over. "What happened to you?"

"I met up with an old acquaintance." To Lil, he added, "Daisy will be thankful to know you are well."

Lil got up on unsteady legs and embraced Fidelio. "Is Daisy here? Is she all right?"

"She is fine, though quite worried about you." Fidelio said. "Sheriff, I am surprised to see you here."

Robertson laughed. "Sometimes upholding the law can be hazardous to your health."

"Jesus God, did they work you over," said Lil, clucking her tongue. "Bill, we got any of those bandages Jim's wife brought us?" He shook his head, so she tore a strip off the bottom of her dress and began to bandage Fidelio's wounds.

All around them, the conversations of the prisoners, which had been a continuous low murmur, grew louder.

"Hey Zack," growled a hulk of a man from nearby. "Is that feller the Mexican who used to come to our meetings?"

"I believe it is," said a scrawny man with droopy eyes. "I hear he's a spy for the owners."

"Seems to me like he's a queer," said a third man.

"Shut up, everybody!" Haywood shouted. The prisoners fell silent. "This man is my friend. I'll clobber anyone who touches him."

"I'm with Haywood on that," Robertson added.

"Thank you," Fidelio said. "I understand their anger, considering the appalling conditions."

"Probably won't be for much longer," Bill said.

"Is that meant to be reassuring or ominous?" Fidelio asked.

"He means," said Robertson, "they're going to ship us all to Denver for trial, where they'll have juries full of anti-union citizens to send us up the river."

"Or worse," Bill added.

⊗ ᚠᚼ ⊗

"You say this town is too dangerous for a woman," Wilhelmina said, "Yet you were the one who got shot. Thank goodness it didn't hit any vital organs."

Hank was about to reply when Aldous Bunker burst into the infirmary. "Wilhelmina! Are you all right? I've been looking for you everywhere."

"Good gracious, Uncle, I'm not a little girl. I can take care of myself."

Bunker's expression darkened when he saw Hank. "Obviously not. I told you he was no good." He grabbed his niece's arm. "Come along. I promised your folks I'd keep you safe."

"You can't order me around," she snapped as she pulled her arm free.

"I've had quite enough of your insolence!" cried Bunker. "Staying out 'til all hours and always writing in that blasted notebook. It's bad enough I let you come here with me. I'll be writing to my sister about this, young lady." He stormed out and slammed the door.

"I guess this means I'll be sent to bed without supper." Wilhelmina giggled at her own joke. "So tell me, where *is* Fidelio right now? I should have known he'd be behind this."

"Like I said, I don't know; he got captured," Hank said. "You still haven't told

272

me why you're here. Some hot news story? Maybe to hear Peabody speak?"

"Don't change the subject. You *lied* to me." Her blue eyes flashed as she berated him. "You said you were going away on business."

"This *is* business, union business," Hank said. "We aim to get proof of the rotten things Bell is doing and tell the people of Colorado. If they knew the truth, they wouldn't stand for it."

"You are such a hypocrite!" Wilhelmina snarled. "You *lie* to me and then go traipsing off on this insane mission with that self-righteous Cuban fop. And you have the nerve to treat *me* like a child, to act like my journalism is some kind of silly girlish diversion."

"Sweetie, that is not fair. I support you all the way. And I'm sorry I didn't tell you, but... I was afraid you might want to come along, and I didn't want you to get mixed up in this."

"Then you don't know me at all. I would never be involved in such madness. Do you know what I think? You don't trust me. You were afraid I'd tell my uncle, and that he'd alert the authorities."

"Willie, you know I..." Hank's words were slurred; the morphine had taken full effect.

A man burst in the door. "Fire's getting closer! Bell says we must evacuate!"

"My goodness!" Wilhelmina said. "Are you able to walk?"

"You bet," laughed Hank, "After the shot, I don't even feel the bullet in my ass!"

"Henry MacMillan, watch your language! Now come along."

"Sorry, dumplin.' That morphine's making me feel all woolly in the head."

They got outside just in time to see two guardsmen escorting Fred Seeley down the street with his hands cuffed behind his back. Fred turned his head and stared at them.

"Keep moving, Injun!" The soldier jabbed him in the ribs with the butt of his rifle.

"I demand to see an attorney," Fred said.

"Shut your mouth, Squanto. Don't say nothin' 'less we ask you a question."

Hank kept his mouth shut; he couldn't afford to draw attention to himself. He watched as the men took Fred down the street to the east end of town where they'd seen that camp. "I think they're taking that man where to they're holding the strikers," he told Wilhelmina.

"So why are we following? Are you going to do something crazy like break

273

them out of jail?"

"Ha, I sure wish I could. Fact is, I think they're holding Fidelio there."

Wilhelmina's fair face reddened with anger. "Henry MacMillan! Time and time again I warned you not to associate with those people. And Fil – I mean, Fidelio, he's the worst. I am beginning to doubt your ability to ever be a good husband. I need a man who's going places in life, besides prison."

"But, Willie..." Hank's response was cut short by shouting and gunfire.

"Spider!" a Guard captain was shouting. "It's gone berserk, stop it!"

Hank and Wilhelmina turned around to see a military spider, stomping down the middle of the street. The soldiers continued to shoot at it, but their bullets had no effect. Nor did it shoot back; it just kept coming. Who was controlling it, friend or foe?

"It's like my uncle's spiders, but with a Gatling gun underneath!" Wilhelmina dug around in her handbag and found a tiny notepad and pencil. Lacking a camera, she began to sketch the giant automaton.

"Watch out!" Hank grabbed her arm and pulled her into an alleyway between two buildings. "What if it started shooting? Or stepped on you? It'd squish you like a bug!"

"Stop interfering! Danger is part of the job." She bent down to pick up her notebook and brush the dust from her skirt. "Look at this, it's all filthy. May I go now? I'm missing my story."

Hank grimaced. "Just be more careful!"

It didn't take long for them to catch up with the spider. It had stopped dead a block away. The guardsmen were staring at it, dumbfounded. The captain broke the silence. "Don't just stand there, you nitwits, shoot it! Aim for the spot just an inch above the left shoulder. On my mark..."

Each man chambered a bullet and pointed his rifle at the spider.

"Ready..." shouted the captain. "Aim..." A deep hum issued from the spider.

"Jee-zus!" cried one of the soldiers as an invisible force wrested the gun from his hands. It sailed through the air, slammed onto the spider's leg, and held fast.

In quick succession, the guns were snatched away. Regardless of how tightly their owners held on, all the weapons ended up stuck firmly to the spider's body. One of the men screamed and clutched broken fingers. Another cursed the loss of his pocket watch. Hank looked back at Wilhelmina just in time to see the buttons popping off the front of her dress.

"Good gracious!" Wilhelmina's dress fell open, revealing ample bosoms spilling out from the top of her corset. She shrieked and pulled it closed. "What in heaven's name? Is this your doing, Henry?"

"No, Willie, and nobody saw." Hank quickly stepped in front to shield her from view, then blushed and turned his back to her. Under his breath, he muttered, "It's got to be Nick."

The humming stopped and the guns clattered to the ground. With its claws, the spider gathered up its plunder, depositing everything into a container on its back.

Hank turned back to Wilhelmina, who was frantically digging in her purse with one hand. "Look!" he whispered excitedly, "On the spider's shoulder! It's Tarantela, hitching a ride!"

Wilhelmina just glared at him as she found some pins and fastened her dress closed.

"Take cover!" ordered the captain. "We're going to fight fire with fire!"

Three more military spiders approached from different directions and converged on the first. All three opened up with their Gatling guns. Hank, Willie, and the other spectators dove for cover. One unfortunate man cried out as he was hit. Bullets dented the first spider's flank as it spun in a tight circle. One by one, the attacking spiders stopped shooting. Were they running out of ammunition?

All at once the trapped spider ceased rotating and fired a burst at one of its opponents. A lucky shot pierced the other's coolant tank. The damaged spider emitted a cloud of vile-smelling mist and froze in place. The first spider knocked it down and scuttled down the street.

It was pursued by the two remaining spiders, until a second one froze. Hank saw a small metal creature on its back – somehow Tarantela had leaped on and sabotaged it. Hank couldn't help himself; he let out a rebel yell.

"Where is it going?" Wilhelmina quickly checked her repaired dress and grabbed her notebook. "I must see what happens next!" She ran down the street after the spider.

"No! It's not safe!" Hank sprinted after her, grunting in pain despite the anesthetic.

Two blocks down the street, the two remaining spiders squared off like boxers, throwing punches with their great metal claws and dodging nimbly. The magnetic spider took a fierce blow from the other and toppled. The soldiers cheered, until the downed spider stuck out a metal leg and swept its adversary off its feet. It then jumped up and sat on its foe. A handful of the bystanders – those not wearing

275

Guard uniforms – shouted and applauded.

After a brief humming noise, the attacker stopped moving. The first spider continued down the street.

"What on earth?" Wilhelmina asked.

"I reckon it wiped out the other guy's magnetic brain," Hank said.

"Amazing!" She resumed writing, "'I'll call it, 'The Battle of the Mechanical Monsters.'"

"Good idea," Hank said. "You stay there and finish your story."

"You can't tell me what to do!" she huffed.

"That pin on your dress is metal," Hank warned. He left her there fussing with her bodice and pursued the spider as it headed toward the courthouse. No doubt Tesla was controlling it, and maybe the little one as well, but from where? Hank was impressed. He hadn't realized the range of Tesla's wireless extended that far.

In a moment Wilhelmina was behind him, calling his name. Hank wished he could have talked her into staying someplace safe, but if she insisted on facing danger, at least they would face it together.

They followed the spider past the courthouse to a fortified camp at the edge of town. The guards raised their weapons, but like before, these were taken by the spider's magnet. The camp's fence bowed outward. The barbed wire strained against its posts, then snapped in a dozen places.

The big spider found itself bound by the fence wire, which had become wrapped around its legs and was now snagged between their articulated segments. It stumbled and toppled backwards into the street. It lay on the ground, limbs struggling against their confinement.

A bearded man in filthy work clothes emerged from the tented shelter within the now-open outdoor prison. He held his hands up. "Don't shoot!"

"You can all come out," shouted Hank. "The spider took the guards' guns."

The other miners were all crowded back into the enclosure. After the bearded man waved to them, they came forward, becoming a stream that nearly turned into a stampede. Despite their lack of weapons, the guardsmen closed in around them in a circle at the open section of fence.

"Stand firm, men!" ordered a guard commander. "Don't let anyone leave!"

Haywood strode forward like a giant as the men parted around him. "We can take 'em, brothers!"

"Solidarity!" cried the miners. They surged forward into the guardsmen. The fight began with fists and soon escalated to rocks and boards; now and then a man would fall and lie in the street bleeding. Hank stayed by Wilhelmina's side, guarding her as she scribbled feverishly in her book. Though the miners were gaunt from their confinement, their anger gave them an edge.

Just then a large horse-drawn wagon arrived, packed with men in dirt-stained laborer's clothes. One of the union men pointed. "It's the scabs!"

"Wait!" Haywood stepped over a soldier he'd just knocked unconscious to address the newcomers. "Brothers, this is not your fight!"

"Don't listen to him!" ordered one of the drivers, apparently a supervisor. "We're here to kick some commie ass!"

He was answered by cries of outrage from the other employees. "Hell no!" one of them shouted. "I ain't no hired thug!"

"Any man who refuses this order will be fired!" the supervisor shouted.

"Well then, I quit!" cried another of the 'scabs.' He jumped out of the wagon and walked away. The others followed him en masse. Seeing the wagon was now empty, the supervisor hurriedly turned the horses around and headed the other way at a gallop.

"Hank!" someone called. Fidelio emerged from the camp, a bandage around his chest. He and Fred were helping Lil walk. One of her legs was wrapped tightly with what looked like a torn-up shirt. The three of them navigated around the ongoing brawl, which continued in the center of the street.

"Hank, where are you going?" said Wilhelmina, looking up from her notebook.

Hank ignored her and limped across the street. She followed along behind him.

"I thought you was a goner, *amigo!*" Hank said as he gave his friend a hug. "Lil, are you all right?"

"Hell of a lot better now!" she said. "Where's my Daisy?"

"I'm sure she's around someplace." Hank said.

"Miss Hill!" Fidelio exclaimed. "I am surprised to see you here!"

Wilhelmina had just joined the group, notebook in hand. She gave them a forced smile and continued writing.

Now another group filtered in from all directions, composed mainly of women and children. Many of the women and the older boys brandished clubs, hatchets and butcher knives.

277

Wilhelmina gasped. "Who are these people?"

"The strikers' families, I reckon," Hank said. "They been cooped up in their houses on account of the martial law."

Haywood threw a ferocious punch, felling another guardsman. "You can't win!" he yelled to their opponents. "We've got reinforcements. Time to give up!"

One by one, the guardsmen fell back, away from the camp and the prisoners. From their midst came a red-haired man, bruised and bloodied but still defiant. "You cowards! Are you afraid of a bunch of women and children?"

"You'd better be afraid!" shouted a short Mexican woman.

"We're tougher than the lot of you!" cried an elderly lady.

"Yes!" Wilhelmina exclaimed, shaking her fist, still clutching her pencil. Seeing Hank and Fidelio's shocked expressions, she went back to writing.

Despite his pain and exhaustion, Fidelio knew he had to do something. He left Lil in the care of Hank and Fred and approached his old adversary. "Hopkins, call off your men. End this fight before innocent people are hurt!"

"I do not have that authority," Hopkins sneered. "Besides, can you guarantee your union thugs will not try to take revenge?"

"Of course they will not! They want only to sit down at the table and negotiate!"

"You think I'm a fool? Come on and fight like a man." Hopkins laughed. "Oh I forgot, you're not a man!" He charged forward, causing Fidelio to jump out of his way. Unable to stop, Hopkins ran into a large woman standing at the sidelines. She raised a massive fist and punched him, causing him to sprawl into the dirt.

"Do you require assistance?" laughed Fidelio.

Hopkins picked himself up and raised his fist. "Not from you, sissy boy!"

The pain fell away as anger and adrenaline urged Fidelio forward. He closed in on his adversary, punching furiously. Twice he connected, but Hopkins took no notice. The redhead responded with a fierce left hook to his injured chest. "*Ayy! Puto!*" Fidelio staggered backwards.

Infuriated, Fidelio charged into Hopkins, knocking him down and landing on top of him. The crowd shouted encouragement as the two rolled in the street, punching and kicking. Hank forced himself to remain silent as he watched with clenched fists and grinding teeth. He had no plans to fight, but he was ready to jump in if things got out of hand.

"This is barbaric," Wilhelmina said. "Hank, make them stop!"

"Settle down darlin,' Fidelio can take care of himself." Hank smiled. It was a side of his friend he had never seen.

"Fight like a man," Hopkins gasped, "you fucking queer!" His vile words brought a gasp from the ladies in the crowd.

Wilhelmina's eyes went wide. "How uncouth! What on earth is he talking about?"

"The man's a jackass." Hank said.

"Well, I never..." Wilhelmina said. "You don't need to join him in his foul language."

Haywood put two fingers in his mouth and whistled. The crowd fell silent. "Break it up! Let's have a fair fight! Give them room, everyone!" The miners and soldiers fell back, forming a makeshift boxing ring around the combatants.

They stood, and resumed their match. Fidelio took a deep breath and tried to keep moving. His chest ached under the damp bandages. Hopkins, red-faced with fury, swung his fists like a lunatic, the sweat flying off him like a dog drying itself. Fidelio realized that, before every attack, his opponent would always grit his teeth and hunker down.

That made all the difference. Each time his opponent readied a punch, Fidelio dodged. Hopkins was still agile, however; Fidelio only connected with one or two punches. Then, as Hopkins made one more frantic advance, Fidelio landed an upper cut to his jaw.

Hopkins wobbled, swayed, and collapsed into the dirt. Haywood grabbed Fidelio's arm and raised it to the sky. "I give you... the victor!"

The miners and their families erupted in cheers. Two soldiers picked up the unconscious officer and carried him away. The rest of them slunk away or stood, watching sullenly.

"Let's head for the storehouse," a miner shouted, "where Bell's got our food locked up!"

"That's right!" shouted another. "Our families are hungry!"

"Then you, Sam and Manny are in charge of getting it," Bill said, "The rest of us are going to have a chat with the Governor."

A parade of workers and their families headed toward the remains of the wildfire at the outskirts of town. The crowd thinned substantially as many stayed to tend to the wounded. Hank, Fidelio, Fred and Robertson walked together. Lil rode beside them on a borrowed horse.

"I'm a damned idiot!" Hank realized he'd lost track of his fiancée. "Where's

Wilhelmina?"

"There," Fidelio pointed ahead. "She is speaking to Big Bill."

"She's a-playin' reporter again," Hank said. "If only one of the papers would hire her on."

"Is that your girl?" Lil asked Hank.

"Well... yeah," Hank said.

"She's got spunk," Lil said. "Where's Daisy? I can't wait to see her."

"And Ooche?" asked Fred.

"Haven't seen either of 'em," Hank said. "Sure hope they're all right."

Halfway to their destination, they encountered a horse-drawn carriage coming their way. It halted; the animal reared at all the noise and commotion as the driver tried to turn it around. In a moment the crowd had surrounded them. Undaunted, Sherman Bell handed the reins to the Governor, and then stood up on his seat.

"By the authority of the Governor," Bell shouted. "I order you to return to your homes!"

An angry murmur went through the crowd.

"If you stand down at once," continued Bell, "I will urge leniency!"

"Can you believe the balls on that man?" Lil said.

"General, be reasonable," Peabody said in a quavering voice. "I am willing to negotiate."

The crowd parted to allow Haywood to step forward. "The union accepts your offer of negotiation. We demand a general amnesty and restoration of our jobs with back pay."

Melissa Choyce for her unique "Time to Get a Watch" font which I've used for scene dividers.Hank. A dozen hands grabbed his arms and tugged on his shirt. Despite the protests of Fidelio and Haywood, there was no calming the mob's fury. "No! Stop!" Hank gasped as a knee slammed into his groin. He tried to pray, but something inside him snapped. "Spaniards!" he cried, then began shrieking in terror.

"Release that man!"

The mob ignored the order and lifted the thrashing, struggling Hank in the air. At the whining sound of hydraulic actuators and the crunch of metal feet on the dirt street, people looked up in curiosity. "Spider!" someone shouted. When they heard the clicking of the rotary magazine of the Gatling gun, they stopped in their tracks and began to back away.

The approaching metal monstrosity set Hank into a frenzy, and he broke free from his captors. In his panicked state Hank tried to flee, slamming into a group of people who had been watching from the edge of the street. The men he had knocked down grabbed him and began punching him until the voice called out again. "Stop!"

The crowd parted. In the center of the opening stood Tesla. Around his waist was a rope, tied to the halter of Radmila the mule, walking by his side. In his hands, he held a shiny metal box covered with switches and dials. Behind him loomed an eight-foot-tall military spider.

"Did you not hear me?" Tesla moved a lever on the box, and slowly the spider's Gatling gun swiveled to face the crowd. "Put that man down – gently!" The miners lowered Hank to the ground and stepped away, letting him fall to his knees in the dirt. He curled himself into a ball and covered his face with his hands.

"Get up, Hank." Tesla extended a hand to help him up.

Hank stared up at his rescuer. The setting sun shone around the spider like a halo.

"I take no side in this dispute," Tesla proclaimed. "But if anyone attempts to harm anyone else, I may be forced to act." To underscore the threat, he punched the control box, causing the spider's Gatling gun to scan across the crowd.

Fidelio and Fred rushed over to grab the befuddled Hank and lead him out of the crowd. Hank was grateful, though the shame of his episode made him want to crawl in a hole and hide.

Wilhelmina ran up and embraced him tightly. "Are you all right, darling? I thought those ruffians would kill you!"

"I'm... all right," Hank said between ragged breaths. "Willie, Stop! Let me breathe." He pushed her away, ignoring her shocked expression. "Nick... how?" he asked Fidelio.

"Do not be angry," Fidelio said to Wilhelmina. "He is not in his right mind." To Hank, he said, "I am proud of Nikola. I did not expect him to take such bold action."

Hank watched silently as Wilhelmina stormed away. He did not pursue her. The expression on his face was like a whipped dog. Fidelio put a hand on his arm and said in a half-whisper, "There is no reason for shame. She does not understand."

"Your plan worked!" Fred exclaimed, slapping Fidelio on the back. "But I didn't expect Tesla to be the one to carry it out. I wonder if Ooche put him up to it."

"Was someone slandering my name?" They looked up to see Ooche on horseback.

Fred laughed, "You old rascal, I figured you were behind this!"

A moment later, Daisy joined them, also on horseback, a worried expression on her face. "Has anyone seen Lil?"

"She is fine, Daisy," Fidelio said. "She is resting on the bench in front of that house." Without another word, Daisy jumped off the horse and ran over to embrace her.

Hank looked around for Wilhelmina, and saw her standing with Big Bill, apparently waiting for a chance to speak to the Governor. She looked up and gave him a nasty glare. Not ever having experienced war, she just didn't understand his shell shock. He'd need to find a moment and have words with her about that.

Sherman Bell, who had been watching the goings on with increasing disgust, stood up in the wagon once more and addressed the remaining soldiers. "What is wrong with you? Are we to surrender to a mob of women and children and a broken-down machine? Governor, if I were you, I would never submit to this extortion. I wash my hands of this affair!" He got out of the wagon and stormed away.

The Governor stared at the crowd for several seconds, then sighed "All right. I hereby declare a general amnesty and pardon for everyone in this town."

A few hoots went up from the crowd. Haywood held up his hands for silence.

"Furthermore," Peabody continued, his voice shaking, "I shall convene a commission to investigate recent events, including," he coughed, "excessive use of force by Guard troops."

"What about our jobs?" someone shouted.

"Lastly, I shall meet with your employers and urge them to restore your jobs."

"I move we put this to a vote!" cried someone.

"I second!"

Haywood said, "It's been moved and seconded we accept Peabody's offer. All in favor?"

The crowd thundered "Aye!"

"I declare this motion passed by acclamation."

"Praise the Lord!" Hank said to Fidelio. "Doubt it all you want, but I believe a heavenly hand guided Nick to show up here when he did."

"Certainly it was fortuitous – for you," Fidelio said with a smile. "That reminds me – there is something I must say." He waded through the crowd to the spider that kept its silent watch. "Everyone, your attention please! Let us acknowledge the hero of the hour, Nikola Tesla!"

The response was deafening. "Hip – hip – hooray!" Radmila joined in, braying loudly.

Tesla bowed, his face reddening. He turned his attention to straightening Radmila's halter.

Hank went up to Fidelio and clapped him on the back. "You got a gift for speechifying. You ought to become a citizen like Nick, then run for office."

Fidelio laughed. "That, my friend, would truly be a miracle."

Chapter 25 – The Journey Continues

With the emergency lifted, Fidelio expected his life to go back to normal. This did not happen right away. The town of Cripple Creek was in shambles. Its mayor wrote a guest column in the reinstated *Weekly News* requesting that all citizens pitch in to help. Fidelio felt obligated to participate, since the illegitimate children of his creation had caused much of the destruction.

He was loading the Steamer with tools and supplies, much of it donated by Tesla, when Hank rushed over.

"Hold on, *amigo,* I'll ride along and help. You're still using a cane, for gosh sakes."

Fidelio smiled and held it up. "I am becoming rather fond of it." The staff was mahogany, topped with a horse's head in brass. Beneath was a compartment containing magnifying lenses and other tools. "Your aid would be most welcome. My motorcar only has two seats, however."

"Don't worry. Willie ain't comin' along. Her parents are here visiting from St Louis."

"That is unfortunate," Fidelio said, "She could be writing about the reconstruction effort." Secretly, he was relieved at the news.

The days were long and exhausting. There was damage to the courthouse and many of the shops. The Catholic church required a thorough cleaning after its use as an infirmary. Several homes on the outskirts had burned, though thankfully no one was hurt in the fires. Fidelio and Hank volunteered to help rebuild the union hall, which Bell's troops had destroyed.

Being experienced with electricity, Hank took on the task of providing the hall with built-in wiring, an amenity that was normally reserved for the rich. As he knelt on the floor fastening cables to the building's frame, two burly men approached him, one dark and Latin-looking, the other blond and fair-skinned.

"*Buenos dias, señor,*" said the darker man. "Are you Henry MacMillan?"

Hank stood up and dusted himself off. "Not sure I should own up to that," he said with a grin.

"We felt bad about what happened to you the day of the breakout," the man continued.

"Yes. We did not know about your shell shock," said the blond man. "You served our country and we treated you terribly."

Hank shrugged. "'Twas just a misunderstanding, that's all."

"A bunch of us wanted to say we was sorry," said the first man, "and to thank you for all you done for the workers. So we made this." He thrust a leather pouch into Hank's hands.

"Oh, it ain't necessary; I got all the reward I needed..." He opened the pouch and was speechless. "Holy Moses, what a beaut!" It was a handmade bolo tie, with the eagle insignia cut from a twenty dollar gold piece and mounted on an onyx background. At the top in gilt lettering was the inscription 'FREEDOM.'

"Gosh fellas, I don't know what to say." Hank removed his hat and put on the tie on immediately. "I know these ain't exactly my Sunday go-to-meetin' clothes, but with this on, I feel like I could go anyplace. Thank you."

"You're welcome," the first man said." Both shook Hank's hand. "By the way, where's your Cuban friend?"

Fidelio had been watching from across the room. "I am here."

"I believe this belongs to you," the second man said. "We made a case to keep it safe." He handed Fidelio a velvet-lined wooden box containing the Mercier pistol.

"Why thank you! I thought this was gone forever!" Fidelio shook their hands and the two men returned to their work.

"What amazing luck!" said Hank. "Maybe one of these days you'll actually get to use it. If you need any lessons, I got a bronze medal in the annual skeet shoot in Queens, New York."

"Is that so? I shall have to take you up on that offer."

That following week, Fidelio and Hank rejoined Tesla at his laboratory. Fidelio was eager to resume his work after abandoning it for the last several weeks. Even Tesla's own projects had been neglected. He had been busy constructing a stable behind the lab for Radmila.

As Fidelio began work on one of the broken Tarantelas, there was a knock on the door.

"I'll get it." Hank was at the door in an instant. "Fred, Ooche! Welcome, friends! Step inside and pull up a chair."

"Yes, please come in," said Tesla. He did not look up from the piece of gray ceramic floating in the air above a tub of bubbling liquid. "I am continuing my search for a better cryomagnetic material. Perhaps you would like to observe."

"Thank you," said Fred as he and Ooche entered. "Though we can't stay long. We just wanted to say goodbye, and express our gratitude for your hospitality."

"You are the ones who deserve thanks," Fidelio said. He wiped his hands on a rag and came over to greet them. "Without your help at Cripple Creek, our effort might not have been successful." He looked past them out the doorway. "Is that your automobile?"

"Yep, it's mine," Fred said. "It's a Ford Roadster. Just got it last fall."

"May I have a look?" Fidelio asked. "With so much happening, I never got the chance."

"Certainly."

The men all went outside, except for Tesla. Hank took the opportunity to roll a cigarette. Fidelio made a circuit of the vehicle and scrutinized the engine as Fred held open the hood.

"Uses gasoline rather than kerosene," Fred explained. "Not as smooth as a steam engine, but it's convenient, with those 'gas stations' popping up all over."

"It appears to be well designed, for an internal combustion automobile. The storage compartment is rather small, however. You fellows must not have much luggage."

"We are not obsessed with material possessions like the white man," Ooche said. "Or the mostly-white man." He smiled at Fidelio as he spoke.

Fidelio sniffed. "Science cannot be done with the mind alone. One needs equipment, tools, and most importantly, parts with which to build things."

"He's only pulling your leg," Fred said with a smile. "We're big supporters of science and progress, especially your inventions. If fact, I'm quite keen to invest in it."

"I am gratified to hear that," Fidelio said. "I have worked hard to convince the mine workers to accept this innovation, even though I have as yet seen no reward. At this time, however, I must remind you of my continuing difficulties with the Patent Office, which will take some time to sort out."

"We've got faith in you," Fred replied. "Anybody who could invent something as amazing as Tarantela can sure as hell win against Springfield's lawyers, especially since you've got right on your side." He pulled a card from his vest pocket and handed it to Fidelio. "This is my address in Muscogee. They forward my mail to wherever I'm at. Please keep me apprised of any developments."

"I certainly will," said Fidelio.

"It's a shame you can't stick around for a spell," Hank said.

"Yes, it is unfortunate," Ooche replied. "It is a long drive back to Muscogee."

"Official business?" Fidelio asked.

"Opera business," Fred replied. "Tallulah sent a telegram. The influenza is going around. Luckily, they have enough performers to go on, but they're short-handed with the crew and security. So we'll drive to Muscogee, leave the car there and take the train to New Orleans."

Hank took a last drag of his smoke and stubbed it out on a convenient hitching post. "Give my regards to Tallulah, would you? With all the hullabaloo, I ain't had time to write her."

"I'm certain she understands," Fred said. "We'll definitely relay your greetings."

Everyone said their goodbyes. Even Tesla paused from his labors to emerge from the lab and bid them farewell. The men all shook hands and embraced in turn, except of course for Tesla.

⊗ ⼍⼈ ⊗

The following week, Haywood returned to Denver to resume his chairmanship of the Western Federation of Miners. One of his first actions was to start a petition to remove Governor Peabody from office. Fidelio volunteered to gather signatures in Colorado Springs.

Outside the mining district, the voters were not particularly supportive of the effort. Though he filled a few pages with names, Fidelio encountered many who were apathetic or even hostile. "I don't know what you people want," said a man in a top hat. "Governor Peabody handled the crisis quite fairly. He gave those troublemakers far better than they deserved."

At the Gold Dust Saloon, there were rumors that Haywood would run for governor. To Fidelio, this seemed like an excellent idea. He wrote to the union leader to pledge his support.

Haywood's response came quickly. "I'm flattered by your endorsement," he wrote, "but I must decline. I've always viewed government as a tool of the capitalist oppressors. I cannot be a part of that system. By the way, have you heard about our friend Sherman?"

Fidelio chuckled; he had read the story in the *Gazette*. In Denver, a grand jury indicted Sherman Bell for abuse of power and unlawful imprisonment. The indictment was later withdrawn, when President McKinley let it be known he would pardon the General, likely at the behest of Vice President Roosevelt. Still, Bell's pride was so wounded that he slunk off to Venezuela to aid in the fight against the British blockade of that bankrupt nation.

Not long after her parents' return to St. Louis, Wilhelmina had a big argument with Uncle Aldous. She moved out of his mansion and rented a room from Mrs. Tyler. That made Hank happy, because she was now closer, and they could see each other more frequently.

Yet relations between Hank and Wilhelmina were still strained. One evening at the boarding house, she once again mentioned his 'episode' after being rescued from the mob in Cripple Creek. The distant rolls of thunder and the lightning flashes visible through the window provided an ominous background for their discussion.

"I'm trying to understand your affliction," she said curtly.

"War changes a man," Hank said. "If you ain't been there, you can't possibly understand."

"But it's been four years," Wilhelmina said. "Yes, I understand you were sick with cancer for much of that time, but I would think by now you would have recovered all your faculties."

"It ain't – I mean it isn't – all that easy. Can you love a man who goes off his rocker now and again?"

"Oh, you sweet man, of course." She gave him a long, sensuous kiss.

Fidelio did not share Hank's joy about their rapprochement. He was not happy to see her at the laboratory every midday and at the boarding house each evening.

One morning on the way to the lab, Hank confronted him with a surprising accusation. "Whenever Willie's around," he said, "you seem like you're powerful angry about something."

"Do you honestly think so? I believe it is she who views me with disdain."

"No, she's not like that. Come on, let's have it. What's your beef with Willie?"

"Very well," Fidelio said. "I am convinced that someone stole Nikola's remote control. Shortly thereafter this exact circuitry found its way into the mine spiders and the military spiders as well. This is a design it took Tesla months to perfect, after

288

which it took me weeks to adapt it to Tarantela. The notion that they developed it independently seems implausible at best."

"I don't like where you're going," Hank declared. "Just who are you accusing of this? Just because you and Willie don't get along don't mean you can blame her for stealing your gadget."

"My feelings about her have nothing to do with it," Fidelio said. "She is the only person who had both motive and opportunity."

"Well, then," Hank said, "we got nothing to talk about, 'cause there's no way she'd do something so low-down and sneaky."

"Perhaps you do not know her as well as you believe."

"That sounds like an accusation," Hank snarled. He clenched his teeth and unthinkingly raised his hand in a fist. "If I weren't a peaceable man, those'd be fightin' words."

Fidelio huffed. "In the past I might have suggested a few rounds of boxing to clear the air, but in practice it did not turn out well."

Hank nodded. "We got to work together, so let's keep it civil-like. I don't want to hear you talking dirt about Wilhelmina no more, all right?"

"Very well; you have a deal." Fidelio walked away in a huff, got into his car, and did not return to the laboratory until late in the day.

The argument created a gulf between the two men. Hank continued to work with Tesla, but Fidelio began spending several days a week away from the lab. When Hank questioned him, he said, "This is a critical time for the union, and I want to do whatever I can to help."

Hank doubted the union really needed Fidelio's help. Things seemed to be going well for the WFM. After the fracas at Cripple Creek, all the owners agreed to negotiations, except for Aldous Bunker. His statement appeared in the *Gazette*. "As long as I live, I shall never capitulate to these Marxist bullies." Instead, he put the mine up for sale. Shortly thereafter, he sold his mansion and returned to his home state of Missouri.

Hank and Fidelio barely spoke to each other, except for minimal communication during their work. To Hank the end of their friendship caused an ache in his chest. He longed to escape those bad feelings. Maybe he'd seek other employment, as Wilhelmina had suggested.

One evening Hank and Wilhelmina were dining out, and things between them were going well. She talked him into splurging on a bottle of champagne, and they laughed and talked like they had at the beginning of a courtship.

As the waiter arrived with the pitcher to refill their water glasses, he accidentally knocked over Wilhelmina's purse. The catch popped open and something clattered onto the wooden floor and shattered into several pieces.

"Aw, shucks! Let me get that for you, sweetie."

"Please! I'll get it, Hank," she said, almost jumping from her chair to grab it.

Hank was quicker. "What in tarnation?" He gathered up the gray, brittle shards into his hand. Obviously they had fit together in a disc of something that looked like fired clay. "Hey, this looks just like one of Tesla's chill-o-netic experiments. How'd it get into your handbag?"

She coughed as if choking on something. "What is that? I've never seen that before."

Hank shook his head. "That seems mighty unlikely. It didn't just sprout legs and jump in."

Wilhelmina's face flushed red. "Are you accusing me of stealing? If so, just come out and say it."

"I ain't saying that," Hank said. "But it does look suspicious."

"I said I've never seen it before. Why won't you believe me?"

"I'd like to," Hank said, "but when you see the dog in the chicken coop with eggshell on its face, a man's got to wonder."

"What's that supposed to mean? Who's this 'dog' you're talking about?"

Hank sighed in exasperation. "It's just an old sayin', Willie." He wrapped the pieces up in his handkerchief and stuffed the package in his pocket.

"I can't believe you have so little trust in me," she sniffed. "How do know that *somebody else* didn't put that in there to set me up? I think you should take me home."

Despite alternating between tears and increasingly implausible excuses, Wilhelmina was unable to convince Hank of her innocence. "Maybe we oughtn't get married," Hank said as he left her at the Tyler residence. She wept by the door as he drove off. He was still angry and told himself to stay strong, but the image of her crying made the tears roll down his face as he drove home.

The next morning, he told Fidelio what had happened. "You were right all along, I reckon. If she stole Tesla's test stuff, she probably did take that controller box. I hope you can forgive me for getting all riled when you were just trying to help."

Fidelio was remarkably restrained. "It is all right, *amigo.*"

Hank half-expected Wilhelmina to come to the lab and plead with him to take her back, but she did not. After a few days had passed, he borrowed Tesla's car and drove to the Tyler house. "Miss Hill no longer resides here," Mrs. Tyler said sharply. "She has accepted a stenographic job with the *Denver Evening Post.*"

Hank's first impulse was to drown his misery. Tesla indulged him by providing the whiskey. The inventor shared a drink with him and offered consolation, but when Hank began sobbing he was clearly at a loss. Tesla returned to his work and left Hank to his sorrows.

Fidelio arrived at the lab early the next morning to find Hank asleep on the floor. "Hank, wake up!" Hearing his friend moan in response, he said, "I heard what happened."

"Ohh... my noggin feels like it got hit by a baseball bat." He looked up at Hank. "I promise you, I ain't gonna ever drink like that again."

"I would not blame you. Though I would agree that some wines have an agreeable taste, I will never understand your fondness for whiskey."

Hank laughed, and then groaned. "Well it don't like me all that well either. So you heard about Willie running off to Denver."

"It is for the best," Fidelio said. "She was not the woman for you. A man of your morals and integrity should not be married to a thief."

"Deep down, she ain't a bad person," Hank said. "I betcha her uncle put her up to it."

"Perhaps. Nevertheless, she made that choice, despite the potential harm to your employment, not to mention enabling the automata as more efficient killing machines. What I find particularly disturbing is that she stole from Nikola as well, after she and her uncle had broken off their relationship. For whom could she be working?"

Hank shrugged. "I don't expect she figured on all the horrible stuff they did with the spiders. But taking that cryomagnetic disc, that *is* mighty queer – uh, pardon my choice of words. But it don't matter, 'cause I'm done with that woman."

The next day Hank was his old self again. "I've been a real jackass these last few weeks," he said to Fidelio on the way to the lab. "Hope we can put all the bad blood behind us."

"I would be a poor friend if I could not," Fidelio replied. "The emotion of love can have a profound effect on a man's judgment."

"Yep." Hank nodded, and the matter was settled.

Fidelio could sympathize; he knew the pain of loneliness all too well. Still, he believed Hank would find an honest woman someday.

Busy as he was with his daily labors, Fidelio remained involved with the union. In their ongoing negotiations with the owners, the biggest sticking point was the automata. Most of the rank and file wanted to ban them completely. Fidelio strove to persuade them otherwise with an impassioned speech at the WFM local.

"There is a natural human desire to stop the clock and keep things as they are. But as my friend Nikola Tesla has said, it is fruitless to fight progress. In any case, my intent in creating the first spider automaton was not to replace human workers. Rather, I aimed to prevent deaths and injuries, by utilizing it only for the most dangerous tasks."

In the end, the union accepted a compromise which was, on the surface, more permissive than Fidelio's proposal. The contract allowed the use of automata, only if existing employees were re-trained for their operation and maintenance.

This proved to be a dilemma for the companies, since re-educating their current workers cost far more than bringing in specialists who already knew the trade. Thus the automata collected dust in the storehouses; most were sold or returned to the Springfield Company.

The military spiders met a similar fate. Officially, they belonged to the Pinkerton Agency, as the Colorado Guard had no budget for such devices. These automata were seized to settle a lawsuit by the town of Cripple Creek against the company. The town sold most of them for scrap.

Fidelio used his contacts to procure the mine spider Tesla had used in the battle, purchasing it with his share of the proceeds of the sale of the horses. At the lab he studied its design, comparing it with Tarantela's original blueprints. Like the small one they had procured earlier, this was a near-perfect match, except for a few structural changes that were required to support the machine's greater size. This, Fidelio felt, proved beyond a doubt that his ideas had been stolen.

Every day, Fidelio checked his postal box for a response from the Patent Office. He was surprised to receive one instead bearing a North Dakota postmark, with the address hand-written in flowery script. Inside was a letter which read:

"My dear Fidelio,

"I write this letter not in a business capacity but as a friend, so please consider the information herein to be confidential.

"You will shortly be hearing from the attorney of Charles and Edna Wagner. As subscribers of the *Denver Evening Post,* they were surprised to see an article about a patent dispute between you and Springfield Arms over the 'arachno-automaton.' They are quite upset that no one informed them of this issue at the time that they purchased shares in your venture. Charles confronted Antoine, who informed them that we had not been aware of the issue, either.

"Antoine was fit to be tied. He urged Charles to seek a remedy though the courts. I personally believe you are an honest and forthright man, though the article was quite slanderous, implying that your claims of a 'stolen prototype' were fraudulent. I pray that this dispute can be resolved fairly and that all your hard work and ingenuity will not have been in vain.

"Sincerely, Medora Vallambrosa"

"¡*Maldita sea!*" Fidelio crumpled the letter into a ball, and was ready to discard it in the post office's refuse bin, when he thought better of it, smoothed the letter out, folded it, and stuck it in his pocket. He had not been so angry since his argument with the Marquis so many months ago. No, he shouldn't put the blame on Medora. She had only been trying to help.

Fidelio had never felt so overwhelmed. Should he hire that Gellman fellow? He had no idea what type of law the man practiced. He decided to stop at the general store for a copy of the Sunday *Post.* The 'funny pages' were his guilty pleasure and he had missed the *Katzenjammer Kids* for the last several weeks. Once cheered up, he would decide on a course of action.

The *Post* did not provide solace. The headline read, "SECRET WEAPON REVEALED: How Mechanical Spiders are Winning the War in the Philippines." He skimmed the article, which confirmed that Isabelle's 'rumor' had been true. His heart had never hurt so badly, save for the time he had lost Rodrigo. He did not return to work that day; instead he took a long, aimless drive through the countryside. On returning home, he retired to his room without speaking to anyone. Soon there came a knock on his bedroom door.

"Open up, Fidel. Mrs. Johnson said you was in there moping, and that ain't like you." When Fidelio made no response, he came in anyway, to find his friend lying on the bed with all his clothes on. Without a word, he handed the wrinkled papers to Hank.

Hank read the letter, his features clouding with anger. "Dagnabbit, that bastard Wagner hires a shyster before he even gets your side of the story. Ain't that just like a banker? Makes me wonder who in Denver knows about your troubles."

Fidelio gave a long sigh and decided not to point out the obvious. "There is more. Look at the newspaper."

Hank picked up the paper from the dresser and let out a low whistle when he saw the headline. "Lord have mercy on us all." He sat down next to his friend. "I'm sorry, Fidelio. I don't know what we're gonna do, but by gosh we've got to do something. That invention is yours, and here they are, using it for the Devil's work."

"I would like nothing more than to wrest control of Tarantela's children from these criminals and put an end to this atrocity. Yet I cannot take legal action, because I am out of funds. My father refuses to extend me any more credit. He was particularly angry to hear how I sided with the union in Cripple Creek. Fighting a lawsuit takes money."

"Well..." Hank began, "How much money are we talkin' about?"

Hank had hoped that discussing the problem would make Fidelio feel better, but that was not the case. That next morning he had to knock three times on his friend's door to get him out of bed. At the lab, Fidelio spent the entire day in a fog, mindlessly tinkering with the same spider.

As they drove home that evening, Hank decided to take action. "You've got to snap out of it, *amigo*. You've always been a fighter, and I can't believe you'd give up."

"I appreciate your concern," Fidelio said. "But you are not responsible for the situation I find myself in. That is my own fault entirely."

"Now don't you get discouraged," Hank said. "You've got plenty of proof to get your rights back from those invention-stealing crooks. We can't fight 'em from Colorado, though. We've got to go to Washington and bring the war to them."

"You are correct," Fidelio said as they got out of the car, "But my bank account is empty. I have alienated my father, as well as the Vallambrosas and Wagners. Nikola has a generous nature, but I cannot in good conscience ask him for help. He has financial problems of his own."

"Then you'll have to find another Samaritan," Hank said as they walked to the house. "You know how when my uncle passed away, he left me a big piece of his ranch. That was mighty nice of him, but I got no desire to go back to the cowboy's life. All in all, it's back-breaking work for too danged little money. So I'm going to sell that land, which ought to get us a pretty good lawyer to argue your case."

Fidelio stopped in his tracks and stared at Hank. "No! I could not accept your money. I would not feel right about it."

"Now listen here, Fidel. You've taken care of everything since day one. Consider it payback – also an investment. Promise me a share of the profits, and when the greenbacks come rolling in, we'll have more than we could possibly need."

"You are a true friend." Fidelio embraced Hank, then quickly regained his composure and stepped back. "If you can make sacrifices, so can I. I shall sell the Steamer. A quality automobile like that should have held much of its original value."

The next day, Fidelio took out an ad in the *Gazette*. On the day of its publication, they received visitors at the lab, a local businessman and his wife. "It is in reasonable condition," the man said. "I'll offer you five hundred dollars, not a penny more."

"I am sorry, I must have at least a thousand," Fidelio said.

Eventually they reached a compromise at eight hundred. The man handed over a sack of golden eagles, and Fidelio handed him the key. He stood for a long time on the front steps, watching the man drive off in his beloved Steamer.

Hank emerged from the lab and stood beside him. "You done a good bargain, Fidel. Only problem is, how do we get to Washington now?"

"With this, of course," Fidelio held up the sack. "We have plenty for passage on the Trans-America Zephyr to Washington, not to mention travel expenses. Or we could take the train, if you think air travel is too extravagant."

Hank grinned. "I'm a man of simple tastes, but another Zeppelin ride? Hoo doggies, count me in!" He clapped Fidelio on the back. "This is a new chapter in our lives. The Lord is shining his face on us, I just know it."

"Perhaps He is," Fidelio said with a smile.

"We better talk to Tesla," Hank said. "After all he's done for us, we owe him the courtesy of a couple weeks' notice."

"Of course," Fidelio said. "I will be saddened to leave this place."

Hank had acquired few possessions during his time in Colorado. Most of these he gave away to charity, except for what he could fit in his old traveling trunk.

When the day came, Tesla said, "It has been a pleasure working with the both of you. As you know, I do not shake hands, but I will make an exception this time."

Hank had to laugh when he realized that Tesla was wearing the rubberized gloves he used for his high-voltage experiments. The scientist extended his hand awkwardly, shaking Hank's hand and then Fidelio's. "I wish you the best of luck in all your endeavors."

"Thank you," Fidelio said. "I apologize for any unwarranted assumptions or rash behavior on my part."

"Rash behavior? I don't recall anything like that," said Tesla.

Hank rolled his eyes skyward and resisted the urge to shake his head.

"It's been a real honor to be part of your team," Hank said. "Someday the young'uns will read about you in the history books, as one of the greatest inventors in history."

Fidelio looked stricken, until Tesla interjected, "I'm sure Fidelio will be in the books as well, and you, too, Hank, just like Alexander Graham Bell and Watson."

Their farewells completed, the two friends waited in front of the laboratory for the taxi that would take them to the airfield. Hank had his trunk. Fidelio had a suitcase, two fiberboard boxes and three satchels containing everything they would need in their upcoming legal battle.

Hank gazed wistfully at Pike's Peak, wondering if he'd ever come back. He felt a pang of regret as his mind drifted back over the last few months. This was where he had met Willie and lost her. As ornery as she'd been, he'd miss her pretty face, her independence and determination, maybe even her fiery temper. No, he wouldn't miss *that*.

Then, in his mind he heard the lovely strains of "*Sì, mi chiamano Mimì.*" It made sense; Tallulah had always been the real girl of his dreams. Without thinking, he began to hum the tune.

Fidelio, who had been reading Jules Verne's *Voyages Extraordinaires*, looked up from his book and smiled. "I can guess what person is in your thoughts."

Hank shrugged. "Me and Tallulah are from different worlds. It ain't meant to be."

"Do not despair, Hank. Who knows what the future holds? But even if the two of you never marry, you will always be friends. Friendship is a thing more precious than wealth or even knowledge." He turned away, lest Hank see his glistening eyes. "Ah! Our ride has arrived."

With that, they climbed into the taxi and were on their way.

Coming soon from Nakota Publishing:

Diana's Fury

In the high-tech wars of the future, women have the upper hand.

Mirjana Lovac, US Navy drone pilot, is one of the elite few who can master the neural interface to the new generation of unmanned aerial vehicles. The downside: due to bandwidth requirements, pilots must be stationed near the front lines. Mirjana's future looks bright until a terrorist attack strands her in the jungles of Borneo with a bitter rival. Can the two women put their differences aside long enough to get out alive?

Diana's Fury is the first in a planned series of adventure novellas set in the near future, when warfare is dominated by drones, and only women can pilot them.

Coming to Amazon in late 2015.

Upcoming Sequel from Nakota Publishing:

Fidelio's Insurrection

A Novel by Vaughn Treude

Chapter 1 – A Significant Decision

"The United States Court of Appeals for the District of Columbia has reached its decision." The gray-haired judge peered down at the sheaf of papers in front of him and adjusted his spectacles. He squinted and frowned, then took off his glasses and wiped them with a handkerchief.

Fidelio leaned forward in the straight-backed wooden chair, holding his breath so he would not miss a word. On his left sat his attorney, Viktor Szabo, who smiled and nodded curtly. On his other side was his friend and business partner Hank MacMillan. The former cowboy's forehead was beaded with sweat; he pulled on his necktie to loosen it, and fiddled with the stiff collar of his new shirt.

Beyond Szabo sat the opposing counsel, Springfield Arm's best corporate lawyers. They had seemed eloquent compared to Szabo, with his thick Hungarian accent. Yet Szabo was a friend of Nikola Tesla, who described him as "a practical man, the only attorney I can stand to be in the same room with." Despite his many quirks, the brilliant inventor had never steered them wrong.

"In the case," the judge continued in a bland monotone, "of Fidelio Espinoza vs Springfield Arms, Incorporated, the court awards the plaintiff the sum of 100,000 dollars in payment of royalties for infringement of the plaintiff's patent #678012, also known as the Arachno-automaton."

"YEE–" Hank sprang to his feet, arms in the air, drawing stares from everyone in the courtroom. He blushed bright red, mumbled "Beg pardon, your honor," then sat down, leaned over to Fidelio and whispered. "Haw!"

The judge gave Hank a scathing look over his glasses and continued. "As for the second part of the suit, the injunction to bar the defendant from manufacturing the device, this motion is denied in the interest of national security. Defendant will instead receive a royalty of one US dollar on every unit produced."

Without thinking, Fidelio stood up. "Your honor! May I ask a question?"

The judge sighed. "Sir, I don't know how they do things in Cuba, but here in America we stand by established protocol. However, in the interests of fairness, you may proceed."

"What good is the recognition of my intellectual property if I cannot exercise control?"

"Mr. Espinoza," the judge replied, sounding as if someone had awakened him from his afternoon nap, "In each case, the court is required to weigh carefully the interests of all parties. One of these parties is the United States government, which established this institution to promote the general welfare, including the maintenance of law and order and the defense of the nation. Inventions such as yours are necessary to that defense." He picked up his gavel and struck it against the wood block. "This hearing is adjourned."

Everyone rose to their feet at once. "Congratulations, Mr. Espinoza!" exclaimed Szabo, his bearded face breaking into a smile. "It is as good as I would have hoped."

"Thank you," Fidelio replied, shaking the man's hand. "Though I am disappointed at the failure of the injunction, I cannot fault your services. Your work has been exemplary."

"The good guys win again," Hank said, a big grin on his face. "First we beat 'em on the patent, and now the dirty rascals have got to pay up. Too bad about the second part, though."

Fidelio approached the court clerk and quickly verified that they had correctly recorded his father's mailing address. "We will send a copy of the judgment there, sir," said the clerk, a skinny fellow not far out of his teens. "Will this also suffice for the royalty checks?"

"Thank you, but no," Fidelio said. "For those I shall give you my postal box address. How shall it be paid?"

The young man looked at the documents. "Ten thousand payable immediately, the remainder to be paid monthly, over a maximum period of two years."

"That will have to do," Fidelio said. That first check, he realized would go entirely to his attorney. After that, he would need to send no more letters to Havana begging for money. Even Fidelio's stern, humorless father would have to admit that his so-called 'harebrained schemes' had borne fruit.

To Fidelio's dismay, Springfield's head counsel approached them in the hallway as they exited the courtroom. "Well fought, Mr. Szabo." The attorney shook his opponent's hand. "And Mr. Espinoza, though I don't share your philosophy, I respect your dedication to your ideals."

Fidelio nodded. "Thank you, Mr. Eckelstein."

The second Springfield attorney, a stocky bearded fellow named Knowles, stood behind his partner, glaring at Fidelio. As Eckelstein turned to depart, he said, in a low voice. "Espinoza, I've heard all about you and your rabble-rousing in Colorado. I suggest that you go back to Cuba where you belong."

Before Fidelio could answer, Hank stepped between the two men and said, "Now that weren't a very charitable thing to say."

Knowles' frown became a scowl. "As far as I'm concerned, you're worse. You're an American, consorting with this foreign agitator. You're nothing but a traitor."

Hank grimaced; his hands made fists. He took a deep breath and steadied himself. "I served this country in the Spanish war. Did you?"

"Even if the he'd been willing, with a flabby physique like his, I doubt that the Army would have accepted him," Szabo said with a wry smile.

Knowles turned and walked away without a word.

"Capitalist parasite," Fidelio hissed through his teeth.

"I was itching to slug that bastard," Hank said. "Had to remind myself that someday, like all of us, he'll have to stand before the Lord. I 'spect he'll have some explaining to do."

"Indeed," Fidelio said. Though he did not share Hank's religious beliefs, divine retribution seemed appropriate in Knowles' case.

As they exited the Federal courthouse, Hank slapped his friend on the shoulder. "No need for the hang dog look, amigo. You're a genuine tycoon! And this is your own earnings, not your old man's. Yours to do with whatever you want!"

"True," Fidelio replied, "Though it is less than half of the sum we were asking."

"It is still a substantial amount," Szabo said from behind them. "As I told you, it is a common tactic; we ask for more than we expect, and with luck we get a reasonable result."

Fidelio nodded. "I understand."

"You could use a portion of the money for good works," the attorney continued. "Though it would be wisest to reserve the lion's share for investment. I could recommend several corporate securities with a good potential for profit."

"I don't doubt you could," said Hank, "But if you ask me, Fidelio ought to use it to work on a new-fangled version of Tarantela, something you don't got to share with those Springfield sons of bitches."

"Agreed." The prospect of besting the death-merchants made Fidelio feel somewhat better. "And now let us get something to eat. Mr. Szabo, would you care to join us?"

"Thank you, but no," the Hungarian replied. "I need to prepare a brief for my next case." He extended his hand and once again shook both Fidelio's and Hank's. "Best of luck to the both of you. I hope to work with you again, and tell Nikola I said hello."

"Most assuredly," Fidelio replied.

"I say we celebrate," Hank said. "Let's find the best eatery in Washington and have some big ol' juicy steaks. It'll be my treat."

"Oh no, my friend, you have done enough. I can certainly afford to buy dinner for the both of us." He looked at the street in front of the Federal courthouse, busy with both automobiles and horse-drawn carriages. "Where can we hail a taxicab around here?"

"There's one!" Hank said, pointing. He put two fingers in his mouth and let out a shrill whistle that made Fidelio wince. The driver pulled over. "I learned that trick in New York City."

It was a motorized cab with one of the new gasoline engines. The driver's seat was open and the passenger's compartment behind him was enclosed. "Tell me, my good man," Fidelio said. "Where can we find the best steak dinner in the capital?"

"That'd be the Morrison Hotel, in Georgetown, sir." The cabbie replied in a lilting Irish accent.

"Then Georgetown it is."

As they rode, Hank talked about the recently concluded trial. Fidelio did his best to suppress his irritation; his friend was only trying to bring him out of his sulky mood.

"Boy howdy, that Knowles sure was a nasty fellow, weren't he? Made that sourpuss Eckelstein look downright happy-go-lucky"

"Indeed. Those remarks were most unprofessional of him." Fidelio had been glancing through cab's rear window; this time he turned and stared. "Is that motorcar following us?"

"What?" Hank looked back. "By golly, there he is. An electric, no wonder I didn't hear him back there. Well, it don't look like one of the Springfield boys. That hombre's pretty dark, looks like a Mexican."

"Springfield could have hired anyone to surveil us," Fidelio said. "But I expect they will put their energy into appealing the decision. It is unfortunate the judge allowed them to draw the payments out over two years. I shall be surprised if I receive the entire amount of the judgment."

"In that case, amigo," Hank laughed, "you'd best spend the money as soon as you get it, just in case they want it back!"

Soon they arrived at the Morrison. Its dining room had just opened for the evening and was not yet busy. As the maître d' led them to their table, Fidelio noticed a colored busboy, probably just shy of adulthood, diligently preparing place settings on the last remaining tables. He reflected that if the establishment realized that he himself also had some African ancestry, they would likely not welcome him as a customer.

As they ate their meal, the two friends discussed their future plans.

"So what's up next for you, old friend?" asked Hank. "Now that this hullabaloo is over, I mean."

Fidelio shrugged, then took a sip of his water. "I have been so focused on the trial that I have not decided. Now that I have come into money, I am free to pursue political activism if I choose. It reminded me of something Samuel Clemens said in his reply to my last letter."

"Samuel Clemens?" Hank said as he cut a bloody piece from his very rare steak. "Why does that name sound familiar?"

"It should. He is popularly known by his nom de plume, Mark Twain."

"The Mark Twain?" Hank grinned. "By golly, you sure have a knack for hob-nobbing with the high-cotton folks."

"Hob-nobbing? High cotton?" Fidelio chuckled. "You have such a colorful vocabulary."

"What did Mr. Clemens have to say?"

"We were discussing the lamentable state of the world, in particular, the US occupation of the Philippine Islands. He and numerous others in the literary world have publicly opposed this country's continuing war on the people of those islands. I had asked him how we could wake the American people from their apathy, but sadly, he had no ideas."

"Smart feller like him, I'm right surprised." Hank said. "It just ain't right, the way people don't care, considering what the Savior said – as ye did it unto one of these my brethren, even these least, ye did it unto me. Like with the shameful way the Indians done been treated." He took a long drink of his beer, emptying the heavy glass mug. "Too many Christian folk turned a blind eye to that."

At that moment the busboy appeared at their table with a pitcher. "Refill your water, sir?" he asked Fidelio. After doing so, he set the pitcher down on the table, glanced both ways, and pulled a piece of paper from his apron. "A man asked me to give this to you," he said in a low voice, then quickly moved on to the next table.

Fidelio quickly unfolded and read the note. "Ah, so that explains it."

"Explains what?" Hank asked, puzzled.

"The identity of the man who was following us. I could not see his face, but there was something familiar about him. It is our old friend James Hightower."

"You don't say! I'd expect he'd be with the opera back in Chicago."

"If I am not mistaken, the opera is on hiatus for the next few weeks. Did not Miss Tallulah mention that fact in her latest letter?"

"Yep, she did, in fact she used that exact word. I'd been meaning to look up the meaning in the dictionary, but I plum forgot. To me it sounded like something 'bout being hungry."

"You could have asked me," Fidelio said with a smile.

"True enough, but I don't want you to get sick of answering questions from an unschooled cowboy,." Hank grinned.

Fidelio gave a hearty laugh. "You cannot fool me – under that unsophisticated manner of yours lurks a brilliant mind. And now, let us quickly finish our meal. I do not wish to not keep James waiting."

"Not a problem. I can eat like a starving grizzly when I put my mind to it."

They found James in a shady place behind the restaurant. He was leaning against the trunk of an old oak tree, writing with a pencil in a reporter-style notebook. He closed it when the two men approached. "Fidelio, Hank," he said, shaking both their hands in turn.

"You should've come in and joined us," Hank said. "You've already got a coat and tie on. There's mighty good eatin' in there."

"I would have enjoyed that," James said. "Unfortunately, my complexion is a bit too dark for the proprietors' taste."

"Blasted dolts," Hank said, shaking his head. He reached into his jacket pocket, pulled out a pipe and filled it with tobacco from a leather pouch.

James frowned. "I see you've picked up a new habit."

"Our attorney, Mr. Szabo, persuaded him that smoking from a pipe is less of a health risk than a cigarette," Fidelio said. "However, I find both forms equally repugnant."

"Enough jawin' about my vices," Hank said, "What brings you to Washington? Opera business, or," he lowered his voice, "a job for the Elders?"

James glanced in both directions before answering. "The latter," he said. "Perhaps we should have our discussion in a place with a bit more privacy."

"Certainly," Fidelio said. "I know a place that would be ideal. It is not far; we can reach it in just a few minutes."

Hank and Fidelio squeezed into James' electric car and instructed him to drive down the main thoroughfare of K Street. The autumn sun was high in the sky, bringing summer-like temperatures to the capital city. After a few short blocks, Fidelio directed James to turn left onto a side street. Three buildings from the corner stood a colonial area brick building with a sign that said "K Street Gymnasium."

They entered through the front door into a large room dominated by a boxing ring. Several men greeted Fidelio by name.

A practice match was in progress. Two slightly built bare-chested men wearing short pants and padded gloves swung at each other, while a number of spectators stood around the ring shouting encouragement. In other corners of the room, other men jumped rope or worked out on punching bags.

"Pardon the noise," Fidelio said, "but if we stand closely we shall be able to converse without fear of being overheard."

"Do you box?" James asked.

"On occasion," Fidelio said. "But not often, as I do not wish to risk any undue injury. For the most part I come here to keep myself in physical conditioning."

"I didn't know this place existed," Hank said, a knowing smile on his face. "When did you have time to come here?"

"When you were touring all those historic sites," Fidelio replied. "We have been here several months, pursuing legal issues relating to my invention," he explained to James. "Now, how can we help you?"

"Well," James began, "Recently I was appointed to the Council of the Elders."

"Hurrah for you, old man!" Hank said with a grin. "I done forgot that Miss

Tallulah said somethin' about that in her last letter."

"Sadly, I had to resign as her vocal couch," James said, "As this new appointment takes a hundred percent of my time."

"Congratulations," Fidelio said. "What an honor it must be."

"You, an Elder!" Hank grinned. "All joshing aside, you don't seem old enough to qualify."

"It's more a title of respect within the community than of actual age. And yes, it is a great honor. I have assumed the seat vacated by the death of my great uncle. He was eighty-nine years old, the oldest member of the Council. Now I am the youngest Elder in living memory."

"So I assume then," Fidelio said, "that your business must be quite important, if they have seen fit to send a council member and not a mere representative."

"Yes. I was sent here to lobby for statehood on behalf of the Indian Territory. But it is difficult to find Congressmen who are willing to talk to me. They are preoccupied with the recent events in the Philippine Islands."

"Naturally, I support your mission," said Fidelio. "I, too, am concerned about the conflict overseas. It is a grave injustice to the people of that land, made more grievous by the fact that my spider automaton is being used in the furtherance of this outrage." He shuddered at the thought of a giant Tarantela unleashing its Gatling gun on the poor Filipinos as it demolished their villages. "Has the Council taken a stand on this issue?"

"Unfortunately not. The Council is deeply divided, as a result of our actions in the Colorado labor unrest earlier this year. Some feel that by intervening, we have alienated the more conservative members of Congress, thus lessening the territory's chances for statehood."

"Maybe so," said Hank, "But sometimes a man's got to stand up for what's right. As the Good Book says, 'What doth it profit a man to gain the world and lose his soul?'"

"How do *you* feel about it?" By this time the crowd had become so loud Fidelio almost had to shout the question.

"To hell with the white man's war!" At that moment a hush fell over the gymnasium, as one of the boxers had just delivered a knockout blow to his opponent. A number of men stared at James; their expressions were not friendly. Fortunately, the events in the ring drew away their attention. The referee stepped in and felt the fallen man's pulse, whereupon he nodded and raised the arm of the victor. The uncomfortable silence was replaced by cheers.

"This location was more problematic than I expected," Fidelio said. "Come gentlemen; let us head to my quarters. It is rather a long drive, but we can discuss the matter uninterrupted."

The men once again climbed into James' motorcar and rode back to the Fillmore Hotel on the east side of the city. There in Fidelio's small but immaculate room, they discussed the matter for several hours.

It was obvious that James felt isolated within the Council. "Like our friend Ooche, I believe that the best course of action for our people is not statehood but independence. Otherwise we shall always suffer under the yoke of the white man. No offense to those present," James said, looking at Hank.

"None taken," Hank said. "Can't say I blame you anyhow. Though unless you folks can get Texas to follow you out of the Union, you'd still be surrounded."

"It's a pipe dream, I know," James said. "They won't even let the Filipinos be free, and they live half a world away. What bothers me most are the rumors of the terrible cruelties the US Army is inflicting on those people. I wish I had the means to go there, and see it for myself. Perhaps if the American voters could get unbiased information on the situation, they might demand an end to this fiasco."

"I fully support honest reporting," Fidelio responded. "If only there were newspaper publishers with integrity."

The next morning Fidelio rose early, as was his custom. He dressed and went down to the hotel dining room, where he found his friend already seated at one of the tables. He sat down beside him. "Good morning, Hank. After our late discussion, I expected you might sleep a little later this morning."

"Wish I could've done that," Hank said, "I woke up at the crack of dawn when the sun peeked in my window. I rolled over and put the pillow over my face, but it didn't help."

"I had a similar experience," Fidelio said. "Though I was quite exhausted, it took me several hours to get to sleep. I kept thinking about what James told us."

Hank shook his head. "Yep, it's a goldurn shame. But that's man's nature. Being sinful and all, he wants to take what's not rightly his."

"Are you saying that this detestable situation is God's will?"

"Not at all," Hank replied. "It's like in the parable of the Good Samaritan. The Lord puts us here to help them that are in trouble. I ain't keen on going half way across the world; I'd rather take it easy and enjoy myself for a change. Spend some time fishing, and maybe take in a little opera, since I've lately taken quite a fancy to that."

Fidelio smiled. He knew that the acclaimed soprano Tallulah Hightower, whom they had met in the previous year, was responsible for Hank's newly acquired interest in high culture. "That reminds me; you said that you recently received a letter from Miss Hightower."

"Yep, we write each other every couple weeks or so. Why do you ask?"

"Did she mention the Opera's planned goodwill tour to Manila? Is it still proceeding as planned?"

"Yep. They say the Army's pretty much routed the rebels from the area, so it ought to be pretty safe, long as they don't leave the island of Luzon."

"Indeed," Fidelio said. "I have come to a decision. If Tallulah and company can perform Mozart in that war-ravaged nation, I can go there at well. I shall travel to the Philippines immediately to see the situation for myself. While I am there, I intend to do whatever I can to stop the US government's blatant misuse of my invention."

"Is that so?" Hank raised an eyebrow. "And you're going to sail across the ocean all by your lonesome?"

Fidelio shrugged. "Certainly I would prefer to have you accompany me, but given your history and your intense aversion to war, or even loud noises, I should not feel right about asking."

Hearing that, Hank almost choked on his coffee. He set the cup down and put up his hand. "Now hold on there, hombre, I ain't no basket case. Besides, we're partners, and if ain't over, just 'cause you're going overseas. I'm a man who sticks by his obligations. Matter of fact, I think I've even got enough scratch to buy a ticket over there." He reached into his pocket to check his wallet.

Fidelio held up his hand. "That will not be necessary, my friend. Since I expect to receive the first payment from Springfield shortly, I shall have no problem covering the cost of your travel."

"I'd be much obliged. You know, I always thought the Lord brung you and me together for a reason. Count me in, amigo."

About the Author

Vaughn Treude grew up on a family farm in North Dakota. The remoteness of his home, with few children his age nearby, made science fiction and fantasy a welcome escape. His favorite writers were Isaac Asimov, Robert Heinlein, and JRR Tolkien. He always planned to become a sci-fi writer, but the demands of life kept his various projects from completion. After several years as a software consultant, he realized that the same kind of discipline required for writing code could be applied to creating fictional worlds.

Politics have exerted a strong influence on science fiction ever since HG Wells speculated on the future of human civilization, to *1984*, *2001* and beyond. Treude's writings are no exception. His first book, *Centrifugal Force* (Nakota Publishing 2012) was the result of speculation on how a measure of freedom might be achieved in today's unfree world. *Fidelio's Automata*, his second book from Nakota Publishing, returns to the past for an exploration of history as it might have been, set at the time when Wells was alive.